REIN ME IN

**The Cowboys of
Night Hawk**

By Kayla Grosse

Published by Kayla Grosse

Printed in the United States of America

First US Edition: March 2023

ISBN: 979-8-9870546-0-4 (paperback)

Edited by Swati Hedge

Cover art by Nia Oliveira @niaoliveirart

Layout by Nicole Reeves

For those we have loved.
For those we have lost.
And for those left behind.
This book is for all of us.

Author's Note

This book is the first in my new Cowboys of Night Hawk series and can be read as a standalone novel. It contains a happily-ever-after and lots of beautiful and funny moments, but please note it has serious themes of loss, grief, alcohol abuse, and depression.

Thank you for reading, and know I love and appreciate you all.

Xoxo,
Kayla

Rein Me In Playlist

"You Should Be Here" Cole Swindell
"Burning Man" Dierks Bentley
"Boot Scootin' Boogie" Brooks & Dunn
"Save a Horse, Ride a Cowboy" Big & Rich
"Papa Loved Mama" Garth Brooks
"Country Girl (Shake It For Me)" Luke Bryan
"Wildflowers and Wild Horses" Lainey Wilson
"Old Town Road" Lil Nas X
"Wreckage" Nate Smith
"Body Like a Back Road" Sam Hunt
"Brown Eyes Baby" Keith Urban
"Rumor" Lee Brice
"Cowboy Take Me Away" The Chicks
"Suds In the Bucket" Sara Evans
"Burn" Jo Dee Messina
"Wanted" Hunter Hayes
"The Good Ones" Gabby Barrett
"Strangers" Maddie & Tae
"Never Til Now" Ashley Cooke
"With You I Am" Cody Johnson
"After the Storm" Mumford & Sons
"5 Foot 9" Tyler Hubbard
"WildHorse" RaeLynn

CHAPTER 1

Blake

HOME. RANDALL, TEXAS. POPULATION: 5,549.

Once upon a time, that number was 5,550. That was before my life was turned upside down. Before my family's lives were turned upside down.

"Blake!"

My head whips around, long dark brown curls hitting me in the cheek as I do. I need to remember to buy stock in ponytail holders and ball caps now that I'm back home.

"What are you doing down here?" Mom's high-pitched voice cuts through the sound of horses nickering and cattle mooing in the distance.

I pull up my Wranglers over my round hips and tuck one of my curls behind my ear. "I was checking on the new foals," I say as she approaches.

"You've been down here for a long time. I need your help with dinner."

I turn toward a nameless black foal whose little nose is hanging curiously over the stall. I try to touch him, but he shies away. "I thought Carol was coming to cook today," I say.

Mom sighs and leans on her crutches. "Look at me, Blake."

A lump forms in my throat as I turn to look at the lithe five-foot-eight frame of Margie Tanner, one of the greatest horse trainers in Texas.

Her blue eyes are tired, and if you know what you're looking for, you can see the sadness there too. The same sadness that lies in mine, and in Daddy's.

"You came home to help around here while I get back on my feet," she reminds me. "But the entire month you've been here, you just stand in front of Briar's stall."

My eyes begin to burn, and the urge to run back to Tennessee lies heavy in my gut.

"You know that's not true," I say, trying to keep my voice free of anger. "I've been helping around here plenty. Ask George or any of the grooms! Do I have to remind you her foal almost didn't make it? The vet said he needs to be watched."

Mom hobbles on her crutches, and for a moment I feel bad she came all the way down to the barn to get me. Yet, trying to tell Mom what to do...it won't work. Daddy says I get my stubbornness from her, and he's right.

"The foal is fine," Mom argues. "He's almost a month old now, and the vet said he's looking good. Now, let's get back up to the house. You know I can't stand on my feet for too long—and besides, we can't let your dad starve."

"That's dramatic, Mom."

"You know he can't cook. You remember the Thanksgiving of 2006."

Of course I remember, he almost burned the house down. "What happened to Carol?"

Mom's jaw ticks. "Carol's son has the stomach flu. She called to say she'd be out the next few days. That means you're on cooking duty."

The foal tentatively begins to sniff my fingers as I move my gaze to Briar—a sturdy black mare that once belonged to my brother. A stabbing pain shoots through my chest, but I try to ignore it.

"Fine," I huff, "but only if you promise to call me on my cell phone next time instead of coming down here. You're supposed to be resting."

She waves her hand at me. "*Pssh*! I'm fine. The doctors don't know who they're working with here."

I resist rolling my eyes. "I think they do. Mrs. Stubborn USA."

Mom grins, and for a moment I wonder if maybe I can build a relationship with her again after so many years apart, after what happened that day and everything that followed; but I'm not sure if I can, or if I deserve to.

Her voice interrupts my thoughts. "Let's get back to the house. I'm sure your dad's waiting for us."

I give Briar and her foal one last look before heading toward the golf cart at the end of the stable aisle. "Did you drive this here?" I question as I turn to help her get in the cart. She shrugs and I let out a scoff. "Mom!"

"I don't need help," she answers instead, pushing my hand away.

"Let me help you," I chide.

"I don't need it, watch." She throws her crutches in the back of the cart with gusto, then gingerly places her butt in the seat before arranging her casted leg. She smiles triumphantly once settled. "See, I told you."

Holding in an eye roll, I walk to the driver's seat and turn the key already in the ignition. I know if Daddy saw this, he'd throw a fit. But again, that's Margie Tanner for you. She was born to privilege up in Saratoga, New York. She grew up riding Dressage and made the Olympic team when she was in her late twenties, right before she met Daddy. She's always been an independent and strong woman, which I love about her. But sometimes she *really* ruffles my feathers.

I've been away from home for five years now, but that didn't stop us from having a tense relationship. Every phone call we have is filled with silence, or her opinions about what I should be doing with my life, or how at my age she already had me and my younger brother, Reed. I may be twenty-nine (almost thirty), but as I always tell her, I'm still figuring my life out. Though that pisses her off even more. She believes I should either be a career woman or someone's wife, popping out babies.

Without looking at Mom, I ask, "Are you good?"

"I'm good."

I push the gas pedal and begin the short journey up to the house.

"How did you drive the cart down here?" I ask after a moment.

"Probably wasn't the smartest idea, but I used my left leg to push the pedal."

"Seriously?!"

"It's just a golf cart, sweetie. My leg is broken, not my entire body. And with all the horses that need working, I can't afford to watch movies all day."

"I get that, but you need to be careful. If not for me, then for Daddy's sake. You really shook him up with your fall off that ladder."

"Blake," she murmurs, her voice thick. I know what she's thinking about. It's what we all think about every day since it happened.

"Just take care of yourself, okay?" I tell her.

"I am, Blake."

My hands grip the steering wheel as we approach our ranch-style home with white siding and green shutters. Daddy's standing with his arms crossed on the wrap-around porch. It doesn't take a genius to figure out he's upset at seeing Mom on the cart.

Mom lets out a tense breath. "Oh great, I thought he'd be in town for longer."

"I was wondering why he let you drive this thing."

She scoffs. "You know I don't let men tell me what I can and can't do. Not even your father."

I let out a small chuckle as we come to a stop. Daddy is immediately at Mom's side, a frown on his aging face. He's a tall man, around six foot two, with a short salt and pepper beard and hair to match. He's wearing his Silverbelly Stetson and a dark blue button-up shirt with jeans and cowboy boots. A born and raised Texan rancher through and through, he's the one who taught me how to rope and run a working ranch. The one who's always had my back no matter what life choices I've made. I love him to death and would do anything for him.

It's also how I was convinced to move back home after so many years of avoiding it. When he called me about Mom's accident, I could hear the pain in his voice. She'd fallen off a ladder getting hay and broken her leg in the process. It left me no choice but to book the next plane ticket home.

"Margie," his low voice rumbles in its thick, small-town accent, "what the heck are you doing on that cart?

"Oh, Lee. Don't 'Margie' me. I'm fine! You and Blake are both worrywarts."

Daddy looks at me from beneath the rim of his Stetson, his brown eyes sparkling in the evening sun. He's not angry at Mom; he's never angry at her. He's just concerned and overprotective. When I was fifteen, he caught the town hottie, Hunter Brooks, with his hand on my thigh while watching a movie in our basement. I'd never seen reflexes so fast when Daddy had glared at him, warning him to keep his hands to himself or lose them. After that, I always went out on the town with boys instead of bringing them home.

"You know I just want my girl safe and sound. The doctor said you should be resting, not running the place. That's why I asked our baby girl to come home." He winks at me. "Now grab those dang crutches for your mom and come inside." He lifts Mom as gingerly as he can, but that doesn't stop her from hollering.

"Put me down, Lee! I can walk."

Daddy smirks at me over the top of Mom's head, ignoring her demand. "I went out and got us some barbeque from Sweet Cheeks."

I blow out a sigh of relief, thankful I don't have to cook tonight. I've been mucking stalls and painting fences all day, and the last thing I want to do is cook. Though I enjoy it, I don't so much love whipping up a nice meal on the fly.

"Thanks, Daddy. How'd you know I didn't want to cook tonight?"

He walks up the steps and through the front door, heading toward the couch where we have Mom set up. I follow, closing the door behind us.

"I figured you were still out at the barn with Briar's foal," he says as he settles Mom in, arranging her leg so it's elevated and she has pillows under her lower back so she can eat. I can't help but hear the heavy question in his tone. His desire for me to say *why* I've been standing outside that stall—even though he damn well knows. If he thinks I'm going to say it out loud, he's got another thing coming.

When he turns his gaze on me, I can only look at the floor. My heartbeat pounds in my ears, and my cheeks heat. I find myself wishing I could teleport back to my rental in Tennessee so I can pretend like I'm someone else—and that Reed is still alive.

Mom clears her throat. "Well, that barbeque sure smells good. I hope you got my favorite."

Daddy plasters a weak smile on his lips. "Of course I did, Margie. I even got you extra sauce."

When he starts to walk toward the kitchen, I hold up my hand. "I got it. Why don't you set up the TV trays, and I'll put together the plates?"

"Good idea," he says.

I make my way to the kitchen island and start to unpack the containers from Sweet Cheeks, grateful for the distraction. I love my parents, but it's about a month shy of five years since my little brother died. So not only will it be the first time since it happened that I'll be home for the anniversary, but five years of our family avoiding anything to do with Reed or the accident—and five years of me avoiding real life and dealing with what happened that day, and every day after. Needless to say, it's been hard for me to adjust to being home. I think they sometimes forget what this is like for me.

I pull out a pack of warm cornbread, and my throat constricts. Reed's favorite. When I look up, I can see Daddy quietly talking to Mom. Part of me wonders if he got this side on purpose. Or maybe I'm reading into it? Regardless, it's not going on my plate.

"What's taking so long?" Mom laughs. "Are you cooking instead?"

I swallow the lump in my throat. "Sorry! Coming."

I pull out the blue tiffany plates Mom still uses from their wedding, piling them with an assortment of beef brisket, mac n' cheese and coleslaw. In a hurry, I put the cornbread on their plates, acting like the yellow squares are diseased. Before long, I've got their plates in front of them, and I'm off to get mine and a pitcher of lemonade.

After I have what I'm after, I turn back toward the living room. When I lift my gaze, I stop, struck with the image of my parents before me. They're chatting about their recent horse sale and eating their meal. Above the mantel hangs a beautiful picture of our home, Double-Time Ranch, with the morning sun rising behind our main barn and arena. In the corner is a sleek black Quarter Horse, his head held high and ears placed forward. I remember when we got that photo. Daddy was so proud of what we'd built as a family...

"Can't you see it, baby girl? Daddy grins, his arm around my shoulders. "You'll be the best barrel racer in the world—and you'll win with our stable name on your back."

"And she's going to do it on one of the horses I trained!" Reed gloats. "Especially when Briar is ready to go. She'll be a speed demon, I know it. She's already outrunning all the other colts and fillies in the pasture."

I punch him in the arm. "For being so young, you sure think highly of yourself, brother dearest."

"Ouch!" He rubs his arm. "You jealous, Blakey girl?"

I cringe at the nickname. "Never."

"Wow," he scoffs, looking at Daddy with a playful smirk, "the ego on this one!"

I punch him in the arm again, and Mom steps between us. "Now, now, you two. When are you going to start acting like adults?"

"Never," we both say together.

"Earth to Blake?" Mom's voice interrupts the memory. "What are you staring at?"

I blink, my eyes refocusing. "I'm fine. Leg cramp, is all. Guess I didn't drink enough water today."

I sense them both staring at each other, knowing I'm lying through my teeth. I make my way over to the space at the end of the couch with Mom where Daddy has my tray. I tuck into my food, savoring the rich flavor of brisket and spicy sauce.

"There's nothing like Sweet Cheeks in Tennessee," I say to break the awkward silence.

Daddy eyes me. "They've got to have good barbeque there."

I'm grateful he's going along with my subject change. "Sure, but nothing like Sweet Cheeks. This is the good stuff," I say as I take a bite of mac n' cheese.

He smiles around a bite of that damn cornbread. "That's true."

"Oh!" Mom cries, her voice lighting up with excitement. "Blake, I forgot to tell you. You know the Montgomerys?"

I take another bite of food and swallow. "Of course. How could I forget old Ruby Montgomery? She's practically the Mayor of Randall."

"Well, you know, it's been so long since you've been back here…"

"Mom?" I urge her on. I know she hates I haven't been home, and that I've missed every holiday and birthday. But it really was better that way.

"It's been a hard couple of years for them. Early this year, Emmett died of a heart attack on his tractor. Then last month, they had to sell fifty percent of their herd and kill off some of their crops because of the drought."

A wave of sadness washes over me. "Wow. I'm sorry to hear that. Emmett was a nice man—and the drought...that's not good at all." I hesitate, then ask, "Is there anything we can do to help?"

Mom perks up. "Funny you should mention that. The Montgomerys are holding a charity event tomorrow night at Night Hawk to raise money for their ranch."

"Night Hawk." I furrow my brow. "That's the bar with the mechanical bull."

"That's right."

"What kind of event is it?" I'm wondering who in their right mind would host a charity event at a townie bar with a mechanical bull.

"It's rather brilliant. They've recruited single people in town to ride the bull. While they're riding, the crowd can bid on them for a date. Whoever bids right before they fall off wins. Each rider also has a basket with items for their dates, like cookies or a picnic. It's sweet."

I almost choke on my lemonade. "Seriously?"

"Come on, Blake. I think it sounds cute."

"What is this, a CW show?" I snort.

Mom and Daddy have no idea what I mean. So she continues, "Don't be such a Sour Sally. This is fun, and most of the town will be there. We all want to help the Montgomerys out as much as we can."

"You two have fun then. Do they have a website or something I can donate to?"

"Blake! You know I can't go with my leg."

"No, thank you."

"Someone has to go with your daddy."

I shake my head, pushing my plate away, my appetite gone. "I've got to stay and look after the foals."

"The foals are fine, baby girl," Daddy says. "Nothing's going to happen to them."

I pinch the bridge of my nose. "I haven't even been into town yet. Why would I go?"

"To support your community," Mom says, slight irritation in her voice. "You've been on this ranch day in and day out since your plane landed. We've told so many people you're back. This is the perfect opportunity to say hi to them and support the Montgomerys. Maybe even meet someone. I bet I could still sign you up."

Anger ignites in me. She knows I don't ride any more, not even fake bulls. "I'm not riding the bull."

Daddy sighs. "She didn't say you had to."

"I don't see why I need to make an appearance. I can support them from here."

"Supporting your community isn't all about money. I know you know that. What's gotten into you?" he asks gently.

I swallow the lump that's building in my throat. For half a second I want to scream: *You know what's gotten into me! My brother is dead, and it's all my fault!* But instead, I take three deep breaths before speaking again. "You're right, Daddy. I'm tired, is all. It's been a busy few weeks, and I'm still not used to sleeping in my old bed."

"We could buy you a new bed."

"I'm fine." I look into his searching brown eyes, ones that match my own. "Really. I'm sorry I got upset. I'm anxious about seeing everybody again all at once."

Mom pipes up, "That's natural. But people are so excited to see you. I think it will be good for you to get out of this house and off the ranch. Change your surroundings."

As much as it pains me, maybe she's right. Even though the thought of seeing people I went to school with and all of Randall in a crowded space makes me nauseous. At least if I'm with Daddy, I can leave early. He's the kind of guy who likes to make a short appearance and then leave without saying goodbye. We call it his disappearing act. He's actually an extrovert, but he'd rather be on the ranch with the workers shooting the shit instead of at parties.

"You promise I don't have to ride the bull?" I ask. The thought makes my stomach hurt. Not because I can't ride the bull—I used to ride it like a pro in the past—but for other reasons. Ones I don't like to talk about.

"We wouldn't make you do that," Daddy assures me. "Plus, I have a feeling I'll be beating off the men in town with sticks as it is. You won't need to ride that bull to get a date."

I cover my face with my hands. "Good lord, Daddy. You're embarrassing."

"I speak the truth. You're beautiful and smart. Not to mention a great cook and ranch hand. Any man would be lucky to have you." He winks. He's only saying the part about the cook and ranch hand to irritate me.

I throw up my hands, cheeks stained with red. "Fine. I'll go with you. But I want on the record that I object."

He chuckles. "Noted."

CHAPTER 2

Gavin

"DON'T GO DRINKING ALL those shots at once now, ladies. I don't want to have to peel you off the floor."

The table of pretty girls giggle, fluttering their eyelashes at me in a way I've become immune to since working at Night Hawk as a bartender and 'Bull Wrangler.'

"Take a shot with us, Sexy Cowboy!" one of them croons.

"Maybe another time, darling." I laugh, walking away before she can ask again. I find an open spot near the perimeter of the room, tilting the brim of my black cowboy hat so I can get a better look at the large crowd forming.

Night Hawk, once a little townie bar, has become a popular spot for the young crowd on the weekends. We often get city folk in here for bachelor and bachelorette parties. I guess nothing says "celebrate your last night as a single person" like riding a mechanical bull.

I smirk at the thought.

Despite being a small-town country boy, I've always enjoyed being around all sorts of people, which is why I enjoy this 'silly' part-time job, as Momma calls it. People watching, throwing assholes off the bull when they piss me off, forgetting my problems for a few hours—it's exactly what I want after a long day on the ranch.

Night Hawk also provides extra money that I desperately need, and gives me a break from the harsh reality of life. It lets me forget for a moment that if I don't do something drastic soon, the Montgomery Family Ranch isn't going to be a family ranch much longer. I feel the weight of it like a thousand boulders on my chest.

"Looks like we might have a good crowd tonight."

I turn to face my younger brother, Kade. His hazel eyes are devouring some blonde girl who's clearly not from here. She's wearing daisy dukes with the pockets peeking out of the back and some designer white cowboy boots. Her fake boobs spill out from the tiny hot pink top she's wearing.

Kade licks his thin lips like he's an animal in heat, then takes his hat off to give the gal his panty-dropping smile. His damn dimples have been getting me in trouble since he was born. All it ever takes is one 'innocent' smile and I get blamed for whatever goes wrong. Such is the life of an older sibling, I suppose.

I push his shoulder, but he doesn't break eye contact with the lady. "You're working, Kade. Stop trying to sleep with the customers."

Kade winks at the poor girl, and I swear I see her panties fall to the floor. If she's wearing any. He runs his hand through his long dusky blonde hair, then places his cowboy hat back on his head.

"Live a little, big brother. Isn't this event for *charity*? I'd be more than happy to give my time and attention to that hot little number right here."

I notice the way he says charity with spite. He hates that the town knows we're going through hard times. I get it, and I'm not the biggest fan of it, either. But it is what it is. This whole bull riding date thing to help us out was Momma's idea, and it would break her heart to hear that Kade would rather bury himself in a random woman than help his family.

I pull Kade by the front of his shirt, effectively ending his eye-fuck-a-thon with Blondie. If this place wasn't filled with half of Randall, he'd be trying to throw a punch at me for embarrassing him. But everyone is watching us, so I keep a smile on my face and tip my head so it looks like I'm telling Kade something private.

"Be on your best behavior, Kade. This isn't the time to stick your dick in the first thing you see. Momma's here and we have work to do. So smile and act like the man Dad taught you to be."

Kade's face turns hard at the mention of Dad. The muscle in his jaw ticks.

"Lighten up, Gav. I was just having some fun."

"You have fun all the time. Tonight is about work. Now go flirt with the local girls and get all the men excited about bidding on them. We need this money, even if you don't want it."

I let go of his shirt and pat it with brotherly affection. When I step back, I see Momma approaching. Her silver hair is tied high in a ponytail. She's wearing a yellow sundress, and it looks like she's put on a little makeup. Dad would be happy to see her out and about. Since he passed away nine months ago, she doesn't leave the property much. Always too worried about the ranch, her boys, and of course, Gran—who's forever doing things she's not supposed to do at eighty-five years young.

I put on my best smile to greet her. Kade doesn't have to ask me why I look so giddy all of a sudden; he knows this is my Momma smile. He knows because his is the exact same. He plasters his smile on, dimples showing, and turns to face the best woman in our lives.

"You boys got everything sorted?" she asks, looking at the auction paddles I have laid out on a folding table nearby.

"We do. Looks like we'll have a good crowd for this," I tell her.

Kade gives Momma a kiss on the cheek. "All the riders are accounted for. I'd wait a bit longer before we start. Let people get a few drinks in them before the bidding."

Momma pats his stubbled cheek. "Good thinking, baby."

"I'm gonna go work the crowd. Make sure their money is good." Kade winks.

She nods, letting him walk off. When she turns to me, her smile is gone, and frown lines crease her forehead. "You know, your brother is twenty-one years old. Let him make his mistakes."

"Momma..."

"Don't 'Momma' me. I saw the way you two were looking at each other. I know the difference between a friendly sibling chat and a heated one."

I notice her neck start to splotch red, a telltale sign her blood pressure is dialing skyward. It takes everything in me not to say something back or tell her how Kade hasn't been right since Dad died. But she knows, and yet does nothing about it. Sometimes I wonder why, considering she was always on my ass when I was his age about being a good responsible boy, which I have been. So instead, I bite my tongue.

"Sorry, Momma."

She takes a deep breath and pulls at her dress. "I can't believe you boys work here. It's so—"

"It's a job. A job Kade and I need right now. And our boss is letting us use Night Hawk for free."

"I know, Gavin. I wish things weren't like this. I wish..."

"I know, Momma."

She puts her hand over her heart and looks out at the crowd. "It's getting busier. I'm going to mingle. I see Sarah Jane and Mark Gunner."

I follow her eyes to see the older couple smiling at her. "Go on. I've got to raise the music and get the energy up in here. Find Kade in a bit and have him work the bar when the bidding starts."

She gives me a kiss on the cheek and a final forlorn look before heading to her friends. I make my way to the back of the house, pushing my way through bodies. I hear several of the men say my name in greeting; some of them slap me on the back. I know most of the people here, minus the ones who've come in from the city.

Right before I reach the bar, a hand grabs my bicep. I know who it is before I even turn. I can smell her floral perfume over the stale beer and peanut shells littering the floor. The animal inside me wants to push the hand off, but the gentleman in me turns to face her.

"Howdy, Cricket."

"Hiya, Gavin," she purrs, squeezing my arm a bit tighter. "I have an idea to run by you."

Her gray eyes are alive with hunger, and I know she's picturing me with my clothes off. She tucks a stray brown hair that's escaped from her French braid behind her ear, her red painted lips puckering.

I take a step back, but she still has a grip on me. "And what's your idea?"

Her skin flushes, turning the apples of her cheeks pink. There was a time I would've thought she was the cutest thing in the world. A natural beauty, one that has roundness in all the right places and knows how to impress your Momma. Hell, I could've seen myself marrying her, but that time has passed. Now she's nothing more than a persistent thorn in my side. A reminder of the life I thought I had before Dad died—and a reminder of the pain people can cause you.

"Well," she says, leaning forward so her lips are next to my ear, "I was thinking you should bid on me tonight. I'm not supposed to reveal what's in my basket till the date, but let's just say, I've got big plans for us."

"You realize this event helps my family. It wouldn't make sense for me to bid on you."

The corner of her mouth turns up. "I may have been stupid when it came to letting you go, Gavin, but I'm a smart woman."

Before I can comment on the fact that she never let me go, she's pushing a wad of hundreds into my hand.

"My daddy gave me this. But he said I can only use it if you bid on me. You know how much he loves you. You're like the son he's never had."

The money burns my palm. "Are you forgetting why we aren't together, Cricket?" I lean in so only she can hear me, my voice rough with anger. "Because you let some random guy screw your brains out the day after our one-year anniversary. Did you tell your *daddy* that? I'm sure he'd be real proud."

Cricket pushes me away, and my stomach sours. Though I love living in Randall, and most of its people, when shit goes wrong, you gotta face it on the daily. You can't hide from your past here. And Cricket is one part of my past I'd love to bury.

"You're a piece of work, Gavin Montgomery. Forget about this money," she says, grabbing it out of my hand.

I would have never taken it, and she knows that. Yet for some reason, she's been on a mission to get me back since I found her with her skirt pushed up around her stomach and some city boy I'd never seen between her legs. I still can't wrap my brain around what possessed her to do that, and she's never offered me an explanation. My temper flares.

"I don't want your money, Cricket. Go find some other guy to explore your basket—I know that's not a problem for you." She lets out a cry of indignation, and even though she hurt me bad, I regret this entire interaction. Momma would be pissed if she knew I spoke in a dishonorable manner. I was raised to be a better man. Though I often wonder if that man died with Dad.

Her lip wobbles. "You're an asshole."

I stare at her for a moment, an apology on my lips, but instead I keep my mouth shut. I don't have it in me to be nice to her tonight. Not with more important things on my mind. Like ranch work, bills, and my brother. "Goodbye, Cricket," I say, my features stern. I hope after this interaction, she'll finally get the message that I'm not interested. With that, I make my way toward the back of the bar so I can raise the music level and get a moment to myself.

Once there, I thank God the sound system is just outside of eyesight and lean against the wall, putting my head down as I take a large exhale. I do my best to keep my shit together for my family, but it's getting tougher every day. We've all been working hard since Dad died, but becoming the man of the house at twenty-four is the last thing I expected. Though it was always the plan for me to take over the Montgomery Family Ranch, I hadn't planned for it to be so soon. I thought I had at least another ten years or more till Dad retired.

I also didn't expect the worst drought in fifty years to hit us. Or that Dad had been horrible at keeping books and spent way too much money on horses and cattle. Until he died, our entire family thought we were the richest ranch in Texas. But now here we are, hosting a charity event to keep us afloat. Not to mention my family doesn't know exactly how bad things are.

The sound of footsteps has me turning my charm back on. The world may be falling apart, but I have a part to play, and a family to feed.

"You ready to get this party started, Cowboy?" Jake asks, placing his signature red cowboy hat atop his head. He's my boss's son and a good friend. He manages the place now that his dad's got a bum knee.

I give him a crooked smile and look out at the crowd. It's a little after nine and they're looking primed and ready to have a good time. I know because there's a certain energy in the air—one that you learn to notice when you work places like this. Almost like that feeling you get as you count down the seconds before the New Year. These fine people are ready to drink more, bid on beautiful people, and ride the bull.

Even though I hated the idea when Momma brought it up, this crowd is excited. More than excited. And word has spread because there are more people than we expected.

As I'm about to turn up the music, I notice Kade talking to the blonde girl from earlier.

I glance at Jake. "Will you go grab Kade and tell him to work the bar? Fill the folks' beers so they shell out their cash."

Jake follows my eyesight and shakes his head. "I'll try to tear him away. But focus on doing what you do best. You know how to light up a crowd. Hell, you'd probably make more money if you were the one being offered up for a date instead."

I grumble out, "I don't have time for women right now."

Jake laughs. "You're the most eligible bachelor in town, and you know it. How many numbers did you get last night during your shift?"

"I don't know. I threw them out."

"Exactly."

"I'm not a good catch." I gesture to the crowd. "You realize we're here because I'm broke?"

Jake rolls his eyes. "Yeah, but that doesn't mean these women don't want you. You're a smart man, Gavin. Everyone in this town knows what it's like to go through hard times. You'll turn it around. You've got to have some faith." He pats me on the back. "I'll wrangle Kade before he disappears into the alley with that city girl. You get this place ready to spend their money."

I tip my hat at him before changing the song to one I know gets people ready to go. I take another inhale, put my most charming Montgomery boy smile on, and get ready to be the showman I've taught myself to be.

CHAPTER 3

Blake

WHEN DADDY AND I walk into Night Hawk, we're greeted with "Boot Scootin' Boogie" blasting at level ten. I cringe as the notes hit my eardrums, not used to such loud sounds after a few weeks of working the ranch in silence.

Daddy has a smile on his face, the people person that he is. Since he grew up in Randall, everyone knows him. The Double-Time Ranch is trusted; most people come to us to buy foals or get their horses trained. Before Reed passed, we would host big town barbecues and horse shows for the locals.

I tense. Now's not the time to think about Reed. Or the fact that I'm sure everyone here is aware how close it is to the anniversary of the accident. My stomach rolls, but I manage to slap a smile on my face and brace myself for the onslaught of people who are about to come my way. I knew this day would come, but I wanted to avoid it for longer. Mom said that at least this way I could get all the reunions over with at once, since most of the town is here to help the Montgomerys. Maybe she's right.

As I walk further into the bar, the first thing I notice is how packed it is. This used to be a watering hole for locals and a place where kids could drink before they turned twenty-one and ride the bull to impress their dates.

"Well, look at what the cat dragged in!" a male voice hollers above the music.

The people around who can hear him stop what they're doing to look at the excitement. I feel my heart rate pick up and tip my head at some of the familiar faces. But before any can come my way, I'm being picked up and spun around.

A squeal escapes my mouth. "Good lord, put me down!"

When my feet land, I'm met with a red cowboy hat and shit-eating grin. "Jake Buckley. You still wearing that ugly red hat?"

He laughs. "It's my lucky hat. Been wearing it since the day I found it in that State Fair parking lot."

"Oh, please! I can tell it's brand new." I tap the brim of it as he smiles at me before launching in for a hug.

"It's good to see you, Blake. I heard you were back in town and almost stopped by to visit you," he motions to all the people, "but we've been crazy here."

I pat his shoulder. Jake and I were a year apart in high school and often found ourselves in the same circles, given our fathers are old friends.

"I like what you've done with the place. It's very..."

"Kitschy?" he finishes.

"That's the word." Not only has the clientele of Night Hawk changed, but it looks like many of the bars in Nashville. There's country memorabilia on the walls, peanut shells on the floor, and there, right in the middle of the old dance floor, is a shiny mechanical bull.

"My old man said I could change whatever I wanted if it brought in money. Though the new bull is what put us on the map. I started putting videos of the Montgomery boys riding it on social media. The next day we had three bachelorette parties show up out of nowhere. That thing," he points to the bull, "is like magic."

"I'm happy for you." My eyes scan the crowd, wondering where Daddy went. I find his Stetson and see he's talking to June Montgomery and the Gunners. When June catches my eye, she beams at me, and I give her a little wave. She always was nice to me when she came to pick up her oldest boy, Gavin. He and Reed had been friends since they were babies.

"Are you gonna ride the bull tonight? I know you'd give us all a show," Jake teases, eyeing me up and down. I'm not wearing anything special, just my old cowboy boots and a pair of skinny jeans with a faded Garth Brooks concert-T and a natural-colored cowboy hat.

"You're looking good enough to eat," he adds, dark eyes twinkling.

Jake and I hooked up once in high school, but that's as far as it was ever going to go. He's a sweet guy, but I wasn't interested in anything long-term then, and I'm not interested now.

I knock him on the shoulder. "I don't ride anything anymore. Not horses, not bulls, not fake bulls...not Randall boys. I'm here to support the Montgomerys and keep my mom happy."

It's hard to miss the look of pity that flashes in Jake's eyes, but I don't let it get to me. "Now that you're home, maybe that'll change," he says.

"Keep dreaming, Cowboy." My voice is light and flirty, which thankfully makes the pity-gaze disappear.

The sound of glass breaking turns his head.

"I better get back to it. I don't want this place burning down."

I chuckle. "Go!"

He gives me a kiss on the cheek. "Don't be a stranger now, Cowgirl. I want to see you again soon. Even if it doesn't involve riding of any sort."

I shake my head and push him off. He may be a shameless flirt, but I'm glad he hasn't changed one bit in the last five years. It's also nice that he didn't bring up Reed. People tend to immediately offer their condolences when they can't think of anything else to talk about. Sometimes they even try to share how much they miss him; that's the most painful of all.

With Jake now melded with the crowd, I'm left alone without the comfort of someone familiar at my side. I can feel people's eyes on me, but I don't want to make eye contact and discover who they are. Especially if I know them well. Then I'll get stuck in the exact kind of conversation I don't want. Thankfully, Daddy appears at my side right as the town gossip, Abby Allen, starts to make her way toward me. She's an older woman, at least in her seventies, but she likes to run her mouth and get into everyone's business. I grab Daddy's hand and pull him toward the bar, leaving Abby's third degree for another day.

He smirks. "Good thinking, baby girl."

Together, we weave our way through everyone; I smile and say hi to townies who greet me like the good Texan woman I am. Hell, I even hug a few people I went to high school with. By the time we finally get to the bar, I'm ready for a drink.

"Is that Blake Tanner?" the bartender asks Daddy. He looks familiar, but I can't place him exactly.

"The one and only," Daddy answers.

The man behind the bar is way too young for me by the looks of it, but attractive as hell. He's wearing a cowboy hat tipped back so I can see his hazel eyes twinkle with mischief. He looks like the type of boy you'd end up in jail with, after a night making out in the back of his truck and TPing Abby Allen's yard. He's wearing a tight black T-shirt that has Night Hawk's logo on it, as well as worn jeans that make it known he has muscles hiding underneath.

"You don't remember me, do you darling?" he drawls.

I shake my head. "Sorry, I can't say that I do. You look like someone I should know though."

He smiles, causing his cheeks to dimple. Oh, I'm sure this boy's mom had her hands full... probably still does.

The man wipes his fingers on a towel, then holds out his large hand. "Kade Montgomery."

Ah. I should've known. I place my hand in his, and lord help me... he kisses it. "Kade? Wow. You look..."

"I was sixteen when you left town and looked like a starving possum. I'm not surprised you don't recognize me. Though I'm sure you'll remember Gavin. He's always been a looker."

I let out a little laugh. "Well, it's nice to see you again."

"Likewise. What'll ya have?"

"Whiskey neat for Daddy, and I'll have whatever beer you got that's cold."

Daddy tips his hat at the drink order, and Kade gets to work. Once we have our drinks in hand, Daddy hands over some bills—with what looks to be a more than generous tip—and I'm left with no other excuse than to mingle.

"Thanks, Kade. It was nice to re-meet you."

He gives me another one of his swoony smiles. "I'm sure we'll see each other again." Then he's on to the next person, leaving me to wonder why he believes that.

Daddy leads me toward a table in the back that has a clear view of the bull. The crowd is fidgeting, ready to get on with the evening festivities. There's a card table set up near the wall full of auction paddles and a line of young people dropping off their baskets. I recognize one of them to be Polly Carson who was in Reed's grade, which means she's around twenty-four. She's blossomed into a buxom woman who looks like a proper country girl. She smiles at me and I give her a little wave.

As I stand next to Daddy, I find myself wishing I had a close friend in town. Most of them moved away after they married their high school sweethearts or went to college, like my friend Shelby who I lived with in Tennessee for a couple months before I found my own place. The thought makes Mom's opinions of my lack of relationship or career enter my head, and I fight to keep a frown off my face.

"You look like the cheese fell off your cracker," a warbling voice says to my left.

I turn to find Ruby Montgomery at my side. She looks good for an old woman, like someone who's lived her life and enjoyed the heck out of it.

"Ruby! I was wondering if you'd be here."

She beckons me down to give her a hug. She's a little thing, maybe even shrunk a few inches in the last five years; that means with my five-foot-nine height, I have to bend down to meet her.

"Of course I'm here, silly goose. This is my family, isn't it?" She pulls back from the hug, then adds with a teasing wink, "Not to mention you know I like being out past my bedtime."

I laugh softly. Ruby's been known to close out bars around town for years. She's a spitfire and apparently hasn't slowed down since I left.

"It's good to see you," I say.

Her smile wrinkles her already well-lined face. "I told your mom that if I didn't see you here, I was going to come down and drag you out for a drink myself."

"I believe you."

I see yellow out of the corner of my eye before I hear, "Ruby! What are you doing here?"

"June," she tsks, "I'm here to support my family. It was our idea to do this event, after all."

"I know, but I thought you were resting." I can hear the concern in her voice, which makes me wonder if there's something wrong with Ruby, but it's probably because of her age.

Ruby ignores June and pats my arm. "I can sleep when I'm dead!"

I muffle my chuckle, and June looks like she wants to throttle her mother-in-law. I don't know what their story is, but I understand why Ruby wants to be here; she seems perfectly fine, too.

"You need me here to get the boys bidding on these lovely women," Ruby adds. "I know how to make men spend their money."

I bark out a loud laugh this time. "I missed you, Ruby."

She takes my hand and squeezes. "I missed you too, dear. Now, why don't you come work the crowd with me. I'm sure

Gavin will take the stage soon. Wait till you see him do his thing. My grandbaby is an entertainer," she says with pride.

Before I can tell Ruby I'd rather stay near Daddy and get another drink, she's dragging me into the happy crowd as June lets out a huff behind us.

As we walk, a few more people say hi to me, and other acquaintances continue to awkwardly stare. As we find an open spot, the music rises and the lights dim.

"Get ready," Ruby says with giddiness. "He's coming out now."

"Save a Horse, Ride a Cowboy" by Big & Rich blares through the speakers, and every woman in the joint starts to cry like a stripper is about to walk out on stage.

Before I see a face, I hear a low drawl; a true country man's voice that vibrates through my feet and up to the top of my head. My toes curl in my boots and I'm now very aware that this is exactly the reason why these women are going nuts.

"Ladies and gentlemen! Are you ready to have a good time tonight?"

My eyes search for the voice belonging to Gavin Montgomery, but even with my tall stature, I'm having a hard time seeing where he is. Eventually, I spot the top of a black cowboy hat moving through the heated bodies.

The crowd cheers, and Ruby and I are smushed a bit closer to the front so we're in the middle now. Concerned about the older woman, I glance at her, but she couldn't care less. Her eyes shine bright, and she's hooting and hollering like the rest of the crowd.

The still faceless Gavin waits for them to calm down a bit, then says, "I *know* I am. And you know what I'm REALLY, ready for?" The crowd's cheers go crazy. "To see some good-looking people riding the one, the only... TORRRRNAAADOOOOO!"

As he speaks the bull's name, he must hit a controller because it comes to life, shaking and spinning about under a spotlight. It's comical, but effective.

I turn my head to the right just as the nicest backside in Texas jumps up on the old stage near the bull. Gavin's jeans are tight and faded, his cowboy boots worn, and his T-shirt matches Kade and Jake's—except his is cut off at the arms to show his muscular biceps. I haven't seen his face yet, but my eyes are drawn to the way his veins run from his forearm to his hand, gripping the handheld microphone.

I think back to the last time I saw Gavin. It was at our Ranch; he would've been only nineteen and I twenty-four. He was a sweet boy who was quiet when he came around. He and Reed were always off getting into something with their little herd of troublemakers. Just like with his brother Kade, I guess I never really noticed him. I was so absorbed in winning barrel racing titles and kissing boys my own age.

Gavin turns, and his masculine face looks out at the crowd before he makes eye-contact with his mom and gives her a wink. Girls I don't recognize are going wild, yelling at him to take his clothes off like he's in Magic Mike. He could be, but this place is packed full of people we've known since before we were born, and his family. I can't imagine this feels comfortable for him, but who knows? I don't know anything about Gavin Montgomery.

Once he's turned off the bull, he opens his big arms and tells the crowd to settle. "Now, tonight is a little different from a usual night at Night Hawk. So before we start, I'd like to say on behalf of the Montgomery family, we appreciate y'all being here tonight. Again, the people of Randall have shown up for their own."

Cheers of "*Yeehaw*!" "*We love you, Gavin*!" and catcalls ring through the crowd. I must admit it warms my heart.

When he turns his full gaze toward me and Ruby, his green eyes connect with mine like he knew I'd be standing here. I can tell he knows who I am by the blanched look on his face. He swallows, his Adam's apple bobbing as he continues to stare. Within seconds, someone yells his name, and he turns his stage smile back on in a well-practiced manner.

"Alright folks, a few ground rules," he says into the mic, no longer fazed. "If you've decided to participate in the date auction, you have a card on you that gives the lineup of each rider that's up for bid. Riders, we'll call your name when it's your time. Once you're on good 'ole Tornado here," he wiggles the bull again, "the audience can bid on you only while you're on the bull. Once you fall off, the bidding ends, and the last lucky cowboy or cowgirl who's raised their card is the winner of your date."

The air is pulses with energy—these people are ready to start bidding.

"Papa Loved Mama" by Garth Brooks comes on as Gavin calls up the first girl, who happens to be Polly Carson. She looks nervous, but I already see her eyeing one of the young Corbin boys. I can tell the blonde one has the hots for her by the way he's staring at her chest and ample butt.

"Come on up here, Miss Polly. No need to be shy now!" Gavin calls.

She blushes when he gives her a crooked smile. I watch the way his arms flex as he helps her walk along the cushioned area around the bull. Then, in a move that has half the room wishing they could bid on Gavin, he lifts Polly up like she weighs as much as a two-string bale of hay. Which is nothing. She blushes harder as he rights her on the bull, showing her where to put her hands before patting her thigh in a friendly manner.

Gavin walks off the bouncing mats, closing a small, padded gate behind him. When he's back up on the small stage, he holds up Polly's basket. It's a cute little wicker one that's wrapped in pink cellophane.

"Gentlemen, this here is Miss Polly. If you don't know these fine folks here tonight...well then, you've either been living under a rock or you're not from around these parts." He smiles as he says it, laying his accent on thick. I don't think he normally talks like this, but it sure gets the people going.

"Polly is twenty-four years old. She's sweeter than honey, and just so happens to be studying to be a large animal vet, but also enjoys swimming and baking. You know what that means, fellas..."

"I'll never go hungry!" the blonde Corbin boy yells, still looking at Polly like he's ready to jump her bones.

"He's talking about what's in the basket, you idiot!" Ruby yells at him, giving me a look that says, "*Men. Ugh!*"

Gavin shakes his head while he laughs, before turning back to Polly. "Hold on tight, darling. Bidding starts at one hundred!" he yells into the mic before shaking the bull. Polly lets out a squeal and grips her thighs around the machine. The shaking causes every bit of her to jiggle, making the crowd erupt in cheers.

"One hundred!" the Corbin boy calls out, lifting his paddle.

"We got one hundred, do I hear two?" Gavin spins the bull gently, making sure Polly doesn't fall off right away to end the bidding.

"Two hundred!" a gentleman yells.

"Two hundred-fifty!" the Corbin boy counters. Gavin vibrates the bull, then spins Polly a little faster. She lets out another noise and for a moment, I think she's going to fall. The audience cheers her on, and the women start yelling pointers on how to grip with her thighs.

"We've got two hundred-fifty! Come on, fellas, don't be shy. He holds up Polly's basket and smells it. "Pretty sure there's freshly baked cookies in here." He wiggles his eyebrows and then spins the bull again.

"Two seventy-five!" a third man yells.

"Three hundred!" The Corbin boy says, shooting his shot again. His brother tugs his arm, giving him a look that tells him to stop bidding, or he's going to be in trouble.

Gavin looks over near us. At first, I think he's looking at Ruby, but I realize he's eyeing me again. God, he's sexy. Maybe the Montgomery boys just mature into sexy cowboy gods—or something landed in Randall's water supply after I left. *Dang...*

"I hear three hundred!" Gavin echoes, never taking his eyes off mine.

My cheeks flush as a man yells another bid at three twenty-five.

Getting nervous under Gavin's gaze, I look back to Polly, who's still hanging on—granted, the bull isn't moving that fast. When her eyes lock on the Corbin boy, it's almost like she's pleading with him to bid on her again.

The Corbin boy ignores the chiding of his brother, holding up his paddle and yelling, "Three-fifty!" His brother smacks him on the head as Gavin gives Tornado a wild jerk. Polly goes flying off, landing on her plush ass. The crowd makes an 'aww' sound before they start cheering again.

My eyes find Gavin's once more, and he winks at me. He definitely threw Polly off on purpose so she could get her date with the Corbin boy.

Gavin walks over to Polly, helping her up and handing the basket to her. "Good work, Miss Polly! Now off you go. And congrats to Tim Corbin for winning this pretty gal here. Enjoy the cookies."

The audience laughs, and Polly blushes pink. Tim runs up while people slap him on the back. Once he reaches Polly, he kisses her on the cheek, and she hands him her basket.

Gavin shoos them off the stage. "Run along, now!"

"I told you my grandbaby is good at this," Ruby says. I jump a little, having completely forgotten she was right next to me.

"You could say that again," I chuckle.

"He was staring at you." She smiles. "I saw the look on your face, too. Looked like sparks were flying out of your head."

My cheeks burn. "Ruby! He's your grandson, and he's younger than me. I'm also not looking for a man right now."

She shrugs. "None of those things mean anything."

As I'm about to respond, the music lowers, and Gavin's full-toned voice echoes over the mic. "Before we move on to the next person on the list, I have someone special I'd like to bring up on the stage."

Ruby raises her eyebrows, and I think he's going to call her up, or maybe his mom. But when he locks eyes with me again, a mischievous smile forms on his lips, and my stomach drops.

Good Lord, please, no.

"A beloved member of our town has returned to us," Gavin says.

I shake my head, my body going stiff. The crowd turns, even causing the people from the city to look at me. I shrink back into Ruby, frantically looking for the emergency exit so I can run. My eye catches Daddy's, and I can see the frown on his face. He didn't know this was going to happen. At least that's something.

Ruby nudges me forward. "It's alright, now. Go up there and say hello to the people. Everyone's been wanting to hear from you."

Gavin continues, "Ladies and gentlemen, welcome on up our very own National Barrel Racing Champion..."

My mouth goes dry at my old title—one that is no longer relevant; nor one that I want. It only gets worse when people do a drum roll and I know I'm being backed into a corner. I stare into Gavin's eyes, shaking my head back and forth as I plead with him to stop, but the bastard just smiles. Smiles! And even though I desperately don't want to go up on stage, everyone is here. I don't think I can embarrass myself or my family by not going up there.

"Miss Blake...Tanneeerrr!!!" Gavin elongates every syllable, and the crowd cheers. I wave at everyone, but my feet don't move.

"Come on now, Miss Tanner," he drawls into the mic.

"We don't bite!" someone yells from the crowd.

Gavin puts his pointer and middle fingers together, then makes a 'come hither' motion with his hand. I stand strong, finally saying, "I'm fine right here, Cowboy."

He only shakes his head and motions for me to come to him. Before I know it, my name is being chanted throughout the crowd, and people are nudging me to the stage.

I shoot a quick glance at Daddy and he only nods his head. He knows I'm stuck. If I don't go up, I'll look like a coward. Not to mention a fool. I'm stuck between a rock and a hard place.

With a smile on my face, I push back my shoulders and take a step forward. But not before I silently say every bad word I know to Gavin Montgomery.

CHAPTER 4

Gavin

I CAN FEEL KADE and Jake's curious gaze on me all the way from the bar, but I don't give them the satisfaction of acknowledging them.

I heard Blake Tanner was back, but I tried not to think too much about it. Considering how tragic Reed's death was to our town, thinking about her meant thinking about him. About the loss of a friend, a brother.

But then I took the stage and saw her. Her brown eyes were wide and her cheeks were stained pink from either a natural blush or the heat, maybe both—and I couldn't take my eyes off her. Instantly, I wanted to get Blake on the bull and bid on her, rational thought be damned. Her presence alone made me forget where I was for a moment and what I was supposed to be doing, which is never the case. On any regular night, Matthew McConaughey could walk in and I wouldn't have missed a beat. But this woman...

When I was a kid, I had a little crush on her, one I didn't entertain because she's Reed's older sister. But in the years she's been gone, Blake has transformed into something else. I can't help but notice how her heavy breasts strain against the faded Garth Brooks concert tee she's knotted at her stomach, revealing a tiny peek of luscious skin that I want to bite with my teeth. And how her coffee-colored hair is curlier and longer than the chin-length style she once wore. I've already started to fantasize about wrapping it around my fist as I run my hand down her bare back.

Before my thoughts slip further down the gutter, I turn my eyes on Gran and her questioning gaze. I can't tell if she disapproves of this little stunt or not, but she's been trying to push me into the arms of every available woman in town, so this should make her happy. But I had meant what I told Jake: I don't have time for women, nor the money to properly treat my date the way I liked to—but I also haven't seen or been in a room with Blake Tanner in almost five years. It's like someone has electrified my body and opened my chest wide, stuffing butterflies in. It's a feeling I haven't had since Cricket ripped my heart out and stomped on it.

My stomach turns, and for a moment I try to stop myself from making what I know is an irresponsible decision. I should not be letting a pretty woman throw me off, especially one I don't know well, but my body, my heart, has other ideas. It wants to find out who she is now, and what she's been up to the last five years. It wants to throw caution to the wind and be like Kade for once: a man who does what he feels like and enjoys life. Suddenly, I don't want to be responsible; I don't want to be Gavin Montgomery, the head of the house. I want to be young and free. I want Blake.

I lock eyes with her again, and my final decision is made. I'm going to have that date with her, even if I have to make a fool of myself to do it. Even if the entire town gets pissed at me, it will be worth it.

With the sexiest grin I can muster, I give her the 'I see you' motion, followed by pretending to lure her in like a fish. When she doesn't move, the crowd does the work for her and starts to nudge her forward. Unable to stop the motion, she takes one step toward the stage, then another. I watch as she puts her shoulders back and transforms from a shy woman into the confident Champion Barrel Racer I knew back in the day. Back when Reed was still with us, and she rode a horse as if she was born to do it.

At her shift in energy, people part like the Red Sea, as if I'm Moses waiting to receive her. The music around us fades as her body sways toward me. I'm salivating at the sight of how her jeans hug the supple skin of her well-rounded thighs and generous stomach. Lord, I've got it bad already.

When she finally reaches the stage, I offer her my free hand, hoisting her up next to me. It doesn't escape me that her touch sends a shock to my system—which only enforces my decision to do what I'm about to do. As she stands straight, warmth builds in my belly at her height. Blake's taller than most of the women in town, which is a nice change. I don't have to bend down too far to look her in the eye...or kiss her. And by the way her plush lips are pouting, I want that to happen as soon as possible if she'll let me.

"Y'all, let's give our sweet Blake Tanner a big welcome home!" I say into the mic, spinning her out and back in. She's not expecting it, so when she stumbles into my arms, her soft body hits my hard chest. She lets out an oomph before placing what I call a 'Bless Your Heart Smile' on her face and uses her free hand to wave at the cheering crowd.

Eventually, her eyes flit down to our interlocked hands. I think she forgot I was holding it, but I've been enjoying its soft warmth. I don't get a chance to relish it much longer, because she pulls back and steps away from me.

I leave her standing to my right before addressing everyone in the crowd again. "Now, you may be wondering why I brought the beautiful and talented Miss Tanner up to the stage."

"Get her on the bull!" one of the townies hollers.

Blake waves her hands and politely declines, but she's not getting off that easy. Though the years have been kind to her physical form, it doesn't take a genius to see by the rigidness in her stance that she could use a little fun. Not to mention, this town talks. After Blake left, it was apparent that the girl we once knew had changed because of the accident...not that anyone could blame her. Grief changes a person. I would know.

What I don't know is what she's been doing all these years. But now that I have a closer look at her, it sure as hell doesn't look like she's happy. I've seen her happy before, and this is not it. An intense desire to make her laugh fills me from head to toe. I hope I'm not reading the situation wrong. I could just be an idiot, and she's only uncomfortable because of me getting her up here, but my gut is telling me it's more than that. I can only hope the bull and a date with me might shake her up a bit. Maybe it will remind her of who and what she is to this town. Maybe it'll help her feel more comfortable.

I give the crowd a big Montgomery boy smile. "For all the young'uns that weren't around when Blake Tanner was the best thing in Randall since sliced bread, let me bring you up to speed. At twelve years old, she started winning barrel racing competitions all over Texas. By the time she was a teen, she was winning junior championships and riding better than most of your elders." The older men of the town chime in, yelling words to back me up.

Blake flushes, bowing her head in humble grace as I continue. "She then went on to win numerous rodeos while setting records. When she was twenty-four, she ranked fifth in world standings, and even topped a million dollars in career earnings."

Before I can finish, the people begin to chant, "*Ride the bull! Ride the bull!*"

"Y'all!" she yells after a few seconds, putting out her hands to quiet them down. "Y'all are sweeter than honey, I almost can't stand it." Her saccharin voice hums as she says it. She's laying her accent on thick, almost comically. I can't say I don't love it.

Then, in a move that surprises me, she saunters over and takes the mic from my hand. The crowd lets out a collective chuckle as she brings it to her lips.

"Thank you, Gavin, for the warm welcome and tooting my horn. I'm happy to be home. Y'all are welcome to come on down to Double-Time Ranch anytime you like."

I raise my eyebrows at her words. Given she's been home for a month, and this is her first appearance in town, I highly doubt she wants to see anyone at her ranch.

"But I think it's time to get back to why these fine people came here," she finishes with a too-sweet smile.

"We want to bid on you, Blake Tanner!" Jake says from the bar. He looks at her in a casual flirtatiousness; even though this is Jake's MO, I want to punch him clear across the face. When I lock eyes with him, he gives me a knowing look. Like he understands exactly what my plan has been from the moment I laid eyes on her. I hope he doesn't think that she's going home with him.

"No boys, I'm out of practice." She laughs. "You've got plenty of women, younger women, to choose from."

She gazes out in the crowd at her dad, Lee Tanner, as if she's hoping he'll swoop in with his Stetson and slam his boot up my ass. God help me, but he looks...relieved? Blake presses her lips together, like she's afraid. Confusion and curiosity fill me as to why she's refusing the silly bull ride with so much gusto. That woman can ride any horse or bull and ride it well. I've seen her stay on a horse that tried to run her through a goddamn wall and make it out without a scratch.

"Ride the bull, Blake Tanner!" Mark Gunner's boy yells before he flashes a wad of cash in his hand. I guess the entire town wants to take Blake Tanner on a date. Too bad they don't know she's going to be mine.

"Come on, Blake! We want to see you ride!" Polly adds with a Cheshire cat grin. That turns the crowd up again, and this time they get damn rowdy. To the point if she doesn't get on that bull soon, they may storm the stage and put her on it. Not that I'd let them.

She turns to me, contempt on her face. We stare at each other for what seems like an hour, but in reality, it's seconds. I lift an eyebrow at her and try to reassure her with another smile, but she stares me down as the people's cheers get louder. Maybe this is stupid; I didn't intend to actually make her angry.

"You got this, Blake!" a voice yells above the hollering. I know it's Gran's from the familiar scratchy tone.

Blake's eyes flick to hers, and in one last feeble attempt, she says, "I don't have a basket."

That's when Abby Allen yells, "I'll make you one, darling! Don't you worry."

The crowd goes wild, and I give Blake a smile that rivals even Kade's. It doesn't work on her in the slightest because she shoves the mic against my chest and makes her way toward the bull. It's a nice view, watching her walk away from me in those tight jeans, but I'm ready to watch her ride Tornado and win a date. I can only hope she'll forgive me for doing this later. When I follow her into the bullpen, I go to help her up onto the bull, but she turns and stops me.

"I got it, Cowboy."

She hops up on that thing like the champion she is, putting one hand on her hat to keep it in place and holding on with the other.

I raise an eyebrow at her, as if to ask, *"Are you sure about that?"*

She taunts me back out loud, "Do I look like I need both hands?"

The people shout out their 'oohs' and 'ouches' like she's hurt my feelings.

Laughing under my breath, I say into the mic, "Get ready for the ride of your life, Miss Tanner."

I walk to the stage and see Kade there. He's riling up the crowd and getting them ready to bid on this rodeo star. As the music turns up, he leans to speak into my ear, his voice low, "What the hell do you think you're doing?"

"Getting myself a date," I tell him, my voice sure.

I watch him swallow hard. His eyes crease with anger. I don't blame him either. I'm being a hypocrite. Not just to him, but to Cricket, too. I would never have bid on her, but now I'm going to go spend my own money. Thankfully, it will come back to me, but Blake Tanner is going to fetch a pretty penny. Probably more than any of the people on our list. She's an enigma, a woman wrapped in mystery after having been gone for so many years. Not to mention attractive as hell and a spitfire. Every Texan man's dream.

Kade grunts. "You're a selfish asshole."

He's right, at least in this case. But at the same time, this is the kind of stunt he would pull if he felt even half of what I'm feeling right now for Blake; I have no doubt in my mind. That thought helps me push back the guilt I'm beginning to feel, even if deep down, I know I shouldn't be doing what I'm about to do.

I bring the mic to my lips again. "My brother Kade here is going to run the bidding on Miss Tanner." The crowd hollers. As I hand the mic to Kade, he instantly clears the look of unrest from his features and goes to work. Before he can get a word out, I'm hopping off the stage and grabbing a number left on the table. I can feel all the eyes of the room on me, and I hear a few gasps of shock, but I don't give a shit.

"It seems my big brother has decided to join the bidding," Kade says into the mic.

"How is that supposed to work?" Mark Gunner's boy yells.

"Oh, let him be!" Gran says back. And that about ends that. I'm sure she'll take it upon herself to do some recon later to make sure people aren't upset. She's always been good at making the folks of Randall happy. She has that charm about her.

Kade keeps his smile on and says, "Alright then, Jake, turn up the music."

"Country Girl (Shake It For Me)" by Luke Bryan saturates the room, raising the already buzzing energy up. I make my way toward Gran so I have a better view of the woman I'm about to win a date with.

Gran's eyes are twinkling as she says, "You son of a gun! I approve, but that sweet woman is not happy with you. Not to mention your Momma and Kade won't be happy about the money we're about to lose."

She's right on both accounts, but I'll have to worry about both things later. I've already made my bed.

I keep a casual look on my face as I call out to Kade, "Let's do this thing!"

My eyes reconnect with Blake, still sitting atop Tornado with her fierce gaze trained on me.

"You ready, Miss Tanner?" Kade asks. She tips her hat at him and grips her thighs around Tornado, which makes me think a lot of dirty thoughts. Ones I'm sure the other men in this bar are thinking, too.

"Get ready, ladies and gentlemen, because the bid starts at one hundred!" Kade hits the button controlling the bull and gives Tornado a little spin.

"One hundred!" someone calls.

"One-fifty," I call back, raising my paddle.

"Two hundred," another man yells before Kade can say a word. I think it's Mark Gunner's boy, but I'm not paying close attention.

My eyes are trained on Blake as I bid and Kade starts to make the bull buck a little. She may be out of practice, but her body remembers how to ride.

"We've got ourselves a professional, gentlemen!" Kade calls, making Tornado spin faster. At this point, fifty percent of people would have fallen off, but not Blake.

"Two-fifty," I call again, raising my paddle.

"Three hundred!" This time, I know that voice. It's Jake. Goddamn bastard.

"Three-fifty," I immediately say back.

"Three-seventy-five!" another man yells.

To my annoyance, Kade bucks the bull harshly to throw Blake off, but she doesn't move an inch. Her hips are undulating with the movement of the machine; hell, she doesn't even look bothered by it. The crowd goes wild. Clearly, they're loving this.

A few new men shout bids, bringing the total up to five hundred. Now I'm wondering why I gave my brother control over this auction. I should've stayed up there and thrown Blake off the bull after I bid one hundred. More guilt flares at the thought of taking this much money away from my family, but I can't stop myself now. I'm in too deep.

As the bids get higher, and the crowd gets louder, Gran says into my ear, "What are you doing, boy? Bid again before she falls off!"

"Seven hundred!" I yell.

Jake calls back, "Eight hundred!"

"Yeehaw!" Kade crows, right before he turns Tornado up to the fastest speed we have. Blake is holding on for dear life, but I can tell she's getting tired. She's been on for a long time.

"Nine hundred," I bid quickly, seeing she's about ready to fall.

"You sure you got that much money, boy?" some drunk Randall townie yells, but I ignore his jab.

I lock eyes with Kade. I know he's about ready to do some trick we know to throw people off, usually the drunk assholes we want to embarrass. But Blake has already proven she's got skills, and it's time to end this auction.

"One thousand!" Jake yells, causing people to gasp.

Gran elbows me in the ribs as I look once more at Kade. I see he's a little sorry, but not enough to stop himself from spinning Blake so wildly that it's almost guaranteed to give her whiplash.

I raise my paddle and open my mouth, but I'm too late. With one last buck, she finally falls, landing on the padded surface beneath her.

As the people go crazy, yelling words of love to Blake, I feel the blood beneath my skin start to boil.

"Jake Buckley," Kade says, "come on up and get your lady!"

Your lady. Bullshit.

My eyes narrow as Kade meets my more than angry gaze.

*Oh...*my brother is a dead man—and he knows it, too.

CHAPTER 5

Blake

ONCE I'M OFF THE bull, I make a beeline for the emergency exit, not caring about the people screaming my name or my wobbling legs. I push open the door and finally let out the breath I've been holding in. The heat of the summer night doesn't do anything to cool down my flushed skin, but I'm grateful for the fresh air.

After I've taken a few deep breaths, my brain finally catches up to what happened in the bar. That asswipe Gavin Montgomery is a piece of work. I've never encountered a man more full of himself, more oblivious to a person's signals, than him.

Then he went and pretended he wanted to bid on me so he could get more money for his family? What a bastard.

"You look like you could start a fight in an empty house."

The voice of my *date* makes me stand a little straighter. I force a smile his way. "I'm fine." The fib tastes like acid on my tongue, but I've already been embarrassed enough for one day.

Jake pulls out a pack of cigarettes and offers me one. I tell him no as he takes a half-used one out for himself and lights it up.

"I know it's a gross habit. But my gramps smoked, then my dad, now me. I guess it runs in the family." He chuckles to himself.

"You shouldn't have to pay that money for me, Jake." The words come out of my mouth before I can stop them.

He takes a drag of his smoke and puffs it out away from me. "I love the Montgomerys like my own family. I was planning to bid on someone tonight, anyway. Having you up there made the choice easy."

"It's not fair, though."

"What's not fair?"

"Gavin planted himself in the audience and Kade made sure the bull wasn't going that fast up until the end. They purposely made the bid draw out so they could get more money. The whole thing was a set up."

A barking laugh leaves Jake's mouth, startling me. "Blake Tanner, are you blind?"

"Excuse me?"

He takes another drag of his cigarette. "You heard me."

My eyes narrow. "I don't know what you're playing at."

"Gavin wanted to win that bid. He did this whole thing on his own. It wasn't planned. When he called you up on stage, I swear Kade's pretty head was about to pop right off his body. He was so pissed."

Curiosity fills me. "Why?"

Jake stubs the end of his cigarette on the wall before throwing it out. "You'd probably have to ask him that."

My brain is trying to put all the pieces together, but I don't understand. I don't know the Montgomery boys well. Ruby and June are the only members of that family I'm super friendly with. What Gavin pulled in there baffles me. The only answer is that he did it to get more money. Jake has to be wrong.

I cross my arms over my chest. "Then why did you win the bid?"

"Honestly, I wanted a date with you. We could be good together..." he trails off, his eyes wandering my body like they had earlier.

"Jake—"

He cuts me off. "But as I said, the Montgomerys are family. I wasn't going to let Gavin make a complete fool of himself or miss out on all that cash. They need it more than Dad and I do. This place has been good to us," he adds, looking back at Night Hawk. "And Gavin has made it what it is. I owe him."

My heart clenches for Jake. It's clear from his tone that he really does love them.

Jake continues, "And Gavin wanted you, honey. Make no mistake. If we weren't friends, he'd probably punch my lights out for what I just did. But at the end of the day, their family gets what they came for, and I get to have you for a night."

I snort as he grins at me like a cat who caught the canary. Which is definitely how I feel right now. A bird who's in the jaws of death, unable to move.

I fidget nervously. "I'm still not sure what to believe. Are you sure it wasn't a stunt?"

Jake puts his hand on my shoulder, the smell of nicotine invading my senses. "You've been gone for a long time, Blake. Things around here have changed. But one thing that hasn't is how the people of this town show up for one another, and the fact that we're all honest with each other. Gavin is a good man, and so is Kade. Gavin wanted to win you, but I knew that Kade would be pissed if Gavin spent a thousand bucks on you and stopped their family from getting what they needed. This whole event is to support them, after all."

"So Kade threw me off after your bid?"

He removes his hand from my shoulder and nods.

"I thought you said you wanted a date with me, Jake."

"Jesus, woman," he chuckles, "you're busting my balls here."

I shake my head at him. "I'm only trying to understand!"

"I've said it a few times now, but I'll say it again. I want to go on a date with you, Blake Tanner. Even if it's to catch up as friends. The question is, can you handle me?" He looks at me with a wolfish grin, his dark eyebrows raised in question.

I shove him in a friendly way. "Did you see me in there?"

"I did. It was amazing to see you in action again."

My throat tightens. The endorphins of the ride are starting to come down, and the reality of what I did comes rushing back. Riding the mechanical bull...it's a lot different from riding a live animal. Different from riding a horse or barrel racing. My cheeks burn as I remember Gavin telling the entire crowd my history. A history I want to forget.

"I hope you burned it to your memory, Jake, because that's the one and only time you'll see me riding anything again. You're lucky as it is! If the entire town hadn't been inside, I would've given Mr. Montgomery the finger and hightailed it home."

Before Jake can speak again, the door opens, and Daddy's Stetson comes into view. I let out a sigh, grateful he's here so we can leave.

Jake goes still and takes off his red cowboy hat. "Howdy, Sir."

Daddy nods at him. "You treating my baby girl right?"

"Of course. Just sorting out our date. Does this Friday evening work for you?"

I open my mouth to say I'll pass on the date, but Daddy sees what I'm going to do and steps in, saying, "That works for Blake."

Jake eyes me and I feel like a fifteen-year-old girl again.

"But the foals?" I try.

Daddy shakes his head. "This man bid a lot of his hard-earned money to take you out and help the Montgomerys. The foals are fine tonight, and they'll be fine on Friday."

When my gaze connects with Jake, his dark eyes shine with question. I know he's wondering if I'm going to follow Daddy's orders. The Blake he knew once wouldn't have. But now things are different. I'm his only living child. A child who took off when shit got hard. I don't have the heart to let him down again. So I swallow my pride.

"Friday is fine," I answer.

Jake blinks at me, as if he expects me to say, *"Kidding!"* and flip him the bird.

"It's settled, then." Daddy nods, putting his hand out to shake Jake's.

My gut churns. I've never felt more like cattle in my entire life. Apparently moving home has made me some kind of prize. I knew coming here tonight was a bad idea! I should've refused harder, but as Jake's solemn gaze just told me I've completely lost my backbone, not that I didn't know it already.

Jake puts his hand in my father's, shaking it sternly.

The door opens for a second, and Kade's head pops out. He winks when he sees me, then grabs Jake's attention. "We need you inside, it got busier."

Jake salutes him, then bids us farewell. "I'll pick you up at seven on Friday."

My head jerks in acknowledgement before he follows Kade back into the bar. Through the open door, I can see Gavin on stage, a sheen of sweat on his forehead. For a moment, his eyes lock with mine, and I swear he looks pissed. I don't know what for—I'm the one who gets to be upset. Right before the door closes, I finally get my chance to flip someone off.

When he sees me do it, I swear he smirks, but the door closes before I can know for sure. Once the light is gone from inside, I'm met with the silence of Daddy's disappointment.

"I expect you to act more mature than that, Blake."

I grasp my hands behind my back and instead start walking to the truck. He sighs behind me, and the gravel crunches under his boots as he follows me.

Once at the passenger door, I try to open it, but it's locked. He never locks it, which means he just did it so I couldn't get in. Once he reaches me, he puts his hand on my shoulder.

"I know this isn't what you wanted."

I let out a snort. "That was embarrassing. I haven't seen these people in years. I don't even know Gavin Montgomery! He had no right to do that, and you know it."

"He was trying to be nice. He wanted—"

"He was being self-serving. It was rude and a real dick move."

"Watch how you talk."

I kick the rocks and dust at my feet. "I would like to go home. I'm done being treated like an animal for the evening."

"You know that isn't what this was about."

"Do I, though? As far as I can tell, I was given to someone for a thousand dollars against my wishes. I had to take it because I was in front of people that have known me since I was born; some people who I've never even met! And don't even get me started on the fact that I don't get on horses anymore, and the same applies to mechanical bulls!"

Daddy holds my shoulder firm as I try to take a step back. "Calm down, Blake. There's no reason to get this upset. This was just some fun for the town. Gavin is raising money for his family, and we came to help. You helped. It's a harmless date with a kid you grew up with. It doesn't have to be more than that."

My mouth goes dry, tears stinging the corners of my eyes. "I thought you were always on my side."

He sighs. "I am on your side."

"It sure as shit doesn't feel like it."

"Blake—"

"I said, I'd like to go home."

Daddy stares me in the eyes and then says, after a long moment, "How about we go to The Diner like old times?"

My heart pounds, so much so that I can hear it beating in my ears. Bile rises in my throat, and I want to throw up right at his feet. When his dad, our Gramps, was alive, he would say that milkshakes were the cure for all sorrows, all hurts...pretty much anything. It was a Tanner family tradition to go to The Diner to have milkshakes at any sign of trouble.

The last time we went was the night before Reed died. He was arguing with Mom about having me take Briar to a competition in Tennessee. The mare was only four and had a very unpredictable temperament, which made her a less than desirable pick for competing at such a high level. We all knew she wasn't ready yet; but Reed wanted to prove to everyone, especially Mom, that he was ready to start taking on other horses to train for various disciplines.

So we went to The Diner that night and they talked it out. But it was easy to see that Reed was going to try his hardest to get her ready in time, regardless of what anyone told him. He wanted to be known as one of the best horse trainers in Texas, like Mom, and nothing and no one was going to stop him from doing that.

Three weeks later, I was on a bus to Tennessee, but not for a rodeo...

"Baby girl, where's your head at?"

The roaring in my skull fades as I clench my fists to keep from sobbing. "I'd really like to go home," I repeat.

Daddy reaches up and catches a tear on my cheek I didn't realize escaped. "We have to talk about what happened with Reed at some point. It's eating you up from the inside out."

I want to laugh. Hell, I almost do. "You and Mom don't talk about it, so why should I?"

"That isn't fair, and you know it. Your mom and I have worked hard to get where we are—but you keep running from it."

I swear if I was a color right now, I'd be red. "Either you take me home right now, or I'll walk." It's miles away, but I'd rather walk till sunrise than stand here any longer.

"Bla—"

"Please! *Please* listen to me," I plead. "I've had enough for tonight."

He takes a breath, then blows it back out again. The door to the bar creaks open as Daddy finally unlocks the truck. I'm glad about it, too. Because I see a black cowboy hat and broad shoulders that I know belong to Gavin Montgomery. Before he can catch my eyes, I open the door to the truck and hop in, locking it behind me as if I'm being chased. God finally must be doing me a solid because Gavin doesn't approach. Though I'm sure he would've, if Daddy wasn't outside.

After a few long seconds, the driver's side door opens, and Daddy hops in. Thankfully, he doesn't try to talk to me again before starting the ignition. As he pulls out of the parking space, I stare out the side window, and look at Gavin. He's got a bottle of water in one of his large hands as he sends me a wave. I don't flip him off this time, choosing instead to stare at him with all the anger I can muster. Hopefully, it's the last time I'll ever look upon his stupidly handsome face.

CHAPTER 6

Gavin

IT'S AFTER FIVE IN the morning, and I'm exhausted. I've only slept a few hours, but my mind won't let me rest. Every time I close my eyes, I see Blake Tanner's beautiful but pissed off face staring at me like I'm the worst person on the planet, which makes my insides twist with shame.

In retrospect, what I did was an assholish thing to do. What's worse is that my plan failed. Thanks to my little brother and Jake.

"If you frown that much, your face will get stuck that way."

I look up from the kitchen table, giving Gran a morning nod. I'm not much of a morning talker. Hell, I don't talk much outside of MCing or bartending at Night Hawk. I've always been the kind of man who stands silently next to his friends unless he has something important to say. Which makes last night's loss even more embarrassing. Serves me right for trying to act more like Kade.

I point to the coffee pot. "Coffee's fresh."

Gran makes her way over to the counter. She takes her favorite ruby red mug out of the cabinet and fills it to the brim. She drinks black coffee, like me. When I was a kid, she used to let me have a few sips of hers every morning. Grandpa used to say it's why I have such a bitter personality.

After she sits next to me at the table, her questioning look has me squirming in my seat.

"I didn't get a chance to chat with you last night since I left early with your Momma."

I take a sip of my coffee. It's hotter than I expect, so it burns my tongue. "We did alright. Kade counted everything up. It will cover some of our expenses, but not all of them. We're going to have to sell off some of the pigs."

Gran drinks her coffee as if it's room temperature. "I actually wanted to chat with you about Blake."

"I should get to work," I mumble. I make a move to stand, but Gran places her hand on my arm and tugs me down. She may be old, but she's stronger than she looks.

"The sun's not even up yet," she says. "You can take a minute to chat with your Gran."

I sit my butt back down like a good boy. I may be the head of the family now, or so I'm constantly reminded by Momma, but Gran is the true leader, the matriarch of the Montgomery family. Even when Grandpa was alive, and when Dad held his place after he passed, Gran had been the glue. She's lived and worked on the land since she was born. She knows when we're going to get rain and when a sow won't take during breeding season. She can also tell exactly what you're feeling without you having said a word. In grade school, Kade used to tell the kids she was a witch. It was funny until we started getting brooms and capes stuffed in our lockers.

Gran's eyes crinkle as she performs her neat magic trick right before my eyes. "You're upset about what Kade did last night, but you're also upset you let your emotions for Blake Tanner get in the way of your well-crafted persona. I'm sure there's guilt from the money we lost sprinkled in there, too."

I chuckle. "Have you been watching Oprah reruns again, Gran?"

She smirks. "Maybe."

"I don't know what came over me. I shouldn't have done it."

"I'll admit that you could have asked the woman out in a normal fashion. You didn't have to cause a scene to do it."

"I sense a 'but' coming?"

"But…it was nice to see you smile last night. And not that silly trademark Montgomery smile you and Kade give everyone all the time, but one that went all the way to your ears."

I mull over her words. Maybe I was happy, but Blake wasn't. "I saw her before she left with Lee. She flipped me off."

Gran snickers. "You can't blame her. You made her ride that bull in front of all those people."

"I didn't make her."

"Maybe not physically, but that girl was raised right. With everyone around, chanting the way they were, there's no way she could say no. I also know how hard it is to say no to a Montgomery man, especially one as handsome as you."

I tap the side of my coffee cup. "Now I feel worse than I did before."

"I was just as bad. I encouraged her to join you on stage." Gran ponders for a moment before she continues. "But when I looked into her eyes last night, I could tell the poor thing carries the weight of her brother's death on her shoulders. I thought maybe being up there would help. She used to love being the center of attention."

Gran's taken my thoughts from last night right out of my mind. I sigh. "I suppose that still doesn't make what I did right."

She takes another sip of her coffee. "Why did you do it?"

"You know why, Gran."

"I want to hear you say it."

I thread my hands through my short sandy hair, now nervous. "She just—she made something fire up inside me that I haven't felt in a long time. Maybe not even since before Dad died."

Gran hums in a teasing way. "Your eyes did always watch her a little bit longer than I thought they should. Especially considering you were ten and she was fifteen. You also remember her barrel racing record impeccably."

"The whole town knows her barrel racing record. People still watch the old tapes at bars for fun."

"That may be true, but the way you looked at her last night, it reminds me of the way your grandpa looked at me when we first met."

Gran and Grandpa were a love story that could be one of those cheesy romantic comedies. They met when they were kids and married when they were only eighteen. Grandpa died when I was a teenager, but Gran still talks about him as if he's alive, always keeping him with us.

I stand up to put my empty cup in the sink, then turn to grab my cowboy hat from the table. "Either way, not only did I embarrass Blake, but I didn't even win the bid. I got too full of myself...too high on the adrenaline of a chance to win and woo her like we're still in the 1950s. Now Jake gets to take her out."

"You know," Gran says as she stands, "you could head on over to Double-Time and ask the sweet girl on a date."

I grind my teeth. "Like she'd say yes to me now."

Gran reaches up to pat my cheek. "You're a Montgomery. If we want something, we go after it. Since when did a little wounded pride stop you? I saw the look of determination on your face last night. I also saw the way Blake looked at you. She wasn't looking at Jake Buckley like that."

A fire in my gut sparks. "You're sure?"

"If there's one thing you can bet on, Gavin Montgomery, it's that I'm never wrong."

I crack a real smile at her. "No, you aren't."

Double-Time Ranch is massive. The plains roll expansively with greenish brown hills off in the distance and smatterings of trees. The drought has been unkind to all of us this year. Even the neon grass that usually stands out around the main stables has gone dry, making the red barn look a little worn.

It's still beautiful. The kind of barn you see on postcards from Kentucky.

But even with the drought, the Tanners have been lucky. Their horse breeding and training program hasn't slowed down. Though I'm sure their hay prices are through the roof, they can afford the price jack. Lee and Margie have even taken it upon themselves to donate a lot of supplies and money to other families like mine who've needed help. They're admirable people, ones that have deep roots in Randall.

My dad used to tell me all about how the Tanners once ran a similar operation to ours, raising and selling cattle, pigs, and growing cotton. That is until Margie met Lee and changed their business into what it is now. The horses they breed and train are some of the best in Texas, if not the United States. With their history, it's not a surprise that both Reed and Blake ended up being the best riders I've ever seen. It's in their blood. And Blake has once again proven her natural talent while riding the bull last night.

My mouth turns dry as images of her hips moving in time to Tornado's flips and spins saturate my mind. I blink my eyes a few times to try and remove them from my memory. I'm not here to chase down a piece of ass for the night. Even if Blake Tanner has one of the best, if not *the* best, asses I've ever seen. She's way more than some buckle bunny to pick up. She's...well, I'm not one hundred percent sure yet. But I do know that I want her, in whatever way she'll allow.

"Is that you, Gavin Montgomery?"

I turn on my signature smile as Margie Tanner comes hobbling over on a pair of crutches. I knew about her accident right after it happened. We were all grateful she only came out of it with a broken leg. This family, the people of Randall, we've suffered enough losses.

Taking off my hat, I walk to her in greeting; not wanting her to hobble for longer than she has to. "Sure is, ma'am."

"Oh, quit it with that 'ma'am' stuff. You know to call me Margie."

I lean down and give her a kiss on the cheek. I don't see too much of Margie these days. A couple years back, I bought a horse from her, but I don't have a reason to come out here anymore. I see Lee a lot more because of his frequent runs into town for feed and other supplies. He also buys a cow or two off us every year. But since Reed's death and Blake's departure, it isn't like it used to be when I'd come here to hang out with Reed.

"*Margie*," I say with a smile. "How are you feeling?"

She pushes bits of brown curly hair flecked with silver behind her ear. "I'm managing. It's nice to have Blake back to help around here. But I get restless at home. So," she chuckles, "I sit in a chair and tell the exercise riders what to do."

"I'm glad to hear that."

"What brings you out here this evening? Feels a little like old times."

It surprises me, but sadness licks at the back of my throat. "I—well, I was coming to see Blake."

Her forehead rises. "Trying to get her to ride the mechanical bull again?"

I bite my inner cheek, feeling shy. "I suppose you heard about that."

"It was front page news this morning."

I blanche. "I sure hope you're kidding."

"Nope. Local newspaper snapped a shot. Was on my front porch this morning."

Shit. Gran must have hidden the paper from me.

"I'm sorry if I brought unwanted attention to Blake and your family."

"I've got no problem with it. I wanted Blake to participate, but she refused. I'm shocked she went up there in the first place. I thought maybe she got drunk or something till Lee told me what happened."

"Margie—"

She shakes her head. "I'm not upset with you. But I haven't seen Blake all day. Which means she's probably at the swimming hole, sulking."

My chest tightens. The Tanners' spring-fed swimming hole holds a plethora of memories. Ones I haven't thought about in a long time. Summers were spent there with lots of the other kids our age. Blake and her friends didn't spend much time there since they were older, but I remember Reed saying they would take the horses when it got hot, just the two of them.

"Oh, then I won't bother her. Thanks for your time, Margie. Hopefully I'll see you again soon."

Before I can make my escape, she stops me with a hand on my arm. "Don't try to run away now. I was actually going to send one of the grooms out to go get her for dinner. Why don't you grab her and join us? It's just some frozen lasagna, but it's tasty."

My stomach knots at the thought. "I think I've already done enough to anger Blake. I should probably hit the road."

She raises an eyebrow at me. "Didn't you come here to talk to her?"

I let out a low laugh. "I did."

Her head turns at the sound of horseshoes on concrete. A groom walks up with a chestnut quarter horse, fully tacked.

"George, bring Fancy over here, would you?"

"Sure thing," he calls back, walking the pretty mare over to us.

Margie takes the reins from George. "You remember where the swimming hole is?"

"I do."

"Take Fancy there, and you can chat with Blake. Then you'll join us for dinner."

Margie's eyes are full of determination. Like Gran, she's clearly scheming.

"I'd like that," I finally say. Because it's true. I do want to talk to Blake. And I would like to have dinner with the Tanners.

Blake is going to be another story though, which makes me nervous about what's to come.

With a smile, Margie puts the reins in my hands. Once I've got Fancy, George leaves, and I adjust the stirrups to the length I need for my height. After I've mounted, I look down at Margie again.

"My, my, Gavin. You look straight out of a Western."

I tip my hat. "I've been told that a time or two."

"Don't dawdle too much."

I nudge Fancy forward and smile. "I'll bring Blake home safe and sound. And on time for dinner."

I can hear Margie laugh as I make my way down a path that will eventually lead me to an open field. From there, it's probably a forty-five-minute ride if I walk Fancy the entire way. But the sun is getting lower in the sky, and the longer I wait, the more I find myself itching to see Blake again.

Even if she flips me off when she lays her eyes on me, it will be worth it to be in her presence.

CHAPTER 7

Gavin

I GIVE FANCY SOME time to warm up before I push her into a nice trot. Like all the Tanners' quarter horses, she moves smoothly and responds to all my cues. Once we have a rhythm, I ask her for nice lope. As we ride along the plains, our bodies in sync, I find myself enjoying the time alone.

Ever since Dad died of his heart attack, it's felt like one thing after another. The drought and the loss of crops and cattle are only part of the problems we have. Kade is one of the bigger ones, at least in my book. Sure, he does his jobs and helps around the ranch, but he's been going to the sleazier bars in the city the last few months. Often, he's hungover in the morning and looks like shit for half the day. On top of that, he's been sleeping with every woman who offers. And when you look like Kade, a lot of women offer.

I know I shouldn't be surprised by his actions. Our family was raised on stuffing emotions down. And Kade looked up to Dad as if he were made of gold. So once he died and passed the ranch to me, as was the Montgomery family tradition, it hit Kade hard. He expected Dad would split it between us since we weren't living in the "old times" anymore, but he hadn't.

I tried to tell Kade that it was because of tradition only, but I know the truth now. That we're so far up to our ears in debt the ranch doesn't belong to any of us anymore. I've hidden the truth from my family to spare my dead dad's pride...to let them all keep thinking he was a god, but Emmett Montgomery was just a man. A man who didn't know how to spend money or make the right investments. The drought is going to be the final nail in our coffin, but it's also a great excuse to try and protect the memory of the man who raised me.

I let out a tense breath, pushing Fancy into a gallop. She's a fast little thing. Probably one of the horses they use to train younger barrel girls. Taking a deep breath in, I enjoy the way the early summer air fills my lungs and the sun warms my face. Sadly, the heat doesn't do much for the growing pit in my stomach when I think about the reality of our situation. If we lose the ranch, what will my family do? What will I do? This place is all we know.

A few vultures fly overhead, and I think they're warning me to turn around. Grief, debt, and an unknown future are all I have to offer. Maybe I'm an idiot for even entertaining the idea that a woman like Blake Tanner would want to be with someone like me. Especially someone she already despises.

Ahead of me, a tree line comes into view. It's the only green patch dotting the brown plains for miles, so it's hard to miss. I'm surprised more of the young kids in town don't know about this place, especially during hot days like these. Maybe they play video games now instead of cooling off in spring water. Hell if I know. All I know these days is work, paperwork, and Night Hawk.

I slow Fancy down, not wanting her thudding hoofbeats to alarm Blake and have her take off without me being able to catch her. Though Fancy is fast, I'm sure whatever horse Blake has out here is faster.

We come to a walk a few hundred yards from the opening that leads down to the bank. It doesn't take me long to notice there isn't another horse tied up. I swear under my breath, wondering if I missed her somehow; or Margie is wrong and Blake is hiding somewhere else.

I dismount and give the mare a pat on the neck. She nudges my shoulder as if to ask for a carrot. Chuckling, I rub her face to scratch away some of the salt from her sweat. "Sorry, girl," I say softly. "I don't have anything for you."

Fancy nudges me again, but this time as if to tell me to walk on. I pat her once more, then find a shaded hitching post with an in-ground watering hole for her to drink from. Once she's safely tied, I make my way through the trees toward the pool of water that's hidden inside. The spring is a lot smaller than I remember, but in a way, more magical. Like a hidden oasis that feels as if you've stepped outside of Texas.

I look again for another horse, but I still don't see one. What I do see though is a pair of jeans, a light pink T-shirt, work boots, and a cowboy hat on a rock near the waterline. The same cowboy hat I saw her in last night. Which means she's swimming, and with a lot fewer clothes on.

My pants are suddenly tighter, and even though I was raised better, I walk closer to the water as my eyes search for the woman who now haunts my every waking and sleeping moment. Thankfully, it doesn't take long to spot her. The evening sun catches through the trees and her hair swims behind her in the clear water as she floats. For a moment I think she's naked, but the angle her body is at reveals she's wearing a pair of white cotton panties that sit below her belly button and a purple bra that barely covers her ample chest. I bite the inside of my cheek to keep myself from making a noise.

Fuuuckkk. There's nothing I'd like to do more than swim out to her and take my time discovering the skin underneath those scraps of fabric. But I'll have to settle for her fair skin and the dark triangle of hair I see outlined under the wet cotton of her panties. Shit. I've turned into a perve. This is not what I was expecting to find here.

I stand at the rocky bank, debating my next move. If I keep staring, I'm very much a perv, but I don't know what to do to get her attention. I start waving my hands and call her name, but it's almost as if she's asleep. Her body drifts so her head is facing toward me now, and I get a pleasant view of the tops of her breasts. The water droplets clinging to her collar bones and fleshy skin makes my lower part stir again.

"Blake!" I yell. When she doesn't answer, I put my fingers to my lips and give a loud wolf whistle. She startles, sputtering as she tries to find her footing in the hip-deep water.

"Calm—" But I don't get the words out in time because a small rock hits me in the chest. "Fuck!" That woman has an arm on her. "Don't throw rocks at me, Blake. I'm not going to hurt you."

She ungracefully blows water out of her nose, pushing her wet hair back so I can see her eyes. It's comical the way her skin is pink from too much sun, giving her a lobster like glow, yet her glare and stance scream murder.

"What the hell are you doing here?" she screeches, her voice a few octaves higher than normal.

I give her a wide grin. "Your mom asked me to fetch you for dinner."

She places her hands on her flared hips, chest heaving. Damn, her skin really is red now that I can see it properly.

"You forgot sunscreen," I tell her.

Her face is dazed from being pulled out of her peaceful float, and she's trying to figure out why Margie would ask me to fetch her for dinner. When I say the sunscreen bit, she looks down at her body, finally realizing she's practically naked.

"Turn around, Gavin Montgomery! Turn around RIGHT NOW," she seethes.

With one last look and another scream from Blake, I snap myself out of my lust-filled stupor and turn around. She's swearing under her breath as I hear her splashing back to the bank. The sound stops, then I hear another curse word.

"You okay back there?"

"No!"

I start to turn around, worried she's hurt herself, but all that gets me is another small rock pelted at my shoulder this time.

"Jesus, woman! That hurts."

"Then stop trying to look!"

I rub my shoulder. "I thought you needed help."

"Keep facing the other way or I'll make sure it hits you in the head next time."

"You'll kill me."

She mumbles, "*Good*," under her breath before she lets out another string of curses. I smirk to myself. For some reason it makes me happy knowing that good 'ole Blake Tanner is a potty mouth. I wonder if she curses in front of Lee, though I highly doubt that.

After a few minutes she lets out a grunt before tapping me on the shoulder. "You can turn around now, Perv."

When I face her, Blake's scowling at me. My eyes are directly drawn to her pink T-shirt, which is being soaked through by her wet bra. She slaps me on the shoulder before covering her breasts. "Eyes on my face, Perv!"

Her tone is commanding, which doesn't help the situation I have going on in my pants. I'm hoping her eyes don't scan downward like mine have been doing.

"Sorry," I say truthfully, my eyes meeting hers. "I didn't know you were swimming in your underwear. Like I said, your mom sent me here. I rode Fancy." I almost want to punch myself after I finish that sentence. This woman completely throws off my game. I should've said something charming to make her smile. Not something a bumbling teenage boy with no chest hair would say.

Blake's eyes dart through the trees to where Fancy is standing and waiting like the good mare she is. I guess she thought I was lying.

"How the heck did that even come to be?" She pushes some of the wet hair off her forehead, beads of water still dripping down her skin like raindrops.

I shove my hands in my pockets. "I came by to see you. Margie said you'd be at the swimming hole, then gave me Fancy to ride and find you."

A huffing noise leaves Blake's pretty, rose-colored lips, "Well, you've seen me. So get right back on Fancy and go home to your family."

I'm glad I didn't say Margie already invited me to dinner. She'd probably tell me to go fuck myself and then ride off on Fancy into the setting sun, leaving me here to rot.

Blake steps away from me, then grabs her hat off the rock and places it on her wet head. Before she can run off to hell knows where, I grab her arm gently. The warmth of the skin beneath my hand tells me her sunburn is going to hurt like a bitch tomorrow.

"You'll have to put aloe on your burn as soon as you get home."

Blake pulls her arm away. "Is that what you rode all the way out here to tell me?"

I let out a sigh. "The sun is starting to set. Why don't you go grab your horse and we can ride back? I'll talk to you on the way."

"I walked."

No wonder she's burnt. "You walked here?"

She tries to move away again, but I step in front of her.

"Out of the way, Perv. I'm not in the mood."

"I'm here to apologize for last night, not to fight with you."

She snorts. "Really? I thought it was to spy on me like a Peeping Tom."

"I didn't mean to—"

"I don't care what you meant to do. But I've got to start walking home so I don't get eaten by coyotes." Between the sunburn and the anger, her rounded face is now beet red. I'm messing this up royally.

"I only wanted to talk to you. Really, I didn't mean anything by it."

"Which part? The peeping or the fact you embarrassed me and sold me off to the highest bidder last night without my permission?"

I rub my hand on the back of my neck, now feeling younger than a teenager. More like a boy being scolded by his momma.

I sigh. "I'm sorry for all of it. I wasn't thinking last night, I—"

She removes her hands from her chest and I do everything I can not to look down. Fuck me. How do I tell a woman I saw her and all I can think about is how much I want to have her? How somehow I know she's meant to be mine?

She taps her foot in annoyance. "You?"

Removing my cowboy hat, I run my fingers through my hair. I notice that she stares at my short locks, following the movement of my fingers and the flex of my hands. She licks her chapped lips and I find myself unable to form words again.

"Gavin?" she asks, her tone impatient.

"I wanted to bid on you," I finally say, letting the truth linger in the air between us.

Her saddle brown eyes burn into mine. "That's all you have to say?"

"Well, that, and I was hoping you'd consider letting me take you on a date sometime. To make up for what I did."

Blake lets out a balking laugh. One that makes me flinch. Though I don't show it on the outside, I feel like an idiot. An idiot whose pride has been wounded twice now in less than twenty-four hours. After a few seconds, she continues to laugh, which only makes my hurt feelings worse. Those hurt feelings slowly turn to anger.

When she eventually stops laughing, she sees the hard line of my mouth.

"You're serious?" A final bubble of nervous laughter leaves her lips.

"I don't find what I said funny. But apparently a man being interested in a beautiful woman is something to laugh at."

Blake stands taller, a similar look of fortitude crossing her features as it had last night before she came up on stage. "Your pretty words don't make up for humiliating me," she spits.

"In case you forget, I was humiliated, too."

Shaking her head, Blake walks away. Her long legs stride past Fancy and before I know it, she's making her way back home down the dirt path.

Fuck me. I said the wrong thing again. I jog to Fancy and mount swiftly. Since I'm on a horse, it doesn't take me long to catch up to Blake, even with her long legs. I pull fancy in front of her, effectively cutting her off.

"Get on," I tell her.

"Not a chance."

God, this woman is as stubborn as a goat. "It will take you over an hour to walk home, and I'm sure your sunburn is starting to hurt."

"Let me be." She walks around Fancy, and I pray to God to help me out.

I nudge the mare into a slow trot, keeping up with her. Blake doesn't look at me, but there's no chance I'll let her walk back alone with the sun going down. I hop off Fancy and she doesn't even have to ask me what I'm doing. Silence fills the air, the sound of dust, hooves, and footsteps our only soundtrack.

About twenty minutes later, Blake starts walking funny. Her clothes are still wet, and I'm sure they must be chafing against her raw skin, though she'll never admit it or get on the horse with me so she can prove some kind of point.

"Would you please get on Fancy? If it's about me being on the horse with you, I'm happy to walk."

"I'm fine," she grits. Her face tells a different story.

For a moment, I study her profile. Her long hair is drying, making her curls return in pretty springs. Her cheekbones are defined and her chin round. I even see a smattering of freckles on the bridge of her nose that have darkened from her time in the sun and tiny lines developing in the corners of her eyes. With the way the setting sun diffuses across her face, it becomes apparent that Blake Tanner isn't the young and hopeful rodeo star I once admired from afar. She's hardened. But it doesn't stop her from being the most beautiful woman I've laid my eyes on.

Blake turns her head my way. "Quit staring at me."

I clench my fist around Fancy's reins. "Then quit being stubborn. You're in pain."

Abruptly, she stops, turning to face me again. The chest of her shirt is mostly dry now, which makes it much easier to concentrate on her face.

"I didn't ask you to ride in and be a knight in cowboy boots. You can take Fancy and go home. I'm fine being alone."

Her words strike me as meaning much more than being alone on a walk. I'm trying to be patient, but I'm tired and thirsty, and her refusal to be smart is setting me on edge.

"What's your problem, Blake?"

"My problem is that a man I don't even know ruined my evening two nights in a row!"

Her words sting because there's truth to them.

"I'm not a stranger, Blake. And I came to apologize, not argue. Don't you think you're overreacting a little?"

Blake scowls. "You have no idea! You, you...UGH!" She throws her hands up and stomps off, cursing under her breath.

"Would you stop walking away?" I call after her. Lord help me, but this is not going the way I hoped. I knew she would be upset, but why this upset?

"I'm trying to walk home," she bites out.

"Please get on the horse, Blake."

"Leave me alone, Gavin," she parrots. I block her way once more. "Get on the horse."

"Kindly fuck off!" she yells in my face, her voice explosive. Her voice seems to echo for the briefest of seconds, but I know it's just in my ears. Then silence envelops us.

Abruptly Blake steps back, her expression aghast, as if she didn't plan on exploding like that. Regret flashes across her face.

"Blake—"

She cuts me off. "I'm not getting on Fancy. I'm not. I'm sorry I yelled at you, that was impolite. Either you can walk back with me, in silence, or you get on Fancy right now and ride off. Tell my parents I'll get to them when I get to them."

"I'll walk with you," I say without question.

"Silence," she warns me again. "Or I'll tell Daddy you ogled me when I wasn't aware."

The image of Lee looming over me has me shutting my mouth. I'm a big guy, intimidating in my own right, but Lee Tanner is a true Texan. The kind that's humble and nice to everyone, but wouldn't hesitate to murder you if you did wrong by someone he loves.

"Noted."

"Alright," she says with a nod. "Let's get on with it, then."

CHAPTER 8

Blake

ALL I WANTED WAS one evening of peace. One where I didn't have to worry about making dinner or attending charity events or Mom talking about my lack of social life.

I needed time to think about what happened last night: how I broke my riding ban even though it was on a mechanical bull; how Gavin Montgomery makes me so angry, yet there's something about him that makes me want to look twice. It's probably because he's stupidly attractive, but it annoys me nonetheless. All these things, and that dang newspaper article, drove me to walk to the swimming hole, a place I haven't been to in years.

It's a long walk from the ranch, but my feet carried me to the banks, like an invisible force was pulling me there. Eventually, I found myself floating in the cool water, happy memories of Reed and me together on a hot day with our horses prancing through my head. At first I thought the memories would be too much, but it turns out it's just what I needed. Until Gavin Montgomery appeared out of nowhere.

His boots crunch as he walks beside me, but he's quiet now. Without his incessant questions, I have more time to focus on the pain of my sunburn. Since I didn't plan on walking to the swimming hole, or floating in the water for so long, I've burnt to a crisp, which Gavin so nicely pointed out. If I wasn't already red, my cheeks would have shown my blush. I can still feel the heat of his gaze moving over my practically naked skin like a starved man.

Not that I would ever admit it to him, but his attention is flattering. I haven't exactly spent my time away dating or hooking up with guys. The few times I had gone looking to maybe have a fun night, Tennessee only offered me attention from men I didn't feel the same about, so I stopped trying. But the way Gavin looks at me, the way I was bid on last night and hit on by Jake, it reminds me that I'm hot and desired in a way I haven't let myself be since the accident. And what Gavin said at the spring is true—I'm beautiful.

Maybe it's the sunburn, but I feel like this whole thing has lit a fire inside of me. A kindling of one, but a fire nonetheless. Even my emotions are less bottled than normal, which I displayed during my outburst at Gavin and my fight with Daddy last night. Who knows, could my anger be a good sign? I've spent so long feeling numb that I forgot what it's like to fight for something, even if it's my own wants and desires.

I bite my lower lip as a sharp pain lances through my skull. Apparently said emotions give me a headache. When the pain persists, I can't stop a small groan from leaving my mouth. I bring my fingers to my temples to try to rub the pain away, but the movement only makes my skin hurt. *Great*! I should've drunk more water at the spring and at least grabbed sunscreen before I left the house earlier.

Gavin takes in an audible breath. "Are you alright, Blake?"

His voice is intense. There's something about it that both soothes me and grates on my nerves.

"I'm fine," I clip. "Only a headache."

Gavin puts out his hand to stop me, and Fancy stops with us. Before I can stalk off again, he puts his finger under my chin and forces me to look into his evergreen eyes. Good heavens, he's handsome. So handsome it almost knocks the wind out of me. *No*! He's a jerky-perv, remember? I need to stop thinking about how hot he is. It's the dehydration talking!

As he tilts his head to study me, the setting glow of the sun illuminates his features. I frown when I notice the sunken impressions under his eyes from lack of sleep and the way his irises hold something private, painful. Pain a young man like him shouldn't have. But I suppose he has a lot to take care of after his daddy died last year, and everything going on with their ranch.

I internally groan, and the guilt of treating him poorly after he came all the way out to apologize fills me. Especially given his circumstances. And despite his prior jerkiness, Gavin's demeanor screams like he's being genuine now, like he cares about my wellbeing. And Jake did tell me that he didn't plan out last night like I assumed, and Jake has no reason to lie. Maybe I overreacted? But Gavin did embarrass me and perv on me just now. *Ugh*! This whole situation is confusing, and I don't know what to think anymore.

Gavin and I continue to stare at each other, his long finger not leaving my chin. Did I mention he has great hands? *Stop it, hormones!* The air starts to feel thicker than chili, and my chest constricts. At first, I think it's because my body is having a silly reaction to Gavin Montgomery's touch, but then my vision starts to close in. As the world begins to shift, I don't hit the ground like I expect to. Instead I'm locked between two arms of steel and a warm chest.

"Whoa there!" I hear Gavin say, but it sounds far away.

I press my eyes together as Gavin lowers us toward the ground and he manages to keep my back from touching the dirt. I try to blink away the black spots in my vision as he holds me delicately. Surprising for such a large man like him. It's comforting, but also painful because of the sunburn.

"Can you open your eyes?" His voice vibrates around me. I shiver at the feeling. "Blake?"

After a second, when I feel able to, I pry my eyelids open as Gavin maneuvers me so he can bring one hand to my forehead.

"Blake, you're burning up. I think you might have heatstroke."

I groan out loud this time. Figures I would get heatstroke when my only means of support is the man I'm trying to loathe—even if I'm starting to question my choice more with the feel of his arms around me. I close my eyes again and turn my face into his chest, then inhale. This time I'm for sure blaming my actions on the heatstroke.

Goodness, he smells good. Really good. Like hard work and worn leather. When he chuckles, I think I die inside. Maybe I sniffed too hard. To distract from my shame, and the way I'm feeling, I try to push him off, but he holds me tighter.

"You have to get on Fancy, Blake. It's getting dark, and you need a cold bath and some painkillers."

My eyes snap back to his concerned ones. "I don't ride."

"I gathered that. But you're sick, and we still have another mile or so to go."

"I'm walking. Now let me go."

"Most stubborn woman," he mumbles under his breath. "But as you wish."

He releases me, my upper half landing on the ground as he leans away. It's only a few inches, but I grunt anyway. I close my eyes again and breathe. Man, I'm dizzy. That's when I realize the last thing I ate today was some eggs and toast for breakfast. I really did set myself up for success, didn't I?

"You lying there isn't going to get us back to your place any faster," Gavin chides.

"I'm getting up," I mumble.

He sighs loudly. "If you can't get up, I'm either going to have to call your folks to bring the truck out, or you're going to have to get on Fancy."

"I don't—"

"Ride, I know. But those are your options. Unless you want the third one."

I look up into his smirking face. "What's that?"

"I sling you over my shoulder and carry you."

This time, my cheeks do flush. I look up at the coloring sky, the sound of crickets starting to buzz in my ears. If I get on Fancy, I—part of me would rather die out here.

You're being an idiot, Blakey girl.

I squeeze my eyes shut as Reed's voice rings in my ear. Great, now I'm hearing his voice. I really am sick. But that voice in my head is right. If Reed were here, he'd be calling me an idiot to my face.

I open my mouth. "Help me up, please?"

Gavin offers his hand to me. When my fingers wrap around his, electricity tingles up through my arm like it did last night when he touched me—though I ignored it then because I was so angry. He must feel it too, because when I'm standing in his embrace, he's staring at me like he's struck oil. The tension in the air returns, but this time it's not because I'm going to faint.

Out of the corner of my eye, I watch as he brings his hand up to rest on my cheek, then my forehead again. "We should get you home."

"I can walk—"

I'm cut off by him lifting me up and settling me in his arms.

I squeal like a pig. "Gavin Montgomery, put me down this instant!"

"I told you the third option. Be glad it's a bridal carry instead of a fireman's," he says as he starts to walk, Fancy right behind us.

My eyes are level with a smattering of dark blonde hair on suntanned skin coming through the top of his long-sleeved blue button-down. And while I would kind of like to enjoy the show from a safer distance, I don't feel well. And when I don't feel well, I get grumpy. Which means I'm not in the mood to play around.

When a wave of nausea moves through me, I pound on said chest weakly. "Put me down or I'm going to throw up all over your nice shirt. I'm dead serious!"

Of course, he doesn't listen. After a few more paces, I think I'm going to make serious on my threat. His shirt is going to be covered in puke, and I won't be sorry. I hold my hand over my mouth as I see headlights in the distance.

Gavin freezes, the cease of movement making it easier for me to stop from being sick. I feel him let out a tense breath as he gently sets me down. I close my eyes to reset my equilibrium but find I'm swaying again. Before I can say anything, Gavin's arm is around me, holding me in place.

When the truck becomes clearer, I see it's Daddy's, so I try to push away. The last thing I want is for him to get any ideas about why Gavin Montgomery has me in his arms. Or share that information with Mom. I'd never hear the end of it.

"You'll fall if I let you go," he says, tsking.

"Then let me fall!" I cry, frustration getting the better of me.

Gavin's face turns toward mine, the truck's headlights defining his solid features. He looks serious, his gaze penetrating like it was when he stared at me from the stage last night.

"I'd never let you fall, Blake Tanner."

I almost tell him he technically let me fall into the dirt even if it was only a few inches, but I stop myself. He means what he's saying. Though I can't decipher his tone or why he's saying it. The words seem too...*personal*. Yet we don't even know each other. He's an annoying acquaintance at best. A once-friend of Reed's that I never spent more than a couple hours with at a time, and now a thorn in my side. How can he make such a promise? But for some reason, I believe him.

When the sound of the truck door slamming interrupts us, I tear my gaze away to meet Daddy's. He's dressed down for the evening in sweatpants and a T-shirt, though it doesn't make him look any less intimidating.

"Blake?" he questions. "What's going on?" He looks at Gavin's arms around me, then at my disheveled appearance. It's getting dark now, but the lights of his truck make it clear that my skin looks red and angry.

"Sir," Gavin drawls, "I think Blake has heatstroke, maybe sun poisoning. I was trying to get her home but we ran into a few—"

I cut him off. "I wouldn't ride Fancy and that meant I had to walk. I started feeling sick, and well, here we are."

"I'll take her now." Daddy gives Gavin a nod. "Thanks for looking out for her."

Gavin nods his head back. "My pleasure."

As Daddy and Gavin have their man-protector moment, I leave the comfy weight of Gavin's embrace and take hold of Daddy's outstretched hand.

"You alright, baby girl?"

"I'm probably dehydrated and have low blood sugar."

"She has a bad sunburn," Gavin adds.

I roll my eyes. "Anyone can see that." I'm very ready to get in Daddy's truck and go home. I'd love to pretend this entire incident with Gavin Montgomery didn't happen. Especially the smelling part.

"You alright following us on Fancy?" Daddy asks.

"No problem, sir."

"I think we'll have to take a raincheck on that dinner, too."

My skin prickles. "Dinner?"

Gavin's eyes flick to mine, a small, entertained smile playing on his lips. "Mrs. Tanner invited me to have dinner with y'all tonight."

I tense. "Did she now?"

Daddy grins. "You know your mom. Always trying to take care of people. But I got worried when you weren't back and tried to come sooner, but she made me wait till now. She insisted you both were fine."

It's just like Daddy to worry, and it doesn't surprise me Mom made him wait to come. I bet she was hoping Gavin and I were getting it on at the spring. He may be hot, but nothing is going to happen between us. No matter how many burning looks he gives me, or how good he smells. The attention may feel nice, but that's not why I came home. And I'm sure I won't be here forever.

I grimace at Daddy. "I see."

"There's plenty of extra food, Gavin. After you hand off Fancy to George, come up to the house. Margie is making you a plate to take home."

"That's awfully kind of her," he says with a smile. Then his eyes turn on me. "I hope you feel better, Blake."

I stare back. "Thank you."

I should say thank you for catching me. Thank you for staying with me instead of leaving me to pass out in the middle of the dirt, alone. But instead, I turn away from his gaze and walk to Daddy's truck.

CHAPTER 9

Gavin

By the time I get home from the Tanners' ranch, it's after nine in the evening. Getting out of my truck with food in hand, I see the porch light is on. Kade is sitting in one of the rocking chairs holding a beer. I haven't seen him all day, and I'm surprised to see him now. He's usually out by nine and home after two in the morning.

As I walk up the steps, he eyes me, a look of cold indifference on his face.

"When Gran said you were out, I nearly keeled over," he says before taking a sip of his beer.

I sit in the chair to his right, setting the food on the porch.

"I go out all the time."

A sound similar to a laugh leaves his chest. "You go to Night Hawk for work, then come back. I hardly call that going out." He leans back in his chair. "For instance, when was the last time you kept a woman's bed warm? You could use a good lay."

My fists clench around the wooden arms of my chair. Kade is baiting me. He knows the answer to his question. "I know you're upset about the auction last night. You can say that instead of trying to goad me."

He finishes off his beer, then sets it on the small table between us. That's when I notice the other empty bottles already there.

"I'm trying to figure you out, Gav." He looks at me with question, the lines of his face showing me how tense he is despite the alcohol.

I run my hand over my stubbled jaw. "There isn't much to figure out."

This time Kade does chuckle. "I beg to differ. You're always on my case about this and that. Yet you live by your own rules. Rules which I can't seem to figure out."

"I disagree."

"You can think what you want. But one minute you're telling me to keep my dick in my pants, then the next you're pissing all over Blake Tanner. A woman you don't even know, mind you."

I wish I had a beer. Or maybe a glass of whiskey. It's been a long day—a long year—and with Kade's horrible behavior since Dad died, I don't think I deserve such severe judgment.

With a short breath, I push down my bitterness. "I went and apologized to Blake. I was out of line for what I did, and I was a hypocrite to you and Jake last night. I really am sorry for how I acted. And for almost taking that money away from our family."

"You think that makes it all better?" He puts his forearms on his knees and drops his head like he's defeated.

"I'm not sure what you want from me," I tell him seriously.

"I want you to admit that you're a selfish asshole."

My body goes tense at his insult. He called me that at Night Hawk before I bid on Blake, too. But this feels deeper. Like he's finally voicing how he feels about Dad leaving me the ranch.

"Kade—"

"You know what I think, Gavin?" he cuts me off. "I think you're afraid. Afraid to not be the perfect responsible saint that everyone thinks you are. That's why you judge me all the fucking time." He spits out the last part.

"I'm not judging you, Kade," I say seriously. "I'm trying to help you."

He laughs condescendingly. "That's another thing. Always trying to be the savior. I didn't ask for you to save me. Dad gave you the ranch, but that doesn't mean you're equipped to run it. Hell, you can't run it. We held a goddamn charity event last night to beg for money from our friends."

The anger I've been trying to cap pushes to the surface. "I'm doing the best I can. And if you'd talk to me like a man, you'd know that."

"Jesus Christ! What do you think this is? I *am* trying to talk to you right now."

"You've been drinking, and I think you're going to regret how you're speaking to me in the morning."

Kade shakes his head. "You know, for a second I thought you bidding on Blake was a good thing. But then I saw how you wouldn't take no for an answer from her. How you forced that broken girl to get up on the stage for your benefit. That's why I did what I did. I would've let you win, Gavin. But like I said, you're a selfish asshole. You don't deserve to take her out on a date. And I think you know that, or you wouldn't have gone to apologize to her."

"Enough!" I growl.

Kade reaches over and pats me on the arm. "I see I hit a nerve. At least you're showing some type of emotion. Maybe I should thank Blake for turning you into a human again."

I shake his arm off and stand. "I'm going to leave before *I* say something I regret. You should stop drinking so much."

He stands to meet me. "I'm fine."

"You're not."

He shakes his head, his body sagging. "People change, Gavin. You've changed, too. Even if you don't realize it. I used to admire you. But now, I just see a scared twenty-four-year-old kid trying to act like a man."

His words cut me like a knife, yet the nagging voice in my mind reminds me that I haven't been truthful with him, or with my family. That deep down, I know he's right. I am scared, and I've been scared for a while now.

Kade takes another step forward and puts his hand on my shoulder. "Last night I saw a glimpse of my brother, not the fake bullshit one you show to the town when you perform at Night Hawk, or when you tell Momma and Gran you've got shit handled. But Blake is just like us. And maybe she doesn't need the perfect Gavin Montgomery to save her."

Just like us. His words ring in my ears, and I deflate. "You actually see me that way?"

"You see me as your alcoholic, sex addict brother. At least you're still better than me."

"I don't see you that way."

"Don't you?"

We form a sort of a stand-off, his eyes hard as he stares at me. I wish more than anything right now that I could bring Dad back, to put things back the way they were before. But here we are. Reality doesn't care if you're in pain. Life moves on, and you're expected to move on with it. Unfortunately, Kade doesn't know how to do that, and if I'm honest, I don't think I do either.

I place my hand over Kade's on my shoulder and squeeze, trying to convey that I love him. Even when he's pissing me the hell off. I don't say anything because I don't think words would do any good right now.

After a few tense seconds, Kade's eyes turn glassy. "When are you going to realize it, big brother? We're the same; you just choose to pretend like it's all going to be okay, when I know it won't be."

"Kade..." He takes a step back, his balance off. Shit, he's more drunk than I thought.

"I'm going out."

"Like hell you are!"

He turns on his heel and starts to walk down the porch steps. I follow, intending to drag him to his room like Gran used to do when he was five, but I stop in my tracks as headlights appear.

"I've got a ride," he spits out. "I'm not as much of an idiot as you think I am."

I blow a breath out, happy at least he's not trying to drive drunk off this property. He moves toward the black truck heading down the gravel road. When I eventually see who it is, I feel like I've been stabbed in the back, because the person behind the wheel is the last person I thought I'd see tonight.

When the truck comes to a stop, Cricket's gaze pierces me through the darkened windshield. What the fuck is Kade thinking? First this outburst almost out of nowhere, and now he plans to spend the night with Cricket?

Kade doesn't have the balls to look me in the eye this time as he opens the door to the truck. "I'll be home in time for chores tomorrow. Don't wait up."

He hops in the passenger seat, and I can't help but stare at Cricket. She looks smug, which only makes my stomach churn and acid burn my throat. Not only have I now been betrayed by a woman I once cared for, but my little brother.

I guess as the saying goes, when it rains it pours.

The truck backs up and I'm left with the sound of spitting gravel and my own heartbeat pounding in my ears. Maybe I deserve this treatment, or maybe this is Dad's way of looking down on me from heaven and telling me to get my head out of my ass. Either way, I do know one thing—Kade is right. I have a savior complex. And after last night and today, I know Blake is hurting. And trying to break her out of her shell when she isn't ready is a dick move. Then today, I gave her a bare minimum apology, then tried to get her on Fancy after she told me she didn't ride anymore.

Fuck. What started out as a way to get a date with Blake has turned into a pile of cow shit. I should've listened to myself when I told Jake I didn't have time for women. I should've realized those vultures over my head were a sign to turn around today. Kade's clearly gotten worse, and I have the ranch to figure out. I shouldn't be chasing after Blake, no matter how much chemistry we have, or how much I want to be the balm to her hurts and catch her when she falls.

I've been a romantic fool. An idiot one, too, because I didn't even sweep the girl off her feet, at least not the way I planned. I look at the now cold plate of food Margie gave me sitting on the porch and decide I will not do any more to woo Blake Tanner.

As Kade said, and as I see clearly now, she's a broken woman, and I'm a broken man. Burden settles heavily in me as I feel the familiar weight of my family's situation drag me down. I may have been able to ignore it for a few hours, but it's not going to disappear because a beautiful woman comes back to town. It's time to get back to work.

I grab the plate of food and instead of heading to bed, I go to the backyard where our small guest house is, which is where Dad's (now my) office is set up. Maybe if I get creative, I can figure out a way to get us out of this hole we've been dug into. Though that would take a miracle.

More than a miracle.

CHAPTER 10

Blake

FIVE YEARS AGO

SMOOTHING OUT MY JEANS over my generous hips, I give myself a smile in the mirror. I look good enough to eat, if I do say so myself. Once upon a time, I would have wished for a smaller body like most of the other girls in town, but my squishy parts make me happy because they also make me different.

My friend Shelby likes to joke that my boobs, ass, and lack of tiny waistline are a beacon to the men in our town, telling them that not only do I have extra cushion for certain activities, but that I could provide them with a hell of a lot of babies. The attention is nice sometimes, but these men all know that if they married me, I wouldn't be popping out babies. Instead, they'd be accompanying me to horse shows and raising foals to be the next best thing. Maybe one day I'll pop out a kid or two, but that isn't a dream I have right now.

With one last look in the mirror, I throw on another sports bra to stop the girls from bouncing too much—the woes of having a large rack—then put on a teal plaid tank top. I'm going to have to wear extra sunscreen so I don't burn, but it's way too hot to wear long sleeves. As I'm about to grab my cowboy hat, a pounding on the door makes me jump.

"Blakey! What the hell is taking you so long? We gotta get going before it's too hot!"

I roll my eyes at the voice of my little brother, Reed. He may only be nineteen to my twenty-four, but he's my best friend.

He's also reckless, annoying as hell, and a pain in my side. Mom even jokes that maybe we were twins in another life with the way we act. Maybe she's right. Even with our age difference, I've always felt like Reed is my other half. We both have similar goals, personalities, and even look alike with our rounded features and dark curly hair. The only difference being that I stopped growing at five foot nine, while he towers over me like some freckled giant.

Opening the door, I give him a grin while placing my hat on my head. "I'm ready."

"I was going to call a search party."

I pat him on the cheek. "Yeah, yeah." As I walk away, he shakes his head. "Are you going to stand there or are we going for a ride?" I yell back at him.

He catches up and knocks me on the shoulder. "You're something else, Blakey girl."

We make our way down the steps and stop at the kitchen to see Carol. She's worked for our family since I was a baby, coming to cook and clean every couple of days. It's a luxury many people don't have, which I never take for granted. Between training horses, training myself, competitions, and trying to have a social life, there isn't time for cooking.

"Hey, you two," she greets us. "I packed a bunch of things for your ride. All saddle bag safe," she adds with a wink, tossing her long red ponytail behind her shoulder.

Reed runs up and kisses her over-blushed cheek, then snatches an apple from the bowl in front of her before taking a large bite. "Thanks, Carol baby," he says through the food.

I make a gagging noise. "You're disgusting."

Carol smiles warmly before pushing a satchel toward us, followed by a bottle of SPF fifty. I rub it all over my face and arms, Reed doing the same, before we head toward the door.

I stop and yell at Carol, "If our parents ask, we won't be home until late afternoon. We're taking the horses up to Prickly Pear Pass." Or the PPP as we like to call it. It's one of the longer horse trails that has tons of cacti and vegetation along its route. It's a great trail to run the horses and have a good time. It also leads to a small man-made lake where we like to cool off.

"Got it. Good thing I packed you extra sandwiches. Remember to take extra water, too."

My body warms with Carol's mothering. Our own mom is great, but also extremely busy. Especially now that Double-Time's horse breeding operation is growing. It's nice to have Carol looking out for us when Mom can't.

"Thanks, Carol. We'll see you next week."

I run outside, the screen door banging behind me as I catch up to Reed. Once I reach him, I throw the pack at him. "Your saddle bag is bigger."

He chuckles as he slings it over his opposite shoulder, putting his arm around me. He takes a deep breath, smelling the air full of hay, horses, and Texas earth. "This is gonna be ours someday, Blakey girl. Can you imagine it?"

"Then I'd have to imagine Mom and Daddy being dead. Not to mention all the responsibility," I tease.

He shakes my shoulders a bit. "Okay, fine then. I'll take it all. You'll probably be off traveling the world anyway. I know how much you want to do that once you've won all the barrel racing titles you desire. Maybe I'll come with you for a few weeks. I've always wanted to ride the Icelandic Horses with the sheepherders."

"Has anyone ever told you that you watch too much Travel Channel?"

"Are you making fun of your little brother's dreams?"

Nudging his arm off me, I grab his hand. "Of course not. You know I would never. You've never laughed at mine."

He squeezes my fingers, his hand strong. "Never. Not to mention you've already conquered half of yours, Ms. Barrel Racing Champion, fifth in the Nation, all-star American, Pride of Texas—"

I cut him off with a blush. "Yeah, yeah. And someday I'll be riding the horses you trained into the winning circle. Briar just needs a little more work."

He releases a loud laugh that makes me laugh, too. "You're so kind to me. But I like your honesty. It makes me better." His eyes shine, and I lean in to hug his fleshy middle.

"I'm glad you feel that way."

"Now only if Mom would believe in me like you do." Reed pulls away, making his way toward the tack room to grab brushes for our horses.

I follow him, taking the red caddy from his hand for my horse, Winchester aka Win. He's a seven-year-old pure black Quarter Horse with the mind of a racehorse and the personality of a lapdog. I've raised him his whole life and consider him my heart horse. There will never be another one like him for me.

"You know Mom believes in you, Reed, but Briar isn't ready yet. She doesn't want anyone to get hurt."

He sets his jaw stubbornly and huffs. "You sound just like her."

I grind my teeth at his reaction as I watch him walk off down the barn aisle. Sometimes I forget how touchy he is about this topic. It's like igniting a bomb.

"Don't be like that, Reed," I call after him. "I'm looking out for you!"

He turns, his blue eyes that look like Mom's staring right at me. "I know you are. But that mare is going to be a winner. I know it."

I blow out a tense breath. "I know she is, but you need to be patient. The best trainers are. You've got to remember that just because you want something doesn't mean it's yours for the taking. You need to earn it."

Reed stares me down for a moment, eventually cracking a small smile. "Since when did you become a walking motivational quote?"

I shove him. "Get your horse ready."

He holds up his hands in surrender, "Fine. But I'm taking Briar on the trail."

My stomach sinks. "Reed, you know she's been spooking a lot lately. I thought you could take Figaro or Max."

"I'm going to take Briar. It's good practice for her. She needs to learn, and what better time than on a trail with one of the best riders in North America?"

"If you're trying to butter me up, it's not working."

"Come on, Blakey! Live a little! Dad isn't around to scold us. Mom is off working another expensive-ass Dressage horse. You worry too much."

"And you don't worry enough."

He shrugs. "Come on. We're wasting the best time to ride. It's going to get hot, and I want to be at the lake before then."

Reed isn't going to budge, and we're wasting time. He's an adult now, even if he doesn't act like one sometimes. I have to let him make his own choices and decisions, like I make mine.

"Fine. Go tack up your horse. I'll meet you out front in twenty."

It's only mid-morning, but it's already in the high seventies, and humid as all get-out. But the heat is somehow soothing to my nerves.

I pat Win's neck as we walk through a small puddle of water on the ground. He's such an easy-going guy. To my surprise, Briar walks right through it as well.

Reed gloats, "I told you she's doing better. I've been working her every day."

I know he's been. I've seen him get up early before the grooms even arrive to work without people's eyes on him. I used to do the same thing when I was his age, afraid of other people's judgment. I think part of the reason is that he constantly compares himself to me. The oldest daughter who always gets attention for winning and doing things most people would never dream of doing. Reed feels like he has to live up to my accomplishments. I've tried to tell him otherwise, but I can see the jealousy getting the better of him sometimes.

"She looks great," I tell him, because I mean it. She does.

"Never doubt me, Blakey girl!"

I smile at him. "I don't."

"What do ya say we let the horses stretch their legs a bit. Maybe a little race?"

I contemplate for a moment. We're about to come up on some more narrow areas of the trail with a bit of terrain. Not that the horses can't handle it, we've raced it a million times before. But Reed was on a different horse.

"I'm not sure."

He lets out a groan. "You just said you didn't doubt me."

"I don't, but—"

"Last one to the lake has stall duty on weekends for a month!"

"Reed!" I yell, but he's already taken off. Win starts dancing in place, ready to take off after Briar. "I guess we have no choice, Win. Let's get him!" With a very cheesy, "*Yah!*" Win and I are off to the races, speeding down the plain toward Reed. I hold the top of my cowboy hat as the wind flips my braid about so it whips my back.

"Yeehaw!" Reed cries happily up ahead.

I lean down and say into Win's listening ear, "They may have a head start, but let's show them who's boss!"

With a kiss and a squeeze, we pick up even more speed. I can't help my own call of happiness as I see us get closer and closer to Reed. I live for moments like these. The feeling of a powerful being beneath me, nature around me, wind in my hair, and Reed by my side. It's heaven on earth.

For a moment, I close my eyes and enjoy the sound of hoofbeats thundering along the plain. Peace settles inside me, and I smile serenely.

Snap!

My eyes fly open and a horrible shrieking whinny hits my ears. My heart plummets when I don't see Briar and Reed in front of me anymore as my brain tries to register what happened. I keep Win moving as my eyes search until I spot Briar on the ground, her painful cries imprinting into my soul. I pull Winchester to a stop and jump off.

"Reed!" I scream. "Where are you?!" So far, all I can see are some cacti around.

"Reed!" I yell again, this time my eye catching a flash of white near Briar. It's his hat.

I cry out his name even louder, straining my voice. He's still not responding, and Briar won't stop screaming. Win is standing near her now, and I wish more than anything we brought George or one of the grooms with us. As I'm about to turn my head, I finally spot Reed behind Briar, face down in the dirt, unmoving. I take off at a sprint and fall to my knees once I reach him.

"Reed! Oh my god, Reed!" I cry. My first instinct is to turn him over but I don't know how injured he is. I've taken a little first aid but I'm not sure what to do. I gently put my hand on his shoulder and add pressure.

"Come on, baby brother, can you hear me?" My voice begins to shake and my body goes clammy when he doesn't move. "Reed! Come on, Reed. Please, stop fooling around." Still nothing.

"To hell with it!" With a prayer, I put my hand under his neck to support it as I move him onto his back. His eyes are open, but he's limp in my arms. For a moment, I think he's playing a joke.

"Reed..." My voice is quiet, realization taking hold as I notice his eyes aren't responding, they're...vacant. The noise of an injured Briar plays in the background as I put my ear to Reed's mouth. He's not breathing. This time, I tap his cheek as tears well in my eyes.

"Reed, come on!" I plead, but he stares above into nothing.

A sob escapes my throat, and I scream for help. I scream and I scream, and I have no idea if anyone can even hear me, but I keep screaming.

"Reed Tanner!" His name blends in with my scream. "Reed Tanner, if you don't wake up right this instant, I'll—" I run my hands through his short curly hair, feeling the softness under my touch.

I let out another anguished cry. "Reed, please. Please, Reed!"

But he's gone.

CHAPTER 11

Blake

PRESENT DAY

I BOLT UP IN bed, my breath ragged, my heart pounding a mile a minute. I feel as though I've watched a horror movie. Only it's one about my own life.

My skin is irritated and warm, and I'm twisted in my sheets like I tried to tie them in a knot with my body. It's been a while since I've dreamed about the accident so vividly. I should've known that going to the swimming hole could trigger one. And with the anniversary of that day looming, I'm even more prone to bad dreams.

Tears burn my eyes as the fear I felt that morning sits in my body like poison in my veins. I check the clock on my nightstand and see it's only four in the morning. After the situation with Gavin yesterday, I showered, put aloe on, and forced food down before face planting in my bed. Even though my body could use more sleep, I'm wide awake now. I untangle myself from my sheets and look over my skin as I head to the shower. It doesn't look as bad as it did last night. I'm still pink and a little sore, but not enough to be mistaken for a lobster.

I strip off my pajama shorts and tank top and turn the water to cold. Nothing like a freezing shower to cool you off and strip away the sweaty evidence of a nightmare. I take a few breaths in and out, preparing for the shock of cold against me, then jump in. My breath leaves my body in a whoosh as I acclimate to the frigid water. After a few moments, it becomes easier to tolerate and starts to feel good. I started taking cold showers while living in Tennessee. It's a trick I read online while looking for ways to help my panic attacks. It helps regulate the nervous system, or something. All I know is that it works.

Once I've washed off and cleared my mind a bit, I hop out of the shower and dry off. When my eyes meet the mirror, I find myself unable to look away. I've changed a lot in five years. Most people do, but when I used to look in the mirror, I saw a confident woman who was ready to take on the world. One who had every opportunity at her feet and plans to travel and win more titles.

Now I see someone who outwardly looks fine but is consumed by her sadness. A coward who ran away because she couldn't bear to stand in Reed's empty room, or feel the town's pitying looks on her, or know that her parents were constantly waiting for her to break down or talking about euthanizing Briar. Thankfully, they were able to save her after she broke her leg stepping in that gopher hole, but that didn't make it any easier to be around the ranch.

Tears well in my eyes again, and I can no longer look at myself. I don't know why I can see those things and yet not change them.

Why is it so hard to get up every day and act like a normal human being? Somehow, my parents have done it—or at least enough to function—and they lost their baby boy, their only son.

I swallow the lump in my throat and drag a comb through my hair. One thing I do know is I've done enough crying. Enough to fill an ocean. But no matter how much I cry, it won't bring Reed back. And it doesn't help me feel any better. Whoever said "cry it out" needs to take it back.

Once I've brushed my hair and applied sunscreen for the day (don't want to forget that again), I throw on a pair of loose jeans and T-shirt with Double-Time's logo on it. The less fabric that rubs against my already sensitive skin, the better. Quietly, I make my way down the steps. Daddy shouldn't be up for another hour, and Mom will follow shortly after.

With my work boots on and my hat in hand, I set out for the barn to get started on my morning chores. I may not ride anymore, but I do enjoy the physical labor that comes with mucking stalls and grooming horses. About a year ago, a friend of mine suggested I try connecting with horses again when I drunkenly admitted I missed them. Riding wasn't an option, but I started to volunteer at a place that rehabilitated racehorses off the track.

The first day, I had a panic attack in the parking lot, but it got easier over time. It was cathartic to work with injured horses, many who had similar leg injuries that Briar had. In a way, it felt like Reed sent me there. But cleaning horse poop, filling water buckets, and doing some light groundwork with them is about all I can handle. Riding is too much, too painful.

The morning air is heavy with humidity as I reach the stable doors. A few of the horses whinny, knowing that my presence means breakfast is soon to follow. But first, I have a certain foal and mare to check on.

Briar and her unnamed foal are at the end of the aisle in a double stall. I can already see his little nose over the door. Happiness peeks through my sadness when I think of how much Reed would've loved this baby. Even though Briar was young when Reed died, he always talked about how one day he'd breed her and maybe get a beautiful black colt like Winchester. And this foal, he looks almost exactly like a mini version of him.

Once I reach the stall, I hold out my hand and the colt nudges my fingers. I feel that bit of happiness fall away as more thoughts of Win fill my mind. About a year after I left town, still deep in grief and denial of what happened, I gave Mom permission to sell him. He was wasted at Double-Time since he needed a high-caliber rider, and there weren't any people who were looking for a horse like him in town, so it was a unanimous decision. It's one of the many things I've regretted—and part of me wishes I kept him. But it wasn't fair to let his talent go to waste, especially a horse who loved barrel racing as much as him.

Briar gives her baby a push and brings her head over to me. "Hey, sweet girl." I scratch her ear in the spot I know she likes. "You're a good momma, aren't you?"

I let out a breathy laugh when she knickers, as if to say, "Of course I am."

My gaze falls to her dark eyes, and my throat closes. Horses' eyes have always been what drew me to them in the first place. They hold so much wisdom, as if you can see the world in their depths. In Briar's, I see a horse that my brother loved, a horse that faced trauma and recovered. She may not have gotten the titles that Reed wanted, but she's a survivor.

She puts her nose in my hand, and I can't help the tear that falls from my eye. "I miss him, Briar." She pushes me again, this time a little more forceful. "You miss him, too?" Her head bobs. I'd like to think she's telling me yes.

I exhale shakily as I study her long face and brush my fingers along a healed cut below her eye. When her baby comes up and tries to nip me for attention, a chuckle escapes my lips. I scratch both their faces and try to blink away my tears.

"Think of something else, Blake," I mutter to myself.

When Briar's whiskers scratch against my palm, an image of Gavin's stubbled jaw line appears in my mind. My cheeks stain red, and my sadness is replaced with embarrassment. I can't believe he saw my half-naked body, and then I literally collapsed in his arms and smelled him. What was I even thinking?

"How's unnamed lookin'?" I jump at the sound of Daddy's voice and throw a hand over my chest.

"Daddy! You know better than to sneak up on me like that."

He lets out a laugh, pushing his Stetson up so I can see his eyes better. "I went to check on you. I thought after all the hullabaloo yesterday, you'd still be sleeping."

I give him a look. "Really?"

He stuffs his hands in his pockets and stands next to me. "I suppose not. I couldn't sleep and figured you'd be down here."

I scan Daddy's face. He's looking at me like he always does. With love and concern. While away, I'd missed his face, the Daddy's girl that I am. When I left, I thought maybe I'd be gone for a few weeks, max; but a few weeks turned into months, which turned into years. My parents came to visit me occasionally, but we've been good at pretending everything is fine, or at least tried to.

Not that I give them a choice to act otherwise. I never want to talk about what happened. Once they accepted that, they stopped trying to push me. Still to this day, they haven't heard all the details from my lips. I told everything to the police and the poor farmer who happened to hear me screaming and found us. That information was eventually given to them by the authorities.

"Are you alright after yesterday?" Daddy asks, breaking the heavy silence.

I push a smile on my face. "A little sore. Nothing I can't handle."

"Good, good." He stares at the foal, a pained look on his face. "He needs a name."

"I'm scared to give him one," I blurt out, not sure why I admitted that. Daddy's face mirrors my own surprise, though he tries to hide it.

His eyes lock with mine. "Why's that?" He knows why, but he wants me to say it.

"I'm afraid I'll name him, and he'll pass away." I pause, debating if I should continue. But as I look at Briar, I feel like I need to. "A name makes him real. It makes him permanent. I can't handle burying something of Reed's if he has a name." As soon as I say it, I feel a weight lift, but also an unbearable sadness replacing that heaviness.

Daddy stands taller and clears his throat. When he speaks, his voice is clouded with emotion. "I think it's safe to say this boy is in the clear now. Your Mom thinks Reed's been looking out for him. He always wanted—" He stops.

"Daddy," I say quietly, "it's okay."

He clears his throat again, not letting the tears fall. I've only seen him cry once in my life, and that was the day Reed died. It's almost too much to handle, but I force myself to stay strong. This is the first time I've talked to him about Reed since before I left. I don't want to lose it.

Daddy continues, "Reed wanted this foal. It took Margie a long time to finally make it happen. Then last year, she woke up one morning and said Reed came to her in a dream. Now here we are. I know she doesn't show it, but she's been as scared as you about this little fella. But he's fine now, and he's going to be a strong one. You know I can tell these things." He half-grins as he runs a worn hand over his face.

There's a second of silence before the colt lets out a super high-pitched whinny. Daddy and I both wince, then let out a bark of laughter.

"Maybe that was Reed's way of saying you're right."

"I'd like to think so…" Daddy trails off.

In a flash movement, I grab Daddy around the middle. With my arms locked tight, I hug him so hard I think I'm squeezing his organs.

A surprised *"oomph"* escapes him before he hugs me back. I hold back my tears as he embraces me just as tight. In his arms, I feel safe, protected, like I used to when I was little. It's nice but it's also a lot of emotions I'm not prepared to fully feel today. I think I've hit my limit after this conversation. So before I start sobbing, I pull back to look into Daddy's glassy eyes.

"I'll figure out a name for him. Just give me time. I want it to be a good one."

"I'm sure it will be," he assures me. He steps back and stuffs his hands in his pockets. It takes about half a second for him to collect himself and erase any emotions from his features. It's very impressive.

"Now," he says, a sly grin settling on his lips.

"Oh no. What's that look for?"

"Are you going to tell me what was going on with you and that Montgomery boy when I came upon you last night?"

"Daddy!"

He chuckles. "Alright, but so you know, your mom was asking me a million questions. None of which I wanted to think about or answer."

I groan. "Nothing was going on!"

"If you say so."

I huff. "You're as bad as Mom! I'm going to get to work before I smack you good." I stomp off with his laughter chasing me.

"Blake!" he calls, stopping me in my tracks. I turn toward him. "Yeah, Daddy?"

"I love you."

My chest tightens. "I love you, too."

CHAPTER 12

Blake

FRIDAY, THE NIGHT OF my date with Jake, comes around quicker than a flash flood. Our resident town gossip Abby Allen dropped off the basket she made for me earlier today. I'm glad Mom was the one who intercepted her at the house while I was out working.

I've heard through the town grapevine that Abby hasn't stopped talking about what Gavin did at Night Hawk. Mom confirmed she also heard he came to visit me earlier this week. How the hell Abby finds out about these things is beyond me, and freaky.

I run my hands over my hips, feeling the soft fabric of my red sundress under my hands as I look out the living room window, waiting for Jake's truck to pull in. For a fleeting moment, the memory of how warm Gavin's touch was against mine haunts me. The damn Cowboy has been a constant figure of my daydreams these past few days, which is annoying since I'm trying to hate him. It's been harder after what went down between us led me to having such a great talk with Daddy. But then I remember why I'm getting dressed up and leaving the safety of the ranch. Because Gavin Montgomery put me in this situation.

Anger simmers, but not enough to convince my body that it one hundred percent hates him. I chew on my lower lip and have the urge to throw up my hands at how confusing this whole thing is. It doesn't help that I had an inappropriate dream about him the other night. One that involved him very much naked. The thought has me blushing.

I wish he'd never come to apologize to me. Then I wouldn't have the imprint of his hands on my cheek or his arms around me. I wouldn't even think of him calling me beautiful or the electricity I felt when our hands touched. I shake my head and remind myself that even if I had a reason to like him, it's been almost a week, and he hasn't tried to contact me at all. Which leads me to believe that I'm right about him after all, and the whole thing at Night Hawk was a stunt. Or if it wasn't, he came out to the ranch to apologize just to save face. Or his mom made him come.

"Why do you look so upset?" Mom says from the couch, a book in her hands. She's resting today, which is unusual. She must have overdone it.

"Because I'm going out on a date," I say.

"Don't be dramatic. You'll have a good time. I bet there's something unique in the basket Abby made you. Or maybe a sweet treat."

I glare at said basket that's sitting on the coffee table in front of her. "I wonder if she hid a bug in there to record the date. That way she can tell everyone in town how it went."

Mom cackles. "You never know."

I turn back to the window at the sound of Jake's truck coming up the drive. According to the old clock on the wall, he's right on time. I move to grab my cowboy hat and a small purse Mom let me borrow and take a calming deep breath.

"Have a good time. I know Jake isn't the one you have feelings for, so enjoy catching up with a friend."

I bite the inside of my cheek. "I don't have feelings for anyone."

Mom hums to herself. "Keep telling yourself that."

Instead of taking the bait, I say, "I shouldn't be home too late."

"Take all the time you need. You can come home tomorrow morning if you want!"

Sighing, I open the door before Jake can come up to the house.

"Don't forget to take your basket!" Mom calls.

I flip around and grab it off the table and give her an annoyed smile. "Bye, Mom."

She kisses the air and goes back to her book with a smug look on her face. "Have a nice evening. Don't do anything I wouldn't do."

Lord help me. Before she can tease me more, I make my exit. Jake is stepping out of his truck as I do. He whistles and removes his red cowboy hat to admire the view. "Damn, Blake! You look like a snack. You match me on purpose?" He points to my red dress, then to his hat.

I laugh. "Actually, it didn't even cross my mind."

He stumbles back in jest like I've wounded him. "You sure do know how to make a man feel good." His tone is sarcastic.

"It's a special trait of mine." I smirk. Once I'm in front of him, he leans in to kiss my cheek, then takes the basket from me.

"I don't know what's in it."

Jake smiles. "Should we open it now or you want to go grab a drink first?"

"You don't want to know?"

He shrugs. "It's not important. Plus, I bet you'd rather chuck that thing in the garbage and see where the night takes us. Picnics and pleasantries be damned! Or at least, that's what the old Blake Tanner would do."

My chest warms. He's right; that is what the old Blake Tanner would do. And maybe tonight I can let go and pretend to be her.

He nudges my shoulder, his eyes alight with mischief. "Come on, Blake. Let's go have some fun. Let loose a little." He holds up the basket, then pretends to throw it.

"What if there's actually something good in there?" I tease.

"You're right. Maybe it's got her lemon squares. Those are tasty and cannot be thrown out at any cost."

"You haven't changed, Jake Buckley."

"Why change perfection?" He winks. "Let's go to Night Hawk. We drink for free." He puts air quotes around 'free.' "It's also line dancing night, so I can promise you no bull riding."

It's funny, I didn't think about that. Instead, I'm wondering if Gavin is working. Though I'm not going to reveal that to Jake.

"I don't know. Why don't we go to Big Dog instead?" I suggest. I think it's probably best I stay far away from Gavin right now. I'm trying to keep my wandering mind off him, not see him in that Night Hawk uniform again.

Jake makes a face. "That bar has become a place where the old men in our town go to reminisce about the time when they could walk without limping."

"I'm sure it's not that bad."

"Night Hawk—and I'm not trying to impress you—is the best place in town now. Trust me, you don't want to go to Big Dog. We'll be drinking warm beer all night as I fight off men trying to be your Sugar Cowboy."

"Sugar Cowboy?"

"You know, when a man—"

I put my hand over his mouth like I used to do when he pissed me off in high school. "I get it."

He smirks around my palm, and I remove my hand.

"Night Hawk?" he asks.

"Fine. Night Hawk."

The ride over is amusing. Jake pretends to be my travel guide, showing me "The New Randall." Which is the same as it was when I left. I find myself laughing like I haven't laughed in a long time. I'll take it to my grave, but so far, I'm kind of happy that Jake got me out and about after all. Though I'm saving my final judgment until after the date is over.

Once we park, Jake forces me to stay in the truck so he can open my door. He helps me down and holds my hand tight as we walk into Night Hawk. For how early it is, this place is packed.

Jake reads my face. "Don't worry. Since it's Friday, we get a lot of people from the city in for our line dancing. We offer lessons at six-thirty, then people dance till close."

"That's clever. Who teaches the dances?"

"Believe it or not, Kade Montgomery."

I think of the young man I met the other night. I can see him having dance moves, especially since he probably gets more women that way.

"I believe it."

"He's a great dancer. Gavin's amazing as well. He'll teach when Kade can't."

I ignore the comment about Gavin and try to not picture him moving his hips as I continue to walk toward the main area full of small tables littered with people, none of whom I recognize. Kade is on the dance floor, calling out moves into a mic as "Old Town Road" by Lil Nas X plays. I watch him for a second and smile. I can't see his feet, but I can tell he's moving like a pro. The faces of the dancers around him are smitten. They're clearly falling for his charm.

I make a move to the bar, but Jake stops me. "Let's get a table. I'll go grab us some drinks." He puts his hand on the small of my back and takes me to a high-top with a view of the bar and the dance floor, which is right next to the bull.

He pulls out my chair for me. "Best seat in the house."

I bat my eyelashes playfully. "I feel honored."

Chuckling, he steps back and asks, "What'll you have?"

Last time I was here I made the mistake of going with a beer. I may be smiling and acting like my old flirty self with Jake, but my insides are churning. I need something to take the edge off. "Whiskey."

"Ooh! You trying to get drunk, Cowgirl?"

"Not sure about that, but it sounds like the drink I need right now."

"Alright, then. I'll be right back. Don't run off while I'm gone."

"I'll try not to." He starts to walk off, but not before he stops to shake his well-defined ass a bit.

"If you leave, you'll miss all of this. Think about that!"

I let out a snort. Jake is an attractive man. He's tall, muscular, and his russet skin has darkened from time spent in the Texas sun. He has beautiful ebony eyes that one could happily stare into. I remember the first time I met him; my teenage self swooned. He's as nice as they come and has always treated me with respect. He'll be a great partner for some other woman. I just don't feel more than friendship with him. I'm going to have to be careful I don't lead him on or make him think there's a chance between us. We should probably talk about it.

As I wait for him to return, I hear Kade call out some dance moves. It makes my mind drum up thoughts of Gavin again. I haven't seen him yet, so maybe he's not working tonight. I tap my fingers on the tabletop, disappointment entering my system. The feeling upsets me since I should be glad he's not here. I grit my teeth and try to focus on the music instead of my silly thoughts.

Jake thankfully approaches after another minute. He sets down my drink and bows softly. "Whiskey for the lady."

"Thank you."

He raises his beer. "Cheers to a good night with an old friend."

Relief fills me at his words, my body relaxing. He must see it, because he puts his beer down and places a hand on my shoulder. "We may not have seen each other in a long time, Blake. But I watched you as I walked over here. You're nervous and in your head. I know you didn't want to come tonight, but I meant what I said. This night can be two friends catching up. I'm not expecting anything from you."

I place my hand over his. "Thank you, Jake. You know I like you, but I want to be friends."

He sighs and shifts his body back. "I'll admit, I was hoping maybe you'd change your mind after all these years."

"I'm sorry, Jake."

"No sorry needed. You know I'll always care for you." He pulls his hand back, putting it over his heart. "Though my heart may never recover." He grins, a teasing smile on his lips.

I flick his shoulder with my finger. "You'll be fine. I'm sure there's plenty of wonderful people who come through this bar just waiting for Jake Buckley to sweep them off their feet."

"But none of them will ride the bull as good as you."

I let out a laugh. "You never know."

"You never know," he echoes. He holds up his beer again. "To a fun good night with a good friend."

We clink glasses and I take a sip of the amber liquid. Right away I know he gave me top shelf. "Special occasion?"

"Blake Tanner is back in town, and she's on a friendly date with me at my bar. That's the occasion."

I match his smile over my tumbler. "If anyone had to win me, Jake, I guess I'm glad it was you."

He quirks an eyebrow at me. "You guess?"

"Who else would give me free top shelf whiskey and a night free of questions like: "Tell me how you really are, Blake?" Or "Why don't you ride anymore, Blake?" Or my favorite, "We're so sorry for your loss, Blake."

"Good thing I wasn't planning on asking you any of those things. I do have one question for you, though."

"Oh?"

He sets down his beer and holds out his hand. "Dance with me?"

"Ummm," I fumble. "I haven't danced in a while."

"What happened to bringing out the old Blake for the night?"

I sigh. "I don't think I ever agreed to bring her out."

"Come on, Blake! You used to love to dance all night long!"

A breathy laugh escapes my lips. "Ok, fine! Just promise not to laugh."

He makes an X motion across his chest. "Cross my heart."

I down my drink, then slam the empty glass on the table. "Let's go."

"Damn, girl. You chugged the fine stuff down like it was water."

I grab his hand, then lean forward so my lips are near his ear. "Then you should've given me the cheap stuff."

He throws his head back and laughs. "Let's dance the night away, Blake Tanner."

CHAPTER 13

Gavin

WHEN I ARRIVE AT Night Hawk, the parking lot is nearly full. My eyes fall on Jake's truck as I pull into a spot reserved for me. He told me he'd be out with Blake tonight for their *date*, so I didn't expect him to be at Night Hawk. Which only means one thing. Blake Tanner is inside.

I've done a horrible job at taking my mind off her. I keep thinking about her beautiful body floating in the spring and the way her soft skin felt against mine when I held her. These daydreams made it harder to stay away from her like I planned, which only added to my foul mood. One that was worsened by Kade's lack of apology. Not to mention the constant calls from the bank and severe sleeplessness. Gran started calling me Prickle Pants, which didn't help anything. If only she knew why I'm in such a bad mood all the time. But I can't tell them, not yet. I have a lead on some government subsidies and grants that might be able to dig us out a little, but I'm not sure if we qualify.

Rubbing my face, I take a moment to collect myself before entering the bar. This place is usually my escape, but with Kade working the dance floor and Blake inside, I'm starting to think I should call out for the night. But I'm a better than that—and calling out would only make Jake ask questions. Ones I can't answer.

At least the loud country music and the sound of people having a good time drown out my looping thoughts. I scan the crowd, because I'm a glutton for punishment, and find the brim of Jake's red hat. He's dancing with Blake and is pert as a cricket. I would be too if I had my hands on Blake Tanner's delicious hips. She looks good enough to eat in her red sundress. Her legs are shapely, and her arms toned from working the ranch. If I hadn't sworn off wooing her, I would knock Jake out and ask her to dance.

Great. Now I'm thinking about what her body would feel like pressed into mine, swaying in time to the beat of the music. And what her hands would feel like clinging to me as I dipped her and brought my lips to her neck. My cock comes to life, and I curse myself for letting her get to me so fast. We haven't even made eye contact yet. Snapping myself out of my lust, I make my way to the bar, hard-on uncomfortably pressing against my jeans. I'm grateful I can hide behind the bar top for a moment till my lower half calms down.

After a few deep breaths and making a mental list about all the work I need to get done at the ranch, I calm down enough to move. I wash my hands and go to greet the other bartender, Stu. He's a year older than Kade and makes the best mixed drinks. Which is why we have him work on nights like this so the city girls can have their Palomas and Hurricanes.

"You look like shit," he says with a grin.

I let out a terse laugh. "That's kind of you."

"Now that you're here, I'm gonna go on break. Mind manning the bar?" he says as he slides several drinks to the girls in front of us. They're all trying to catch my attention, but I ignore them.

"No problem. I got it handled."

He pats me on the back then turns to the women. "You ladies enjoy your drinks. Don't let this one scare you, he won't bite. Hard."

Stu smirks at me before leaving me to the rabid bunnies. It's clear they came here looking for 'real life cowboys.' I usually hear that several times a night. The city girls want me to tell them in detail what I do on a daily basis. When they find out it's mostly hard work, it bores them. Not sure what they're expecting. For me to shoot people on the plain?

One of the women bats her eyes at me while taking a sip of her fruity drink. "What's your name, Cowboy?"

"Montgomery." I often give out my last name to patrons when I'm working. Keeps things professional. It doesn't always work, and sometimes they find out anyway. Especially if Kade is working and blabs about me being his brother or a townie calls me over.

She giggles. "That's an odd name. Mine's Alexis."

She holds out her hand and I shake it for formality's sake before asking, "Can I get you ladies anything else?"

Alexis looks defeated but I can't find it in myself to care.

The women shake their heads and one of them convinces her friends to head back out to the dance floor, leaving me to tend to the rest of the customers. For a brief minute I let my eyes catch Blake. Kade is talking to her and Jake, showing them a move. Blake laughs when Jake gets it wrong, and a pang of jealousy thrums inside me.

Another customer interrupts my view, and I scold myself for even looking again. I'm here to do a job, not peep the woman I told myself I'd leave alone.

I put on a smile and look at the customer in front of me. "What can I get for you?"

I'm lost in the rhythm of making drinks, serving customers, and settling bar tabs. There are times my eyes find Blake, since her height and curves make her stand out among the carbon copy women here tonight. But mostly I keep my head down. I'm unaware of how long I've been here, but we're busy and I hardly have time to breathe.

As I'm pouring a round of tequila shots, a thud on my back pulls me from the pattern. Jake tips his hat back, a sheen of sweat coating his forehead.

"Busy tonight," he says.

"It is."

"Did you see Blake out there? That girl likes to say she's not great at dancing, but she knows how to move."

"I hadn't noticed," I lie.

"You should go ask her to dance!" he chirps, his tone genuine.

I sneer at his suggestion. "Is that the alcohol in your system talking?" I push the shots of tequila at the customers, then look at Jake.

He's got a wide smile playing at his lips as he says, "No. Figured you might want to."

Stu handles the next customers as I give Jake my full attention.

"Why would you suggest that? You won the date fair and square. And if you hadn't noticed, I'm working." I move to grab a new bottle of tequila on the back wall, but he stops me.

"Come on, man. You practically stamped your name across Blake's forehead last weekend when you got her up on that bull. Besides, she and I have established we're here as friends. She's made it clear that's all she wants from me. I'll admit, it stung a bit, but she's been looking at you since you got here. She thinks I haven't noticed, but I see her wandering eyes. I'm not the kind of man who steps in between something. I'm not a second choice." He smirks at the last part. "Go ask her to dance, Gav. I'll cover for you."

I'll admit there's a part of me that feels relieved at his words, but then I'm also not. I want to dance with Blake, but I also want to stay true to my word. She doesn't need someone like me in her life right now, and I need to focus on my crumbling ranch.

"I'm good," I bite out. The words feel sour on my tongue as I watch Jake grind his teeth.

"And if I tell you that you have to dance with her, or I'll fire you?"

"I'll punch your face in," I say seriously.

Jake shakes his head. "Seriously, Montgomery. What's your issue?"

Frustration builds inside me. I wish he would leave it alone. "My issue is you're preventing me from working."

"I'm trying to help you out. Literally telling you to go after the girl I'm crushing on."

"That's on you."

"Come on. You're being an idiot."

I roll my shoulders back and look at Jake in the eyes, my expression stern. "Blake doesn't want anything to do with me, and I don't want anything to do with her. I made a mistake putting her on that bull. The end. Now go enjoy your prize." My words come out like fire, burning me as I spew them. I know I'm being an ass, but my patience is worn thin.

Jake's eyes dart behind me and some of the color leaves his face. I turn to follow his gaze, only to be met by Blake's. Her features are blank, her bright red painted lips pressed in a hard line. She heard what I said, which makes me feel sick.

"Blake," I find myself sputtering, but she cuts me off.

"Whiskey. Make it a double."

She's not going to care if I apologize, so instead, I pour her the drink. She goes to take out cash, but Jake stops her.

"I told you that tonight is on the house," he says.

Her eyes meet mine as she brings the glass to her mouth, her pink tongue darting out sensually as she puts her perfect lips over the rim. She tilts her head back, coffee curls cascading over her shoulders as she gulps the amber liquid down. When her eyes return to mine, I try and think of anything else except how hot that was.

"Another," she says, pushing the glass toward me.

Jake hovers his hand over the glass. "Take it easy, Cowgirl."

Her eyes don't leave mine. "Another."

Jake sighs and removes his hand. I pour another shot for her and wonder how much she's had prior to these. It doesn't look like much since she's coherent and intentional with her actions. After she downs the drink, she licks her lips, and I swear my cock twitches.

"Are we dancing, or should I find another partner?" she asks Jake, though her eyes fall on me as she says it. Is she wondering what my reaction will be? If she's hoping for jealousy, she'd be right. The thought of another man's hands on her makes me grit my teeth.

A small smile plays at her lips as Jake says, "As if I'd let one of these city boys get the chance. I paid good money for you, Blake Tanner."

"Good," she chirps. "I'll see you out there."

Turning her ass to us, Blake walks back to the dance floor with an extra sway in her step, flipping her hair over her shoulder as she does. Now I'm convinced she's trying to get to me. I showed her my cards too soon, and now she knows anything she does will have my blood pressure rising.

Jake smacks me on the back, and I let out a tense breath. "Wow, Montgomery. Nice job pissing off the woman you're crazy about even more."

I glower him. "I'm not crazy for her."

He lets out a boisterous laugh. "Yeah, I'll make sure to tell that story during my best man's speech at your wedding. But for now, I'm going to go dance with a beautiful woman and pretend I'm the one she wants."

Jake walks off, still laughing to himself as I grab Blake's empty glass from the counter and take another patron's drink order. The man rattles off what he wants as my eyes drift back to Blake on the dance floor. She's once again having a good time, my words forgotten. Or at least that's what it looks like.

Her curved body sways in time with the music as she laughs at something a girl says next to her. God, she's beautiful. And I insulted her, *again*. I pour the drink order as I watch Jake grab and spin Blake so her back is to me and I have a perfect view of her glorious ass. It doesn't take a genius to know what Jake is doing. When I meet his knowing gaze, I see it written all over his face. The bastard is trying to make me see what I'm missing out on. And it's working.

I turn my body so I'm no longer facing the couple and check the clock on the wall. I've only been here for two hours, which means I'm going to be tortured for several more. Grabbing an empty glass and a bottle of whisky, I pour myself a finger before drinking it down, grateful for the burn and heat it offers me. After downing another, I put on my Montgomery smile and get back to work.

It's going to be a long night.

CHAPTER 14

Blake

JAKE AND I HAVE been dancing for I don't know how long. The whiskey I drank has finally gone to my head, and my body is buzzing with a feeling that seldom inhabits me: fun.

Kade is a great instructor, and even though he stopped teaching a while ago, he's been on the floor dancing with all the women and getting phone numbers stuffed in his jeans' pockets left and right. Not that I blame them, he's an attractive guy, but *wayyyy* too young for me. He's also related to the way too hot bastard named Gavin Montgomery. My now enemy. Well, not enemy, but I want to pretend he is so I can hate him. After his little comment about me being a prize, he can go screw himself. At least I got to have a little fun teasing him at the bar.

"Penny for your thoughts, Miss Tanner?" Jake asks as he spins me out. We've been doing our own thing for a while now, not bothering with all the steps.

I clear my mind of Mr. Hot Bastard for a moment as I look at my friend in front of me. Despite my interaction with Gavin, tonight's been great. The booze is good, the company is great, and Jake makes having a good time easy.

"I'm thinking I'm glad I came," I say truthfully. "Not that my daddy gave me much of a choice," I tease, thinking of how he embarrassed me in front of Jake after the auction.

Jake watches me thoughtfully. "I was a little surprised you let him do that. I've seen you go toe-to-toe with Lee Tanner before. You usually win."

"It's complicated."

Jake nods. "Most relationships with parents are. But—" He doesn't finish his sentence because Stu, the other bartender working, interrupts us. He leans down and whispers something in Jake's ear, then walks away.

Jake frowns. "I'm so sorry, Blake, but I've got to go take care of something."

Concern fills me. "Everything okay?"

"Sounds like the old man fell. He's okay, but I gotta go."

"I'll come with you—"

"No, no. Why don't you stay, have another drink, and dance with some fine young men?"

"Jake—"

He grabs my hands. "You have a good time now. I'll arrange a way for you to get home."

I shake my head. "I'll call Daddy. No worries."

Jake leans in and kisses me on the cheek. "Thanks for the date, Blake."

Before I can say anything else, he takes off, and I'm left on the dance floor. For a second, panic sets in. Jake was a great security blanket, protecting me from curious eyes. Now I feel a little like I'm stuck in the middle of the ocean with sharks all around me. I wring my hands in front of me and debate what to do.

"Blake?" I hear my name above the noise. I turn to find a sweaty Polly next to me with two shots in her hand. "Do you remember me?" she asks.

"Of course, I do." I smile at her.

She smiles back. "You looked a little scared after Jake walked off in a hurry, so I thought I'd come see if you wanted a drink and maybe some company. There are also some cute guys here that I've seen staring at you!" She steps closer to me and points toward the bar. "Including a certain hottie bartender who bid on you the other night."

When I follow her finger, sure enough, Gavin Montgomery is staring at me again. When our eyes meet, he doesn't avert his gaze. He's really a piece of work.

"Despite what you may think, he's not interested."

"I'm not so sure about that." Polly laughs. "But if tall, hot, and beefy doesn't do it for you, there's plenty of guys from the city peeling your clothes off with their eyes if you want to have a little fun without strings. I wouldn't blame you if you did." She hip-checks me to look at a table across the room. "Like that guy over there."

My eyes connect with the man she's speaking of. He's wearing a cheap cowboy hat, a white T-shirt, and jeans. I can see he's also wearing steel-toed boots. He probably doesn't even know why you'd pick a steel-toed boot over a regular one. But Polly is right about one thing: he is cute, and he's looking at me like he might take me out back and screw my brains out if I ask.

My cheeks flush. It's been many years since I've taken someone in the heat of the moment with no strings. Mr. Wannabe Cowboy tips his hat and my body buzzes at the idea. Not that I want have sex with him, but a dance or kiss with a random stranger would be exciting. Especially with Gavin watching. Because if he thinks he can ask me out one minute, then call me a prize the next, he's got another thing coming. For a second, I wonder if the alcohol is talking, but then I find I don't care. My conversation with Jake about bringing out the old Blake rings in my ears and I decide, to hell with it.

"What do you say?" Polly holds out the shot for me.

I take the glass from her hand and my lips turn up. "I say, sounds fun!"

She hollers then holds her glass up to mine. "Yes, girl!"

I down the shot after we clink them together, the sweet drink entering my already buzzing system. As the heat from the liquor settles in my gut, I attempt to drum up the courage I need to approach a stranger.

Polly takes the empty shot glass from me. "Relax, Blake. Do you need another shot?"

I shake my head. If I have another shot, I might end up on the bathroom floor instead of having some fun. My eyes stray to the bar again to Gavin. I shouldn't continue to look at him, but it's as if I can't help it. His gaze finds mine and my stomach flutters. Then for a moment I swear he looks regretful. Which he should feel, given how he's treated me so far. We stare at each other for another beat, the heat in my belly no longer from the alcohol but from my traitorous and confused hormones.

"Blake?" Polly chimes. "Looks like that guy is coming over here."

As her words register, I notice Gavin's features harden, his eyes now tracking who I assume is Mr. Wannabe Cowboy on his way over to me. Gavin clenches his jaw, his look turning fiery. His jealous reaction gives me a thrill, and it pushes me to continue with my plan of some random fun. Another bonus is it will take my mind off Gavin's attractive yet annoying face.

"Care to dance?" a deep voice interrupts my thoughts.

I turn to meet the blue-green eyes of Mr. Wannabe Cowboy and smile nicely at him. With the burn of Gavin's focus on my back, I gather what confidence I can find and nod.

"I'd like that."

"You two have fun," Polly sings. I watch as she goes off to join Tim Corbin and his brother. I didn't see them show up, but by the way Polly skips over to him I think I know where her night is heading.

Mr. Wannabe Cowboy gives me a half-grin and offers me his hand. I take it, and he pulls me closer, the warmth of his body melding into mine. I find myself thinking about how different it felt when Gavin and I touched. There's no spark with this man, though I suppose that's not always the point of a no-strings-attached dance, or whatever the hell may come from this.

As we begin to sway, I move my hands to his shoulders. To stop my thoughts from convincing me this is a bad idea, I ask, "What's your name?"

He pulls me even closer. "Mark."

Mark. I don't know why I thought this man would have a more interesting name. "It's nice to meet you, Mark." After a few awkward moments pass and his hand slides closer to my ass, I arch an eyebrow at him. "Aren't you going to ask my name?"

"Would you be upset if I already know it?"

I stiffen. "Stalking me, are you?"

He pulls me closer so I can feel what he's got going on beneath his jeans. I admit it's impressive, though again, it doesn't excite me like I thought it would.

"Nothing like that, darling," he answers. "But apparently you're famous in this town. People at the tables were talking about you." His accent is thick and different than I'm used to, like he's from Alabama or Arkansas.

My eyes dart from booth to table, taking in my surroundings. In the last hour, more people I know have arrived. Several of them are drinking and doing their own thing, but a few of them are watching me and Mr. Wannabe Cowboy. I mean, Mark.

I'm reminded through my alcohol-induced haze that I'm not anonymous here, and maybe it's time I head home. If I continue to dance with this man, or have him follow me outside, people will talk about it either way. Maybe I'm not ready to bring old Blake out to play. The thought of Abby Allen telling my Mom I left with a stranger has the shot I drank trying to come up.

The man's fingers dig into my hip and he leans down to my ear. "I've been watching you all night. You sure know how to move." In his strong grip, I shiver. Sadly, it's still not from attraction. I take a step back and try to keep a friendly smile on my face.

"You know, I think I'll have to pass tonight," I say.

He steps forward into my space again, clearly not taking the hint. He grabs my hips and pulls me back, this time his hand on my ass. "Come on, Blake." My name on his tongue really does have a gag forming in the back of my mouth. Why did I want to hook up with this guy? The endorphins I felt from dancing must've blocked my better judgment.

I put my hands on his chest and push back, but he's got at least a few inches on me and a lot more muscle. "I said, I'll have to pass for tonight. Now if you'll please step back," I say calmly. This isn't my first time dealing with a drunk boy who thinks if he pushes hard enough, he'll get me to say yes. I also learned long ago how to enact S.I.N.G. (solar plexus, instep, nose, groin) from Sandra Bullock in *Ms. Congeniality*. I'm not opposed to doing that here if I have to. Even if I've never actually had to use it before. How hard can it be to knee someone in the balls, at least?

"I'll make it worth your while," he drawls.

"I—"

"The lady asked you to step back."

I turn to face who I already know is standing there. Gavin looks menacing, his cowboy hat tipped back, and his square stubbled jaw set in a straight line. If looks could kill, Mark would be flat on the floor. I don't need Gavin's help, but damn if I'm not turned on by the way he looks right now.

"We were just dancing, no need to interrupt," Mark says. When he still doesn't let me go, Gavin reaches forward and grabs the man by the front of his shirt, nearly pulling the guy up from the ground. The crowd around us gasps, and I'm thrown into embarrassment.

"You asshole," Mark spits, trying to shove Gavin off of him.

"You're done here for the night, bud." Gavin lets Mark go, pushing him back so he stumbles. When Mark makes a move like he's going to try and clock Gavin across the face, Kade appears at his brother's side, looking equally as menacing.

Heavens above. This is not how I planned this night to end.

Marks gaze bounces between the brothers. "I was just dancing with her. She wanted it."

I open my mouth to stop any further embarrassment, but Gavin lunges at the man before I have the chance. The sound of skin hitting skin echoes, and Mark goes down like a sack of grain. Several men in the crowd get up, readying themselves to defend Gavin if needed, but Mark scrambles up from the floor and holds his hand in surrender, his other grasping his now bleeding lip. Even if he wants to fight back, he knows he can't take on an entire bar.

"For fuck's sake! You people are nuts. You can have your easy lays."

This time it's Kade who lunges for the guy, but I'm faster. I jump in front of him so he nearly bowls me over, but it stops this stupid fight from going any further. The bar goes quiet, and I realize someone turned down the music. Now I'm never going to be able to show my face here again.

"Let this idiot leave. His words don't mean anything," I say quietly so only Kade and Gavin can hear. Kade looks at said idiot, then back at me. Eventually he nods, and steps around me to grab the guy by the back of the shirt.

"Time to leave. You're not welcome in our bar anymore," Kade bites out.

The man grumbles and calls me a few other names that have me standing in front of Gavin, so he doesn't end up in jail for murdering the guy. Once Kade has shoved him out the door, I'm left with the eyes of way too many people on me. So I do the only thing I know how to do. I pretend I'm perfectly fine.

With a smile on my face, I yell to the bartender, "Stu, I think it's time to get these fine people a drink. A round of beer on me!" Everyone lets out a cheer. "And don't forget to turn up the music."

Much to my relief, music floods the room, and Stu starts to pass out beers. I hear a few people cheers me, including Polly, but my eyes are on Gavin, who looks like he's about to either yell at me or shove me against a wall to kiss me—maybe both. I can't help the warmth that pools in my belly, which reminds me that it's really time to leave. I've had enough for one night.

"Tell Jake to put it on Daddy's tab. I'll square up with him the next time I see him," I say to Gavin. Before he can speak, I breeze past him, ignoring anyone who tries to get my attention as I head toward the door. It's not until I'm outside that I realize I've got no way to get home unless I call Daddy like I told Jake I would. I pull out my cell phone from my purse and see it's one in the morning. Shit. Daddy will have a heart attack if I call him now.

I let out a breath. "Guess I'm walking."

"Like hell."

I jump at Gavin's voice. Will this man ever leave me alone? "I'm an adult woman. I can walk home." "You really can't take help, can you? It's going to take you hours to walk home. Not to mention it's dark, we're in the middle of nowhere, and you've had a lot to drink. So unless you'd like to get murdered, I suggest you let me give you a ride home."

I roll my eyes. "I'm not going to get murdered. You know how safe Randall is."

"I didn't say by a person. Though who knows where that dick is that we just kicked out. Either let me take you home, or if it's me that's the problem, I'll get Kade to do it. But you're not walking, and that's final."

I cross my arms over my chest and stare down Gavin Montgomery. "Aren't you supposed to be working?"

"Kade and Stu got it handled. Now, will you let me drive you? Or do you want to keep arguing with me?"

I huff. God, Gavin Montgomery makes me so angry I could scream. Before I can question what I'm doing, my feet carry me toward him and I press my finger into his hard chest. "Who do you think you are? You think you can boss me around all the time and get me to do anything you want because you're a sexy cowboy?"

A grin splits Gavin's lips as I realize what I said. *Seriously, Blake?* That was for sure the alcohol talking.

"I'm not trying to boss you around. I care about your safety, Blake."

I shove my finger further into his chest so I know it hurts. "Why? You don't know me. You never knew me. And you've made it clear that you want nothing to do with me. So why do you care if Mr. Wannabe Cowboy or an animal tries to eat me?"

Gavin doesn't answer, instead a symphony of cicadas surrounds us, with the occasional notes of music that drift from the bar. I wish I could tell what he's thinking, but his simmering eyes are unreadable. However, I'm close enough that I can see the way his jaw clenches as he watches me, and how a few days without shaving has revealed darker blonde hair growing in on his pretty face. It makes him look older, sexier.

My body shifts a bit in awkwardness, but I can't force myself to step back. There's a pull between us, one that's hard to ignore when we're this close to each other, and harder still with all the whiskey in my blood.

I push him with my finger again. "Hello, Gavin? I asked you a question."

My voice finally makes him react, and his eyes blink. "You're Reed's sister. He'd want me to take care of you."

I feel like I've been punched in the gut. I shove him with more force than I mean to, enough that he loses his balance.

"You're a real asshole!" I howl.

He grunts as he rubs his chest. "Stop trying to injure me. I'm being nice!"

In another act that surprises me, I run at him so we're backed against the brick wall of Night Hawk. I try to shove him again, but he grabs my hands before I can.

"Let me go!" I huff.

"Not until you calm the hell down and stop trying to hurt me."

"I'll stop when you stop hurting me!" The words ring around us as I struggle against him.

In one swift move he turns me so I'm now the one up against the wall. Locked against him, my movements are futile, so I stop fighting him. He drops his head, our hats bumping together before he lets out a breath. "I didn't mean to hurt you, Blake. I—"

I test his grip a little, but he's holding tight enough I still can't move. When he brings up his gaze to meet mine, I want to turn away, but I can't.

"That didn't come out right. Blake—damnit, I like you and—*fuck*!"

I like you. My heart hammers in my chest as he finally lets my arms go. They fall at my sides, but I can't seem to move away from him.

"I don't understand you," I say quietly.

He lets out a sad laugh. "I don't understand me either."

"You're so hot and cold. And if you're only doing all this because you think Reed would want you to—"

"No!" he cuts me off. "I said that because I was trying to push you away." He stops and his eyes drop to my mouth. He darts his tongue out, wetting his lips before his gaze flicks back to mine. My body ignites with fire again, and without thinking about it, I press my hips into his. He lets out a small groan before bringing his hand up to brush his thumb over my cheekbone. His touch feels like fire, causing my mind to think about certain indecent thoughts I've been having.

Gavin puts his finger under my chin, gently pushing the pad of his thumb into the flesh below my bottom lip. "Tell me to walk away, Blake," he breathes out. "Tell me to walk away and I will. I'll never bother or hurt you again."

My mind reels with every feeling I've had about Gavin Montgomery in the last week. Including how I wanted to make him hurt moments ago. I called him hot and cold, but I'm the same. Because right now, I just feel hot. And reckless. Maybe I can blame the alcohol tomorrow, even though deep in my gut, I know I'm sober enough to tell him to walk away.

"Blake," he says again, his voice like rough waves over my body.

"What if I don't tell you to walk away?"

He runs his finger down my jaw again. "Then you'd be stupid. Because I'm not good for you, baby."

I bite my lower lip and try to make sense of his words. I don't know what he means by that, but all I can think about is the way he called me 'baby.' It keeps playing over and over in my mind like a broken record.

I suck in a breath after a moment. "We have that in common."

His finger stops stroking my cheek, and he looks at me in question. Though I've never said such words out loud, I don't feel like I'm a good person to be around. It's one of the reasons why I didn't come home until now, and why I haven't let anyone get close to me. I'm just a sad woman who can't move on. Who would want to be around that?

Gavin's eyes search mine as he brings his hand up to remove my cowboy hat. With its removal, I feel naked. Exposed. "Blake," he says, his voice revenant. "I meant what I said at the spring. You're beautiful and I'm—" He plays with one of my curls, running it through his fingers before his eyes connect with mine again. "I know I shouldn't ask, but I need to kiss you. Even if it's just this once."

His ask is pleading, desperate, like how my body feels. Before I think more, I press my chest into his and reach up to push his hat from his head. It falls to the ground in a thump and his face tilts so our lips are close enough for me to feel his breath. Tomorrow, I'll blame this on the emotions of the night, on all the alcohol I consumed—but tonight, I want to kiss Gavin Montgomery.

So, I do.

CHAPTER 15

Gavin

IT TAKES ME A moment to register Blake's pillowy lips against mine. It's when her fingers grip the short threads of my hair that my body finally reacts. I grab the back of her neck and press her further into the brick wall, groaning against her mouth as her softness melts into me.

I've thought of this moment, despite my best efforts to stop it, and now it's happening. Blake's lips are searing, and the heat of her body drives me to near insanity. When she tugs on my hair, a sound akin to a growl vibrates through me as I press one of my hands against the wall to ground myself. I press my hips forward to let her feel how hard she makes me, and she moans into my mouth. I take advantage of the opening and slip my tongue inside, tasting her like the fine wine that she is, or should I say whiskey?

Her hand moves from my hair, and she doesn't waste any time finding my ass. Her nails dig in through my jeans, and it takes everything in me to not take this further. The thought alone of Blake in my bed almost makes me lose it. But if I'm going to throw away my sanity, I need to woo her the proper way.

I pull back reluctantly and kiss her lips in a few short pecks before resting our foreheads together. She keeps her eyes closed as I try and catch my breath, her brow pinching together in thought.

"Blake," I say, my voice rough. "Don't overthink this." When her eyes finally open, they're full of lust, but I can also see the effects of her whiskey and dance-a-thon wearing off.

"I—"

I press my lips to hers again in a quick kiss. "Don't. Please don't."

She closes her mouth and nods. "What now?"

I let out a breathy laugh and she follows. We're still plastered to each other, and I can faintly hear people leaving Night Hawk. Which means last call must've happened.

I tuck a piece of hair behind her ear. "I'll take you home."

For a second, I see the disappointment on her face; it's quick, but my heart pounds at the sight. I brush my thumb over her kiss-swollen lips.

"Don't worry, Blake Tanner. This isn't over. Not by a long shot." I mean what I'm saying, too. Because even though I asked for one kiss, I should've known one kiss would never be enough.

She bites her lower lip and moves to speak, but before she says anything, she takes notice of the patrons leaving. A blush like the way her sunburn looked envelopes her cheeks. Time to leave before she thinks about the kiss too much and regrets her decision. Because even though I didn't plan for this to happen tonight, I know I will never regret that kiss. Even if it's all I get for the rest of my life.

I grab my hat from the ground, then take her hand and lead her to where my truck is parked, ignoring everyone's stares. As soon as we're at the door of my black Ford F150, I open it for her. She gets in, and I close it behind her. Before I get in the driver's side, I shoot Kade and Stu a text to let them know I won't be around to close the bar. I'll have to make it up to them, or at least to Stu. Kade left early enough times with a random woman to not make me worry about paying him back for this decision.

Once inside, I see Blake looking out the window with her hand on her stomach. Before I can ask if she's feeling okay, her stomach growls so loudly she laughs.

I thank her stomach because this gives me an in. "Would your folks mind if we made a pit stop before I take you home?"

She eyes me, her dark eyebrow up in question. "Where might that be?"

"The Diner." For a moment, she stills, and I wonder if she has something against The Diner. "I can take you home, no problem," I add.

She shakes her head. "If you're not tired, I could use some dinner."

I grip my steering wheel. "Jake didn't feed you before he gave you drinks?"

She snickers. "Calm down, Cowboy. Abby Allen made us a basket, which probably had food in it. But we came here instead and left the basket in his truck. It was more my fault than his. I wanted to have a fun night out." It looks like she's going to say more, but she stops herself.

That's still no excuse for not feeding her, but I let it slide. "Alright then, I'd love to take you to The Diner if you'd like."

She studies my face, her gaze penetrating. I probably look tired because I was before that kiss. But for Blake, I can stay up forever, even if only to look at her.

"Let's go," she finally agrees.

I give her a small grin before I start the truck, its engine coming to life. The Diner isn't far from here, and it's the only restaurant in town that stays open past eight at night. Which means it will probably have some locals there, maybe even a few truckers passing through. Blake knows that, which has me all the more eager to get there before she changes her mind.

Country music plays softly from the radio as we drive along the darkened roads. Blake's so quiet that I think maybe she's fallen asleep, but she's focused on the barely visible landscape beyond.

"You're a good dancer," I say to break the silence. Even in the dark I can see her blush at my words. Damn, she's pretty. I wonder if her whole body blushes that way.

"Thanks. Daddy taught Mom how to dance after they met. Mom loves two-stepping and line dancing so much that she taught Reed and me as soon as we could learn."

Reed's name from her lips gives me pause, but she doesn't seem to withdraw at the memory she's telling me.

"Gran made Kade and me learn in middle school. Said we'd never be able to impress girls if we didn't learn," I say.

"Kade does dance well. He had the whole place in love with him by the end of the night. Maybe even me a little too."

Envy bubbles inside me. Which is ridiculous since I know Blake is just teasing. "Don't get too attached to my *little* brother," I emphasize that word on purpose, "because you haven't danced with me yet."

She laughs. "You think you're better than him?"

I give her one of my smiles as we pull up to The Diner. "I'd bet money on it."

She grins back as I turn off the engine. It's the first time she's given me a smile that's more than something you'd give a passing acquaintance. It's beautiful. She's beautiful.

"You're staring at me again," she says.

"I can't help it. I like staring at you."

She lets out a breath and turns to open her door. *Shit.* I embarrassed her again. I get out but she's already making her way inside. I catch up with her in time to open the door, but she walks through and goes to the counter where the waitress, Lyla, is standing. She's a sweet girl with an olive complexion, dark brown hair, and curvy features. She just graduated from high school and helps the owners run the place from time to time on weekends. I doubt Blake knows who she is, but by the look on Lyla's face, she knows who Blake is.

I clear my throat, and Lyla looks up at me. "Hey, Gav. No Jake with you tonight?" Her eyes look behind me, and I can tell she's disappointed. She always did have a crush on him.

"Nope. But we'd like a table." I put my hand on Blake's lower back. Her body is warm beneath my palm, and it puts a pleasant feeling in my belly. Like a warm, relaxing afternoon.

"You're Blake Tanner, right?" Lyla asks.

Blake smiles shyly. "I am."

"I knew it!" Lyla squeals. "I know you don't know who I am, but I grew up watching recordings of you riding. I even took some lessons down at your ranch. Oh boy! I've competed here and there myself, but I'm not nearly as good as you. I'd love to take you out for pie sometime and pick your brain on your riding style, I watched—"

"Slow down there, Lyla," I cut her off. "I think you drank too much coffee tonight." Blake looks about ready to bolt. Maybe I shouldn't have brought her here.

Lyla blushes. "Oh, I'm so sorry. I get excited sometimes, and I word vomit all over people."

Blake waves her hand like it's not a big deal. "You're fine. But I don't ride anymore. You'd be better off asking one of the rodeo guys we've got for help. They're good at what they do."

Disappointment colors the girl's face, and I feel bad for her, and for Blake.

"Lyla, how about that booth in the back there?" I point to the most secluded one. We won't be completely away from prying eyes, but thankfully there aren't many people here right now. Just a few drunks and people I know who will keep to themselves.

"Sure thing," she says, less pep in her voice this time.

I gently nudge Blake forward till we get to the booth and seat ourselves. Lyla hands us each a menu. "Thanks, darling." I wink at her. The look and pet name do exactly what I'm hoping, because her disappointment vanishes.

"You're welcome. Can I start you with drinks?"

"Two waters and I'll take a decaf coffee. Blake?"

Her eyes flick to Lyla's, and she forces a half smile. "I'll take a milkshake, chocolate."

"Whipped cream?"

"Sure."

Lyla jots it down and heads off to make our drinks. I give Blake a questioning look at her choice.

She shrugs. "I used to come to The Diner with my family. It's a tradition to get milkshakes." The answer is a simple one, but the pain is obvious behind her words. And now that she's told me, I remember that little fact about the Tanner family.

"Reed mentioned that to me once. At least, I think. It's been a while."

She fiddles with a gold ring she has on her middle finger, so much so that it starts to make me anxious. I put one of my hands over hers to quell the action. When she gazes up at me, there's fear in her eyes, more than I expected her to show.

I squeeze her hand. "Relax. You don't have to talk about him with me if you don't want to."

She looks at our hands on the table but doesn't pull away. I have no idea what's going through that head of hers, but I'd give anything for her to let me in. But I don't want to force it. I'm happy enough that she agreed to come here with me, especially with what happened up against the wall of Night Hawk. Before I can say anything more, Lyla arrives and places our drinks down. The action inspires Blake to remove her hand from mine, leaving a feeling of loss inside me.

Blake stares at the milkshake in front of her. It looks like something out of a movie. It's got fluffy whipped cream and a cherry on top of the sweet chocolaty mixture below.

Lyla smiles. "Here you go. Do you know what you two would like to eat?"

We haven't looked at the menu yet, but Blake says, "I'll have the House Burger with grilled onions, your special sauce, and cheese. Fries done extra crispy." My kind of woman.

"You want your usual, Gav?" Lyla asks.

"Actually, let's change it up. I'll take what Blake's having. Been some time since I had a burger."

"Sure thing. Be back in a jiffy."

Lyla leaves, and Blake pulls her treat toward her. She stares at the whipped cream for a bit but doesn't take a drink.

"Everything alright?"

"I—" she stumbles over that singular word. "I've never told anyone this before but, Reed hated whipped cream."

The warmth returns to my stomach at the fact that she's sharing this with me. "He did?" I ask, encouraging her to say more.

"He used to lie to our mom that he liked it. But he thought it had the consistency of wax. He never told her because it's one of her favorites. It was a stupid reason, but sometimes I saw him shoving it into a napkin when she wasn't watching."

I let out a chuckle. "Reed hated seeing people sad. Even if that meant pretending to like their favorite thing because he thought it would make them happy."

Blake gazes at me, her dark eyes thoughtful. "You're right about that."

With an exhale, she takes the cherry from the top and brings it to her mouth. I'm not sure if she's aware, but she sucks the juice out of it then pulls it off the stem. It's sexy, and not something I should be thinking about after she was so vulnerable with me. But I'm learning that anything Blake does sends me over the edge. I have a feeling I'm going to end up taking a record number of cold showers if we hang out more often.

After she swallows her cherry, she looks at me with curiosity. "I told you something personal. So tell me, what's your deal, Gavin Montgomery?"

"My deal?"

She uses a finger to swipe some whipped cream from her milkshake, then places the digit in her mouth and sucks. With the eye contact she makes as she does it, I *know* she's taunting me this time. She's good at diverting me from deep topics.

"Yes, your deal," she repeats. "You embarrass me in front of the entire town, show up at my home and watch me like some perv, ask me out, then I don't hear from you for a week. Then tonight, you basically called me Jake's property, and said you want nothing to do with me. Which I think is a lie since, well, here we are."

I let out a chuckle. "Straight to the point, then?"

"After everything, I think that's for the best. Don't you?" Blake's gaze penetrates into me and I find myself becoming nervous.

"From the start, I laid my cards on the table. I didn't lie when I came to see you, but what you heard at the bar tonight, that *was* a lie."

She takes a sip of her shake. Her eyes close for a second to savor it, like her taste buds remember the last time she drank one. When she opens them, she doesn't seem sad or upset, but she does look inquisitive.

"And why did you lie?"

"Because I didn't think I was good enough for you," I answer.

She pushes her drink to the side, folding her arms over the table in front of her. It gives me an ample view of her chest, but I try to keep my eyes on her face.

She cocks an eyebrow at me. "You said that before. Please explain."

Letting out a breath, I give Blake a long stare. "My family is broke."

She purses her lips. "And you thought that's reason enough to act so hot and cold?

My lips curl upward. "Look, I—" Before I can continue, Lyla returns with our food. She puts the steaming plates of greasy food in front of us and fills up my coffee.

"Can I get y'all anything else?"

"I'm good," Blake and I both say at the same time. Lyla smiles and heads off to help more customers that came in. Without wasting any time, Blake dips a fry in her shake and puts it in her mouth.

I cringe. "That's disgusting."

"Oh no! Are you one of those men who judge women's food choices?" I can tell she's joking by the twinkle in her eye as she dips another fry in the ice cream.

"Hell no. But that's just wrong."

"Have you ever tried it?"

"I'm good." I dip my own fry in ketchup.

Blake takes another golden stick off her plate and dips it in the shake before leaning over to hold it up to my lips. "Zoom, zoom, goes the airplane. Open wide!"

I can't help but laugh at how ridiculous she's being. The whiskey is still in her system, or maybe I'm getting a glimpse of the pre-accident Blake. Either way, I like it.

"Come on, Gavin. Open wide. It's good, I promise."

I look at the concoction in her hand. The ice cream has started to drip down onto her fingers, so I take the opening and grab her wrist. She lets out a small gasp of surprise as I use my tongue to lap up the sweet, melted cream before taking the fry into my mouth. When I pull back, chewing the salty and sweet treat, Blake's pupils are dilated.

I let go of her wrist and pick up another fry of my own. "Not bad. But you taste better."

Blake's eyes blink rapidly before she sits back. "You need better taste buds."

"I don't think so." I half-smile, biting another fry.

She shakes her head as she picks up her burger. We sit quietly for a few minutes as we dig into our food. While we do, I can't help but watch her enjoy the meal. The poor thing must've been starving, which reminds me I want to have words with Jake later about not feeding her pre-alcohol.

"Why do you look pissy?" she asks.

"Nothing to worry about," I assure her. I don't want her to know I'm imagining all the ways I can rough up Jake Buckley.

She puts a few fries in her mouth, then pushes her nearly empty plate away. "I think if I eat anything else, I'm going to wake up regretting it."

"You should drink more water and take some painkillers when you get home."

A small smile pulls at her lips. "You love giving me advice."

I give her a questioning look.

"First the aloe, now this. You can't turn off your caretaker button."

I wipe my fingers off with a napkin and push my plate away too. "I'm not going to apologize for looking after people I care about." My voice comes off with a slight edge; my fight with Kade is still fresh. She doesn't know that he told me something similar, or that he talked about her, but her words sting nonetheless.

"Gavin..." She sighs my name, making the hairs on my arms stand on end. "I didn't mean it in a bad way. I've been on my own for a while now, and I'm not used to people fussing over me. Unless you count the phone calls from my mom while I was away, but those have reduced in the last couple years." Blake shifts uncomfortably in her chair, like she told me a big secret.

I rub my eyes tiredly. "I know you didn't. Sorry, I snapped. It's been a long week."

She taps her blunt fingernails against the table. "Do you have someone taking care of you?"

Her question stuns me. I honestly don't have an answer for her. Growing up on a ranch as big as ours, I matured fast because of all the work that had to be done. Kade and I were treated more as small adults than children. That didn't mean we weren't cared for or loved, but we were never coddled. Since Dad died, I've been working harder than ever before. So no, nobody takes care of me, but I think I'm doing an alright job of taking care of myself and my family. Though they might disagree when they learn what I've been keeping from them.

Blake opens her mouth to say something, but Lyla comes over with the check. This girl has impeccable timing.

"Can I get y'all anything else?" she asks.

"I think we're good," I answer.

She smiles and looks at Blake. "It was nice meeting you, Blake. If by chance you change your mind about grabbing a coffee sometime, let me know."

Blake forces a smile. "Will do, Lyla." Lyla gives her a curt nod before walking off.

When I see Blake reaching for her cash, the blood in my veins heats up. "Put your money away, Blake. I asked you here, I'm paying."

She tips her head to meet my gaze. She wants to argue; it's in her stubborn nature. And I know what people in this town think, especially after that charity event. But I can pay for a damn burger at a greasy diner.

"I'm paying." My words are a demand this time, not a question. She licks her lips, but puts her purse back down. At least she finally listened to me.

After I've sorted the bill, we head out. I place my hand on the small of her back again, tipping my hat at those I know scattered in a few of the booths. Blake knows some of them, but she doesn't do more than give them a humble smile in greeting. Once she's in the truck and we've started our way toward Double-Time, my brain keeps repeating what she said, *"Do you have someone taking care of you?"*

Blake is lost in thought too, which makes the drive to her home a quiet one, but surprisingly not awkward. After about fifteen minutes, we approach the dirt road leading to her home. It's dark, but in the distance, I can see her folks left the porch light on for her. After I've thrown the car into park, she unbuckles her seatbelt.

"Thanks for dinner," she says.

Thanks for dinner. The words are so mundane after what just happened between us. Which feels like more than a heated kiss and a shared cheap meal.

"I'll walk you to the door."

"You don't have to."

"I'll walk you to the door," I repeat.

She lets out a sigh, mumbling something under her breath about neanderthal cowboys. It makes me grin. She can call me what she wants, but I'm a gentleman, even if I haven't acted like it over the last week. Now I'm going to change that.

We both get out of the truck, and I press my hand to her low back once more. It fits so well there. I wonder what the skin underneath feels like. Swallowing my lust, we make quick work of the distance from my truck to the Tanners' door.

"Thanks again for dinner," Blake says.

I reach up and tuck a piece of soft hair behind her ear. The urge to kiss her again is strong, but I don't know if it's welcome. What we shared at Night Hawk was passionate, in the heat of the moment. Now she's had time to think, time to talk to me, and I don't know where we stand with each other. But I do know what I would like from her, and it doesn't involve staying away anymore.

"Thanks for joining me," I answer. "For talking to me."

Blake studies me like I'm a map. It makes my insides twist in some kind of way. But I let her stare, and I wonder what she sees.

"Good night, Gavin." She takes a step back and opens the front door.

I tip my hat and give her a crooked grin. "Good night, Blake."

Our eyes connect again through the screen door, that studious gaze still there. After a moment I turn to walk away, but her voice stops me.

"Gavin?"

I turn back. "Yes, Blake?"

Her cheeks look stark now, her sad eyes illuminated by the porch light. "You shouldn't care about me," she murmurs.

I clench my fists at my sides, but before I can answer, she closes the door and locks it. My stomach turns over, and I regret eating that burger now. Blake may think I shouldn't care for her, but she's sealed her fate. I'm going to do everything I can to show her how much she deserves to be cared for. How much she's already cared for.

I just have to figure out how to break down those concrete walls.

CHAPTER 16

Blake

I KISSED GAVIN MONTGOMERY.

It happened two days ago, and even as I sip my black coffee, it's all I can think about. The coffee tastes bitter and burnt on my tongue, but that doesn't stop me from drinking a third cup.

"Good morning," Mom chimes, coming in on her crutches.

"Morning," I say quietly. I've been getting up at five the last two days so I could avoid her. But by the cheeky look on her face, I think my luck has run out. Damn it. I shouldn't have slept till six this morning.

"You and Jake have fun the other night? I've been trying to get you alone to ask how it went, but you're sneaky."

I adjust the Texas Longhorns ballcap on my head. It's not my usual cowboy hat, but I left it in Gavin's truck and haven't had time to go get it back. I ignore her comment about being sneaky and answer with a simple "It was a good time."

Mom sits in the chair next to me, propping her crutches on the table. Although it's early, she already has makeup on and her hair in a slick bun. I only managed a little mascara and some ChapStick before I headed downstairs.

Mom smiles happily. "I knew you'd have a good time. Though I didn't expect you to be out so late."

My anxiety springs to life. I know what's coming next.

She continues, "I also happened to notice it wasn't Jake's truck coming down our drive after two in the morning."

I start to stand, but she touches my arm and urges me back down. "You can sit and have a conversation with me, Blake. I know we don't do it often, but I'd like to talk with my daughter."

Letting out a sigh, I sit stiffly in my chair. "For someone injured, you sure have a lot of strength."

Mom blows out a breath through her lips. "I injured my leg, not my arms. Plus, these crutches sure are giving me a workout."

I steeple my fingers nervously. I was really hoping she was asleep when Gavin dropped me off. I should've known she was watching.

She raises a manicured eyebrow at me. "Don't you have anything to say?"

I shake my head. "He gave me a ride home."

She hums, studying my face. Under her gaze, I feel like she can see everything that happened. Hell, she probably knows. I'm sure someone told Abby Allen who probably called Mom and replayed the events at Night Hawk and The Diner to her. I know I've been replaying them for the last forty-eight hours.

"You look guilty." Mom smirks.

"Can we talk about this later? I should get to work."

Mom reaches forward and places her hand on my forearm. "You never want to talk to me, honey. Your Daddy told me about your fight last week. And what you said about naming Briar's foal. Why can you talk with him about that kind of thing, but you can't talk to me about your night out? I know something happened between you and Gavin. I don't need a town gossip to know that."

I pull out my arm out from under her and fold my hands in my lap. She frowns, tucking back into herself.

"I'm just tired," I huff. "We can talk later."

"You look fine to me."

I tense. I don't want to talk about this with her. I don't even know what to make of what happened. And the last thing I want is for her to marry me off in her mind to someone I only kissed once.

Mom sighs and leans back. "What happened to us, Blake?" Her voice sounds tired, resigned. It makes something in my heart clench. "You used to talk to me. But ever since," her voice wavers, "ever since Reed's death, you act like you hate me and I don't know why."

My eyes burn. "I don't hate you." I know it sounds pathetic as I say it, but it's true that I don't hate her. Our relationship is...complicated.

Growing up, she put a lot of pressure on Reed and me to be the best. Whether it was riding, school grades, or cleaning our damn room, she expected us to be great. I still felt that pressure even after I left town. It was as if she kept judging me from afar because I couldn't get my shit together. And now that I'm home, everything that we've left unsaid for so many years hangs between us.

Mom waves a hand in front of my face, and I realize I spaced out.

"Where did you go just now?" she asks.

I pick at the cuticle around my thumb. "It's not important."

She says my name again, this time in a quieter voice. "Please tell me what I can do to make this right. I lost one child, but I feel like I lost both."

Her words stab me like a million needles. My throat constricts, and I turn my face away from her. "Can we not talk about this, please?" My question comes out weak.

Mom shifts, putting her hand on my leg now and squeezing it tight. "We have to talk about it, Blake."

I let out a shaky breath. "I didn't come home to talk about my feelings, I came to *help*."

"So you expect me to let you walk around like a zombie half the time and stare at Briar and her foal, like if you stare hard enough, Reed will appear?"

My chest tightens, rocks tumbling around in my gut. "Like I said, I don't want to talk about this." There's harshness in my words, but she's pushing it.

"It's time we do. We can't be like this anymore, Blake. It's hurting me."

I raise my voice. "Please don't try to manipulate me into talking!"

"Blake Margaret Tanner, I'm doing no such thing." Her voice has turned from pleading to scolding. "I'm only trying to talk to you!"

"You are talking to me," I say snidely.

"Don't get smart with me, young lady. What happened to my respectful daughter?"

I almost say that she died the day Reed did, but instead I pull my face from her grasp, anger set on my face and cheeks heated. "I don't know what to say to you. But forcing me to talk isn't helping."

Mom's chest heaves as she moves her hand to my shoulder and grips it tight. "I thought you left so you could process what happened, but I should have never let you walk out that door. You need to talk to me, Blake. Or if not me, I can have you talk to my therapist in New York. She does virtual—"

I push my chair back and stand from the table. It's a knee-jerk reaction, one I didn't think about because Mom is using me to support her weight. With my body no longer there she falls forward from her chair onto the floor. It's not a long drop, but with her leg it's enough to hurt her. Mom lets out a pained sound, one that stuns me. Before I can do anything, Daddy comes rushing in to the kitchen from the den.

"What the hell is going on in here?" he bellows, moving to Mom's aid as I stand there, still as stone. "Margie! Are you alright?"

"I'm fine, I'm fine," she chants, but I know I hurt her.

Daddy's eyes find mine, disappointment riddling his features like the day I told him I was leaving town. I should be helping Mom get up, but I'm still frozen.

What have I done?

"Blake," Daddy snaps. "Tell me what happened." He helps Mom up in her chair again, but I can only stare at him like a deer in the headlights.

"I—I—"

"It was an accident, Lee," Mom gets out in a wince. "Please calm down." It *was* an accident, but that doesn't make it right. God, I keep screwing things up. I keep hurting people I love.

"I—" I try again, but words escape me.

Daddy's mouth is pressed in a hard line, waiting for me to explain. But for the life of me, I can't get my voice to work. My body is screaming for me to run, to say something, but I can't get my mouth to move. Before I can think about what I'm doing, I turn on my heel, taking the keys to Mom's Jeep that are on the hook by the door.

Daddy yells for me to come back. He could chase after me, but I know he's too worried about Mom. Tears fall down my cheeks, and I don't know what I'm planning to do or where I'm going. All I know is that I need to get off this ranch before I do anything else.

Once I'm settled in the Jeep, I pull out of the drive like a racecar driver and speed toward the main road, eyes squinting from the bright morning sun. It's not until I'm a good mile or so away that I pull off to the side and explode into sobs. It's as if I'm possessed. Cry after cry rips from my throat as I hiccup for breath. Even when Reed died, I didn't have this reaction. I cried, but not like this. This feels different, like the last thread inside of me has finally broken. But the look on Mom's face when she fell, on Daddy's when he saw me just standing there…it's horrifying.

I place my head in my hands as I feel the weight of everything pressing me down—the upcoming anniversary, the mistakes I've made for five years. Every memory and thought feels like it's pulling at me from the inside out. In a way, it's as if something inside me is dying all over again. I don't know how long I sit there and cry, but when it finally recedes, my throat is raw and my head is throbbing so hard I feel like I'm going to pass out.

I glance in the rear-view mirror to see my red face. I look like I've been put in a dryer and set on high. My hair is a mess, mascara runs down my cheeks, and there's snot dripping from my nose. I wipe it off as I debate what to do. I can't go home, but I don't have money or my phone to go anywhere either. As I debate, I see a familiar black truck heading toward me.

"Shit." I frantically try to make myself look presentable. I know that once he sees a car on the side of the road, he's going to stop. For a good Samaritan of Randall, not stopping when seeing a car potentially stranded would be a sin.

Sure enough, I see the brim of Gavin's hat before I see his face. He drives by, eyeing me as he does. I don't think he knows it's me at first until he does a double take. He turns around like I knew he would and parks behind me. I look at my face again and curse some more. This man has an uncanny ability to find me in states I'd rather not have anyone find me in. He must have an internal "Blake is a hot mess" barometer.

Gavin hops out of his truck and approaches. I roll down the window because I don't dare get out so he can see the full scope of my hot-messy-ness. And I'm not wearing any shoes. I ran out of the house so fast I didn't even think about it. Fuck my life.

He stops in front of my window, looking sexy as usual. My cheeks burn brighter with embarrassment as he eyes me, concern evident on his face. It's similar to the way Daddy looked at Mom while she lay on the floor. The realization only makes the pain in my chest grow harsher.

"Blake, what's wrong?" He tries to open the door, but it's locked.

"Hi, Gavin." As soon as the words are out of my mouth, I want to cry again at how dumb they sound. "Just out for a little drive." My voice sounds like a smoker who smokes a pack a day.

Something's obviously wrong, and there's no way for me to hide it.

He eyes me cautiously. "It's only after seven in the morning."

"Yeah. I was actually coming to get my cowboy hat. I've been missing it." I mentally pat myself on the back for coming up with that so swiftly. Though I won't be able to explain my missing shoes.

He stuffs his hands in his pockets, his caring eyes never leaving mine. "Did your car die?"

I bite my lower lip. "No, it didn't die."

He rubs his hand along his stubbled jaw, and for a fleeting moment, I forget my issues and remember what his bowed lips feel like against mine. *God help me.*

"Do you need help?" His words settle into me, his deep voice soothing. *Do you need help?* Yes, I do. But I don't say that.

"Just getting my favorite hat back."

"It's back at the house. I took it inside with me the other night."

"Oh," is all I can manage to say.

"Why don't you follow me home and you can grab it?" He's talking to me as if I'm a scared deer, like I'll bolt any moment. He's probably right. I can still feel myself teetering on the edge.

I grip the steering wheel tighter. "Don't you have somewhere to be?"

"It's not important. I can do it later."

"Ummm...."

He leans forward on the door to bring his eyes level with me. He's not fazed by the way I look, which I guess is a plus. Or he's secretly got eye problems. "I make a mean omelet. Why don't you come back to my place and have a cup of coffee, wash up, and get your hat? We can leave your Jeep here if you'd like."

My eyes dart down to my socked feet, which is a mistake because his eyes follow the movement. I hear his intake of breath, but he doesn't ask me where my shoes are. Instead, he asks, "What size shoe are you?"

I let out a soft laugh. "I have big feet."

"Your feet are perfect. Now, what size shoe do you wear?"

I bite the inside of my cheek at his comment. "Women's 11 wide or men's 9."

"You can borrow a pair of Kade's old shoes. We keep some around in case our seasonal help needs a pair. Pretty sure they're around that size."

My heart clenches again, but for a different reason this time. This thing between us, whatever it is, is new. And our interactions haven't been the nicest. Yet, he hasn't expected anything of me or judged me. It's why I shared about Reed hating whipped cream. Why I've been able to open up to him at all.

"Okay, I can follow you there."

He gives me a soft smile and stands, patting the hood of the car. "Great."

I nod and roll up the window. I can't believe I'm following him back to his ranch. I hope his family isn't around. The last thing I need is for more people to see me like this. Especially after what happened very publicly between us.

Once Gavin pulls ahead of me, I follow his truck in silence. His ranch isn't too far from here, so it doesn't take long for us to arrive. It's got a gravel road that leads back to his home and the massive amount of land they own. Everything is brown like some of the cows that graze on it. It makes my heart ache. There was a time when these plains would have been much greener and lush, even in the summer.

Eventually, we turn into the driveway where a modest white house sits. He drives around the back, and a smaller guest house comes into view. After we're parked, Gavin strides over, eating up the ground with his long legs. I open the door and move to get out, but he stops me.

"Let me grab some shoes from the mud room first. I'll be right back."

"Thanks." He rushes off and comes back in the blink of an eye, holding an old pair of brown cowboy boots. I reach for them, but he gets on his knees and gently takes one of my feet in his large hands. He brushes off the debris on the bottom of my sock from when I ran away, then puts one boot on before doing the same with the next.

The entire experience has me stunned into silence. I've never had someone handle me with such gentleness before. Even back when I'd had boyfriends and flings, this never happened. I'm a sturdy woman, one who used to ride fast horses and could rope a cow with the best of them. Men didn't look at me and think, "She's a princess." But that's how Gavin makes me feel right now. The little girl in me who loved Disney movies is having a moment.

Once he's secured my boots, he taps my feet. "Perfect fit." He smiles, standing to offer me his hand. Without a second thought, I take it.

CHAPTER 17

Gavin

THE LAST THING I expected to find on the side of the road this morning was Blake. It took me by surprise, but as soon as I saw her, my need to comfort her and care for her kicked in. She hasn't said why she was crying, but my guess is it has to do with Reed and the impending anniversary of the accident. I've heard people talking about it and wondered how she's faring. But whatever happened, it's obvious it wasn't good. I'm just glad I was the one to find her.

It also happened to be a coincidence that I was already on my way to Double-Time to return her cowboy hat—though I'd never admit that truth to Blake. I spent the last couple days debating when would be a good time to contact her and woke up this morning with the need to see her. I didn't think I'd find her out of sorts on the side of the road. I lied when I said it was at my place because I knew she needed a friend, if you could call me that.

Blake stands silently next to me as I push open the door to the guest house. I don't live here, but it has a small kitchen I keep stocked, and a full bathroom for showers and washing up. With Blake in this state, I've never been more grateful for it. In the short time I've spent with her, I think she'd hate coming face-to-face with anyone right now. I know the look of someone hanging on by the skin of their teeth and I'm afraid if I even talk too loudly, she'll crumble.

Blake clears her throat. Shit, I'm staring at her again. I squeeze her hand that's still in mine, enjoying the warmth of it. The urge to pull her into a hug and tell her she's okay, that I'm here for her, is strong. But I don't know if that's overstepping.

"The guest house is more private," I finally say.

"Okay." Her voice is hoarse, making that urge greater. Instead, I take her into the house, still holding her hand.

She looks around the space. It's not very large, but it's decent. At one point, it was used as a house for seasonal help, but then Daddy made it into his office. I assume because the ranch started bleeding money and we couldn't afford to hire all the extra hands. There's still a full bed in the living area since the bedroom is where the office is. I use it from time to time when I'm too tired to walk to the main house, and a two-person table to eat at next to the small kitchen.

"Do you live here?"

"No, just do office work, mostly. Why don't I show you to the bathroom, then I'll get some breakfast and coffee going?"

"Thank you," she says quietly.

"Of course." I let go of her hand to guide her to the bathroom. When she feels the pressure of my palm on her back, she doesn't shy away from my touch but leans into it. Between the handholding and now this, I'm happy she's relying on me. That she feels comfortable enough to let me touch her when she's vulnerable.

Once we're at the bathroom, I move ahead of her into the tiny space to grab a towel from the small cabinet below the sink. "There's some cheap shampoo and soap in there, but it does the job."

She takes the offered towel, her fingers brushing over mine. Our eyes find each other when our skin makes contact. This bathroom is a cracker box—and Blake and I are not small people—so we're standing close to each other again. In the harsh light from the vanity mirror, I can see her face better. The skin around her eyes is puffy and red, and mascara runs down her cheeks, but she's still perfect.

I can't help but imagine what it would be like to wake up to her every morning. What it would be like to strip her bare and worship every freckle, fold, and dimple of her body. As if she can read my mind, Blake averts her eyes and pulls the towel to her side. I blink and try to remove the images of her naked body from my mind.

"I'll leave you to it." I step around her, brushing against her as I do. A breathy noise escapes her lips, which goes straight to my lower half. Thank God I'm leaving this bathroom. I hear her thank me under her breath as I close the door and lean against it. I will the blood to go to anywhere but my cock and take a deep breath.

It takes me a minute to return to normal, turning my thoughts instead to brewing coffee. As I do, a plan formulates in my mind. I got a bit of work done from five to seven this morning, but there's a lot more to do. The downside of working a massive ranch with little help is there's always something. Today, Kade and I have to push some cattle to the north pasture. But with where our relationship stands, it's fixing to be awkward as hell. But if Blake helps instead, maybe it will take her mind off her problems for a while. We'll have to take ATVs instead of horses, but I'm willing to spend the money on the gas to be with her today.

I shoot Kade a text to let him know plans have changed. At some point, the two of us will have to talk, but right now I don't dawdle on it. I focus instead on cooking a two-egg omelet for both Blake and me along with two slices of fresh bread I've toasted in the pan. We'll need to have something in our stomachs with the long day ahead. As I'm placing the plates and cups on the table, Blake comes out of the bathroom. Her hair is still dry under the Texas Longhorns ballcap she wears, but her face is clear of makeup, and she looks refreshed.

She entertains a small smile when she sees the omelet and coffee. "Thanks for doing all this."

"It's no trouble. Take a seat and make yourself comfortable." I gesture for her to sit in the chair across from mine. "Feel any better?"

She sits and takes the coffee between her hands. "A little, thanks." She takes a small sip from the mug and grimaces. "Dang. You make a strong cup of coffee."

I let out a chuckle. "Sorry. I should have warned you that the Montgomerys are into extreme dark roasts. I've got fresh milk if you'd like."

"That's fine. It's clearing the cobwebs."

My lips turn up slightly. "Funny you should say that. My old man used to say the same thing."

Blake looks at me thoughtfully. "I'm sorry for your loss."

I clench my fingers around my mug. "Thank you."

Blake rubs her eyes tiredly. "Sorry, I didn't mean to bring that up. I hate when people say that to me, I don't know why I did."

I exhale a tense breath and place my hand over hers. "You don't have to apologize. It took me by surprise, is all. My family doesn't talk much about what happened to him. In the end, he passed doing what he loved. That's all one could ask for, I suppose."

"It must be hard." She says, picking at the omelet now, her gaze pensive. I don't think she's talking about my dad anymore.

I squeeze her free hand so she looks at me. "Loss is hard. It doesn't get easier with time, either. I know people say that but, we all know it's not true. Sometimes when I walk in here, I expect to see my dad at his desk swearing at the computer, then I remember."

Blake puts down her fork and opens her mouth to speak, then closes it. Pain etches in her features as if she wants to share something, but it won't come out. "It's okay," I assure her. "Just because I shared doesn't mean you have to."

She takes a deep breath, determined to share. "Do you know why I don't ride?"

My mouth goes dry, surprised this is what she wants to share. "Because of the accident?" I ask, my thumb stroking the top of her hand to let her know I'm here for her.

A single tear manages to escape her eye, and she lets it fall. "That day, I was out there for a long time after Briar stepped in that gopher hole and Reed—" Her voice cracks.

"Blake, you don't have to tell me this."

"No, no. I want to." She takes another breath. "My cell phone had no reception. And if it weren't for that farmer out in the field, I would've had to carry his body back on my horse and left Briar there to possibly die."

I feel the weight of Blake's grief and swallow down the lump now in my throat. It's hard to imagine her out there by herself with Reed in her arms. No wonder she has such a hard time. She's suffered a trauma that no one should ever have to suffer. I can only imagine if it was me instead of her, and Kade instead of Reed. It's a terrible thought.

She continues, "I spent over an hour screaming and begging Reed to wake up. I told myself I'd never ride a horse again if he didn't wake up, and I—" She stops.

I scoot forward and gently wipe away the tear from her soft skin. Her eyes meet mine as I cup the right side of her face in my hand. "You wanted to sacrifice the one thing that meant the most to you to have him back."

She nods. "Eventually I realized that even if I didn't make that promise to myself, that being around horses, the ranch, this town—it was too much. I felt like I was suffocating, like if I didn't leave, I'd never be able to take a deep breath again. So, I left." A look of shame crosses her features as I rest my hand back over hers on the table.

"You did what you needed to do to survive, Blake. That's all a person can do."

A soft noise leaves her throat, and I think she's going to let out a sob. Instead, she composes herself. "Is that what you're doing?"

I run my hand over my jaw. "Barely."

Her face darkens with concern, and I find myself wanting to confide in her. Tell her the truth about my ranch. Especially after she confided in me. My rational side is telling me it's too soon for us to be sharing this deep. Only days ago, we were at each other's throats, and now here we are, spilling our guts at eight in the morning.

She stands, making the decision to stop the vulnerable conversation for me. "Maybe I should go." Her voice is conflicted. I don't think she wants to leave, but I can see this is her attempt at building her walls back up.

With the option of her walking away, the desire to keep my secret from her evaporates. I'd rather share a million secrets than have her leave right now.

I get up to block her path. "Don't leave."

She stays quiet as we stand facing each other. Time moves slowly around us, and I find myself moving closer to her like a moth drawn to a flame. I've never felt like this with anyone before. Like if I don't touch her, I may cease to exist. It's idiotic, and a feeling I thought only occurred in movies. But it's real. At least, it is with Blake.

When I'm close enough to kiss her, she whispers, "What are we doing, Gavin?"

I twist a curl of her hair around my finger. "We're talking. Getting to know each other."

She lets out a small breath, her eyes darting to the floor. "I keep telling you things I've never told anyone, and I don't know why."

My body buzzes at her words. "Well," I say as I lift her chin, "that makes two of us."

"I'm not supposed to like you." Her lips turn up as she speaks, and I smile back at her.

"And I told myself I'd leave you be."

Blake's eyes scan my face before landing on my mouth, her body leaning in as she sucks her bottom lip between her teeth. The action only lends itself to my desire to kiss her, but the angel on one shoulder tells me not to after the morning she's had. Though the devil on the other wants me to throw caution to the wind.

"Blake." Her name spills from me as I bring my thumb up to her lip and pull it away from her teeth. I rub the small indents she's made there, and for a second, all I hear is the sound of our breathing.

"I'm supposed to hate you," she says again, but there's no gusto in her words.

"But you don't," I state for her. "And I can't stay away from you."

Her eyes dart to my lips again, but before I can lean in to claim them, she's kissing me.

It takes me only a split second to respond, my mouth opening to hers. She groans when she tastes me, the sound making me hard. I moan with her as I revel in the softness of her lips and the feeling of her body pressed against me. I become absorbed in the woman before me as I glide my tongue along hers and savor her.

When I press my hips into hers, Blake becomes a woman possessed with need. She pushes off my hat and runs her blunt nails over my scalp, causing a shiver to go up my spine. She pulls me closer and kisses me deeper, neither of us coming up for air. Her lips are addicting, and thoughts of stopping no longer cross my mind. Even if they should.

When my hand reaches her waist, I clutch the plush skin there, and she releases a resonate sound of pleasure. The vibrations send me over the edge, and the strain of my cock against my jeans becomes almost unbearable. I start to move her back toward the full-size bed on the other side of the room. I don't know how far she wants to take this, but I want to be able to touch every inch of her. Even if our clothes stay on.

Blake doesn't resist my action. She continues to plunder my mouth like she's on a mission for treasure. She tastes like strong coffee and sugar; a taste I could get used to. Once her legs hit the back of the bed, I grab her lower back and rest her down on the hard mattress. I brace myself over her, but she doesn't like the lack of connection. She brings her hands to my hips and pulls me down so I'm now on top of her, whimpering as our lower halves touch. Blake shows me no mercy as she wiggles against my hardness.

"If you keep that up, I'll embarrass myself."

She laughs as she pulls me into another kiss. After a moment I pull my mouth from hers and suck the spot where her neck and collarbone meet. She shivers, pushing her amazing breasts into my chest as she grips my shoulders. I make a mental note to remember her response, hoping I get to explore that space at length if—*when*—this goes further.

"*Gavin*." Her voice is husky and breathless. I lift my head to meet her hooded eyes and dilated pupils. *Fuck me*, she's a sexy vixen. I'd do anything she asks right now.

"Blake," I mirror back, kissing up her neck again.

"I shouldn't want this, but I do. I want it."

I tug on her earlobe with my teeth, eliciting another breathy moan from her mouth. "You can have anything you want, baby," I mutter. "There are no shouldn'ts with me."

Her eyes lock with mine. "You don't want to stop?"

I rest my head in the crook of her neck. This is my last chance to tell her we're moving too fast. That she might regret if we do anything more than kiss, but I don't. I'm too selfish in this moment. I want her, and she very much wants me.

"I'll repeat it again. I'll do anything you want, baby. Just promise me something." I kiss her neck again. "That you'll spend all day with me today."

Her brows lift. "That's all you want?" I don't tell her that by making this promise she'll have to face what we do here when we're through. And once we come down from this high, she won't be able to run.

"That and," I kiss that spot on her neck again, "you have to tell me what you want."

Her shoulders tense, and eyes darken. By her body language I think she might tell me it's over and demand to go home, but instead she grabs me by the shirt and kisses me again. I guess she likes this idea. I pull away and take off her ball cap, tossing it to the floor so I can see her coffee-colored curls.

"I need to hear you say it, Blake."

With her hand still gripping my shirt and our mouths a whisper apart, she finally says, "I promise."

With a growl, I pounce.

CHAPTER 18

Blake

GAVIN DEVOURS ME AS if I'm his last meal. My promise must have flipped a switch in his brain, and now his lips are everywhere all at once. If I was smart, I would get up and walk out the door, but I can't. At this moment I feel...*alive*. It's exactly the kind of feeling I was chasing at Night Hawk by dancing with a stranger, and why I wanted to discover the old Blake again. Only this time, it feels right. So incredibly right.

"Stop thinking," Gavin says, biting my earlobe again. Lord, that's hot. I scoot up on the bed a bit and push him back so I can access the buttons on his shirt. One by one, I undo them, revealing what I've always known is underneath. Hard muscles and tan skin. I want to run my tongue over the impeccable ridges and feel them beneath my fingers.

He lets out a low chuckle at my eager gaze and throws his shirt on the floor.

"Your turn," he purrs. He reaches down and pulls the hem of my T-shirt that's already started to come free of my jeans. Exposed now, gooseflesh breaks out over my skin. I'm wearing a padded black bra, the underwire digging into the skin. I become painfully aware how this position makes me look. My heavy breasts are moving up and down and the expanse of my stomach shows off all her stretch mark-painted glory.

It's been years since anyone has seen me fully naked, years since anyone has touched me like this. He may have seen my body at the spring last week, but this is different. He's so handsome it makes my chest ache.

You're being silly, Blake!, my inner voice says. I bite my lower lip again as he stares, my confidence wavering.

But then Gavin eases my mind. He takes his finger and runs it down my cheek, then my neck, making my thoughts focus back on him. His finger trails to the skin of my cleavage right before he taps on the front clasp of my bra. With ease, he flicks it open, my breasts falling free of their confines.

"Beautiful, baby. Just beautiful," he says with conviction.

Baby. He's called me that a few times now. I don't know where it came from, but I really, really like it. Especially the way he says it, as if he treasures me. It pushes the notions about my body away, reminding me that I like myself as I am, and clearly, he does too.

He takes my hand and tugs me forward, then fully rids me of my bra. He fixates on my breasts hungrily as he lowers me back down to the bed. When I'm about to tell him to look up, he brings his gaze to my lips and kisses me, our naked skin pressing together for the first time. I gasp into his mouth and grind our still clothed hips together. I can feel how hard he is for me, and my entire body thrums in anticipation.

"Tell me what you want, Blake. I want to hear it all."

A breathy sigh escapes me as I open my mouth to his. He tastes so good, and the feeling of his stubble drives me crazy. "I want to feel you," I keen, "all of you."

He grins. "My pleasure."

Gavin starts to lay kisses down between my breastbone, my nipples tightening in anticipation of his mouth. He uses his left hand to massage one breast as his tongue finally finds the other. He sucks the bud into his mouth, his lips working me into a frenzy. The wetness between my legs grows, and I'm positive I've soaked through my cotton panties. When he moves his mouth to the other breast, I arch into it, begging him to give me more.

After he finishes worshiping my breasts, he moves his kisses down my stomach, his lips wet and hot as he traces the faint pink lines of each mark and sucks each pucker and divot. When he reaches the sensitive skin near the waistband of my jeans, his stubble tickles the skin there. I let out a soft laugh and squirm a bit.

"I love when you laugh." He starts to unbuckle my belt. "It's sexy as hell."

He continues to watch me heatedly as he works the buttons down. I laugh again when he shucks them off, as if he's done it a million times before. For a moment he memorizes me from head to toe. When his gaze finally settles on the triangle between my legs, he lets out a groan and drops his head to my thighs. He takes a deep breath, as if he's trying to take things slow but he wants to move faster. Good thing I want to move faster, too.

"Take off your clothes." My voice comes out much more commanding than I plan it to. It feels scary to demand what I want from him, but he did say that's what he desired me to do.

He lifts his head, that silly grin on his face again. "You want a show, Miss Tanner?"

Heavens, he's cheeky. I shake my head. "Just naked."

He chuckles, still making too-slow work of unbuckling his belt. His eyes never leave mine as he removes his boots, then peels off his jeans and socks. The view of him almost naked, staring at me like a hungry beast, has me in a full-body blush. He watches the color rise under my skin, and his mouth drops open. "You're a dream come true," he mutters, and I blush harder.

His hands move to the waistband of his black briefs. I can't stop the hitch in my breath as he lowers them to the ground and steps out of them. When he stands back up to his full height, I wish I could say I'm looking at his face, but I'm not. They're solely on the glorious piece of what I can only call machinery between his legs. He's thick, long, and hard. *Very* hard. My mouth goes dry, all of the moisture in my body flooding to my sex. I bite my lower lip and imagine what he's going to feel like inside me.

He grins. "You like what you see?"

"Lord, yes," I moan. My skin prickles all over and my inner walls clench around the promise of what's to come. This whole experience feels so dirty, so different than anything I've ever done. But for the love of all that's holy, I'm into it. And I'm really into him. His body is young, fit, and the kind you see in those hot and cheesy firemen calendars. Gavin's smile turns sexier as he bends down to crawl back up my body. He kisses the inside of my right ankle, then up my fleshy calves, and lands an open-mouthed kiss on the inside of my knee. I shiver, gooseflesh rippling out over my skin.

"You're so responsive to me," he says against my inner thigh. "I can't wait to taste you."

I throw my forearm over my face and fight the urge to clench my thighs together. I suppose it would be dumb to tell him I've only had oral twice. I had sex quite a bit in my early twenties, but it was always plain sex. Most of my partners were cowboys I met in the rodeo circuit. They didn't worship my body like this or take the time to explore. I never cared since they got me off, but with the way Gavin is sucking on my thigh, I can't help but wonder what his mouth will feel like on my clit.

"Do you want me to make you come with my tongue, baby?" I almost sob. He's reading my mind. "Tell me what you want," he growls playfully. *Damn*. This man.

I eye him between my thighs and say, "I want you to eat me out."

My body turns redder at my words, but a wicked grin displays on Gavin's face. He definitely likes dirty talk. He brushes his calloused hands up my thighs, wrapping his thumbs around the elastic of my underwear. He eases them down and discards them, once again marveling at my curves. The way he stares at me in awe, you'd think I'm a woman in a Renaissance painting.

"Stunning," he affirms yet again. I want to say something, but I don't know what. 'Thank you' seems silly, so I stay silent.

With a devilish look, he kisses up my body to where my thigh connects with my hip. He runs his finger near the crease, and I choke on my own breath. He inhales shakily as his fingers start to inch closer to my wet folds. I want to scream at him to touch me already. He's been torturing me for what feels like hours. Right before he reaches my center, he stops and kisses around my fleshy mons, his large hands massaging my thighs.

"Relax, Blake," he says, blowing a breath over my sex. "You smell like heaven."

I prop myself up on my elbows to look down at the sandy-haired cowboy. For a split second, I think about shoving his head down, but good lord! His slow tenderness is amazing too. So amazing it makes me want to cry—in a good way. I squirm as he kisses around my outer lips, moving his mouth to my inner thigh again. As I'm about to beg for him to touch me, he uses his thick fingers to splay me open and runs a finger through my heat.

He sucks in a breath. "You're soaked for me, baby."

This time I do beg. "*Please. Please. Please.*"

He hums, the vibrations so close to my clit that my body pulls tight like a string. It snaps when he finally puts his tongue to my pussy and licks me in a slow and torturous stroke. He groans loudly in happiness before attacking with vigor. My hips shoot off the bed, and I cry out at finally being touched. To hold me in place he puts one large hand on my lower belly while the other pushes my thigh down to stay open for him. He licks and sucks, his tongue swirling around my clit.

I let my head fall back and I moan. "Yes! Just like that." I slap my hand down over the one he has on my stomach, and he laces his fingers through mine, only making our connection intensify. He maneuvers himself so he can bring his other hand to my opening. He takes two fingers and swipes at the wetness there before he dips one finger in, then two.

"So wet," he groans. "So tight."

"Gavin…" The feel of his fingers inside me is almost too much, but I want more. "I need you. I can't—" He closes his lips over my clit and flicks his tongue in a way that makes me scream. I've never been so loud during sex in my life. I hope nobody else is around to hear us.

"What do you want, Blake?" Gavin asks, kissing the top of my mons.

I gaze down at him through hooded eyes, a bead of sweat dripping from my forehead. "I want you to be inside my pussy when I come."

Gavin's head falls to the inside of my thigh, and he curses. "I knew you had a dirty mouth, baby. But you keep surprising me." I may swear under my breath a lot, but I surprise myself too. I'm just so turned on I can't think straight. He makes my body sing. Now I want to see how high he can make me soar.

I use the hand we have linked together to tug him up. His cock drags along my leg, and I feel his precum on my skin. When he's eye-level with me, he lets go of my hand and braces himself above me. His length lays on my belly, its heat burning me. Gavin's brow is pinched, as if he's trying to hold himself back. That's the last thing I want, so I reach between us and take him in my hand. The hiss out of his mouth sounds like he's been burned, but his face morphs into pleasure. He rests his forehead against mine as he breathes in a staccato rhythm.

When I stroke him again, a little stronger this time, his eyes open in warning. "If you do too much, this will be over soon."

I smile up at him demurely. "Do you have a condom?"

He curses. "No. I didn't think this would be happening yet."

Yet. It excites me to know that he wanted this and couldn't wait. I use my thumb to stroke the head of his weeping cock. "I'm on the pill." I finally say. "And I haven't been with anyone in a long time."

Gavin's eyes open completely as he searches my eyes. "I've been tested and I'm good. But are you sure, baby?"

"I want this." I reach up with my free hand to trace his lips with my pointer finger. "Do you?"

Instead of words he answers me with a kiss. I smile against his lips and stroke his cock again, his approval hums against my mouth. He breaks the kiss and entwines our hands together near my head while his other hand wraps around the one I have stroking him. He runs his cock between the lips of my vulva, wetting it. When he hits my clit in the process, we both let out a feral noise. I swear I feel like my entire body is going to combust.

"Do it, Gavin." I remove my hand from under his. "I need you." With one more kiss to my lips he guides himself inside me. His eyes roll into the back of his head and his face goes taut.

"Oh fuck! You're so tight." He presses his pelvis forward and instinctively I shift to bring my legs around his waist. He groans as he sinks further in, letting his head fall to my neck. His hot breath puffs there as he bottoms out. I let out a small gasp of pain as I adjust. He's huge, larger than I've had, but wow, does it feel good, so full.

Gavin stays there for a moment, our bodies locked together in the most intimate embrace possible. Was it only a few days ago that we disliked each other? Feels stupid now. Once he's gained his composure, he shifts to look into my eyes. "How do you feel?"

"I need you to move. *Please*." He pulls out, watching my face carefully for any signs of discomfort. When I show none, he pushes back in. "Yes!" I cry, "That feels..." *Amazing. Delicious. Sinful*. But I can't form the words.

Gavin thrusts his hips in a nice rhythm, and the friction is so perfect I almost want to cry. I move my hands to his back and press my nails gently into his broad shoulders. He lets out a satisfied noise and uses his mouth to suck at the space right above my collar bone again. I dig my heels into the muscles of his ass to push him deeper inside me. The action spurs him to move quicker and with more precise movements. When I press my hips up, he stops for a moment and grabs a pillow.

"Lift up," he commands. I do as he says, and he slides the pillow under my butt. When he moves again, the new angle immediately sets my body on fire. I let out a sob of pleasure as he thrusts into me again like it's his one and only job. "You're amazing, Blake. Your pussy feels like paradise." His comment almost makes me giggle, but it's cut off when he punches his hips forward and hits my g-spot. Instead, I cry out loudly as my entire body tingles. His lips seal over mine and our tongues tangle together.

Needing more, I move to touch my clit, but Gavin smacks my hand away. "Do you want me to touch you, baby? I told you to tell me what you want.'

I drink in a breath. I think I got wetter from his damn words. "Yes," I breathe out. "Touch me, Gavin." He does as I ask, bringing his calloused fingers to my clit. I cry out again, my vagina clenching around him. I know my release isn't far off, and by the look on Gavin's face, his isn't either.

"I'm going to come," I say against his lips. I run my short nails down his back and bite his bottom lip while I purposely squeeze my inner walls and moan. "Faster."

"Jesus," he grunts. He thrusts rapidly, the sound of our skin-to-skin contact echoing through the small room. He kisses me with purpose, and my release is so close I can taste it. I press myself into him so he's hitting that sweet spot over and over again. Gavin's back tenses and he picks up his pace. "Yes, Gavin. Yes! Right there!" He continues to pound into me, and I scream out as my orgasm crashes through me. He rubs my clit in a torturous motion as I crest. My insides flutter and shake at the intensity of it all.

"Oh, fuck," Gavin chokes out. His body stills as I feel his own release happen, the warmth of it making my toes curl. I grip him tighter. I love the way I feel so full, so cared for. As if I'm flying high in the clouds. It's never felt like this, and if I'm not careful, I could easily find myself addicted to this man.

As we come down from our high, Gavin buries his head in my neck, his breaths labored but body relaxed. It isn't until I feel his release leaking out of me that I shift. I suppose this is the not-so-fun part of not wearing a condom during sex.

Gavin's head turns, his evergreen eyes darker than usual. He has a look on his face I don't recognize, but it's not anything bad. He looks happy. Blissful. I imagine I look the same way.

Then, he comes in for a kiss. It's a lazy one that makes me forget about the mess between my legs and the sweat now drying on our bodies. The kind of kiss that can evaporate my problems and sadness. Lord help me, I'm *so* screwed.

CHAPTER 19

Gavin

I SIT NEXT TO Blake on the bed as she runs a washcloth over her body to remove the remnants of my release from between her legs. It reminds me that we didn't use a condom, something I haven't done before. But Blake is different. The feeling of us connected so intimately is something I want for the rest of my life. For every single day.

We make eye contact, body flushing when she sees me watching her movements. I just worshiped her entire being, but the only part I haven't seen is her naked backside. Which I bet is just as delicious. My cock wakes up again at the thought.

Her eyes flash down, and she swallows. I reach over and grab her hips to pull her to bed. She squeals at the sudden movement and lets the washcloth drop to the floor as her body collides with mine. I arrange us on the bed so we're face-to-face and our legs tangle together.

"Hey," she whispers.

I smile gently at her and stroke her cheek bone. "Hey." I kiss her nose, and then her lips. "That was…" But words aren't enough for what we experienced together.

"Yeah," she returns. Her voice is breathy and sexy as hell. Her stomach presses into my hard length, and she bites her lip. "Already?"

A chuckle escapes my lips. "You're beautiful, naked, and pressed up against me."

"Maybe you *are* too young for me. If we go again right now, I might die."

I reach forward and gently pinch the underside of her breast. She cries out in protest, but I lock her in my arms so she can't escape. "Don't be so dramatic. You're not that much older than me. I think you'll ride me fine if I get you going."

She hides her face in my chest and I chuckle. Being here in bed with her after having mind-blowing sex is not what I planned for us today, but I'm damn happy. All the reasons I told myself this wouldn't work between us have disappeared. As far as I'm concerned, Blake Tanner is everything I want. Fuck the rest.

I run one of my hands down her back in complete bliss. At this angle I can see her ass and it's as sublime as I expected. It even has cute little dimples that I want to bite and suck for an entire evening. It isn't until my phone chimes that our cocoon breaks. Blake pulls away, as if the noise has brought her back into her body, into reality. I turn her chin to mine before she can think too much. "You promised, remember?"

She bites her bottom lip. "Don't you have work to do? I'm keeping you from it."

"Nothing you can't help me with," I say with a smirk.

"What are you planning?"

"We have to push some cattle to one of our other pastures." Her body goes rigid. "No riding involved, baby. We can take ATVs." Blake still looks unsure, but after what we shared, there's no way I'm sending her home. And I already let Kade off the hook, so I do need her help.

"I haven't pushed cattle in years."

"It's like riding a bike. You'll do fine."

She sighs. "You're not letting me out of this are you?"

"Nope," I say, popping the P to emphasize my point.

I stand up and try to ignore the fact I still have a hard-on. Granted, I've had a hard-on since I laid eyes on her at Night Hawk last week. I've gotten used to the blue balls by now.

Her eyes find my cock as I hold out my hand for her to take. Not going to lie, I feel pretty damn good about myself with how she's admiring it. But I know what she's doing. "If you think sex is going to distract me from this, you're wrong." Although she's not wrong. I could be very much persuaded, but I'll keep that a secret.

Her cheeks go pink again as she puts her hand in mine. Once she's standing, she drops my hand and gathers her clothes with a huff of frustration. "Let's go then."

I smile to myself, glad my plan is in motion.

Pushing cattle isn't the most exciting thing, but it has to be done. I look forward to it now that Blake stands next to me, her cowboy hat placed on her head instead of the ballcap. Kade messaged me back a thumbs up emoji, so at least he acknowledged he's not needed for the task. Momma also messaged to let me know that she and Gran went to help at the food drive. I'm glad I don't have to explain why Blake Tanner came out of our guesthouse before noon.

As we approach the garage where we house the ATVs, Blake takes in our land. "It looks the same." She smiles. "Bigger than I remember."

"Time can do that, make us remember things different." I bend down at my knees to pull the manual garage door up. After it's open, Blake goes to one of the covered ATVs. There's a lot of dust on it.

"Haven't used these in a while, huh?"

I shrug. "Kade and I prefer using horses." She bites her bottom lip, and I realize I shouldn't have said anything. "Blake, it's fine. These will do the job. Don't worry about it." I smile to try and lighten the mood. She just nods. "Why don't you take the cover off that one and I'll grab the key?" I continue. Without answering, she uncovers the ATV while I do the same with mine. Once I have the keys, I put one in her outstretched palm.

"You remember how to ride one of these?" I tease, knowing full well she does. I saw her and Reed race on them when we were kids.

She playfully rolls her eyes at me as she swings her leg over and hops on. She looks good in her T-shirt and jeans, like a real cowgirl ready to work. For a moment I let myself fantasize about what our life could be like together. If I can figure out a way to save this ranch, I'll get to spend my days with her. We'll have to figure out logistics and all that, but waking up to her, working by her side all day, and falling into bed with her at night sounds like a good life. One I'm willing to fight for. Her soulful eyes penetrate mine and I wonder if it's what she'll want, too. I don't even know if she plans on staying here after Margie's leg heals.

"You okay?" she asks.

I swallow the sudden lump in my throat at the thought of Blake leaving town. There's no way I could leave with her, even if I wanted to. "I'm good," I manage to get out, smiling through the sick feeling in my stomach.

She turns the key, and the ATV comes to life. A smile lights up her face at the sound. I wonder if she's been on one since she's been home; it sure looks like she's ready to race off and make me catch her. Not that I mind. But she doesn't know her way around our ranch and would have no clue where to go. We have a lot of property. It's easy to get lost if you don't know where the hell you are.

I start my own vehicle and call out, "Follow me!" She grins wider. The excitement radiating from her almost has me calling off the whole thing so I can fuck her right over the seat while she screams my name. Maybe another day.

With Blake hot on my trail, we get past the barns and out onto the open plains. We slow down and drive next to each other, the early summer sun shining down on us. The woman next to me looks happy. A far cry from how I found her earlier. I still don't know why she ran away without shoes, but I'm glad she looks better. More than better. I think the last time I saw her this free and happy is when she was barrel racing. My chest swells thinking I might have something to do with her being a little more carefree. I feel better too. Like I have someone in my corner, someone who will listen to me and support me. I don't think I've ever felt that, not even in my past relationships.

Blake picks up speed a little. "Where are we heading?"

I bite the inside of my cheek to hide my grin. I know exactly what she's going to do once I tell her. "Why? You think you can beat me there?" I edge myself a little further ahead of her. She purses her lips and gazes in the distance. If you look closely, you can see the cattle coming up ahead. It doesn't take a genius to figure out that's where we're heading. It takes Blake all of twenty seconds to spot the herd, the younger calves grouped together by a water tank.

Her lips curve up in a mischievous smile. "See you there."

"Bla—" but it's too late. She's taken off like a bat out of hell, cackling as she does. I go full throttle in an attempt to catch up, but the dang woman is too far ahead. Instead, I enjoy the humid air whipping across my face and the sight of Blake having fun, her long braid whipping behind her as she speeds along.

It's not lost on me that this is as close to riding a horse as she's gotten since Reed. I don't know if she realizes that the adrenaline rush she's chasing is similar to galloping one of her prized horses down a plain or competing, but I sure do. It's a beautiful thing to witness. I only hope she doesn't regret letting herself enjoy life a little, because she deserves to feel good.

When I crest the top of a small hill, the first thing I see is a worn natural-colored cowboy hat. My stomach sinks as Kade comes into view sitting atop his Paint horse, Willy. I lay on the breaks and bring my ATV to a stop beside Blake. Her cheeks are pink from racing and the smile she worked so hard to put on her lips fades quickly. My temper flares, and I'm left wondering why Kade's here after I told him not to be.

"Howdy." Kade grins as he gives Blake one of his two-dimpled Montgomery smiles.

"Hey, Kade." She shifts uncomfortably, biting her lower lip like she often does.

"We've got this handled, Kade, so you can ride back home," I say without preamble.

The air goes taut with tension as Kade stares between Blake and me, as if he can read that we just fucked each other's brains out. Eventually, he breaks the awkward silence by addressing Blake.

"Sorry if I ruined your *date*. I didn't see Gavin's text till after I went to go find him when he didn't show up at the stables. I thought you two would be preoccupied for the rest of the day, so I came here to push the cattle all by my lonesome."

Fuck. He saw us having sex. Or at least he heard us. My gaze tries to catch Blake's, but she's gripping the handles of her ATV so hard I think they might break off. I could kill Kade right now for ruining everything I tried to build with her this morning. And by the brash way Kade's acting, I think he was hoping we'd show up, knowing I'd be upset. The thought alone has me wanting to knock some manners into him. I don't care if he desires to hurt me, but there's no need to embarrass Blake in the process.

Kade opens his mouth again, but I cut him off. "That's enough, Kade."

He turns to me at my warning tone. "I'm not doing anything, Gav. Just talking."

My fists ball at my sides. "I told you we wouldn't need you here."

He shrugs. "Like I said, I thought you'd be preoccupied. I was trying to do you a favor."

Bullshit. If he really meant that, he would've sent more than a thumbs up response to my message. But I'm not going to fight with him right now.

Blake looks up and tries to act like the fact my brother knows we had sex doesn't bother her, though it does. It bothers me too. I want to keep something so perfect between us. I'll do well to remember that I don't get to have perfect things or perfect days. It's how life is out here.

Blake blows out a breath. "I should head back. You two have work to do, and you don't need my help now."

Kade locks eyes on her, the smugness leaving him when he really gets a good look at how uncomfortable she is. "You should stay, Blake," he says, his tone lighter. "The more the merrier." I think he means it too, by the warm way in which he smiles at her now. He likes Blake; he has no reason not to. He's only trying to get under my skin, but that means he's also hurting her in the process. I'm hoping that look means he's realizing that now.

"It's okay," Blake tells him. "I have work to do anyway at Double-Time."

Kade rolls his shoulders back and sighs. "You really don't have to run off. I'm sure the charity event gave it away, but we're not exactly hiring extra help these days." The tone of his voice is bitter, and I know Blake hears it. I swear if it was possible, steam would be coming out of my ears. I find myself wishing Blake *would* leave, only so I can speak with Kade in private.

Blake pushes a loose strand of hair behind her ear. "I, um," she gets out, stumbling on her words. Now she feels pressured to stay, so I make it easy for her.

"You remember the way to the ranch?" I ask her.

Blake's shoulders relax and she nods. "Of course."

"Head back and put the ATV in the garage and the key on the workbench."

"Sure." Blake starts her ATV up and sends one last tense smile to Kade before meeting my eyes again. I feel awkward saying anything in front of him, so I settle for an invite.

"I work another shift tonight at Night Hawk. Will you stop by?"

Blake swallows. "I'll see what I can do."

At least that's something. "I hope to see you there," I add. "Now get back safe." I try to tell her through my body language what this morning meant to me, but it's impossible to do. I'll have to hope she makes it to Night Hawk so I can tell her with my words, and maybe my mouth, too.

Kade clears his throat, and Blake flushes. Without another glance at either of us, she takes off, leaving an empty feeling in her wake, and the nagging desire to pummel my brother.

CHAPTER 20

Gavin

"REALLY, GAVIN?" KADE BREAKS the silence once Blake is gone from our sight. "What the hell are you thinking?"

"What am I thinking?" I bellow. "You embarrassed her to make *me* angry. Do you feel better now?"

Kade clutches his split reins, knuckles going white. "Would it make you happy if I said no?"

I sigh. "No, it wouldn't."

He blows out a breath. "I thought you were going to leave Blake Tanner alone."

"I can't do that." Fuck, it feels good to say that out loud.

Kade grunts. "You can."

"I can't."

"You think sleeping with her is going to make her any happier? It won't. It sure as hell won't make *your* problems go away either."

Rage swells in my belly. He's the one being a hypocrite now, and he knows it. "And you think drinking and fucking my cheating ex-girlfriend is going to make yours go away, Kade?"

He bares his teeth. "You don't know my problems, Gavin. You have no fucking clue. And I didn't fuck Cricket. She picked me up and took me to the bar."

I take off my hat and run my fingers through my hair. "And how do I know you're not lying?"

Kade stares me down, his features tempered. "You don't. But I'm telling you I didn't sleep with her. I wouldn't do that."

"So you did that to make me upset? Like what you just did here with Blake?"

"You pissed me off."

"This behavior is childish, Kade. I think you know that."

"And you sleeping with Blake isn't a childish move?"

I run my hand along my jaw and try to remain calm. "You don't understand what's going on between Blake and me. It's anything but childish. Impulsive maybe, but it's between the two of us."

Kade leans back in the saddle and turns his head up to the sky like he's praying for strength. After a long moment, he says, "When did we become enemies, Gav?

I put my hat back on my head and lock eyes with him. For a hot second, I see the little brother I've always known. The hardworking, shameless flirt who told bad jokes and did everything to impress Dad. It's the Kade I've been missing for nine months now. The Kade I once considered my best friend.

I let out a long breath, attempting to release some of the tension from my body. "We're not enemies," I say truthfully. "We're brothers." To my surprise, Kade's lip turns up in a small grin. I can't help but do the same.

We continue to watch each other for a few moments, a sort of silent understanding passing between us. The kind that only family can have. One that says we've both been acting in the wrong, yet we can still make things right.

Willy digs at the ground with his hoof as he starts to become impatient. Kade moves the horse forward, then I see Kade's shoulders relax a bit.

"I didn't mean to upset Blake. She's a sweet woman. And I don't know why I want to hurt you, Gavin. I just," Kade drops his chin to his chest, "ever since Dad's heart attack, and the reading of his will, my head's not been right, and—" He doesn't say the rest, because I already know. But I'm glad he's finally talking to me. I'll take his sober anger over his drunk antics any day.

"I know, Kade." I pause for a moment. "If I could ask him right now why he did what he did, I would. But it doesn't mean this ranch isn't still our family's. Papers don't mean shit. This place is yours as much as it is mine. Same goes with Momma and Gran."

Kade nods sullenly and moves Willy again as the horse starts to get pissed. The poor guy wants to move some cows; it's what he's bred to do. Not to stand around.

"I'll apologize to Blake when I see her," Kade says. "And I'm sorry for what I said the other night, for what I did."

I have to fight the sudden stinging in my eyes. This conversation is surprising, and not how I expected it to go given how it started.

I exhale. "I'm sorry, too. We've both said and done many things that we shouldn't have. But I need you to know one thing, Kade." He stares at me, expression knowing. "I meant what I said. I can't stay away from Blake. There's something there, and I have to see it through."

In another surprising move, Kade smiles. "I've never seen you like this over a woman before." He's right. I had short-term girlfriends before Cricket, who was my longest relationship, but things with her were always tense. I could have asked her to marry me multiple times, but something always felt off. It's different with Blake...things with her feel right.

"Well," I say confidently, "things change."

Kade moves Willy in a small circle, then stares me down. "Just don't hurt her. Everyone knows she's been through enough. And you have, too."

"We all have, Kade."

He nods. "Should we move these cows before Willy does it for us?"

I let out a low chuckle. "I suppose we should."

"And Gav?"

"Yeah?"

"I'll try to drink less."

Out of all the things we talked about, that stuns me the most. I'm curious if something happened in the last few nights that he's not telling me. He mentioned I didn't know his problems.

A knot forms in my stomach again, and I decide here and now that I need to be more watchful of Kade and try to spend more time with him while we work. Maybe this whole time that's what he's been looking for, but I've been too absorbed in my—*our*—problems to see it.

"If that's what you want, I think that's a good idea."

Kade nods. "Let's get to work."

CHAPTER 21

Blake

I FIND MYSELF IN the stable, where I usually come when I need to be alone. The familiar smells and sounds are especially nice after that awkward moment with Kade. Clearly, I'm not the only one with family drama, and what happened on the plain between the two brothers only inspires curiosity in me.

Briar's foal sticks his head over the stall, and his eyes widen as he studies me. The movement has my prior thoughts evaporating as I focus on him.

The colt is filling out well. He's going to be even more beautiful when he's full grown. Briar is large for her bloodline, and his sire is known to throw fast babies. If he likes to run, he'll be a good barrel prospect, too. Images of me riding him out of the chute into a packed arena fill my mind and my heart pounds.

I touch my hand to the little guy's nose. "That's new," I say to him. "I blame you for these crazy thoughts." Or maybe it's not just him. After this morning with Gavin—not only the mind-blowing sex but the ride on the ATVs—I've changed. I *feel* changed.

The baby nips at my hand. "You're mouthy. Just like Reed." I laugh as I pull my hand away and look at Briar. She's munching on hay, content with the life she has right now. Too many nights I lie awake and wonder what kind of horse she would've been if that day on the trail never happened. I've never asked my parents what it was like to rehabilitate her, though sometimes I've wanted to.

When a throat clears near me, I jump. I know who it is before I look. That familiar feeling of shame returns, but I can't run forever.

"Where did you go?" Mom asks.

I turn to face her. She's leaning on her crutches, hair frizzy from the humid air. When we make eye contact, I'm glad to find she doesn't look angry.

She smiles gently at me. "Can we talk?"

I exhale through my lips. Might as well rip off the Band-Aid. At least I no longer feel like I'm going to cry every two seconds. "Sure."

Mom uses one of her crutches to point to her office down the aisle. Daddy set her up in there, so she has a place to elevate her leg while she does admin work. I try to avoid going in there as much as possible. The main reason being the old family photos she has hung all over the walls. I know it's not healthy that I can't look at them. It just hurts too much to look back at times when we were all together.

As I enter the office, I do my best to keep my gaze trained on Mom. I help her get her leg settled before I sit across from her. She leans back and stares at me. I'm not sure how long we do that, but eventually, the silence gets weird.

"I'm sorry," I blurt out.

Mom's shoulders relax. "I'm sorry, too. I shouldn't have pushed you like that. Especially with it being so close to the anniversary." She pauses for a moment, as if she's remembering the pain of that day. I stay silent as she continues, "I was only trying to connect with you, not upset you to the point you'd run off the way you did."

I rub my hand over my eyes. "I know you were. I am sorry for what I did." I mean that, too. The hours away and my time with Gavin have cleared my head. I know Mom is only trying to talk with me, and I ruined that.

"Can we speak honestly, Blake?" I can hear what she's really saying in her tone. *Can you handle speaking to me, Blake?*

"We can" is all I say.

She leans back and steeples her fingers. When her eyes turn glassy, a stabbing pain shoots through my chest. "I love you, Blake. You're my first child, my baby. You're a beautiful and talented woman that your daddy and I somehow raised. I love you so much that I let you walk out of this house back then because I wanted you to heal. I wanted you to have your independence and the space to be on your own, something you'd never really had before. I never thought you'd distance yourself so much that I'd feel like I lost you." Her voice breaks and the already crumbling walls I've built start to fall.

"Mom, you didn't lose me."

She shakes her head. "But I did, Blake. Your daddy and I both did. You left and didn't come back. It took me falling off a ladder and breaking my leg for you to walk through the door. And now that you're here, it's like you're a ghost. I don't know who you are anymore. You've let your fear control you, and that's not something you ever did."

I can't help it, but anger sparks up at her words. "I can't move on like it never happened, like you and Daddy seem to. That day changed me. It made me this way, and I don't know what you want from me, Mom."

Mom swipes a stray tear from her cheek. "That hurts me, Blake. I think about Reed, about you, every damn day of my life. Just look at this office." When I keep my eyes trained on her desk, she begs again. "Please, Blake. Look around you."

The tender pleading of her voice makes me do it. When I really take in all the photos of me and Reed growing up, I spot one of us with Briar as a foal, in which we're both smiling ear-to-ear. My stomach turns over and I look away.

"I can't keep looking, Mom." My body shakes as I say it. "Please don't make me."

The office goes silent, the sound of our breathing the only thing I hear. Eventually, Mom stands, and her crutches come into view. When I lift my gaze to hers, she puts a hand on my cheek.

"I don't think I'm the one trying to move on like it never happened, honey."

"Mom." My resolve crumbles. "I'm trying, okay? I need time."

She puts her hand down. "Tell me how to help you. Tell me, and I'll do it."

I try to swallow the sadness stuck in my throat. I know I've been unfair to her, unfair to Daddy. But it's been so long since I've had to face this reality. I don't know how to be with her or how to make things better. Nothing I say or do will bring Reed back.

"I just need some time," I say again.

Mom takes a shallow breath. "I've given you time, Blake. Almost five years of it. I don't think that's what you need anymore."

My skin prickles, a feeling of dread washing over me. "What does that mean?"

"I want you to see my therapist. At least try it."

I stand up, careful not to accidentally hurt her like I did this morning. I'm a couple of inches taller than her, so she looks up at me. She's not angry, though, just disappointed, which is always worse.

"I don't want to see a therapist. I tried that—"

She cuts me off with a wave of her hand. "Try again, Blake. Or at least talk to somebody. *Please*. Do it for our family. Reed would hate to see you like this. He'd want you to try to heal."

I snap my eyelids closed to prevent angry tears from falling. I feel like a bull caught in a pen with no way out. "Don't use him on me, Mom. It's not fair."

She presses one of her delicate hands onto my shoulder. "I'm not using him. I'm telling you what I feel in my heart. But you can't keep going on like this. It's taking a toll on all of us. You need to work through this."

Blood pounds in my head, and I want to scream—but I don't. Instead, the image of Gavin's concerned face when he found me this morning enters my mind, and I feel like cold water is being dumped over me. Just thinking of him and how he cared for me, how he listened to me, makes me want to try to be better.

I turn my head from Mom to look at the picture of me and Reed again. Now it's my eyes that I see. The eyes of a girl who was beyond happy, one who didn't have a care in the world. My heart aches to be like her again. I don't think I'll ever be, but maybe I can at least be happy. Happy like I was earlier this morning with Gavin. My mom also deserves for me to try, despite our tense relationship.

Mom squeezes my shoulder. "You're still young, Blake. I know I give you a hard time about not settling down, but you still have time to do whatever it is you want with your life. Reed wouldn't want you to throw that away."

I reach up and brush the tear that's managed to squeeze out of my eye. "I'll think about it."

"Blake—"

"Please, Mom. This is a lot for me. But I will think about it."

After a moment of searching my face, she finally nods in submission. "I guess that's all I can ask for." I let out a long breath. She leans forward and kisses my forehead like she used to do when I was little. "I love you, Blake. Always remember that."

My heart clenches. "I love you, too."

CHAPTER 22

Gavin

I TAKE A HANDKERCHIEF from my pocket and wipe the sweat from my hairline. I'm on a short break while the crowd dances to an upbeat country song.

It's jammed with people who've come to ride the infamous Tornado. Pictures of the charity event last week must've spread around on social media because Jake had to call in a few extra bartenders to help with the crowd since I'm on MC and bull duty.

I scan the room for the hundredth time in hopes I'll see a certain pair of brown eyes staring back at me—so far, no dice.

Jake hops up on stage next to me with a bottle of water. "Looking for Kade?" He grins. He knows full well I'm not looking for my brother. Although I will admit it's odd not seeing him working the crowd and getting drunk on a busy night like this. But after our talk, he decided to stay home. I know Gran's eyes bugged out of her head like saucers when he asked her if she wanted to play cards tonight and shoot the shit like old times.

"Busy night," I say instead.

Jake barks a laugh and slaps me on the back. "I reiterate that I wish Blake fancied me over you, but I'm glad you guys figured your shit out. When I left the other night, I was sure she wouldn't touch you with a ten-foot pole after what you said at the bar."

I take a sip of the water, unsure of what to say back. Jake and the entire town knew about the first kiss Blake and I shared outside Night Hawk a couple nights ago. When I came to work earlier, I was greeted by wolf whistles and pats on the back. I spent the opening part of my shift making sure none of them did that to Blake if and when she walked in. She's been through enough, and as much as I enjoy her blush, I don't want her to feel like she can't come to Night Hawk without being harassed. Though that ship may have sailed between me forcing her on the bull and that city boy who I punched.

The more I think about it, the more I wish I could've spoken to her before she left earlier. God, I hope she doesn't regret sleeping with me or what we've shared. I should've called her after I was done pushing cattle, but I wanted to speak in person.

"You okay?" Jake's voice cuts through my overactive brain.

As his words sink in, a smile turns up on my lips. Because despite all the unanswered questions, I feel better than I have since my life turned upside down nine months ago. I pat his shoulder. "I'm okay."

Jake grins devilishly. "I knew a woman would change your mood. Glad you snagged yourself a good one."

My body hums with warmth. "She is a good one."

"If you want, I can take over. I know you're itching to go find her."

"That's kind of you," I say truthfully. "I told her to come tonight, so I'll wait. It's busy as hell, and I can't leave you in the lurch."

He gestures happily toward the line of people waiting to ride the bull. "People do love you."

"Of course they do." I wink. "Better get back to it before they get rowdy."

"Do your thing, Cowboy."

Jake walks off, and I turn up the music to let people know we're starting back up again. They're yelling, ready to have a good time. I turn on the mic and put it to my lips.

"Ladies and gentlemen!" I say, and they holler. "I know you missed me." A girl in the crowd yells for me to take off my shirt. "Hey now, I don't give the goods away for free." I wink.

"I've got money!" someone screams.

I let out a low laugh into the microphone. "Thanks, darling, but I don't come cheap."

"One thousand dollars!" a voice slices above the crowd. I scan for the person who yelled it, but the lights are too bright.

"Who said that?" I say into the mic.

"I did!"

The crowd parts, and my lips tip up as the sinful body of Blake Tanner comes into view. Never in my life did I think she would be offering me a grand to take off my shirt in front of the entire bar.

"Blake Tanner," I say into the microphone. "That's a lot of money for a shirt."

"Strip tease!" the lady from before screams. All the women in the bar go wild, and the men groan collectively. I can't blame them.

I laugh. "Don't get ahead of yourselves now!" When I make eye contact with Blake, her demeanor screams trouble. She looks good enough to eat in short jean shorts and a pink V-neck T-shirt. Too bad I'm working; I'd rather take her home and bury myself inside her again. But this time, I get to be in charge.

I quirk an eyebrow at her in question. I know I'm in trouble when she winks at me with a wicked grin. "Take off your shirt, then ride the bull," she yells. Oh, she's going to get it for suggesting that.

"Do it!" Jake and Stu whoop from the bar.

My eyes stay locked on Blake's—she's excited. When she crosses her arms over her chest expectantly, I give her a look that says, *"You're serious?"* and all she does is mouth, *"Payback."* I let out a breath. I guess it's true what they say—all's fair in love and war.

The crowd starts cheering, like the night I had Blake get up on stage. My body shakes with laughter as I contemplate giving into pressure. Not that I mind. Taking off my shirt and being ogled doesn't bother me—and I'm *really* good at riding the bull.

"Take it off, Cowboy!" a rabid woman bellows.

"Dang," I say into the mic. "Y'all are a thirsty bunch!"

The people hoot and holler as Blake continues to stand there like this is one of the best ideas she's ever had. She pulls out her wallet and comes up to the stage with a wad of cash. I doubt she carries a grand in her bag, but I think she's doing it for effect.

She proves me right when she holds up a few twenties and says, "Take off your shirt." I have to fight my body so I don't get a hard-on right here on stage—but the way she's looking at me...I forget there's over a hundred people in this bar eating me up right now. I only have eyes for Blake Tanner.

I reach down and grab her hand over the money to give her knuckle a kiss. Then I take the cash for show and stand up. In one quick motion, I drag my shirt out of my jeans and belt and pull it over my head. Everyone goes wild, but my gaze remains on Blake. It's obvious by the way her eyes scan my naked chest that I'm not the only one turned on. But I have a show to do because of her, so I throw my sweaty shirt at her and saunter over to the bull. If Blake Tanner wants a show, I'll give her a show.

CHAPTER 23

Blake

I'm a woman possessed by my hormones. I can't stop staring at Gavin's backside flexing through his tight jeans as he walks with swagger over to Tornado. He motions for Jake to come man the controller before turning back to the crowd to hype them up—not that they need it. This version of Gavin is completely different from the one I'm starting to know, but it's a version of him I enjoy. Minus when he made me ride that damn thing.

But as I said: Payback. Though I need to rethink my methods, because it's clear he couldn't care less that all the women are ready to jump his bones. Some women may be jealous if a man they slept with gets so much attention, but it makes me feel great because he's not looking at them. Which also answers my question on whether he regrets this morning. I know I don't. It feels nice to have shared both my body and private memories with him. I don't know if it's because he's familiar, or maybe because he was friends with Reed, but Gavin makes me feel safe. Who needs a therapist when I have him? Mom probably would disagree, but at least I'm talking to someone. Baby steps.

Gavin beams at me as he hops on Tornado. Women all around me are screaming and throwing dollar bills on the padded area around the bull. It's funny, and I can't help but snort with laughter. When I steal a glance at Jake and Stu, they find it as hilarious as I do.

Jake puts the mic up to his lips. "Cowboys and Cowgirls, this night has surely taken a turn. But I'm ready to see if our boy here can beat his last record of one minute and thirty-nine seconds." The crowd goes wild. That's freaking good for a mechanical bull. In real bull riding, you see if you can make it for eight seconds, but it's a lot easier on something that's not alive and much more predictable. The person controlling it will usually start you off slow and easy.

Jake continues, "So, keep throwing your money, and let's see this cowboy ride! You ready, Montgomery?"

Gavin's eyes stay on mine as he takes the strap with his right hand and grips his thighs around Tornado, his other hand holding his cowboy hat down. He gives me a sexy smile before tipping his head at Jake. "I'm ready."

The bull takes off at the highest speed that's still safe for Gavin, one that won't give him whiplash but still enough to jerk him around. He lets out what I liken to a battle cry that has me shaking with laughter. The women go absolutely rabid, and larger bills start flying. I even see a bra land near him, but I don't care about any of that. Gavin holds on, his hips moving with the fake beast beneath him, abs contracting as he tries not to fall off. That's all it takes for me to imagine riding him like that, my hands on his chest as he grips my hips and teases my breasts. My body tingles with excitement and I squeeze my thighs together to try and quell my arousal.

As Gavin continues to ride, I lose track of how long he's been holding on. At some point Polly arrives at my side and shakes me.

"Holy crud! I can't believe you got him to do this without his shirt on." She giggles in my ear. "I feel like I'm at a strip club!"

I smirk at all the money around Gavin. "It kind of is at this point."

She giggles again. "I can't believe you kissed that fine man. Please tell me you're going to date him!"

I flush. Of course she knows about the kiss; everyone does at this point. Looking Daddy in the eye earlier, when I apologized to him about this morning, was more embarrassing than I thought it would be. But if I decide to stay in Randall for the foreseeable future, I'm going to have to get used to people knowing my business for the rest of my life. Or get better at sneaking around like I did as a teenager.

Polly yells as Gavin gets bucked around, throwing her own dollar bills on the floor. "I'm going to have to see if Tim will do this sometime. It's hot as hell!"

I shake my head. Maybe Jake needs to make male shirtless bull riding a monthly thing. It'd bring in loads of cash.

"Hold on, cowboy!" Polly screams.

I see Gavin's muscles tremble when I catch his eyes. I know he's not far off from falling. I glance at the timer on the wall and see he's close to his record. At that moment, Jake flips the bull and starts to shake it before he spins it around in several circles. I don't know how Gavin does it, but he stays on. If it was me, I think I would've puked. Now the clock is only five seconds away from his previous time, and the crowd starts to count down.

"You can do it!" I bellow. He grits his teeth as his hips pump the air. The moment I can get him alone, I'm going to jump him. I don't even care that he's sweaty, or if anyone sees us. I feel like my body is on fire, and he's the only one who can put it out.

"Thirty-six, thirty-seven, thirty-eight!" everyone chants.

Jake spins the bull even faster, but Gavin still doesn't fall.

"Thirty-nine, forty, forty-one!" And as we're about to call a minute and forty-two, Gavin flies from Tornado, landing with more grace than I would expect after that performance.

Everyone goes wild, including me. Jake yeehaws into the microphone and congratulates Gavin on beating his record. Gavin doesn't care though; he only has eyes for me. For a second, he breaks the eye contact to say something into Jake's ear before he stalks toward me.

"That sure was something!" Polly says.

I jump a little, having completely forgotten she's standing next to me. I think she asks if I want to get a drink, but I don't hear her because I'm watching Gavin. Polly notices because she touches my shoulder and says, "Have fun, girl," before she walks off.

Gavin stops in front of me, baring a sly grin. Before he can speak, I grab his hand and pull him out of the crowd. He follows me willingly, though I'm highly aware of his burning stare on my ass and the warm weight of his calloused hand clutching mine. People catcall and whistle at us as they watch me drag him like a cavewoman on a mission, but I'll worry about the gossip later when I'm not so turned on.

I see the entrance to the back exit behind the bar and decide that's the perfect place to go. The music and yells mute once we enter, but I continue to tug Gavin through shelves of supplies until we're bursting through the back exit and night consumes us. Gavin's hungry gaze mirrors mine, and I lose it. I push him up against the brick wall, which makes him grunt from the force. He recovers quickly, grinning as he presses his hard body into mine.

"Kiss me, baby. Take what you want." His voice is a purr that has my toes curling in my boots. I lean forward and press my lips to his. His mouth opens in invitation, and I don't waste time tangling our tongues together in a sweet dance that makes me moan. Gavin's hands move to my hips so he can press me into him. I feel his erection through his black jeans, and I gasp. With our lips no longer connected, he sucks on the hollow where my neck and collarbone meet. I think it's safe to say that's his favorite spot. He already left a mark I covered up, and now it's going to be even darker.

"Gavin," I say breathlessly. My nipples are hard, and the friction of them against my shirt as our bodies press together is almost too much to bear. He tugs on my earlobe, grinding his pelvis against my heat like he knows how wet I am.

"What do you need, baby?" he says in my ear, his voice gravelly.

"Touch me. *Please*."

He skims his lips over mine in fine strokes. "I am touching you."

When I open my eyes, he's got a mad grin on his face that only makes me want him more. Without words, I move his hand from my hip and press it against me so he's cupping my sex. His eyes shut for a second as he feels the heat there. When he opens them, he uses his free hand to brush the apple of my cheek.

"So sexy." His voice is low enough that I almost don't hear it. He seals his lips over mine again as his hand slips down under the waistband of my jeans and into my underwear. I sigh into his mouth as his fingers find my clit.

"You're so wet," he growls before diving back in.

I move my hands to grip the back of his head as his lips kiss down my neck, then to the top of my breasts. He runs his nose along the flesh as he explores, his other hand working in perfect circles around my clit.

My head falls back, and my mouth drops open. Gavin's touch makes me feel like a goddess. And the way he asks what I want and lets me take it? It's heaven. With him, I don't feel ashamed voicing it, either. With him, I feel brave.

Gavin plunges two fingers inside me, and all coherent thoughts leave me. "That's it," he encourages as his thumb still strokes my clit. *Lord*. He's going to turn me into a sex fiend.

"Gavin," I cry as his fingers fuck me faster. I force my head forward and trap his lips in another kiss. I love the way his stubble scratches my skin, and the taste of his tongue on mine. He's slightly sweaty from being on stage, but it only makes me hotter.

He breaks the kiss and tugs on my lower lip. "Come for me, baby." His voice sends shivers up my spine as I clutch him to me. With another thrust and the delicious pressure on my clit, I feel myself falling. "That's it, baby. You're so beautiful when you let go."

I come hard as he brings his mouth over mine to swallow my cries. When I start to relax down from my high, I press my forehead to his and hold on to him for dear life. It takes me a minute to catch my breath, but when I pull back, he's there with a twinkle in his eye. He takes his hand from my jeans and brings his fingers to his lips. When he cleans my arousal off with his tongue, I feel like I've been transported inside a dirty movie where I'm the star. It's raunchy and hot all at the same time.

Gavin hums around his fingers, that sexy smirk tugging at his lips. My voice catches as he pulls me into him, his hard and impressive length digging into my stomach. I start to trail my hand down his bare chest when a distant sound of laughter makes me pause. In my orgasm-induced haze, I completely forgot we're in public. Thank God we're hidden back here, but it doesn't mean a drunk person or one of Night Hawk's employees won't find us.

Gavin kisses me softly and takes my hand. "When I get off work, you can take care of that, Cowgirl." When I blush, he continues, "If you want."

My heart thuds in my chest. "I do want." He takes my mouth with his again and explores me until I feel like I might pass out from the electricity buzzing between us.

"Stop making out and get back to work!" Jake yells from the door.

I jump what feels like ten feet in the air and press my hand over my chest. "Jesus, Jake!" I cry. Gavin steps in front of me and covers my sexed-up body from Jake's amused gaze. Apparently, he doesn't care that Jake can see his hard-on. I'm just glad I'm still wearing all my clothes. My face burns. I can't believe I got off in public!

"I'll be right in. Now go back inside, Jake," Gavin warns. When the light from the open door dissipates, signaling Jake's retreat, Gavin turns to face me. Surprisingly, he doesn't look the least bit bothered that we got caught. I'm impressed by the confidence he has. It also turns me on that he's so open about his desire and affection for me.

He pulls me to him. "Are you alright?"

I worry my bottom lip. "I forgot we were in public. Do you think anyone saw us? Besides Jake."

"He didn't see anything. And I think we're safe. The cameras don't work back here and I was keeping an eye out. I would've taken us elsewhere if I thought we weren't alone." He pulls me in for a quick kiss, and I melt into him. When I pull back, I have a stupid grin on my face.

"You really made me come in public."

"It was hot as hell. You're one of a kind, Blake Tanner." When he tries to kiss me again, I stop him by pressing my fingers against his puckered lips. "You have to get back to work. But find me later?"

He gives me a shining smile. "There's nowhere else I'd rather be."

CHAPTER 24

Gavin

I GRIN AT MY phone as I take a sip of beer. It's been three glorious weeks since Blake Tanner walked into my life again, yet I can't seem to remember a time when she wasn't in it.

We can't get enough of each other and spend almost all our free time together, which isn't much considering we both have a lot of work to do on our respective ranches. Sadly, I still haven't found anything that can fix my financial problems—but at least I have Blake.

"You're a lovesick puppy." Kade walks into the house with dirt smudges on his face as he heads to the fridge to grab a beer. I stare at the longneck bottle, and his face goes taut. He's been drinking less, but every time I see him with alcohol, I get a little nervous.

He grabs the bottle opener on the counter and cracks it open. "Don't give me that look, Gav. It's been a long day, and it's one beer. Let me fucking enjoy it."

I hold up my hands in surrender. "I didn't say anything."

"You didn't have to." The strain in his voice is evident. It makes my stomach coil. I know it's been hard on Kade these last weeks, picking up my slack. It's getting harder to keep from him why I spend so much time in the office. I know I've got to tell him what's really going on soon. But despite how mad I know he'll be, I'm more afraid that he'll revert to his heavy drinking.

I also want to protect Momma and Gran as long as I can. Hell, Blake doesn't know either—at least not the full scope of it.

Since that morning in the guest house, we haven't spent time talking about our problems again. We've been too busy learning each other's bodies. I especially love the way she cries and throws her head back when she comes, or how she knows exactly the right spot on my ribs that tickles like hell and has me squealing. I smile again at the memory.

"At least one of us is happy," Kade says under his breath.

I wipe the smile off my face and bite back a sigh. I've fucked up again, and I know it. This entire situation is more difficult than I could've imagined. It's been so nice to be happy, to pretend like I'm a normal twenty-four-year-old building a relationship with a magnificent woman.

I take a sip of my beer. "What do you have to say to me, Kade?"

His hard eyes look up at me. "Nothing."

Letting out a breath, I stare back at him. It's my mistake that I thought things were getting better. Kade did seem happier these past weeks, and Momma is smiling again, too. I even caught Gran grinning. But my head's been too far up my ass to realize one half-assed conversation between us isn't going to solve things. It simply plugged the leak for a bit.

I stand up and motion for Kade to do the same. "Let's go."

Kade's eyes narrow. "Go where?"

"We're going for a ride."

Kade looks out the window at the sun low in the sky. "I spent all day working."

"Come on, Kade. Let's do something together that doesn't involve work."

He studies me. "I'd rather go to a bar and shoot some pool. Maybe find a pretty girl to take my mind off things."

I don't take the bait. Instead, I grab my hat and put it on my head. "I think we see enough bars outside of this ranch. Let's go to Devil's Rock."

Kade's body stiffens. Devil's Rock is a canyon that's a good ride from here. Going means we won't get home till late, but I think it's needed.

"We haven't been there since—" He stops. *Since Dad last took us.*

"I think it's time we go. The sky should be clear tonight, and we'll bring our packs like old times."

Kade clears his throat. "Being with Blake has made you sentimental."

I think about Blake, and my entire body relaxes. He's right. "So what if it has?"

He holds up his hands. "Nothing. You're just different."

"So are you," I say back.

His eyes stay fixed on mine until I finally see his body give in and he stands. "Give me twenty. I want to shower."

"I'll get everything together."

He nods, his mouth opening as if he wants to say something, but he doesn't. At least he agreed to go, that's something.

By the time we reach Devil's Rock, the stars are out. We're both going to be exhausted tomorrow, but I think it'll be worth it. Kade and I need time together where we don't work or fight. Devil's Rock is neutral ground, the place where Dad took us when we were kids and teenagers. We learned a lot out here. Like how to make a fire, hunt our own dinner, and other Rights of Passage he deemed worthy of us knowing.

Once we settle the horses, I take off the saddle bags and hand Kade a thick blanket to lay out. We settle on one of the larger rocks overlooking the canyon and click off our headlamps before removing them. The night is still warm, and we've both worked up a sweat riding out here, choosing to work our horses harder for the sake of time. Which means we haven't spoken more than two words to each other since leaving the house. Kade shifts and pulls out a flask I know is full of whiskey. I don't comment since it will only cause problems. He takes a swig, then passes it to me.

"Thanks," I mutter. Whiskey has always been the way Montgomery men relax after a long day, so I'm not surprised Kade brought the flask, or that he picked up our old man's habits of drinking too much. Sometimes I wonder if I'd been more involved in Kade's life this last year, I could've stopped it from becoming an issue.

"Stop beating yourself up, Gavin." Kade's voice cuts through my thoughts. My gaze flips to his. It's dark, but I can see some of his face in the light reflected from the moon.

"What do you mean?

"Maybe I inherited Gran's superpowers. But I can tell what you're thinking, and I know you think my problem is your problem. Hell, I've made you think you're part of my problems, but you're not, Gavin. Dad isn't, either." My curiosity is piqued at his words.

He goes on, "I know why you brought me out here. You want me to spill my guts, fix my problems. But I don't want you to fix me, Gavin. I want you to be my brother."

I contemplate his words as I take another sip of whiskey. "I am your brother. That's why I want to help you so damn much."

He takes the flask back from me and downs another large swig. He screws the cap on, then lies back on the rock to look up at the stars. "Remember when Dad drove us out here in the middle of the coldest week of the year?"

I let out a gruff laugh. "How could I forget that? You were fourteen, I was seventeen. We got in a fight about something stupid, and you hit me. He made us come out here and work it out like men in the freezing cold."

"You really don't remember why I hit you that night?"

I let out a breath. "It was a long time ago, Kade."

He's silent for a moment before he starts again. "There was a senior youth reining competition in Arizona I wanted to enter. Dad asked you to take care of the paperwork because he had some meeting in town, and you forgot. I missed the deadline."

I want to punch myself when I hear the sadness in Kade's voice. That night is foggy. I was a teenager, and Dad started giving me more and more responsibility as I neared eighteen. I also remember that he'd just told me I couldn't go to a "fancy" college, that he needed me to be close to home. I was upset because I saw my only way out of town slip through my fingers, even though deep down, I knew that was a stupid dream.

I run a hand over my face. "I'm sorry, I didn't mean to forget. You know what he was like."

He holds up his hand. "I know. I'm not mad at you. I was never mad at you. I was mad at Dad, but I would've never been able to get a swing in on him. So I took it out on you."

As more memories come back, my muscles tighten. "I don't blame you, Kade. I would've hit me, too."

That makes Kade's lips turn up. "I was jealous of you back then, for getting all that attention, and the fucked-up part is, I still am. Even though I know you had it hard—*have* it hard. I understand he expected a lot of you. I can see how you carry the weight of this," he gestures to the land around us, "but I still get mad that he trusted you over me with it. We all knew you wanted something different, Gavin, but I've wanted to run this ranch since I knew how to work it. Then he left me nothing."

"Kade, I don't know what you want me to say. I keep telling you that a piece of paper doesn't matter, this place is as much yours as it is mine. And you know I love this land and our ranch. I'll do anything to save it."

"I know that. I just don't understand why Dad didn't trust me with the ranch like he always trusted you. It may be only a piece of paper, but that piece of paper means something to me."

I try to stay calm at his words. We've had this conversation before, and it always ends the same way: with him getting drunk, and me working until my eyes burn.

"I've told you before why I think he did what he did."

"I know. It's the same one Momma and Gran give me all the time. I get that he did things traditionally, but that doesn't make it right. I thought he'd break the cycle. He told me he would, he—"

Kade stops himself, and I find myself sitting up straighter.

"He told you what?"

My brother sits and opens his flask. "I said too much."

I clasp my hands on his shoulder. "Kade, what did he say?"

I can see the pain in his eyes even in the dark. "The night before Momma found him in the tractor, we got drunk together on the porch, shooting the shit after a long day like we always did on the weekends. He said he was going to leave the place to me. Then the bastard goes and has a heart attack." He sighs.

Blood rushes to my head, the truth of what Kade's been hiding coursing through my veins. I think he expects me to feel anger at his words, but I don't. He wanted this life since he was old enough to express it, and I've always been the one to want something else. I always thought Daddy didn't understand that, but there's so much relief in knowing that he did.

"Why didn't you say something sooner?" I ask.

He looks up at the stars and sighs. "Why haven't you offered me the place yet?"

His words hang in the air, and I feel as if I've got weights tied to every one of my limbs. "You know why," is all I say. The excuse I've given him before is that the business is unstable. That he doesn't want to deal with all the paperwork he's never been good at. But it's really because I'm a coward and I don't want him to know the truth.

His voice raises slightly. "Your reason is bullshit."

"Kade..."

His hand lands on my shoulder and he squeezes. "I'm not a kid anymore. Tell me what's really going on. Why do you hide in that damn guest house after we all go to sleep and don't come out until sunrise?"

"There's a lot of paperwork. A lot of backlogs," I counter. "I told you it got backed up after Dad died. It's a mess."

Kade watches me, his eyes discerning. It feels like he's looking through me. "Why do I feel like there's something you aren't telling me?" he says.

Kade wasn't joking when he mentioned he has Gran's superpowers. I try to relax and remember all the reasons I haven't told him the truth so he can't see the lies I'm having a hard time hiding.

"Kade," I let his name out in a breath.

"Gavin," he parrots.

I stare into his eyes, the eyes of a young kid who's already struggled so much in life. I just can't tell him the truth yet. Not when he's been doing better with his drinking. Not when life seems to be a little bit nicer around here.

"You can tell me, Gav. What is it?" he urges.

I shake my head to push the truth further down.

"I've told you," I say again, my voice sterner this time. "It's the drought, and we need ways to make money." When he opens his mouth, I continue, "But if you want to help me, then how about you research ways to get a more stable income for the ranch? I've been looking into leasing land out to the people in the city who need space for their animals."

Kade studies me thoughtfully, and I put on the most neutral face I can muster. Eventually, his grip on my shoulder loosens. "Was that so hard?" he asks.

I let myself relax a bit. I don't know if he believes me, but it looks like he's placated for now. I can only hope the probing questions are over for tonight.

"You know I don't like to ask for help. You already do too much," I add.

He rolls his eyes. "Pot, meet kettle."

I let out a tense chuckle. "I'll accept that barb."

Kade half-smiles back. "I have some ideas myself."

This time, I quirk my eyebrow at him. "You do?"

"Maybe. Are you willing to hear them?"

I know he's asking me if I'm willing to let go of a little control, which is obviously hard for me to do. Having him help also means he could get closer to the truth, but if it will ease my tense relationship with him, and potentially save the ranch in the process, it makes it more palatable.

"I'm willing," I say, forcing my tone to be light.

Kade grins. "I suppose that's better than nothing."

I clasp him on the shoulder. "You're a good man, little brother. And I love you."

Kade's eyes are on me again as he says, "I told you. Sentimental."

I shove his shoulder, the energy shifting to a lighter tone. "What about you, are you seeing anyone?"

Kade barks a laugh. "Just like you to turn this conversation back on me." This time we both laugh.

"Well, are you seeing anyone?" I ask again. He shrugs, his body language turning softer.

"Nothing serious. I haven't seen much action since I started staying home and playing cards with Gran."

Now I'm curious. "Who is she?"

"Nobody you know."

"City girl?"

He shrugs. "Not important."

Kade stares out into the night. The moon and stars outline the sharp rocks of the canyon. This place is dangerous if you don't know your way around, but it's also wonderful and wild. I may dream of a different life sometimes, but I do love it. This land is my home, and my family means everything to me.

"Kade," I say quietly. "It's important to me. Your life is important to me."

He turns. "Don't worry, it's not Cricket."

I sigh. "Don't do that. I know it sucks being vulnerable. And I know Dad didn't teach us how to show our feelings, but don't push me away when we just got somewhere."

He grits his teeth, the silence of the night enveloping us. There's a nagging voice telling me I'm a hypocrite for not giving him the entire truth, but I keep repeating the same story in my head.

"A woman and I hooked up, and it got a little rough. I think I spooked her. I don't know why I'm stuck on her, but—" he stops himself, a familiar look of regret on his face.

My brows raise in surprise. Kade and I don't ever go into detail about who we sleep with or what we like in the bedroom. When we were younger, he'd ask me for advice on how to woo girls and things he wasn't comfortable asking our folks, but he's always been a natural flirt and women came easy to him. Especially after he hit puberty.

"Don't give me that look," he glowers. "It's why I keep what I like private. I don't need any more judgment or disappointment in my life from the people I care about."

"Is that what you think, Kade?"

He shrugs. "All signs point to that being the case. First with Dad's bullshit, then Momma's face every morning when I stumble in to work, or Gran when I stopped playing cards with her on—"I place my hand on his shoulder and shake him a little. "No, Kade. You're wrong."

"Am I, though?" His voice cracks.

My eyes burn. "You are. I meant what I said. You're a good man, Kade Montgomery. You've got shit to deal with, we all do. But this is why I brought you out here. You're my brother, and I love you. What you like and do in your own time is for you and you alone. I don't give a shit as long as you're not hurting yourself or others."

A strange smile ghosts over his lips. I think he wants to say something, but he doesn't. For a while, we sit in silence and look up at the stars, listening to the sounds of night. I let my mind drift and enjoy the company of my brother and the memories this place holds for us.

"Gavin?" Kade finally says, his voice quiet.

"Hmm?"

"Thank you for bringing me out here. I'm glad we talked."

"Me too, Kade." *Me, too.*

CHAPTER 25

Blake

"REED!"

I fly up in bed, my heart hammering in my chest. A sob escapes my throat as I try to remember that I'm not actually reliving the worst day of my life. Gripping the sheets, I take several breaths. The early morning light leaks through the curtains, and I squint through my tears. The nightmares went away for a bit, but with the anniversary of Reed's death next week, they've come back in full force.

I chug down a glass of water I keep near my bed, thankful my parents are in the city for Mom's orthopedic appointment. If Mom heard me scream like that, she would force me to see her therapist, an action I've still been avoiding since our conversation a few weeks back. I scrub my hands over my face and let out a breath as I swap my water for my phone.

The time reads past seven in the morning, which is a rarity for me to sleep this late. I guess I needed it. We've been busy repairing a fence that fell in one of the pastures. Mom also got a new horse in from Germany that she plans to train and sell once she's better. That means I've been doing groundwork with him a lot, since she can't. I know Mom wishes I'd ride him instead of staying on the ground, but I still can't imagine breaking my promise. Even if I can't stop thinking about training Briar's colt on barrels after I thought about it once.

My phone lights up in my hand, and I'm grateful for the distraction. When I see Gavin's name on the screen, my heart flutters. Everything with him is perfect. More perfect than I deserve. With him, I almost feel like myself again—well, as me as I can feel without Reed in my life. I've even started hanging with Polly and Jake at Night Hawk and went to The Diner with Daddy once. Things are shifting, and it's been easier since my talk with Mom and Gavin's constant presence in my life.

I open the text to find a picture of the stars with the message: *Went to Devil's Rock with Kade last night. You'd love it out here.* I lift a brow at the mention of his brother. I knew he and Kade were having a rough go recently; that day on the ATVs proved it. But Gavin and I haven't been doing much talking when we're alone, so I don't know all the details. If we could keep our hands off each other, maybe I would know more. But that man is shameless when it comes to touching me. Not that I'm much better. I close the picture and tap out a reply.

You're right, I would love it. Looks beautiful.

It doesn't take him long to message back. My stomach does its familiar flip flop as I read the text.

Morning, Cowgirl. How'd you sleep? :)

My mood dampens as I'm reminded of my nightmare and the anniversary next week. I keep my response light.

Okay. Did you have a nice time last night?

Instead of a responding text, my phone buzzes with an incoming call from him. I pick it up. "Couldn't resist hearing the sound of my voice?" My tone is huskier than normal due to my still raw throat.

"You know I could listen to your voice all day. Especially when I kiss that spot on your neck."

I bite my lip and groan. "Don't you think it's too early for that kind of talk?"

"I've been up since five. I already mucked stalls and ate breakfast."

"Show off."

He chuckles, then asks, "Didn't sleep well?"

I let out a breath. "It's fine. Nothing a pot of coffee can't fix."

He goes silent on the other end for a moment. "I was thinking we could spend the day together."

My spine tingles. "You don't have to work?"

He lets out a huff. "I always have work—but Kade is going to handle it. And I took the night off from Night Hawk duties."

"Is that because I told you my parents would be out of town?"

"Maybe."

"Want to take advantage of an empty house, do you, Cowboy?"

His breath hitches. "And if I say yes?"

I bite my lower lip. "Then I guess you'd better come over. Maybe I'll even steal the good whiskey from Daddy's liquor cabinet."

I can almost hear his smile through the phone. "Sounds like a good time."

"It does." I'm breathless as I respond. Heat pools between my legs as I imagine him on my bed touching me like he did that first morning together. I hear rustling over the phone, and I wonder if he's adjusting himself while he imagines the same thing.

"What time can I come over?"

I think if I told him now, he would. "Since my parents are gone, I've got to work some horses, and—"

"I'll come help you."

I laugh. "You took time off work, and you want to come and do work that's not even your own?"

"It's not work when it's with you."

Butterflies erupt in my belly. "Has anyone ever told you that you're really good with words?"

He laughs again. "Not really."

I shake my head. "As much as I'd love for you to come help me, if you come here before I'm done, I won't get anything finished."

He blows out an audible breath. "Way to dash my dreams of making you come in a secluded corner of your barn."

My cheeks burn. "You're bad."

"Never said I was good," he teases.

"But seriously, that's the reason why you can't come help me."

He groans. "And if I promise to keep my hands to myself like a good boy?"

His words make my lips turn up. Company does sound nice, and Mom and Daddy won't be around to spy on us and make assumptions about our relationship. A status I don't even know. It's not like we've spent much time talking about what we are to each other.

"You promise to be good?"

"I promise," he says.

I don't believe him for a second—but that's part of the fun. "Fine, you can come help."

"I'll be over in an hour after I wrap up some things here," he says.

"Perfect."

"I'm looking forward to it. See you soon."

"See you soon. Oh, and Gavin?"

"Yeah?"

"Make sure to bring an overnight bag."

Now I can really imagine the grin on his face.

"Yes, ma'am."

Watching Gavin Montgomery work is an art form.

He's mucking stalls, but I've never found a man hotter. He's wearing an old white work T-shirt and a red ball cap instead of his usual cowboy hat. I like that I can see the angles of his jaw as it flexes and the curve of his ass through his dark wash Wranglers as he moves. When he catches me staring, he stands and rests his hands on the skinny handle of the pitchfork.

"You finish your stalls?" he asks.

"Yep. You done, too?"

He takes the pitchfork and tosses in a final mess before standing again. "Now I am."

"Want to watch me lunge some expensive horses?"

He studies my face carefully. I know what he's thinking. He thought I avoided horse work all together.

"It's not riding," is all I say. I don't say it with anger, just as a fact.

He leans the pitchfork against the wall and pushes the full wheelbarrow toward me. "Lead the way."

I show him where to dump the manure, then gesture for him to follow me toward the next barn over where we house all the hunters and jumpers. As we walk by Briar's stall, the colt pokes his head out and tries to bite Gavin's elbow.

"Hey!" he says playfully, stopping to tap the colt's nose. "That's not very nice." Gavin pets the foal's long face, and to my surprise, Briar comes to say hello, too. She usually keeps to herself around new people. When he takes in the mare before him, his energy shifts. "You remember me, girl?"

I swear I stop breathing as Briar lets him scratch behind her ear. She makes a soft nicker and my heart cracks in two. For a moment, I'm thrown back to a memory of Reed and Gavin. They were scrawny boys, only sixteen or seventeen. Briar was a filly and deemed ready to start riding. Reed got on first, but Briar spooked, making him fall off the side and into the mud. Gavin and I couldn't stop laughing. Sometimes I forget that he and Gavin were such close friends, that he's the age Reed would've been had he not died. When Gavin notices I'm staring, he turns his attention on me and grasps my biceps gently.

"Are you okay, Blake?"

"You remember Briar?" is all I can manage.

"Of course. She's filled out some, but I'd know that horse anywhere."

My mouth goes dry, and a tear escapes my eye before I can stop it. Then another, and another.

"Hey, hey," he says gently, pulling me into my arms. "I've got you, baby." I bury my face into his chest. His shirt is damp with sweat, and he smells like horse, but I don't care. I take a deep breath and will myself to calm down, but it only makes it worse.

"I'm sorry, Gavin," I murmur against him. "I don't know why I keep crying in front of you."

He rubs my arm. "Don't apologize. You can cry in front of me anytime. I'm here for you, Blake. You know that, right?"

I feel my body warm. We may not have been seeing each other for long, but he's proved that he really is here for me. I'm positive this man would jump off a cliff if I asked him to. The thought makes me smile a little. "I do. And it means a lot to me."

He reaches up and brushes his thumb over my lip. "Do you want to talk about it?"

I shrug. "It's been getting harder not to feel sad with the accident anniversary so close. Then seeing you with Briar—it brought back a memory."

Gavin watches me carefully, his gaze tender. "Which one?"

I recount the scene I remembered of Reed covered in mud, which makes Gavin smile.

"That was a good day. Though Reed was furious for an entire week," he says.

"That sounds like Reed."

"You know, Blake," he says carefully, "we can talk about next week if you'd like. I know this is your first time home since it happened, and it's got to be hard to think about, but as I said, I'm here for you. I want you to be able to talk to me about anything."

I stiffen. We haven't talked about the anniversary—and I've preferred it that way. My time with Gavin has been a welcome distraction, one I haven't wanted to darken with the pain of that day. Hell, his pain too.

"I know I can," I breathe out. "But for now, I'd like to go work some horses. Is that okay?"

He brushes a lock of hair behind my ear. "Of course it is."

I swallow the lump in my throat and kiss his cheek before taking his hand to lead him away from Briar's stall. It's getting late in the day, so most of the staff has gone home and some will return later to do evening chores. Which makes it feel like Gavin and I have the place to ourselves. I swing our joined hands a little and he smiles lightly at me. He's still concerned about my reaction, so I think of something to ask him.

"What's something few people know about you?"

He holds my hand a little tighter and hums. "I'm a pretty open book. Don't think there's much to know that people haven't seen or heard."

I blow out a breath between my lips. "I don't believe that for a second. There must be something."

"Well, I already told you I can dance—and I'm especially good at two-stepping. You know I'm good at being a showman, too." He grins. He's right. He is good at that.

"What about hobbies? What do you like to do?"

A laugh escapes his lips. "I don't know. I spend all my time working."

"Gavin! There has to be something."

"Then tell me what you like to do. Maybe it will give me some ideas."

"Easy. I like to bake."

His expression warms. "Please tell me you make brownies."

I tap his hip with mine. "Only the best."

He stops us in the aisle and pulls my hips toward his. When he leans down, he hovers his delicious lips over mine. "You'll have to let me taste them sometime."

The breath wooshes out of my lungs and I feel ten degrees warmer. "If you play your cards right," I say. He kisses me sweetly before pulling back.

"I think I figured mine out." There's mischief in his eyes as he says it.

"What is it?"

He leans forward and presses his lips to the shell of my ear. "Making you come," he whispers.

I gasp, my thighs clenching at his words. "That's not a hobby."

He kisses down the column of my neck, then back up to my ear again. "I'm making it one." Then he kisses me again—I swear I forget my own name, and the fact he's broken his promise to not touch me while we work. But that was a stupid promise anyway.

CHAPTER 26

Gavin

THE EVENING AIR FEELS cool against my heated skin as I hold Blake's hand in mine. After her question about my hobbies—and her breakdown outside of Briar's stall—I formulated a plan to take her mind off Reed's death day, and hopefully anything else weighing her down.

Blake looks at the building in front of us. "You know, we have honky-tonk in town. In fact, you work there."

She looks pretty in a floral green sundress with her cowboy boots and hat. "We spend too much time at Night Hawk. Also, that isn't a real honky-tonk." I gesture toward The Red Donkey. "*This* is a real honky-tonk." And I'm not lying. This bar is as country as it gets—and one of my favorites. It's a no-frills establishment full of interesting people from all walks of life. Not one person isn't wearing cowboy boots, and most are here to unwind from a hard day's work. It's a few towns over from Randall in the middle of nowhere and hosts live bands several nights a week and on weekends.

"I suppose you're right." Blake tugs my hand, excitement on her face. God, she's beautiful. I'm going to have to fight off men all night. We haven't even entered the place, and already the cowboys lingering outside are staring at us. Protectiveness settles in me, and I pull her into my side. I stare at a man smoking on the wall and have the urge to growl, "*Mine.*" I don't, since that would be ridiculous, but I want to.

Blake smiles innocently at the man, and he winks at her. I grunt, ushering her through the door before I get myself into trouble. Inside, the smell of sweat, sawdust, and stale beer hits my nose and music blares loud over the sounds of people having a good time. Excitement pricks my system and I smile at Blake. It's been a long time since I've had a night out like this where I'm not working. I'm even more thrilled that I'm here with a woman who makes my heart race.

I lean down so she can hear me. "Want a drink?"

"A cold beer sounds nice. It's hot in here!"

She's right. It is hot. This place is old, and it's not like they have money to install air conditioning. It's also big, and with all the bodies squished together, we're in for a sweaty night. I take her chin between my fingers and bring her lips to mine in a short kiss. "Not as hot as you," I say once I pull back. Blake's cheeks tinge pink, and I kiss her again before leading her to the packed bar. As we do, I see a few familiar faces that call out my name. An old buddy of mine, Miles, approaches before we reach the bar and slaps me on the back.

"Well, as I live and breathe. If it isn't the two-stepping champion himself!"

I tense at the mention of that stupid title. Blake eyes me with a wide smile and curiosity.

"Howdy, Miles," I greet him and return the quick half-hug he offers.

Miles takes in Blake beside me and gives her a friendly grin. "And who's this fine young woman here?"

"Blake," she says, reaching her hand out for him to shake. Miles holds it a little too long in my opinion, but I will myself to relax. Just because I want to act like a caveman where Blake's involved doesn't mean I should. And we've only been seeing each other for a few weeks. We haven't even defined what we are yet—we haven't had to. But with the way I'm feeling right now, I'm regretting my decision to bring her to a bar with a ton of horny and drunk men. Especially without knowing if I can call her my girl, even though I already think of her in that way.

"Nice to meet you, Blake," Miles says, breaking my thoughts. "Where've you been, Gav? It's been—""About a year," I finish for him. "My dad died, and I took over the ranch. Haven't had much time to be out."

He pats me on the back. "Sorry to hear that, man. Well, it's nice to see you again. I'm assuming you and Cricket aren't together?" His eyes flash to Blake again before he looks back at me. "She stopped coming around, too."

My hand clenches on Blake's waist. "I'm with Blake." My answer is simple as my affectionate gaze finds hers. Thankfully, she doesn't look unhappy at the mention of Cricket. In fact, there's a familiar blush on her cheeks that I think is because I told Miles I'm with her. A pleasant warmth fills my stomach, settling the thoughts that were running rampant in my head. I put Blake's reaction in my pocket for later, hoping we can talk about where this thing between us is going.

Miles doesn't skip a beat. "You know who you're going to be dancing with, don't you, Blake?"

Her lips turn up. "Apparently a champion two-stepper?"

Miles laughs. "You didn't tell her, Gavin?"

I huff, embarrassment bubbling inside me. "It's a stupid title."

Blake looks up with mirth in her eyes. "And here I thought that title belonged to your brother."

"He's the line dancer." I grin. "I'm the two-stepper."

Miles shakes my shoulder a bit. "This man right here won our championship contest three years in a row. This is the first year it went to someone else, but only because he wasn't here."

Blake eyes me thoughtfully. "I thought you said you didn't have a hobby?"

I chuckle. "Not sure I consider it a hobby. And I told you I like to dance." I lean down so my mouth is at her ear, not caring that Miles is standing there. "Especially with a beautiful woman like you."

She gently smacks my chest. "Then let's get a drink, Cowboy. I want to see those moves."

I give Miles a goodbye nod, thankful Blake gave me a way out. "You heard the lady. It was nice seeing you, Miles."

"You, too. See you on the dance floor." He spins on his heel and walks off, leaving Blake and me standing in a throng of people.

She nudges me with her hip. "The things I'm learning about you, Gavin Montgomery."

"I guess I'm full of surprises." I'm not, really. Blake and I just haven't spent a ton of time talking about things like dance championships. We know stuff about each other, including the big things like my family's need for charity and the trauma of losing our loved ones, but not the normal small things that two people who are dating talk about in the beginning. But with us being here together tonight, I want to remedy that.

After we make nice with a few more familiar faces at the bar, Blake and I settle in the corner with two shots of whiskey and a couple of beers. It's still a bit early, so the dancing is sparse. The bartender said the headlining band goes on in thirty minutes or so, which gives us the perfect opportunity to get to know each other better.

I raise the longneck bottle up to Blake's. "Cheers, baby."

She smiles cutely before tapping her bottle on mine. "Cheers." For a moment, I let myself admire the dark-haired beauty. She's put on a little bit of makeup, enough to highlight her natural beauty, but not enough that it covers her pretty sun-kissed freckles.

"Want to play a game?" I ask her.

She plays with the label on her bottle. "What kind of game?"

"Twenty Questions."

A breathy laugh escapes her lip. "That's not really a game."

"It most definitely is." I move my chair so our bodies are closer. "I want to know more about you, Blake Tanner."

Her body responds to mine being so close. I can tell because her breathing shortens and her ample chest rises and falls as she stares into my eyes.

"Alright, then," she hums. "Do I get a prize at the end?"

My cock perks up at the suggestion in her tone. I lean in so we're almost mouth to mouth as I say, "If you're a good girl and answer everything I ask."

Her breath stops for a second. "And do I get to ask you questions?"

"Only if I get a prize, too." She bites her bottom lip and I bring my thumb up to pull it out. "What do ya say, Blake?" I accentuate the syllables of her name, and a moan escapes her lips.

"Then I say," she grabs my thumb and sucks the tip of it gently, "ask away, Cowboy." When she lets go of my finger, I'm the one holding back a moan.

With a satisfied smile, she sits back and takes a sip of her beer. I have to shift around in my chair so I'm not so damn uncomfortable after how tight she's made my pants. She watches me knowingly, and I have the desire to kiss her senseless, then leave her hot and bothered. But I'll have to save that for later, because despite what my dick wants, I want to get to know her better. Every single part of her, not just her body.

I place my hand on the bare skin of her inner thigh and squeeze. "What's your favorite color?"

She laughs. "That's your first question?"

"These are important things to know," I say seriously.

She chuckles again. "Red."

I think of her in that red sundress from the other night and love her choice. Not only does it compliment her, but the color represents courage, sacrifice, and passion. It's exactly how I see her after all she's been through.

I stow the new information away in the back of my mind. "It's a good color. Now," I smirk, "it's your turn to ask me a question."

She hums. "If you could be any animal, what would you be?"

Interesting question. "Easy. A killer whale."

Her eyebrows shoot up in surprise. "Why?"

"Is that your second question?"

She rolls her eyes. "Just answer it, smarty pants!"

I tap my fingers on her thigh. "They're smart, family-oriented, swim long distances, and most importantly, they're apex predators." As I finish my reasoning, I stroke her inner thigh and I feel her shiver.

"You've really thought about it."

I grin. "They're amazing animals. My turn." I pause for a moment before I ask, "What have you been doing for the last five years?"

Her body shifts a bit, but she doesn't look uncomfortable like I thought she might. "That's a loaded question."

I caress her thigh soothingly. "You don't have to tell me if you don't want to."

She picks at the label of her beer bottle some more, then looks into my eyes. "I lived all over Tennessee. Eventually, I got a job at a coffee shop and well, I just lived there."

Her eyes turn to mine. There's so much sadness in them, not as much as when I first saw her at Night Hawk, but it's there, hiding behind a tough exterior. I tuck a piece of hair behind her ear and my lips turn up.

"What?"

"I'm trying to imagine Blake Tanner working at a coffee shop in a little apron," I say.

She smiles as if remembering it. "It's where I learned I love to bake. I used to make cookies, brownies, and scones every morning. It was...peaceful."

"I could see that."

She sucks in a breath. "Okay, my turn." She taps her finger on her chin in thought. "So you and Cricket, huh?" I clench my jaw as she continues, "How long were you together?"

"You really want to know about that?"

She sips her beer. "Well, apparently you used to bring her here, so…"

I can't stop the smirk that slaps on my face. "Are you jealous, Blake?"

She bites her lower lip. She *is* jealous. Something about that makes me giddy, especially since I had to watch her and Jake dance the night away. I know that night was of my own making, but it was still difficult.

"Just curious," she lies.

I climb my hand higher on her thigh, and she sucks in a short breath. My half-hard cock gets harder. Inconvenient for the topic at hand. I shift again. "Cricket and I dated for a year. She cheated on me, so I ended it."

"Oh, Gavin. I'm so sorry."

I smile at her compassion. "Don't be. We weren't meant for each other." Her thoughtful eyes are still on me as I ask, "And you? Did you see anyone in Tennessee?"

She shakes her head. "Not really."

"I can't imagine how a beautiful woman like you kept men away," I muse.

She chuckles. "I wasn't really looking."

"And now you are?"

Blake moves closer to me this time. "We're really bad at this Twenty Questions game."

I grin. "Well, are you?"

Her mouth hovers over mine. "I wasn't. But then some pushy cowboy made me ride a mechanical bull."

I lick my lips. "I'm glad he did."

"I think I might be glad he did, too." Unable to stop myself any longer, I seal my lips over hers and kiss her like she's oxygen.

She tastes like cheap beer, but hell if I care. We kiss for a long time until someone a table over yells for us to get a room.

Blake pulls back and laughs. I turn to the man who yelled and give him a glare that tells him to back off. He holds up his hands, and Blake snickers, pulling on my bicep so I bring my attention back to her.

"No more fights, Cowboy. We were being a little over the top."

I lick her taste from my lips. "What can I say?" I pull her back to me again. "You're worth fighting for."

She smiles. "Maybe you should be a lyricist. You really are good with words."

As her mouth opens again, the lights dim, and the crowd goes wild. The brassy sound of a harmonica fills the air, and my adrenaline picks up. I take my shot of whiskey and motion for her to do the same.

"To a night of fun dancing together," I declare. "And to you, Blake, for giving me a chance to redeem myself."

Her cheeks color as a smile bright enough to light a room appears on her face. My heart clenches, and it's as if I've been struck by lightning. Some may say it's too soon, but I swear to all that is holy, I fall in love with her right in this moment. Deep down I think I've always loved her, even when I was too young and didn't understand it. It's why I did what I did that night with the bull. It's why I couldn't stop pursuing her even when I tried.

"You're welcome. I'm glad you kept at me, Cowboy," Blake says sincerely.

"My pleasure, Cowgirl."

She brings her glass up to tap mine. "To a night of fun dancing together," she says, echoing my earlier words. Then she leans forward and presses into me, her voice husky as she says, "And to hot sex later in my parents' house."

My body vibrates as I laugh with my entire being.

Good God, I love this woman.

CHAPTER 27

Blake

GAVIN AND I SLAM our empty shot glasses down before he pulls me out to the dance floor. There's got to be at least a hundred people here, if not more. Besides Gavin's friend Miles, and the few people he introduced me to at the bar, I don't see a face I know. It's freeing, and I'm grateful that he's brought me somewhere I don't have to be on my best behavior. For a night, I don't have to worry about gossiping Abbey Allen telling Mom about my public displays of affection.

With pressure on my low back, Gavin pulls me into him and gives me a kiss. "You ready to dance?" The twangy sound of the guitar and bass fill the air—I recognize the song as "Suds in the Bucket" by Sara Evans before the woman on stage even starts singing. It's an oldie, but perfect for two-stepping.

"I'm ready." I smile. Gavin places his hand on my upper shoulder and I put mine over his so it rests on the top of his arm near his bicep, while our right hands come together. For a second, I feel nervous. He said he could two-step, but a two-stepping champion? I can two-step, but not at champion level.

"Relax, Blake. I've got you," he says into my ear.

I let out a breath, and he starts to move us. I find myself stumbling over my feet like a novice, and my frustration rises. My competitive nature doesn't like that I'm failing, especially at something I know how to do. Despite my two left feet, Gavin doesn't falter. He rocks us, then turns me out then back in so I land against his chest much like how he did on stage at Night Hawk. I let out a laugh as my muscles ease.

"You got this," he assures me. "Don't think so much. Feel the music and let me lead."

I think his words are meant to be more than just about dancing. Would it be so bad to let myself not think so much? Let this beautiful man before me lead? He's let me take my own pace so far, even let me use his body. I think it's time I return the favor, let him have what he wants.

He leans forward so he doesn't have to scream over the music. "Quick, quick, slow, slow," he says, his voice a low hum. "Quick, quick, slow, slow." I let his low tones soothe me and the music fill me. "That's it, baby." He kisses my cheek. "You know how to do this, just surrender."

After I start to get more comfortable, and I can feel the alcohol settling into my bones, I become more at home in my body. Gavin notices and leads us in more complicated steps. In my mind I keep saying quick, quick, slow, slow, then he does a hand change and spins me. This time I don't lose my balance.

"Nice," he says.

As the song changes to "Honey Bee" by Blake Shelton, we fall right into step. Other couples are moving around us, but I don't even notice them. We get more comfortable, and Gavin and I start to move as one body. The smile on my face shows him how much fun I'm having, and for once, everything feels perfect. I forget about the upcoming anniversary; I forget about the arguments with my parents or any thoughts of what comes next—it's just me and the cowboy I once thought I should hate.

As the music picks up, he turns me outside to a shoulder catch, then to an inside turn with a barrel roll, then wraps me and sends me back out and around before bringing me in so I brush up against his chest. He pulls me so our lips almost touch, then he dips me. A laugh escapes my mouth before he brings me back to him. This time, our lips do connect. It's a short kiss, but one I'll remember forever. He smiles as he pushes me back out and we begin to move together to the sounds of people cheering around us.

"You're a natural," he says, twisting me out again.

"You're a great partner." His lips turn up and we continue to dance. I lose track of time, and before I know it, the band leaves the stage to take a break and music starts to play over the loudspeaker.

Gavin pulls me to the bar to get a drink, and several people come over to compliment us on our dancing. Gavin graciously thanks them, shining like the star he is. He's amazing at handling people and crowds. It makes me wonder why he never thought of being a professional entertainer or dancer. He'd also be a great teacher outside of dancing nights at Night Hawk. I stick that in my head to ask him later.

Gavin hands me a beer, and we toast. We're both sweaty and my feet are killing me. Even though I've been having the time of my life, I probably won't be able to walk tomorrow. Not that I'll ever admit that to him.

After we drain our beers, he leans forward to give me a lingering kiss. It's sweet and makes my toes curl.

"What was that for?" I ask when he pulls back.

His green eyes sparkle as he lifts his shoulders. "Do I need a reason to kiss my girl?" The tone in his voice has me thinking he's asking more than one question.

I bite the inside of my cheek and blush. "Your girl?"

The corner of his mouth tilts up. "I've been wanting to talk to you about it. See where your head is at with us."

My stomach flips. "You have?"

He puts his beer down on the bar and pulls my body into his so there's no space between us. "We may be new, Blake, but you can't deny we fit together. It's been too long since I've gone after what makes me happy, and you make me happy."

My mouth goes dry at the intensity of his words. Once again, I forget there's people around us. He looks at me like I've hung the moon. And I can't deny that being his girl sounds perfect—and sexy as hell.

He trails his finger down my round jaw. "What do you say?"

"Does this mean I can't see Jake on the side?" I tease.

I squeak as he pulls my lips to his. This kiss is possessive and rough, like he'll lay me on the bar and have his way with me if I let him. When he pulls back, he bites my lip and I swallow a pleasurable sigh.

"Don't joke about that, Blake, or I might have to kill one of my good friends."

I laugh, and he kisses me again. There are more catcalls around us, with some people pushing into our bodies, annoyed that we're hogging the bar space. My hands grip Gavin's biceps, and his gaze turns playful.

"Want to get out of here?" I ask him.

"Answer my question first, baby. Then I'll take you anywhere you want to go."

Excitement tickles my insides, and like him, I decide to do what I know will make me happy. And though it feels scary, I don't want to hide from him or my feelings like I've been hiding from most things in my life the last five years.

I reach up and cup his cheek, locking his eyes with mine. "I'm yours."

His face breaks into a sly smile. "And I'm yours." He gives me a lingering kiss. "Now let's get out of here."

CHAPTER 28

Blake

We pull up to a lookout on the outskirts of Randall. In the time it took us to get here, I thought I was going to jump out of my skin. But Gavin laid out a plan, and he's made it clear he intends to follow it. I know it involves sex, but I thought it would be in my bed back home.

He parks and grabs a pack from the backseat. I have no idea what's in it, or where he got it from, since he's been with me most of the day, but I'm so turned on I'm beyond questioning it.

"Wait here." He grins, not giving me a chance to answer before he's out the door. I hear him doing something in the bed of the truck, but I wait patiently for him.

After a few minutes, he opens the door and pulls me down. He presses his lips to mine before leading me to the truck bed. This place is far enough away from any sort of light pollution, so the only source of light is the nearly full moon and brilliant smattering of stars across the sky. It reminds me of white paint flicked across a black canvas. It's stunning, and the natural light lends me the ability to see outlines of trees and hills, so I can at least tell where I'm going. When the back of the truck comes into view, I see Gavin's laid out a thick blanket, two small camping pillows, and a portable lantern. My insides melt at the care he's taken putting together the modest set-up. Smiling, I climb up without preamble and he smacks my ass as I do.

"Hey!" I yelp.

"It was right there," is his only reasoning.

I shake my head as he climbs up to join me, then pulls us down so we're nose to nose. Once I'm settled, he pushes my hat off my head and breathes me in.

"Hi," he says after a moment, studying my face like he can see every freckle in the darkness.

"Hi," I say back, removing his hat as well. He brushes his finger along the bridge of my nose, then over my lips. When he presses the pad of his thumb into the flesh of my lower lip, I think I stop breathing.

"*All mine*," he whispers. His tone is one of astonishment, as if he can't believe I'm here and I said I'd be his girl. My body shivers with delight as he pulls me closer. Then he puts his mouth to mine—but his kiss isn't tender, it's devouring and hot. As if this may be the last time he'll ever kiss me. My body responds to the power of it, and I open my lips to give him better access, allowing his tongue to stroke mine in long, languid motions.

I feel his cock hardening beneath his jeans, and I let out a moan. His hand travels down my side and when it comes to the hem of my dress, he doesn't waste any time dragging his rough palm up my bare thigh, placing the thin fabric near my belly. He teases the skin there as he kisses me.

Wanting more friction, I hitch my leg over his hip to draw him closer and grind into him.

Gavin lowers one of his hands down to my ass, splaying it over the bare skin he finds there. He lets out a deep vibrating groan as he squeezes the round globe. I knew we would end up naked at some point tonight, so I chose to wear one of the only thongs I own. Judging by his reaction, I'm glad I did.

Gavin pulls back slightly, giving him room to help me remove my dress completely so I'm left in only my boots, said black thong, and a padded bra. I probably look ridiculous, but of course he doesn't care. His gaze peruses my nearly nude form, his body thrumming against my touch as his breath becomes ragged. After he's finished looking, he leans his head back, thanking the heavens for the feast he's about to receive. I let out a shudder, my body tingling in anticipation of having him inside me again. But first, there's something I want to do.

Gavin watches me with his hungry gaze as I sit up, my hands moving to his belt buckle. I think he's stopped breathing completely as I pull the leather free, then deftly unbutton his jeans and unzip his fly. When I start to push his pants down his hips, he makes a move to get up like he wants to take over.

I pin him back down to the blanket with one hand. "Relax, Gavin. Let me take care of you."

"Blake—"

"No. Now it's your turn."

For a split second, I wonder if he's going to deny me, but then a sly smile plays at his lips before he relaxes back down onto the truck bed. "If you insist." His voice is almost a purr, and the sound of it goes straight to my sex, fanning the fire that's already been kindling for hours.

More eager now, I get back to my task, moving to my knees to make it easier for me to maneuver. I put my hands at the top of his jeans and work them down. Ever the helpful man he is, Gavin lifts his hips to make it easier. With the denim now pooled by his boots and out of my way, I'm close enough to view his groin. I can see the outline of his thick cock through his white briefs and my mouth waters. I swear I see it twitch in delight at my proximity, and my inner muscles clench at the reminder of what it feels like to have him move inside me.

"Like what you see?" Gavin questions, his voice flirty. Though I notice his entire body is tense, as if he's trying to hold himself back from pouncing.

Instead of answering vocally, I lick my lips and lean down to press a kiss against his straining length, teasing it gently with a caress of my fingers for good measure. Gavin lets out a hissing noise and turns his head skyward again, the only words on his lips now a string of curses.

Excited to see him so turned on, I don't waste any more time as I push his briefs down to meet his jeans. When his cock springs free, I inhale. I've touched it, felt it inside me, but I have yet to know what it tastes like. I take his heated length in one hand, while I use my other hand to brace my body against his thigh. Looking up at him, I lean forward and kiss the crown, then let my tongue slip out to taste the salty, smooth, skin that's beaded with pre-cum.

"*Blake*," he moans out. The breathy sound of my name makes my nipples tighten and my body hum.

"Tell me how you like it," I say between licks and small kisses.

He lifts his head up, his face illuminated by the small lantern as he says, "Take your bra off."

The command in his voice sends a jolt of lightening through my system. Reluctantly I let go of his cock, pressing my hands to his corded thighs so I can sit back, my butt and thighs meeting my boots. Keeping my eyes locked on his, I move my hands to release the clasp of my bra, slowly dragging the straps down till they're free of the confines. My breasts feel heavy from all the sex hormones coursing through my system, and Gavin's eyes immediately lock on my nipples, his mouth slightly open.

"Now come back here and suck my cock, baby. I want to feel your mouth on me."

Desire floods my body, and my panties are soaked from those words alone. I know Gavin likes to talk dirty, but him telling me exactly what he wants is something else. I like it. It makes me feel wanted and needed.

Leaning forward again, I place myself back in a similar position. This time my sensitive nipples brush against the skin of his thighs, shooting electricity straight to my vagina. I moan as I take him in my hand, then move my lips over the head of his cock, my mouth enveloping him.

"That's it, baby. Your mouth feels so good." His voice is deep and low as he moves one of his hands up to grab my hair. He tugs slightly, and the feeling has me diving down to take more of him.

Gavin lets out a throaty sound and I look up at him from under my eyelashes. He likes that because he groans again before saying, "Suck, Blake. I want to feel you all over my cock."

I hum around him before I hollow my cheeks and do as he requests. I suck and move him further down my throat as I feel the hand that was in my hair move to caress the tops of my swinging breasts. The touch has me whimpering, making Gavin's cock twitch as it hits the back of my throat. I can't take all of him, but enough that the light curls on his groin tickle my nose.

I bring my head back, sucking as I do, then gently dig the nails of my right hand into his thigh as I move back down his length.

"Blake!" Gavin calls, touching his fingers to my cheek. "You're going to make me come, baby."

I move back again, releasing him with a pop. "That's the plan, Cowboy."

As I lean in to put my lips on him again, he stops me. "My turn, Blake."

"I'm supposed to take care of you." The words come out as a whine more than I intended, which has Gavin chuckling.

"Don't worry. You are." He sits up, his cock standing proud, glistening in the lantern light from my work, his clothes are down by his boots and his shirt is still on. It's sexy as hell, and I really want to finish what I started. But instead, he removes his clothes, baring himself completely to me. When his eyes connect with mine, he turns his attention to my remaining clothes.

Gavin takes my hand and lays me back on the blanket before moving down my body, his palms brushing over my naked breasts and stomach. Once he reaches my boots, he removes them, including my socks, then presses his thumbs into the arches of my feet, massaging them. My eyes roll back in pleasure at the unexpected touch. It's brief, but enough to turn me into a massive puddle.

Once satisfied, he trails kisses up my calves and to my fleshy inner thighs before he finds my center. In another dirty and entirely sexy move, he runs his nose along the dampening fabric, then leaves a kiss right where my clit is. I suck in a breath at the touch as he pulls my panties down and throws them with the rest of our clothes. Before I have time to miss the contact, Gavin is back between my legs, licking up my damp folds and exploring my vulva like he's mapping it out for future adventures.

"Oh my god," I keen as he laps at my labia. I grab the back of his head as he wraps his lips over my clit and sucks. My head falls back, and I cry out when he suctions around it again and again. My fingers dig into his scalp to keep his mouth in place, but Gavin has no issue feasting on me, using his hands to hold my thighs open as I squirm.

"Have I mentioned you taste like sugar?" he whispers against my clit. His words are ridiculous but hot all at the same time. "Addicting," he adds, running his teeth gently along the swollen nub—at that I almost lose it.

I clutch his short hair. "I'm getting close."

He looks up at me from between my legs and grins, suctioning harder as he inserts not two, but three fingers inside of me. The myriad of sensations—plus the look on his face—sends me over the edge. I convulse from pleasure while Gavin continues to slowly lick me, shepherding me through the aftershocks of my orgasm.

When my breath returns, Gavin moves up my body, leaving a wet trail of kisses up my thigh, belly, then to each pert nipple. He runs his teeth over the hardened buds, then licks and sucks his favorite spot on my neck. When he's done worshiping every spot of skin his lips desire, he hovers over me so his body is lined up perfectly with mine. I feel his firm cock hot against the fat of my stomach as I push my hips up to feel him better. He leans forward, kissing me slowly—it's hotter than any kiss I've ever experienced.

Eventually he brings his dilated pupils to meet mine. "I was right."

I let out a shallow breath. "About what?"

"Making you come is my favorite hobby."

I laugh. "But you're such a good dancer."

He kisses my lips again. "This is way better."

Our tongues move together for a while longer, our bodies slick with sweat from the heated early summer evening and our activities. I grind into his length again, trying to show him I'm more than ready to have him inside me again. He gets the message because he leans back on his knees to fetch his wallet. He pulls out a foil packet and opens it like a man on a mission before sliding the rubber over his length.

I watch in awe at the man before me. He looks like a god with the lantern and moonlight outlining all the muscles and hard lines of his body. When his eyes return to mine, he watches me, a gentle smile on his lips. It's intense, whatever is happening right now, but I feel like I've never been more seen than I have right now, more adored.

My skin is on fire as I whisper, "You're staring again."

He licks his lips. "I'm committing this night to memory." There's a reverence in his tone that makes me want to cry. "You're so beautiful," he mutters, moving back over to me so he can kiss me chastely. My body shivers with need at his words. "And all mine."

Blood pounds in my ears, and for a split second, I wonder how the hell I ended up here when only weeks ago I was running from everyone and everything. He sips at my lips again and again then puts his mouth to my ear.

"I want you to ride me, Blake. I want to see you as you come again on my cock." The tone he used earlier is back, and my body goes haywire with sensations yet again. I nod as he lies back on the blanket, head on one of the little pillows he brought.

There's adoration on his features as he holds out his hands for me. I accept them, moving my body as gently as I can so I'm straddling him. Once I'm steady, I remove my hands from his and place them on his chest, leaning forward to kiss him, his warm cock pressing into my belly.

My hair curtains around us, fizzy from the humidity and the movement of our bodies as he stares up at me, brushing his thumb over my cheek. I press my lips to his in a gentle kiss before I lean back again, taking his cock in my hand and lining it up with my entrance. Faintly I hear him say something about me being the perfect woman before he shifts his hips up, the tip of his cock pushing inside me. Our breaths hitch together as he stretches me, the burn welcome as I sink down. When my butt meets his thighs, I let out a cry of delight mixed with a touch of pain. He feels so big inside me at this angle, almost too big.

"Relax, Blake." He moves his hands to my waist, stroking his hands along the skin there. "You feel so good, baby. So right."

His words sooth me and send another wave of tingles through my body. I press my hands on his chest again, angling myself so my breasts are above his head and his cock hits that spot inside of me that has me gasping. Gavin takes one of his hands and starts to pinch and play with my nipples, more wetness pooling between my thighs. With my body adjusted, I start to move my hips up and down.

"Yes, Blake," Gavin says, taking the hand from my breast to my waist again. He clutches me, thrusting up at the right time.

"Yes! Just like that," I cry, digging my nails into his skin and pressing myself back so he moves deeper. Fuck, I feel so stretched, so full. This is unreal.

"Ride me faster, baby," Gavin growls, maneuvering a hand between my legs so he's touching my clit.

"More," I chant, clenching my inner muscles around him. He sucks in a breath, pistoning upwards as I bring myself down onto him and move my hips in a small circle.

"Kiss me, baby," he murmurs. I lean forward and do as he asks, our lips connecting as he uses his tongue to open my mouth. His pelvis continues to move but now I miss the angle I was getting from before. I remove my lips from his and lean back, arching a bit, so my hands are pressing on the tops of his legs, then I start to move up and down at a quicker pace, bouncing on his cock.

Gavin swears under his breath, watching my tits move and biting his lip with almost a pained expression.

"God, you make me crazy, Blake. I wish we could do this every night."

I let out a breathy chuckle. "Maybe we can."

He groans as I lean forward again, angling myself so I can brush my clit against his pelvis, and he can fondle my breasts again. The combination of sensations has me teetering on the edge of orgasm.

"I'm going to come," I cry out.

"Do it, baby."

"Come with me."

"Trust me," he says breathlessly, "I'm not far behind."

He rolls one of my nipples in his fingers and thrusts his hips up again. I feel my orgasm coming hard and fast.

"That's it, Blake. Come for me."

I shudder, his words doing me in. With one more thrust of his hips I'm falling apart on top of him. I teeter forward, and in a move that has me squealing, I'm on my back and Gavin is above me. It was so fast I hardly had time to feel the absence of his cock inside. He slides back in easily, hovering over me as he thrusts like a wild man, his lips attaching to my neck.

I cry out again as another orgasm starts to build. How is that possible? Gavin latches on to my lips while he moves inside me, the sound of my arousal reaching my ears at his frantic movements.

"Fuck, Gavin. I'm going to come again!"

"Do it, baby. I want to feel you milk my cock." He grunts as he thrusts, sweat on his brow as he touches his fingers to my clit, swirling around it until I feel like I might cry or scream with pleasure.

I reach up and tug his hair, calling out his name. He lets out a throaty noise, moving his hips once, twice, and pinches my clit at the same time. We both orgasm together, the sounds of our cries surrounding us as Gavin falls gently on top of me, spent.

Once he catches his breath, he pulls out, plastering us together so my back is against his chest and he can kiss my shoulder.

When I can breathe normally, I turn my head to look into his eyes. I commit his satiated and handsome face to memory, just as he'd done with my body earlier.

He half-grins. "What's that look for?"

"I think I found my new favorite hobby."

His smile widens. "Oh yeah? What is it?"

"Multiple orgasms."

A loud laugh booms from his chest, his body thrumming against mine as he pulls me tighter into him. "You're something else, Blake Tanner—but I like it. I like it a lot."

CHAPTER 29

Gavin

MY BODY WAKES UP to a rooster crowing outside and Blake's soft snores. After we had sex under the stars, we cuddled for a bit before I brought her back to her ranch for round two—then we fell asleep in exhaustion from a full day's work and a night of dancing and sex.

I snuggle into her soft warmth, her backside pressing into my morning wood. Even after being thoroughly satisfied, my cock still wants to spend the day inside her. I don't blame him. If I didn't have to get back home, I'd lock her in this house until she couldn't walk.

When the rooster crows again, Blake stirs, pushing herself further into my hardening length. I press my forehead into her shoulder and bite the skin in a playful nip. She moans, turning her head slightly so I can see one of her eyes opening. Her hair is mussed and her gaze sleepy, but I could stare at her for hours and still find something new to look at. Like how some of her freckles make diamond patterns on her cheeks, and there's a small mole on her upper lip that I want to kiss.

"Good morning," she says, her voice painted with sleep.

I twirl one of her curls around my finger. "Morning."

When she wakes up enough to feel my arousal, her eyes go wide and she bites her lip.

I chuckle. "Don't worry about it, baby. That's going to happen every time I wake up next to you." *And every time I don't*, I think silently.

"If you hadn't worn me out last night, I'd consider another round."

I smile into her hair before kissing it, then rub my thumb against her ribcage in a soothing movement. After some time, she starts to doze off, but then the damn rooster crows again. She flips over and presses her head into my chest, grumbling something about stupid roosters.

"Kade hates roosters, too," I say. "When we were kids, he woke up early one morning and moved our entire chicken coop out past the big barn. Gran was pissed at him, but he gave his word he'd go get her eggs every morning just so he could get a few extra minutes of sleep."

Her lips turn up. "Did he keep his promise?"

"Up until Dad died," I admit. Blake tenses in my arms at the mention of him. "He still tries, but he's missed more than he cares to admit."

Blake reaches up and strokes my cheek. "That day we went out to push cattle, Kade was mad at you," she states.

I take in a short breath. "It's been hard since Dad's death. Kade hasn't figured out how to deal with his grief, and he's angry about how Dad left things. It led Kade to self-destructing behavior."

Blake presses her finger into my chin. "I can relate to that."

I know she can, which is why I've tried to avoid bringing up my problems. Especially this close to Reed's death day. I tuck some hair behind her ear. "Grief is a strong thing that's private and personal. But I think Kade is turning a corner. We had a good talk at Devil's Rock."

"I'm happy to hear that," she says sincerely. "And what about you?

"What about me?"

She chews on her bottom lip like she always does. I'm surprised that thing isn't shredded. Her tone is sincere and hopeful as she says, "You know, this talking thing goes both ways. You can tell me what's on your mind. I can help you lighten the load."

I brush my knuckles along her cheek. "You already have enough to deal with, baby. I don't want to burden you."

She presses her forehead to mine. "I want you to tell me. It would help me, I think."

I quirk an eyebrow at her, surprised. "Yeah?"

"Yeah. It will take my mind off...well, everything."

I press a kiss to her nose. "I can take your mind off things in many other ways that don't involve my depressing issues."

She gently shoves me. "I'm being serious, Gavin—and it's not really that. Like I told you before, I want to take care of you. Just like you take care of me."

I puff out a breath. "I've never been good at sharing my feelings."

"You don't say."

I lunge forward and tickle her sides. She squirms erratically, her leg kicking me in the shin.

"Ouch!" I yelp.

She cackles. "You deserve it."

I pin her easily, trying to ignore the way her breasts press into my chest and her hips meld into mine like a missing puzzle piece. I let out a small sigh as I stare down at her probing eyes. "Do you really want to know, Blake?"

"I do. But if you don't want to tell me, you don't have to, I just—"

I stop her with a kiss, letting myself indulge in her lips before our conversation turns serious. My insecurities are coming to the surface, and I don't know how she'll react when I tell her the shame Dad tried to keep hidden from the world for so long. The shame I've continued to hide from those I love. When I finally pull away, I lean down and press my brow to hers.

"If I tell you, baby, will you promise not to judge me?" The weak timber of my tone surprises me.

Blake reaches up and runs her hand down my cheek, her gesture sweet and tender. "I won't, Gavin. I promise."

I lie down next to her and pull her into me so I can see her face. "The Montgomery Family Ranch can't operate any longer. We have a month, maybe two, if we're lucky."

Blake sits up, her face horrified. "Oh, Gavin! I'm so sorry."

"Dad left the place in deep shit. He took out a second mortgage when we were kids and never told Gran or Momma. Then he took out loans and credit cards until he couldn't get a cent more. Since the day the ranch was handed over to me, I've been up to my eyeballs in paperwork, and the bank won't quit calling. I've thought about every way to save us, but the charity event helped to feed the animals and not much more than that."

Blake holds my hand, squeezing it tight. She's silent for a while before she says, "Your family doesn't know, do they?"

Guilt racks me as I shake my head. "They know we're hurting, but they think it's just because of the drought."

She runs a hand through my hair. "I think they'd understand if you told them."

I stay quiet for a second. "They thought Dad was a saint. That he took care of what he needed to. I don't have the heart to ruin his memory. And with how Kade's been—all his drinking—I don't know if he'll be able to handle the truth. It might send him over the edge. Especially now that I've waited so long."

Blake sighs sadly. "I'm sorry you've had to deal with this alone."

I shrug. "It's my own fault, but I've always been the one to take care of the family when Dad couldn't. He trained me for this day. I just didn't think he'd leave me with such a mess."

To my surprise, my eyes start to burn. When Blake notices the change in my demeanor, she melts herself into me, burying her face in my neck. I don't know how she knows I need a moment, but she does. She holds me, letting me work through the shit in my mind.

"When you asked me about my hobbies yesterday, I sort of panicked," I eventually say.

She kisses my jaw gently. "Why is that?"

"At first, I didn't think I had any, but after last night I realized two-stepping really is my hobby...or was. I used to go at least a couple times a week before shit hit the fan." My body goes tense.

"What is it?" Blake asks.

I work a swallow around the lump in my throat. "I feel guilty for enjoying myself. Dad lost his life, and I've been complaining because he made mine harder. I'm being selfish."

Blake shakes her head, then tips my chin. "You deserve a good life, Gavin. Just because your dad left you in a pile of shit doesn't mean it's only your burden, or that you can't be happy."

I tense. "You sound like Kade."

"Gavin—"

I cut her off. "You're not wrong. I'm going to have to tell them, and I realize I'm a coward for not owning up to the truth sooner."

"You're not a coward. I think anyone in your shoes would be having a hard time. I, for one, know how difficult it can be when family and emotions are involved. You're doing the best you can."

The words I spoke to her weeks ago bounce back at me, and I know she's right. I *am* doing the best I can, even if it's been the wrong choice.

She's quiet for a second before I run my thumb along her bottom lip. "What are you thinking?"

"That you're a strong and capable man. That you love your family, your ranch, and that you'll do the right thing."

I hum, staring at her for a while longer, letting my troubles fall away in the depths of her dark eyes.

"Gavin?" She asks a moment later.

"Yeah, baby?"

"If you could do anything besides being a rancher, what would you do?"

A heavy feeling settles in me. The thought of losing the ranch and figuring out what the hell I'd do with my life to support my family is a hard one to imagine, but one I've been thinking about more and more recently as the little money I have left dwindles.

I must be silent for too long because Blake places her hand over my heart. "If you answered from here, maybe you wouldn't have to think so hard."

She has a point. I close my eyes and place my hand over hers. After a time, I say the first thing that comes to mind. "I'd travel the world and pick up odd jobs to get by. Maybe dance through all the honky-tonks." I wink at her.

She smiles. "I've always wanted to travel, too. I did a bit when I raced, but I've never been outside of the U.S. and Canada. I planned on it before the accident but, here I am."

"And what would you do if you weren't a rancher?"

Blake debates what to say next. Her eyes blink and then she smiles. "Travel with you—maybe find stock for our ranch's horse breeding program in other countries."

My mouth goes dry, and I crush her body to mine. "You're making that up."

She laughs. "And if I'm not?"

I hover my lips over hers. "Then it's a nice dream to think about it."

Blake puffs out a small breath, running her hand through my hair. "It is a nice dream."

I seal my lips over hers, knowing I need to get home to work; to pour myself over paperwork again and gather the strength to tell my family I've been keeping a big secret from them.

But right now, I'm content to pretend that it's only Blake and me—minus the million things weighing us down—and the date I know she's fearing on our heels.

CHAPTER 30

Blake

I LOOK UP FROM my laptop on the kitchen table to the floral calendar on the wall. Mom doesn't have anything marked on tomorrow's date except for a small heart in the corner. Not that I would expect her to write "The Day Reed Died" on it, but it feels like it's written there in invisible ink.

It's funny how one day out of the year can hold so much power. How most people will wake up tomorrow, thinking it's just another day, but for me, it's the day I spend three-hundred and sixty-five days a year thinking about. It doesn't escape me, however, that the last few weeks I've been thinking about it less due to a certain insatiable cowboy. In fact, this morning, I woke up happy—or at least happier compared to my usual state. Unfortunately, that only infects me with guilt, especially when Reed will never get the chance to be happy again.

I grit my teeth. I should probably take the advice I gave Gavin. Because deep down, I know I deserve to be happy—yet I can't seem to fully let myself. It feels wrong. I rub my temples to try and clear my negative thoughts. Thankfully I've got a project to keep my mind occupied: Saving the Montgomery Ranch.

Since Gavin told me his secret after our dance and sex-a-thon night last week, my mind hasn't stopped racing. Going into debt is a reality ranchers and farmers have had to deal with for a long time—and the drought has sealed the fate of too many. But that doesn't mean we have to lie down and let it happen, which is why I've been trying to find a way to help.

"Good morning, baby girl." Daddy walks into the kitchen and nods in greeting. It's only past five in the morning, but he's alert. He's probably been up all night thinking about tomorrow.

"Morning, Daddy."

He fills a cup of coffee before pulling out the chair across from me. Close-up, I see how tired he looks as he skims yesterday's paper. I can also tell he's trying not to ask how I am. He must be wondering. With my days filled to the brim with work and Gavin, I've spent almost no time with my parents. They seem happy about it, given I'm no longer a sulking grump or accidently hurting Mom. I cringe at the memory.

"Everything okay?" he fishes.

I push the lid of my laptop down and pick up my warm coffee mug. "Not exactly sure how to answer that question," I answer truthfully.

"That's fair." He sips his coffee.

"What about you, Daddy?"

He contemplates before answering. "It's always hard around here at this time, but it's a little easier this year."

He's referring to me being home. The guilt that's been building in me doubles, and I find myself no longer wanting my coffee.

"Daddy—"

He waves his hand. "I don't want to upset you. Your mom and I are just glad you're here this year, is all. The house has been so quiet—" His voice wavers, but like the old-school man he is, he shoves it down.

Tears prick my eyes. "I'm glad I'm here too, Daddy." He looks at me with surprise. A month ago, I wouldn't have said that, but now, things have changed.

A small smile turns up at the corner of his lips. "Is it because of the Montgomery boy?"

I wring my hands under the table nervously. Why is talking to your daddy about boys so embarrassing? I'm almost thirty, for goodness' sake. "A little," I say truthfully. "But it's more than that."

He nods. "You're different—lighter. I enjoy seeing it." I study his warm features for a moment, and I know he means it. "You know your mom and I have always wanted that for you, right, baby girl?"

I swallow past the emotion in my throat. "I know, and I'm sorry I've been so hard on you both, it's just..."

Daddy places a hand on mine. "You don't have to explain. I wasn't there that day, but trust me when I say I wish I was. I'd do anything to take the last five years of pain away from you."

This time my tears do fall. "Don't say that Daddy."

He squeezes my hand. "I know you don't believe it, but you're a strong woman. You always have been. You like to deal with things on your own, which I'll admit is part of your upbringing. Please know that we're here for you, and we love you no matter what."

I take in his words but don't say anything. Hearing the man I admire most say those words has me reeling a bit, especially since I've done nothing but give him and Mom grief.

After the silence becomes too much, he continues, "Your Mom and I were wondering if you'd come to Reed's grave tomorrow. With it being the five-year anniversary, we've asked the Pastor to come say some words. Several people from town will be there, too. I know it may be asking too much, but we would like for you to stand with us."

My shoulders tense, and I pull my hand out from under his. I've been avoiding thinking about the tradition they have of going to Reed's grave on each anniversary. It's usually just my parents and a few of Reed's friends, like Gavin and Jake. Or at least that's what Mom told me every year when she'd ask me to come home for it.

My stomach turns as I imagine waking up tomorrow, getting ready, and going to stand in front of Reed's grave with potentially half the town's eyes on me. I swallow down the bile and look back up at Daddy's hopeful eyes.

"It would mean a lot to us, Blake."

I know it would mean a lot to them. I know it would mean a lot to all the people who love Reed, too. Gavin, included. Maybe it's time I be brave and do what I should've done years ago: face tomorrow head-on.

"Okay," I blurt out.

Daddy tries to hide his shock, but he doesn't do a very good job. I see the way his eyes bulge a bit, and his skin turns slightly white. He has a right to be shocked, though; my brain is still trying to catch up to the fact that I agreed.

He folds his arms over his chest and eyes me suspiciously. "You took that better than I thought. I guess that Montgomery boy really is doing you some good."

My cheeks turn pink. I know he said that to lighten the mood, but hell, it's mortifying.

"Let's not talk about boys, Daddy."

He chuckles. "Good, because I don't really want to talk about them. You'll always be my baby girl."

My eyes meet his in a tender expression. "I know."

We sit in silence for a few minutes, drinking our coffee and thinking about Reed. When he stands, he taps my computer. "Are you trying to help the Montgomerys?"

Now I'm the one who looks shocked. "How do you know that?"

He half grins. "Doesn't take a genius to figure it out."

I fold my arms in front of me and give him a look. "Have you been snooping?"

"I haven't. But I did make a stop at the bank yesterday, and Gavin was speaking with the loan officer. By the way he looked when he left, I don't think it was good news."

My heart clenches for Gavin and his family. "It's not good."

Daddy sits back down, crossing one of his long jean-clad legs over the other. I see the wheels spinning in his brain. "You know, your Mom and I brought our place out of debt, and look at what we have now."

It's true. Daddy's family had been using our land mostly for cattle before they got married. The Tanner breeding operation was tiny at the time, and only had one good stallion and a couple broodmares. Marrying Mom really turned this place around for them, not to mention Daddy's eye for good stock and Mom's mind for business. They're a perfect team, one I've always admired.

I release a breath. "I don't know if their place can be saved, and I don't want to say out of respect for Gavin, but it's..." I trail off, not having to finish the sentence.

"Have you looked into loans to turn their property into a dude ranch?"

My interest piques. I try to imagine Gavin running a dude ranch, and realize he'd be great at it. He's great at hosting people, and he's personable. Ruby is the same way. Then there's Kade. He'll probably sleep with half the women who come through. I smirk at the thought.

"How'd you think of that?" I ask Daddy.

He lets out a laugh. "Margie's been making me watch all these reality shows on TV while she heals up. There was one on a dude ranch in Arizona."

"I don't know if he can get another loan," I say honestly. "But it's a nice idea."

Daddy comes over and looks at me funny, as if he's trying to tell me something with his eyes. After a time, he squeezes my shoulder. "There's always a way, Blake. Keep searching."

"Thanks, Daddy."

He nods. "Alright. I've got animals to feed and horses to work." He walks to the sink and puts his empty mug down. "See you out there?"

"Yeah. Just going to look at a few more things."

He grabs his Stetson off the table and places it on his head. Right before he walks out the door, he turns to me. "Blake, baby?"

"Yeah?"

"There's always loans that don't come from a bank." I raise a brow at him, but he only winks and walks out the door.

What did he mean by that? He said it like I should know what he's thinking.

I take a sip of my cold coffee before opening my laptop again and entering in loan types. What Daddy said about the dude ranch is a good idea, but if Gavin's maxed out, I doubt he'll get a private or personal loan.

As multiple searches pop up, I groan. Time to dig in.

When I walk into Gavin's guest house later that evening, I know he's shocked to see me. We planned to get together tonight, but not for a few more hours.

He smiles wide as I make myself comfortable on his lap. "What are you doing here?"

I'm holding a few papers in one hand as I wrap my arms around his neck and kiss him hard. This is unlike my normal behavior, but I'm too excited to contain myself. When I pull back, he's dazed, and I can feel him hardening beneath me.

"Keep it in your pants, Cowboy," I say, laughing.

He leans forward and kisses my neck. "Then don't come in here and kiss me like that."

I push him away playfully. "We don't have time for that."

Gavin pulls me back in, ignoring my protests. I let him explore my mouth awhile, enjoying the lingering taste of peppermint toothpaste and the warmth of his hands on my waist. When he starts to lift my shirt, I press my hand into his chest. We're both breathing hard, and he looks awfully proud of himself for winding me up.

"We can kiss later, but right now, I have something I need to show you."

He lets out a groan. "Then you have to get off my lap, or show's over."

I bite back a grin and climb off, teasing him as I do. He groans painfully and adjusts himself. While he does, I admire him in his black T-shirt and jeans. He's sexy at work. Who am I kidding? He's sexy all the time.

"Blake," he chides playfully. "Stop looking at me like that."

I chew on my bottom lip. "Sorry, you just look so good."

"Then let's play." He tries to pull me back into him.

I stop him by holding up the papers I have in my hand. "First, work."

"What work could you possibly have for me?"

I put the papers on his desk and smile. "I've been researching ways to save your ranch."

Several emotions cross his face in a matter of seconds. Is he mad that I'm trying to help? Before I can think too much about it, he grabs my face and plants one on me. It's a strong and solid kiss, one that tells me he's grateful.

When he lets me go, his gaze is full of awe. Or maybe—no. It can't be love, it's too soon. I shake off those silly thoughts and turn his attention to the papers.

"Now, before I say this, I want you to know I didn't tell my daddy anything you told me. But he saw you at the bank the other day and said you walked out stressed, so he asked me how your ranch is doing."

I see Gavin's jaw tighten. "What did you tell him?"

"Nothing all of Randall already doesn't know, but he gave me an idea." I tap the pages I printed off. "Now, by no means am I a business expert, but I did take a few classes at the community college—not surprisingly, the internet has templates for everything these days."

Gavin watches me carefully. I see amusement shine through his expression at my rambling. "Go on," he urges.

"Daddy asked if you ever considered turning this place into a dude ranch."

"A dude ranch?" he questions.

"Yeah, you know, a place where people come from all over to experience ranch life. They get to stay overnight for different amounts of time, go on horseback rides, hayrides, learn how to two-step." I smirk.

"And you think my ranch could be something like that?"

"I do."

He hums thoughtfully. "It's a nice idea. But how would we get the money to start something like that? I'll need to renovate the old hand quarters, maybe even turn this guest house into a suite or something. I hardly have money to feed the chickens, let alone a bunch of city folk on vacation."

I tap the papers again. "I came up with a rough business plan. It outlines everything we'll need to do, the help we need to hire, etc."

The left corner of his mouth turns up. "We?"

"Well, that depends on you."

"Meaning?"

"Just read it!"

He lifts the documents off his desk and leans back. His eyes track over the pages, but he never shows any sign of what he's thinking. My nerves ball in my stomach. I hope I haven't crossed a line by doing this.

After a few minutes, he puts the pages down, staring at them while he thinks. When I can't take it anymore, I place a hand on his shoulder. "Gavin, will you say something?"

"I can't take your money."

A fist clenches around my heart. I had a feeling he would say that. "It's not taking it, it's an investment," I say with conviction.

When his eyes meet mine, they're pained. "This place isn't worth investing in, baby."

I push him back, taking my place on his lap again. This time it's not playful, but I make sure he doesn't turn away from me. "It's worth investing in for me. For this town. For your family. I..." I try to choose my next words carefully. "I care about you, Gavin. I care about Ruby and your Momma, even Kade."

Gavin chuckles at that. He brushes the hair off my cheek and holds the papers up. "I don't know how long this took you, but it's a solid plan, one I never would have thought of. The fact that you'd even want to invest in us," his voice cracks, "it means a lot to me."

"Oh, Gavin," I murmur, squeezing his shoulders, "of course I would. This place matters. This ranch matters to Randall. This town sticks together, remember?"

He gives me a sad smile. "But what about traveling?"

I kiss his chin. "I'll still be able to travel—just not in the beginning. I also want your family to run the place, you can just consider me the bank. Though I don't want you to pay me back until you're earning revenue. I won't consider anything else."

He huffs a laugh. "You really think this could work?"

"Look what you, Jake, and Kade did for Night Hawk. That place is booming. With the help of social media and word of mouth, I'm sure we could make this place a destination spot. Hell, I bet you'll make bank on wedding bookings alone."

"Your daddy really gave you this idea?"

"He did. He even planted the seed of private funding. It didn't occur to me until my fifth cup of coffee that I have my winnings from racing sitting in an account." I don't mention I've got some inheritance from my Gramps as well.

Gavin's brow furrows. "And if it fails?"

I grab his face in mine. "It won't."

"But if it does?"

"Then I'll run off to Europe and find a sugar daddy."

He tickles my ribs. I squeal and try to get off his lap, but he won't let me.

"Stop! Stop! Stop!" I cry.

"Take that back, Blake Tanner!"

"Okay, okay! I take it back," I yell breathlessly.

He finally stops, that same look of awe on his face again. "I can't believe you thought of this and wrote this up all in one afternoon."

"I may have ignored all of my chores, but I'm determined."

He takes my chin in between his fingers and kisses me hard. After he pulls back, he still holds my face. "I'll have to talk to my family about it. I still need to come clean as to why we'll need your help in the first place."

"I understand. I don't expect you to decide now. But I want you to know that it's an option." I point to the papers. "There's also some other ideas in here."

He traces the bridge of my nose. "You're amazing."

I smile. "Doing my part to save my home."

His eyes bore into mine. He knows I'm doing it for a lot more than just saving our community from ruin, but it feels too soon—too vulnerable—to say more than that. This explanation will have to be enough for now.

CHAPTER 31

Gavin

IT'S NOT EVEN NINE in the evening but Blake is sleeping soundly. I wore her out by spending hours thanking her for all her hard work. Sex is an easy way to distract her from thoughts of tomorrow.

I rub my furrowed brow as I sit at the kitchen table with a finger of whiskey and Blake's business plan in my hand. It's a good plan, though I don't care for the idea of taking her money. If it was a small amount, I could deal with it, but it's not.

My eyes find the stunning creature in my bed. The sheet is down around her breasts, and her face is relaxed in sleep. In just over a month, I've become a willing slave to her. She infiltrates my every thought, my dreams. When she sat on my lap earlier and told me of her plan for my ranch, I knew I wasn't just falling in love with her—I *am* in love with her. I've never been surer of anything in my life.

When I'm with her, it's as if everything rights itself. As if nothing can go wrong when she's near me, and with how she's willing to put her own money on the line to help my family. Good God, Blake Tanner is perfect...maybe too perfect for someone like me. But I'm too selfish to let her go now. Not that I could.

Knock, Knock, Knock. I jump up at the sound, my gaze darting to a still sleeping Blake. Not wanting another knock to wake her, I stand and move to the door as quietly as possible. Even before

I get to it, I know it's Kade on the other side. He's the only one who comes to the guest house at this time of night. I open it a crack and then slip out, preventing him from getting an eyeful of the voluptuous body on my bed.

Kade gives me a slick smile when I exit, my disheveled appearance and the way I crept out giving away what I'd been up to before. I punch him playfully in the arm before gesturing to him to stay quiet. He follows me to two old Adirondack chairs I have set up in the backyard. It's far enough that we shouldn't wake Blake.

Kade still has a smirk on his face as we settle in.

I huff a small laugh. "Don't look at me like that."

"Like what?" he teases.

"Like you're imagining what happened in there."

Kade screws up his face. "Blake's a beautiful woman, but I'm still trying to get the image of you going at it out of my head."

I shake my head. It's nice to see Kade more relaxed. Ever since our talk at Devil's Rock last week, he's been in a completely different mood. Gran even asked if he'd been abducted by aliens. And unless he's been hiding it, I still haven't seen him drunk once. He even stopped taking numbers from girls at Night Hawk. It makes me wonder if it's because of the woman he said he spooked, or something else.

"What did you come to chat about?" I ask, leaning back to look at the night sky.

"Gran wanted me to check on you since you didn't come up for dinner. I told her I saw a Tanner truck driving in earlier. She was hoping you'd bring Blake up for pie."

"She's sleeping, and I don't want to wake her." Blake needs her rest. I know she hasn't been sleeping well due to nightmares. Not that she talks about them, but I've seen her enough in the last weeks to know she's plagued by them.

"Are you two dating now, or what?" Kade asks.

I rub the back of my neck. *Dating*...it feels more than that. "It's complicated."

Kade chuffs. "Women are complicated." His words are laced with meaning. Maybe I was right in thinking that woman he mentioned has something to do with his mood change.

"I can't disagree with you there. Though I'm sure they'd say the same about us."

"I'm not that complicated," he says, a stupid grin covering his face at the lie.

I chuckle, looking back up at the night sky. "Keep telling yourself that, little brother."

There's a moment of silence before Kade asks, "I'm assuming you're going to the grave tomorrow for Reed's remembrance?"

"I am. You know I go every year to support the Tanners."

Kade clears his throat. "Gran mentioned she heard through town gossip that Blake's going. Will you be with her?"

My body stiffens, guilt tickling my gut. I'd been so distracted earlier with her plans for the dude ranch, then with sex, I didn't even ask her if she planned on going tomorrow. Earlier this week, I tried to mention it, but it never seemed like the appropriate time to bring it up again. Though part of me hoped she'd go—or maybe I had a feeling all along that she'd be there.

I lick my dry lips. "If Blake wants me by her side, I'll be there. Will you?"

Kade grips the arms of the chair. "I don't know if I want to go to the cemetery."

Randall's Holy Heart Cemetery is the only one we have in town. We buried Dad there. I know Kade hasn't been to visit since it happened, but I've taken Gran and Momma there almost every Sunday since he died.

"You don't have to, Kade," I say honestly. "Go when you're ready."

"Momma will be pissed if I don't show."

"She won't be pissed—"

"But she'll be disappointed." Kade blows out a breath. He sits up and pats his empty pocket in search of his flask. He looks sheepish when our eyes connect. "I swear I've been cutting back.

I haven't had a drink all week, but talking about this makes me want to."

"It's okay, Kade. You're doing great."

He sits back again. "I've been meaning to talk to you, but every time I try, you're with Blake." He smirks.

I rub a hand over my evening stubble. "Well, here I am. Tell me."

He bounces his leg excitedly. "I've been looking into ways to help the ranch like we talked about."

The weight of my untruths come tumbling back into the forefront of my mind. But Kade looks pumped about whatever he's found, so I attempt to keep any evidence of my guilt from my face.

I lift my lips into a small smile. "You have?"

He pulls out his phone and shows me a website he's got bookmarked. "This is a grant website for the state of Texas. It has a list of ones we can apply for. Have you tried any of these?"

I take the phone from him and scroll through. "The ones we can apply for, I have."

Kade nods. "I figured. But have you ever thought of farming more of the land? Agriculture grants are more common."

"Yes, but that requires money and rain. Both of which we don't have."

Kade clenches his jaw. He's frustrated that I'm striking down his ideas so fast—I know that feeling well—but they aren't viable for us. Blake's idea is the first one that seems like it could work.

"What about a loan or a second mortgage?" he asks hopefully.

I bite the inside of my cheek. Kade doesn't know Dad already did that. "I don't think that's possible. With our credit…"

Kade lets out a low growl before taking his phone from me and flipping to another website. This one's for solar and wind energy. "I know it's kind of selling out, but there's a lot of money in leasing our land to alternative energy sources."

"Dad would've hated us doing that."

"Dad isn't here, Gav!" he yells, loud enough I'm sure he woke Blake. "This is our livelihood. You said I could help so I'm trying to help." He takes a breath and pinches his nose. "If we don't do something like this, what else is there to do besides sell to the city or a private developer? Dad would've hated that more."

I sigh. "I'll think about what you said."

"You'll think about it?" he parrots.

"Yes."

He stands and throws up his hands. "I've said it before, and I'll say it again. You're hiding something, and when I find out what it is, so help me God, Gavin—"

I stand up and meet him, my blood pressure rising. "You'll what?"

Kade breathes hard for a moment, his chest heaving up and down with anger. "At least you admitted you're hiding something," he spits out.

My gut twists. "This isn't the time to have this conversation."

My brother stares me down as we stand chest-to-chest. Eventually, he lets out a breath of disbelief.

"Is there ever a good time for you, Gav?

"Kade—"

"Just know that if we lose our ranch, I'm done."

"What does that mean?"

"It means I'm done. Think about what I said."

I look into Kade's pained eyes, the truth is right on the tip of my tongue. My heart is chanting for me to tell him, to end this stupid thing between us. To finally come clean and take whatever hate I get from him.

"*REED, NO!*" a heart-wrenching scream echoes from inside the guest house, making us both flinch. Kade's features transform from anger to sadness for the woman inside.

He pushes my chest. "Go to her."

Now I'm torn. My brother is in pain, but the woman I love is, too.

"Kade—"

He cuts me off. "Just go."

Nodding, I spin on my heel and stalk toward the house. When I get to the steps I turn back to Kade, who's staring after me. "We're not done with this conversation. We'll talk more after tomorrow." Without another word, I go to Blake.

When I'm inside, I don't see her on the bed, but I hear the water running in the bathroom. The door is cracked open, and she's standing underneath the spray of the shower. She's not crying, but her head hangs in defeat.

Once I'm in the bathroom, I strip off my clothes. If Blake notices me, she doesn't give any inclination. It's not until I open the frosted shower door that she looks up, eyes bloodshot. Wordlessly, I take a step into the shower, but she stops me. Before I can ask why, she turns the water from all the way cold to hot. When she's satisfied with the temperature, she moves so I can join her. I don't ask why the water was cold; instead, I pull her into me so she can bury her head against my neck.

"You're freezing, baby," I say against her wet hair, but she only squeezes me tighter, as if trying to shield herself from the world. I run my hands down her wet skin and whisper in her ear that she's okay, that I'm here for her. Words never leave her mouth, but soon her body relaxes.

When our fingers start to prune, I turn the shower off and grab two towels. I hand one to her, letting her stay in the shower since there's limited space. We dry off quietly, but my eyes never leave her as she meticulously wipes the water away, her movements precise and practiced. First drying her arms, then her round stomach and shapely legs. Then she bends over to wrap the towel around her head. When she stands up tall, her eyes meet mine.

"I'll wait outside for you," I say with a gentle smile, knowing she'll need to brush her hair and maybe relieve herself. This bathroom can't hold us both and I want to respect her privacy. She smiles back and I make my way back out to the office. I pull out a pair of comfortable shorts from the small closet. I've been keeping a few personal items down here now that Blake has been spending time over.

Once I'm dressed, I hang my towel over the back of a chair and settle into bed. The pillows and sheets have started to smell like her. She must use a rosemary-scented shampoo because the scent is sweet and herbaceous. It reminds me of the holidays, which warms my insides more. The thought of Blake and her family sitting around our Christmas tree is a wonderful image that I want to come true.

When the door to the bathroom eventually opens, my head pops up to watch Blake walk to the kitchen to grab a glass of water. She's wearing one of my big T-shirts that hugs her frame, though it's long enough to cover her ass. It's adorable, and I enjoy it way too much. After she's finished her drink, she makes her way to bed. I know she's embarrassed that I found her in the shower that way, I can tell by the way she refuses to look at me, but she has nothing to be embarrassed about.

"Come here," I murmur, opening my arms for her. She gets in and lays her head on my chest, one of her hands resting near the crook of my neck.

"Thanks," she puffs against my skin.

"You don't have to thank me. I'm here for you, Blake." The silence of the house settles around us and we hold each other. It isn't until her warmth almost lulls me to sleep that she speaks.

"I dreamt about that day. I usually don't sleep the night before the anniversary because the nightmares get so bad. They feel...so real." Her voice falters, but I let her continue. "I thought I was doing better. Being with you, working on the plan for your ranch today, it made me feel good, useful. I was able to pretend for a bit that I'm not..."

"Not what, baby?" I urge.

"Broken." A small cry breaks through, and she holds me tighter, her eyes refusing to look into mine. Kade called her broken when I first started pursuing her, and I agreed—but now I know better. I tip Blake's chin so I can see her teary eyes.

"You're not broken, Blake. You're far from it."

"I am, though," she says, pulling back. Before I know it, she's sitting up, trying to get off the bed. "Maybe I'm doing okay now, but you don't know what you're getting into with me, Gavin," she cries. "I should go."

My heart hammers in my chest at her desire to bolt. I sit up and pull her back so she can't run. Thankfully, she doesn't fight me, which is a good sign. But her words have me shaken.

"Hey now, don't make rash decisions. We're together, remember? I think you owe me the courtesy of talking through things." My words seem to snap her out of the immediate panic she's feeling, and her features soften. She bites her lower lip, and I squeeze her arms. "Take a deep breath, baby."

Our eyes connect and she inhales. It's choppy, but as she continues to breathe. Eventually, her body relaxes as her adrenaline comes back down.

"That's it," I murmur. "Now let's talk."

She nods. "Sorry."

"Don't apologize. I'm not judging you."

She takes another breath, and I pull her back down so she's lying against me again. "I panicked," she says, her body tense as I continue to rub my hand up and down her back.

"It's okay. I understand this thing between us is new, and what you went through isn't a little thing. But you're not broken, Blake. You're one of the strongest people I've ever met."

"I don't know how you could believe that."

I bring her eyes to meet mine. "Because you went through hell, and you came out on the other side. You may have shit you've got to work through Blake, but so do I. You wear your heart on your sleeve, but that doesn't make you weak. I admire you."

She blinks at me before bringing her fingers up to brush over my lips. "Where did you come from?"

The corner of my mouth turns up. "Well, my folks got married and had sex..."

She chuckles, the mood around us brightening a bit. "Who would've thought that scrawny boy running around with my pesky brother, getting into trouble, would be the one to steal my heart."

I press her into me and kiss her forehead, her words wrapping around my heart like a soothing balm. Hope blooms in my chest that maybe she feels the same way about me that I do for her.

"You know," I say after a moment. "I always had a bit of a crush on you."

She pulls back enough to look up at me. "Really?"

"How else would I have known your barrel racing record by heart? Gran made fun of me after the charity event because of that knowledge." A wide smile arrives on her face and I continue, "I never acted on anything because of our age difference, and because Reed didn't seem keen on any boys liking you."

Blake runs her fingers along my chest. "He was very protective of this old bird."

I chuckle. "You're not old. And he loved you a lot, Blake. He talked about how proud of you he was all the time."

Tears well in her eyes, but the smile doesn't leave her face. She lets what I said soak in before lifting her gaze to mine again. "Tell me your favorite memory of him."

My throat constricts with emotion. I'm surprised she's asking, but I'm more than happy to tell her. I pull her closer so we're practically nose-to-nose. "When we were freshmen, he had a crush on Polly."

"He did?"

"Yep. He talked about her nonstop. But she was already in love with Tim Corbin, we just didn't know it at the time. Anyway, we went to a Homecoming party, and he had this big speech planned out to ask her to the dance. He had no idea that someone spiked the punch. He got hammered and ended up passing out on her shoulder. The poor girl was mortified."

Blake brushes her fingers through the smattering of hair on my chest. "He never told me that."

"Reed was prideful. If anyone even teased him about it, he'd threaten to punch their lights out."

"That I can definitely believe."

The room goes quiet minus the buzz of the refrigerator and the sound of our breathing. I run my fingers along the planes of Blake's face and enjoy this time together.

"Do you want to try and get some sleep?" I ask her a few minutes later.

"You can if you want. I don't know if I'll be able to."

I take my hand from her hair and cup her face, kissing her soft lips lightly. "I'll stay awake with you."

She kisses me again, then rests her head back on my chest. "Thank you for being here, Gavin. For listening and telling me that story."

I close my eyes and hold her tighter. "There's nowhere else I'd rather be."

CHAPTER 32

Blake

I LEFT GAVIN'S THIS morning with a deep sadness, but also a feeling in my heart that's completely new. Together, we'd dozed on and off through the night, but he held me the entire time. We even finished our game of Twenty Questions. I found out that his favorite meal is spicy chili, and he has a soft spot for Taylor Swift music, though I'm not allowed to tell anyone that tidbit.

Spending the night with him made my earlier panic attack fade away and has me feeling closer to Reed. I finally feel as if this day won't swallow me whole and spit me out worse than before. Maybe I can let myself remember my brother, remember the good times we had, and connect with the people he shared his life with. I've always been too scared to let that in, as if remembering him would only make me miss him more. Which in a way, it does, but it's not bad. It's...

Healing.

I walk into my family's barn, seeking out my parents, with my head held a little higher. When I come to Briar's stall and find it empty, I make my way to the round pen. Sure enough, my parents are standing outside the corral. Daddy has his hand on Mom's lower back, and her head is on his shoulder. They're quietly staring at Briar and her baby.

I let myself watch them for a moment. Over the years I've been away, it was easy to pretend my family was better off without me. Even now, I feel like an outsider looking in. I know

I've done that to myself. I left them when they needed me the most because I've been afraid to face them, afraid they blame me for losing Reed.

Mom wipes a tear off her cheek and Daddy kisses her forehead. It doesn't take him long to spot me out of the corner of his eye. He turns his head and gives me a sad smile. When Mom notices his attention is elsewhere, her eyes follow.

"Come on over here, Blake," she says. I do as she asks, sidling up next to her and looking out at the colt who's happily munching on grass while Briar sleeps. Mom puts her hand on my shoulder and squeezes. "We were about to call the cops to come find you," she teases.

Embarrassment hits me as I avoid eye contact. "I'm here."

When I find courage, I turn to face them. I'm met with two sets of concerned eyes. I can't imagine what this day feels like for them, but as I look into their eyes, I come to realize how selfish I've been since Reed passed.

"Talk to them," Reed's voice says in my head. My eyes fill with tears, and immediately Daddy's face goes taut. Mom begins to tear up too, like they can hear Reed as well.

"I'm sorry." My voice breaks.

"For what, baby girl?" Daddy's voice is gentle, like how it used to be when we would hurt ourselves as kids.

"I'm sorry for being so reckless that day with Reed."

He interrupts, "You didn't do anything wrong—"

"No." I stop him. "Please let me finish while I have the courage. Please."

They look at each other, their lips in thin lines. But eventually, they nod for me to continue.

"I'm sorry. You say it's not my fault, but that day Reed asked me to race, he took off and I followed him. If we had just taken our time, or if I had him take a sturdier horse, he might be here."

"Blake," Mom stops me, using one hand to cup my cheek, "do you really think we ever blamed you for that day? It was an accident."

I look into her blue eyes, Reed's eyes, and feel my chest tighten. "I'm sorry," I say again. "And I'm sorry for leaving. I'm sorry for all of it."

After a heavy pause, Mom speaks. "We never blamed you, Blake."

"But—"

"Now it's my turn to talk," she says, her voice even. "Your daddy and I blamed ourselves for a long time. We were gone; we knew Reed would probably take Briar out with you, but we figured we couldn't stop it even if we were home. Your brother was stubborn, just like this entire damn family." She chuckles sadly to herself. "But after a while, when your Daddy and I started healing, we realized that the blame was a way for us to avoid the pain of him not being here. It wasn't your fault, Blake; it wasn't anyone's."

I let her words sink in. Even if they're true, I find them hard to accept. I don't know if I'll ever stop blaming myself, but to just tell them my truth already lifts the weight I've been carrying for five years off my shoulders.

"We hope you know how much we love you, baby girl. And we're glad you're home," Daddy adds, giving me a firm nod in the way he always does when he's choked up.

I look out at Briar again who stands patiently now while her baby tries to drink milk from her. "She's a great mom," I murmur. "Reed always knew she would be."

"We still have to name her colt," Daddy says.

I hum. "I've been thinking about it quite a bit."

Mom lifts an eyebrow. "You have?"

"Unless you have an idea?" I blurt out, not wanting to step on her toes. She smiles and shakes her head. My heart beats fast in my chest as I continue. "I've been discovering recently how much Reed protected me, even if it was from silly things like boys." Mom and Daddy both smile. They haven't heard me talk about Reed, but I can see it makes them happy. "I think he still protects me too," I add, "just in a different way."

"Oh, Blake honey," Mom says softly. "I think that, too."

I nod sadly. "What about Knight?" The colt perks up when I say it, and I can't help but smile. Daddy's eyes follow mine, and he smiles too.

He puts his hand on Mom's shoulder. "I think that's perfect."

Tears fill her eyes again. "I think Reed would have liked that name."

I swallow the lump in my throat. "He would've."

For a while, we watch the baby play. He's growing fast, and once again, I can't help but imagine myself riding him around barrels, feeling the wind in my hair as an announcer calls my name for the win. When I snap out of my daydream, Mom's looking at me.

"I know that look. You're thinking about riding him, aren't you?" she asks.

My back stiffens. Could I really ride again? And on Briar's colt for that matter?

"Thinking and doing are two different things," I finally admit.

Mom tucks some hair behind my ear. "Maybe in time. You don't have to push yourself."

"Thanks," I say. Because I mean that. Mom has pushed me my whole life, so this is a nice change. One that tells me she's trying, too.

"Does that mean you'll be staying with us after your mom heals up?" Daddy asks.

The question surprises me. I haven't put too much thought on the subject. My plan was to always come home, help them out, then—well, I didn't have a plan. I sold what little I had when I moved back home, and Tennessee never felt like a forever place to me. And now with Gavin—my body heats at the thought of him. If he goes through with the plan for the dude ranch, there's no way I can consider leaving, there will be so much work. But the idea excites me, and for once, I'm looking forward to my future instead of dreading it.

I turn my head and give a genuine smile to my parents, one that reaches my eyes. "I think you know the answer to that."

As they both smile at me, Knight whinnies in the background. We all burst out into laughter, and once again I find myself thanking Reed. I think everything might be okay. Okay as it can be without him.

CHAPTER 33

Gavin

THE SUN SHINES DOWN on us as I straighten my sport coat. I stand next to Jake and my family near Reed's grave. We're all here together, everyone but Kade. He hasn't made an appearance yet, which I expected. Momma's eyes keep searching the large crowd for him every few minutes, and it's heartbreaking to watch. I know coming to the cemetery is hard for him, but I wish he would've tried for her.

I turn my gaze to Blake and force myself to breathe. She looks beautiful as always, dressed in dark jeans, cowboy boots and a black button up that has an iridescent shine to it. The Tanners and some of the people who work for them wear cowboy hats like the one Reed used to wear. I'm happy she's here, and she looks okay despite it all.

I think something must've happened between her and her folks, because they're standing close together as the Pastor says a few prayers, their bodies relaxed. I don't see a hint of tension between them, only heartbreak for the memories I'm sure they're experiencing.

Blake makes eye contact with me, and I smile gently. I'd give anything to be holding her hand right now, but this isn't the time or place to let all of Randall know we're officially together, even if I want to shout it from the rooftops.

"Would anyone like to say a few words?" the Pastor asks.

After a heavy pause, a female voice says, "I do."

To my surprise—to everyone's surprise—Blake steps forward. Her eyes are glassy, but she walks confidently to the front. My heart hammers in my chest as she places a hand on Reed's gravestone. The crowd and I watch as she takes a shaky breath before lifting her eyes.

"Reed is my brother. He was my best friend, and everything I wished for in a sibling." She stops to take a break, her hand gripping the stone so tightly her knuckles turn white. "I want everyone to know how much I appreciate that all of you continue to show up for him, for my family—especially when I couldn't." A few murmurs go through the crowd and the pride I feel at watching her stand up there and face her fear is so powerful it almost sends me to my knees.

"Reed would probably say you're all ridiculous for coming here today, but deep down I know he'd love it. He always did want to be the center of attention."

I laugh lightly with the crowd as she looks at the headstone again with so much longing it breaks my heart.

She continues, "I love you, Reed, and I miss you every day."

I meant what I told Blake about her being one of the strongest people I know, and this proves it. After a few minutes of silence, Margie and Lee walk up to stand next to her.

"Thank you everyone for coming today," Lee says. "We're happy—"

The sound of tires squealing violently cuts him off. Everyone there turns to find the person causing the ruckus, and my stomach bottoms out when I recognize Kade's truck in the parking lot. He gets out, slamming the door wildly before stomping toward us. Even from a distance, I can see he's wearing his nice clothes, but they're disheveled.

"LIAR!" he yells when spots me in the crowd. "YOU'RE A GODDAMN LIAR, GAVIN MONTGOMERY!"

Mom starts toward him, but I stop her. "I'll handle it, Momma. You stay here," I whisper.

With a quick apologetic glance at Gran, then at Blake and her family, I take off toward my brother. When I reach him, we're a short distance away from the crowd, but not far enough that people won't be able to hear every word he says.

Kade grabs me by my jacket and shoves me back. "You're a fucking liar!" he spits again.

"That's enough," I attempt to say quietly, already embarrassed as all hell. I'm sure Momma is dying on the inside at the spectacle he's causing.

"You don't get to tell me shit anymore, Gavin!"

I use the force of my larger body to push him further away from the crowd. He tries to struggle, but I'm bigger and stronger. Once we're close to his truck, he gets in my face. He's near enough to me now that I can tell he's sober, just extremely pissed off.

"I was getting ready and wanted to grab something of Dad's to bring with me. I happened to stumble on something at your desk. Any idea what?" he spits.

I stare into the pained eyes of my younger brother. "I was going to tell you."

"Tell me what?" he growls. "That you've been hiding Dad's shame? Or that your new girlfriend is going to buy our ranch?"

I look over my shoulder. Lee and Margie are speaking again, but people are struggling to not look our way. Blake's eyes are staring too, but her features are scrunched with concern. I hate that my brother has ruined this day, this moment for her. That *I've* ruined it with my secrets.

Kade grabs me again and shakes me. "You don't deny it then?"

"Yes, Dad screwed us over, but no, Blake isn't going to buy our ranch. She came up with that business plan and was going to invest in us if we decided to do a dude ranch, but it's just an idea."

He lets go of my shirt and steps back. "Do Momma and Gran know?" I shake my head. "You're an asshole."

"I was planning to tell you after today."

"I don't believe a word that comes out of your lying mouth," he seethes.

I grasp his shoulder. "Let's go somewhere more appropriate and talk. We can sort this out."

He chuckles darkly, pulling his body out from under mine. "We've talked enough."

When he moves to walk away, I try to stop him. "Don't walk away right now, Kade."

"I'll do whatever the fuck I want." He stalks toward his truck. As he grabs the door handle, I try to stop him again, but he reels back and slugs me right in the cheek. I'm not expecting the hard blow, so I fall to the ground, the coppery taste of blood welling in mouth.

For a split second, Kade stares in shock. He hasn't punched me with that much force ever in our lives—and I wasn't expecting a sucker punch. He takes the moment I'm gaining my bearings to jump in the car. I start to get up, but I'm too late. He's driving away just as I get to my feet.

"Shit," I mutter under my breath, holding my bleeding lip.

"Gavin!" Blake appears in front of me, her hands on my cheeks as she inspects my bleeding lip. When she touches the heated skin, I wince.

"I'm sorry I ruined today," I say sadly.

She shakes her head. "You didn't ruin it."

My eyes track over her shoulder to those standing around the gravesite. "People are watching," I say quietly.

"I don't care about them. I care about you, though. Kade really got you good."

My body stiffens as she brushes my wound again. "He found out about the debt, and he saw your business plan."

Blake worries her bottom lip. "You should go after him."

"Gavin," Momma's voice is strained as she comes up beside Blake, Gran not far behind her. Blake steps away but I grab her hand and hold it, locking her in next to me.

Momma's eyes widen at seeing me and Blake together for the first time, but whatever she's thinking gets wiped away when she sees my bloody lip. Tears fill her eyes as she asks, "What was that all about?"

My gaze moves back and forth from Momma to Gran. I know I have to tell them the truth, but I'm worried about Kade. Not just mentally, but if he were to drink and get in an accident, I'd never forgive myself.

Gran studies me, like she knows exactly what I've been hiding this entire time. Hell, maybe she does. She lays one of her weathered hands on Momma's shoulder. "We should let the boys sort it out, June. Gavin will fill us in when the time is right."

I silently send her my thanks, trying to convey through my expression how grateful I am. "Do you think you two could grab a ride home? I have a feeling Kade went to a bar."

"We'll take them," Lee's drawl answers, Blake's folks joining us. I notice the way Lee tries to avoid looking at my hand in Blake's, though I see Margie is thrilled about it—even if she's trying to hide her smile given the situation.

"Thank you, Lee," Momma says. "I'm so sorry for my son—" her voice catches, and my anger at Kade builds.

"It's fine, June," he soothes. "We all got the shit end of the stick in recent years. Let's just make sure we don't have any more tragedy on our hands."

The group tenses at his words as the reality of the situation strikes me. "I should head out," I tip my hat to Lee. "Thank you for taking care of my family, Mr. Tanner." He tips his Stetson back at me and Blake squeezes my hand.

"I'm going to go with Gavin," she says.

"Blake."

"You shouldn't go alone." Her voice is forceful enough that the group flinches.

Margie nudges Lee's leg with her crutch and eyes Gran and Momma. "We'll leave you two to talk."

Momma hesitates, but eventually steps forward to kiss me on the cheek. "Get some ice on that sooner rather than later."

I try to give her a reassuring smile. "I will, Momma. I'll find Kade and be home soon. I know all the places he likes to go. It will be alright."

She gives me a jerky nod and smiles at Blake before walking off. Once she's gone, Blake pulls me behind a truck and out of view. She puts her hands on her hips and stands tall.

"I'm going with you."

I let out a breath and take her face between my hands, kissing her softly to avoid my injury. Once she relaxes, I rest my forehead against hers. "It's better if I go alone. Kade's never punched me like that, and I don't know if I trust him anymore—and I'm sure your family would like you to be with them."

She bites her bottom lip. "Gav, I don't like it."

I smile and pull her lip out from between her teeth. "You called me Gav."

She shakes her head and sighs. "Let me know as soon as you find him."

"Of course. Will you come over later?"

"If you want me to."

"I'll always want to be around you."

Blake presses into me and hugs me tight. Over her shoulder, I see Abby Allen getting into her car. She has a smug smile on her face while she watches us. I let out a chuckle. "I think we're officially a public couple."

Blake awkwardly turns her head to see the town gossip and groans. "No secrets in Randall."

"Now they have more gossip to talk about after this."

She hugs me tighter. "You should go find Kade."

I hold her for a breath longer, eventually pulling back to take my keys from my pocket and kiss her forehead. "I'll see you tonight."

"I'll see you tonight," she echoes back.

CHAPTER 34

Gavin

IT'S AFTER EIGHT IN the evening, and I still haven't found Kade. I have no idea where he could've gone, and he's not answering his phone, either. Jake took it upon himself to look, too, but he's had no luck. He did mention that Kade might've gone off with the woman he spoke about, but I have no way of contacting her.

I take off my boots as I enter the foyer of the main house. I haven't been spending a ton of time here since Blake and I have preferred being alone in the guest house, but when the smell of barbeque hits me along with feminine laughter, I smile. It's been a while since I heard my family laugh like that. I miss it.

As I round the corner, I see Blake sitting next to Gran, a pile of food in front of her and a beer in her hand. I watch them for a moment, letting the image imprint in my brain. Momma is grinning, her cheeks red with laughter as Gran finishes telling an old story about Dad.

Blake snorts a bit, wiping sauce from her mouth. "You're telling me that they released three greased pigs into the high school but labeled them one, two, and four?"

"Yep," Gran laughs. "That way after they caught the three pigs, they'd still be looking for the fourth."

"That's genius. Reed would've loved something like that." At the mention of Reed, I expect Blake to falter, or for the energy in the room to shift, but it doesn't. I can't explain how impressed

I am of her. How happy I am at how far she's come since I laid eyes on her in Night Hawk last month.

"Your brother was a goofball, that's for sure." Momma laughs as she probably remembers the trouble Reed and I used to get into around the barn.

I clear my throat, and the three most important women in my life turn their heads. Momma jumps up and runs to me, giving me a hug before looking at my swollen lip. It's ugly and hurts like hell.

"You didn't find him?" she asks.

"No. Jake thinks he figured I'd come looking and probably went to the city or something." I don't bring up the girl, that feels too private. "Have you heard anything?"

"No. But it says he's read our text messages after we sent them."

"Well, that's something at least."

"Sit down. Let me get you ice for that lip," Momma fusses. "Are you hungry?"

"Starving," I answer as my gaze connects with Blake's, her eyes warm as she watches.

About an hour ago, she texted to say her folks needed some alone time and that she'd wait for me in the guest house. About five minutes before I drove up, I received another text to come find her in the main house. I was surprised at first, but Gran must've intercepted her before she could sit alone and wait for me. I know she's always harbored a soft spot for Blake—it must run in the family.

As I take my seat at the table, Momma places a plate down in front of me, then spoons a hefty helping of barbecue chicken, coleslaw and corn on it.

"You make this?" I ask.

"I did," Gran chimes. "Needed to make myself useful." I know they're all on edge about Kade more than they let on. I'm sure Momma and Gran want to know what sent him to ruin Reed's remembrance.

Gran sets down a beer for me, and I take a swig. The cool hoppy liquid and Blake's presence next to me immediately calms my nerves. She puts her hand on my thigh and squeezes.

"You really need to ice that." She points to my busted face.

"I will after I eat," I reassure her, placing my hand over hers.

Gran and Momma are both sitting now, watching us with interest. Gran smirks. "You two look right together."

Blake tenses, but I don't falter. "We do." My words are simple, but despite how awful today has been, seeing Momma smile at my words makes me feel good. She doesn't smile much anymore, and whatever makes her happy makes me happy. Plus, she's been hoping I'd find someone to settle down with, especially after Cricket. And even though this thing with Blake hasn't been going on long, I have no doubt in my mind that she's the one for me.

"Well, isn't this sweet?"

Everyone turns to see Kade glaring at us like we've committed a crime. His eyes are red, and he looks like he's been through hell. His sport coat and cowboy hat are gone, but he still wears a blue button up and black jeans. He's got it unbuttoned at the top, and I notice there's a red mark on his cheek, as if he's been slapped, along with a scratch near his collar bone.

"Kade!" Momma cries, standing to go greet him. "What happened?"

Kade steps back from her, and Mom's face falls. "I'm fine," he bites out.

She pushes her shoulders back. "You don't look fine."

His hate-filled eyes lock on me. "I think we should all talk about what Gavin and Blake have been hiding from us."

Blake fidgets beside me uncomfortably.

"Blake isn't hiding anything from you, so don't start that." My voice is stern. "You know this is all me."

"Why don't you sit down, young man?" Gran commands. "We can talk like civilized people."

Kade blinks, Gran's tone taking him down a notch. Momma walks back to the table and motions for Kade to sit in the chair between her and Gran. At first, I think he's going to refuse, but he sits, folding his arms over his chest as he turns his gaze back on me and Blake.

Before I can say something, Blake stands. "I'm going to give y'all some privacy. Thank you for dinner."

Kade holds up a hand. "You don't have to leave, Blake. Especially since it seems you've joined my little family quite easily," he finishes snidely.

Gran opens her mouth to scold him, but Momma beats her to it. "Stop being so rude, Kade Montgomery. I've raised you better. Now apologize to Blake."

The room goes quiet. This is the first time Momma has put Kade in his place since Dad died. She's been letting him get away with too much for too long. Pride swells in my chest, and I can tell Gran is happy about it too.

"It's alright," Blake says, moving away from me. "I'll be on my way." Kade stares at her. The way his face contorts, it looks as though he's stuck between knowing he should apologize and remaining righteous in his behavior. When he decides not to say anything, I take her hand. "Wait for me in the guest house. I'll come down soon."

Her skin flushes with the eyes of my family on her. I squeeze her hand, pleading with her to stay. I know I'll need her when this is through. After a moment, she nods.

"Thanks again," she murmurs to Gran, then makes her exit.

Kade taps his fingers on the table, his eyes shooting daggers at me. "I think it's time you come clean, Gavin."

I steeple my hands and meet the three questioning pairs of eyes. "We're going to lose the ranch." Momma shifts in her chair and Gran simply continues to wait for me to explain.

"What do you mean?" Momma asks tentatively.

"When Daddy died, I met with the bank. We've been in bad shape for years, but he never said anything. He took out several loans and a second mortgage—we're behind on payments. A bit of charity here and there is never going to dig us out of the hole we're in. The bank needs to collect soon, or they'll take everything."

A strangled noise leaves Momma's throat. "That can't be true. Emmett would've told me."

"You know that's horseshit, June." Gran shakes her head sadly. "I loved my boy, but he would never admit he was behind. At least not to any of us."

Her words sink in, and I realize I'm a lot more like Dad than I thought. Too ashamed to admit that shit has gone south and I need help. Now look where we are.

"I'm sorry I didn't say anything. I didn't want anyone to worry. I thought I could take care of it, but I'm out of options."

"You're serious?" Momma asks quietly.

I nod my head solemnly. "I'm sorry."

"We can't take out another loan?" Momma's tone is desperate. She knows how much this ranch means to our family and to the town of Randall. I do, too. Which is why I've been fighting so hard to try and save it.

"We're tapped out. I've been looking for options since I found out but—"

"Tell them about Blake," Kade interrupts me evenly. I meet my brother's gaze for a moment, my mouth dry.

I let out a long breath. "Blake thinks we could turn this place into a successful dude ranch."

Gran exhales a sad chuckle. "That would cost a lot of money."

"Blake wants to buy the ranch," Kade grits out.

Momma gasps in shock, a hand flying over her mouth.

I shake my head vehemently. "No, she doesn't. Blake would never want to take our home from us."

Kade stands. "I know what I saw in your office!"

Gran, who's managed to remain calm after all this information, pulls on Kade's arm. "Sit down, boy. Listen to what he has to say."

"I know what I saw," he repeats.

"You saw a business plan, Kade, with her ideas to turn the place into something new. I told you earlier that it's an investment for her. She doesn't want to own this ranch; she wants it to stay ours."

"I don't believe that!" Kade yells.

"Kade, please. I'm sure it's not what you think," Momma says, placing a hand on his shoulder. He shrugs it off, exasperated.

"Nobody just throws around that kind of money without an ulterior motive, Momma."

Anger slithers through every cell in my body. "You may not know Blake well, but you know her enough. She just wants our ranch to survive."

The veins in Kade's arms bulge as he clenches his fists. "The Tanners have the biggest operation in Texas next to ours, you think they don't want to expand their land and make more money?"

"Kade!" Momma scolds. "That's an awful thing to say. You know the Tanners are good people."

He chuckles cynically. It's a sound I've never heard come from his lips, one that's full of resentment and bitterness.

"You're both on Gavin's side then?" His eyes are accusatory, his body vibrating with rage. "You're not even pissed he kept this from you both? He lied to us!"

"Kade," I say sadly, but he stands, cutting me off.

"You're full of shit—just like Dad." He steps back and looks at Gran and Momma. "And you two are just going to sit here acting like you don't care he kept this from us."

"Watch yourself, boy," Gran says. "You don't know what me and June are thinking. I'm pissed, but handling this with anger isn't going to change anything."

Kade grinds his teeth and lets out a frustrated growl. "You know what? I don't need any of you. You can sell the ranch to the Tanners for all I care. You can all go to hell." Momma tries to stop him, but Kade's too fast. He grabs a bottle of whiskey Gran has sitting out before storming off, the door slamming behind him.

We all flinch at the bang before the house is consumed in silence. I hear Momma take a shuddering breath. It sounds as if she's choking on a sob. The pain of it makes my stomach turn.

"He'll settle down, June," Gran tries to calm her. "He's been through a lot this last year. We all have."

"I've been a bad mother to him," Momma says softly. Her eyes turn to meet mine. "You tried to tell me I should step in, and I should've listened."

My heart skips a beat. It's in this terrible moment I truly realize that in my desire to protect my family, I've hurt them even more. Kade is right about me.

"It's not your fault, Momma," I say sadly. "It's mine." "Why did you keep this from us?" she asks, her voice timid.

"I thought I could fix it," I say truthfully. "But Dad really put us in the hole. The drought sealed our fate."

Momma closes her eyes, taking a few deep breaths. When she opens them, she looks at Gran, then back to me. "You really think Blake's idea could work?"

Some of the sadness lifts when I think of Blake's plan—of her offer. "It could. It would be a lot of work, but lucrative if done right. I was planning to show you her business plan later. I just wanted to be there for her today."

Momma studies my face. "You love her, don't you?"

I can't help the small smile that appears when I think of her. "I do."

Gran lets out a long breath, her knobby fingers steepling in front of her. "This family has a lot more talking to do. But that girl has had a hard day—and we ruined it."

I shake my head. "It's my fault."

"As a family, we take responsibility," Gran says. "Now you go be with her. Kade will be fine. Just do me a favor and hide all the keys to the trucks. I don't want him doing anything stupid after he drinks himself silly."

"I will, Gran."

"We'll all talk about this when we've got some fresh perspective. Do you agree, June?"

Momma wipes one of her stray tears. "Yes. I'd like some time to process this anyway. You go, be with Blake. She's probably feeling a whole lot of things right now."

I stand and nod, amazed my family can be so selfless after the information they learned. I feel blessed to have them as my flesh and blood.

I walk over to Gran and kiss her head, then do the same to Momma.

"I'm sorry," I say once more.

Gran shakes her head. "You did what you thought was right. We may not like it, but June and I probably would've done the same. Kade, too. This is a situation we all need to learn from."

I tip my head to her. "You're too good to me, Gran."

She grins. "Now go take care of, Blake."

"I will."

CHAPTER 35

Blake

I WAKE UP WITH the burning need to use the bathroom. I look bleary-eyed at the microwave clock, seeing it's before midnight. After Gavin returned from the main house, we talked for a while about what happened with Kade before falling asleep, both exhausted from today's events. He didn't give me all the details about what happened after I left, but he feels terrible about everything, including what happened at the cemetery. I know because he kept apologizing for it as he held me.

I'm not upset though, and my parents aren't, either. Kade's hurting, and after today I see how much he and I carry our pain in similar ways. He's angry and doesn't know how to deal with his grief. I just hope their family can work it out because I don't like seeing Gavin hurt.

I glance at Gavin one more time, his rugged, stubbled face peaceful in sleep. It's when he's relaxed like this, I remember he's only twenty-four. It makes me wonder if his life wasn't this ranch if we would've ever have crossed paths again. Maybe he'd be traveling like he said, dancing the night away in some bar somewhere far away. The idea makes me smile, though part of me is happy this is where we both ended up. I just wish it was without the loss of our loved ones and all the hardships. I know Reed would've been grossed out about Gavin and me being together at first, but he would've grown to love it.

My bladder protests again, wiping away my thoughts and forcing me to finally leave the warmth of Gavin's embrace. It takes a second to untangle myself from his vice grip on me, but once I'm free, I make quick work of my bathroom break.

After I wash and dry my hands, I head back out to the living room and stop when Gavin lets out a small snore. It's cute, and thankfully not that loud. When he lets out another small sound, I have to hold back a chuckle. As I'm about to reach the bed and wrap myself up in him again, a banging sound from outside stops me. It could be an animal, but my gut has me heading toward the kitchen to look out the window above the sink.

It takes a second for my eyes to adjust, but I see a figure in the distance near the spot where Gavin and I got the ATVs. The figure wobbles back and forth, holding a flashlight that's bouncing light all over. Immediately, I know who it is. Not wanting to wake Gavin, I find my clothes and dress as quietly as I can. If Kade's drunk, the last thing he needs to do is be riding an ATV. And given the fact that he split Gavin's lip open earlier, I doubt waking Gavin to confront him would be good. Maybe Kade will listen to me.

I grab my phone and see a headlamp sitting in a small basket on the kitchen table, so I grab that too. I slip it over my head and leave the guest house before turning it on. I jog to the garage, the sounds of Kade moving around getting louder. Eventually, he comes into view, swearing under his breath as he looks for something.

I flick off the headlamp and clear my throat to alert him of my presence. His head pops up, and he shines his flashlight in my direction, temporarily blinding me. I hold my hand up to block the light.

"What are you doing, Kade?"

"Go back to Gavin's bed, Blake," he snaps.

I suck in a breath at his tone, but I know he's upset, so I don't take it personally.

He stumbles, pulling a cover off one of the ATVs. Yeah, he's definitely drunk.

"Kade," I say again, "I don't think you should be driving that right now."

He chuckles haughtily to himself. "Everyone seems to think they know what's best for me."

His words settle in my bones. "I know what that feels like, Kade. Trust me."

Kade brings his gaze to meet mine. His bloodshot eyes look so sad. It makes my heart break and a sharp pain fling through my chest.

"You know, I told my brother to leave you alone. I told him you were a broken girl." I clench my fists as he continues, "He's broken too, you know? Just like me—like you. He'll never admit that, though. It's why we're going to lose this place."

I shake my head. "You're not going to lose your ranch, Kade."

He huffs an emotionless laugh. "Because you're going to own it, right? Give it to us out of the goodness of your heart?"

"It's not like that, Kade. I think you know that."

"I don't know anything!" he yells.

I hold my ground, not afraid of him at all. "Why don't we go sit down and talk? I know what you're feeling."

Kade ignores me, straddling the ATV before putting in the key and turning on the headlights.

"You may know what I'm feeling, Blake, but it doesn't matter. None of it matters." Kade's body tightens like he's about to start the engine, and my heart beats faster.

"It does matter, Kade. Come on. Let's go chat over some coffee," I try to persuade him, my tone desperate.

He shakes his head. "All everyone wants to do is talk in this town. Except the funny part is, nobody wants to talk about what really matters."

I mull over his words. I think I understand what he's saying. Randall likes to gossip, to have fun, but when it comes to the hard shit, well, there's a reason nobody likes to talk about it at the bar on a Friday night.

"I want to talk to you, Kade. About the stuff that matters." I mean what I'm saying, too. Maybe I wouldn't have wanted to a few weeks ago, but that's changed now. I don't want Kade to feel the way I've felt for the last five years. At least not any longer than he already has. Nobody deserves to feel like their grief is swallowing them whole, consuming all the happy things inside of them bit by bit.

"You don't," he jeers. "You want to sit in your own little world with Gavin. You want to run our family's ranch and do God knows what else. We aren't friends, Blake. Stop trying to do a good deed out of some misguided savior bullshit. It's like my brother's dick has affected you in the worst way possible!"

"Kade! That's not fair and you know it."

"Life's not fair, Miss Tanner—and I think you know that." Kade hits the clutch, startling me to the point where I jump back. "Nice knowing you, Cowgirl!" he yells over the noise.

I make a move for him, but it's futile. Without another glance in my direction, he takes off into the night, dust spitting so thickly into the air that I cough.

"Shit!" I spit out some dust from my mouth, blood pounding in my ears as I debate what to do. There's no time to wake Gavin, and if I don't go after Kade now, he could get seriously injured—or worse. His words, *"Nice knowing you, Cowgirl,"* weren't exactly comforting either. I break out into a cold sweat. On tonight of all nights, if something...

"No!" I scream. Without more thought, I frantically search for the key to the other ATV. I look everywhere, trying to remember in my fear where it could be. My mind is jumbled as I dig through several drawers before I finally spot a shiny silver key on a desk. I cry in relief, climbing on top of the ATV and inserting the key. Nothing happens. I turn it again and again, but still nothing.

"*Damn it*!" I try one more time, but it's hopeless.

I climb off and run outside debating my next move. I think of taking my truck, but I don't know the land here that well. If I hit bad terrain, I'll be forced to turn back. I glance to the barn, and I feel faint at what I know I must do.

"*You can do this*," Reed's voice echoes in my head. It's so loud it knocks the wind out of me. It's as if he's standing right next to me.

I shake my head, tears forming in the corner of my eyes.

"*Go, Blakey girl! Go now!*" Reed's voice says again, louder this time. It should freak me out, but instead, my feet start moving, and I run toward where I think they keep their horses. When I arrive, there are lowlights on in the barn, illuminating the space enough for me to see without my headlamp. At the first stall I come to, I recognize the red roan that has the name Willy plated outside his stall door. He's the horse Kade rode that day when Gavin and I met him on the ATVs. With my decision made, I frantically search for a tack room. Thankfully, it doesn't take me long to find a saddle and bridle that will work.

When I enter his stall, Willy doesn't even balk. He looks at me as if to say, "*What are you waiting for?*"

I stroke his long face. "We're going to go after Kade, alright, buddy? Will you take care of me?" He bobs his head a bit like he understands what I'm asking. I smile, my nerves settling a bit as I throw the saddle on him and do it up like I've done this every day for the last five years, even though I haven't. Once he's tacked up, I lead him out and take a deep breath.

"*You can do this, Blakey,*" Reed's voice echoes.

My shoulders straighten and I ground myself. "You're right," I say into the night. "I can do this."

I put my foot in the stirrup and muster my strength, muscles contracting as I hoist myself up and over onto Willy's back. He doesn't move, perfectly trained and ready to work. When my butt settles into the saddle, a sense of calm washes over me.

I thought the first time back in the saddle would feel strange, but instead, I feel...at home. I pat Willy's neck. "Don't let me fall, boy." He dances a little bit, ready to go find his owner.

With a silent prayer, I flick on my headlamp and spur Willy forward. He takes off into a gallop without much from me, sensing that something is off. With his powerful body moving beneath me, all thoughts of promises to never ride again and any lingering fear leaves my body. I'm only thinking about one thing—help Kade.

I inhale deeply and glance up. The sky is dark and covered with clouds, so I depend on the headlamp to lead the way. Thankfully Kade's ATV left tracks in the dirt so I can follow him. I think of Gavin still sleeping, and regret fills me. I should've got him, but there wasn't time. I can't let anything happen to his brother. The thought urges me, and I have Willy run faster, maybe faster than he ever has before.

As wind whips through my hair, it strikes me that I'm riding. Really riding. I let out a long sigh of breath before it turns into a happy laugh. I never thought I'd be on top of a horse again. I just hate that it's under these circumstances. Lord, I hope nothing happens to Kade.

Willy gallops across the plain, and I can feel him tiring as the long minutes tick by. "Come on, Willy!" I cheer. "You've got this, boy!"

The horse picks up as we crest over the top of a hill, at the same time a crack explodes in the inky night and the sky lights up. Willy spooks, veering slightly right, but he recovers with ease.

"Really, Reed?" I wail. "You choose for it to storm right now?"

In response, rain starts to fall in fat drops. I can't help but laugh. The very thing we've been needing most happens at the worst time. The sky lights up again, but with it I can see further. When the lightning strikes once more and thunder rumbles, I thank Reed again because I'm able to spot some rocky terrain, and right there in plain sight is Kade's ATV.

Thank God. Willy runs toward the ATV without my direction as the rain pelts down harder now. He's probably been here with Kade a hundred times before.

As we approach, I slow Willy to a trot and search for Kade. When I don't see him, I scream his name as loudly as I can—but there's no answer.

I jump off Willy and leave him free standing. I can only hope the storm doesn't scare him off. I pull out my phone to see I have no bars, and suddenly, I feel like I'm reliving five years ago.

I shake my head. "Stay focused." Taking a deep breath, I make my way toward the rocky edge and peer over.

"KADE!" But there's nothing.

The rain is coming down in sheets now, which makes it harder to see, even with my headlamp. I take my phone and turn on the flashlight but it's no use. I curse again as the night lights up. That's when I see him. He's lying on a rock ledge down to the left. I can see blood on his forehead, and I feel like vomiting.

"KADE!" I wail wildly. "KADE MONTGOMERY!" But he doesn't move.

The accident flashes through my mind, those horrible memories I see in my nightmares haunting me as I stare at Kade. Though right now, I see Reed's lifeless body on the ground as I shook him. I swallow down bile. This can't be happening again. It can't. Not to Gavin's family, too.

I feel pressure on my shoulder, and I startle. I turn my head but there's nobody there, only Willy and an empty ATV.

"Get to him, Blake. Get to him now."

I shut my eyes, water soaking my clothes as I take comfort in the warm baritone of my brother's voice. It's time to be the strong woman Gavin and my parents tell me I am. It's time to be brave again.

Feeling steadier, I open my eyes and search for a way to Kade. It doesn't look like there's any way he could've gotten to where he is unless he slipped or jumped. I very much hope it's the former. Shaking that thought away, I murmur a prayer that Gavin wakes up and comes to find us. Because once I get to Kade, I'm going to need help.

I wipe the rain from my face and rush toward the other side of Willy, my feet slipping a bit as mud squelches beneath my boots. Lightening permeates the sky, and I utilize the light to find a slope of rocks twenty feet or so to the right of Kade. When I approach, I see that if I put my butt on the ground, I could slide down to the ledge where he is, then figure out how to get to him from there.

"I'm coming, Kade! Don't worry!"

With one last check to Willy who's still standing by the ATV like a saint, I put my phone under my chin then squat to the ground. My heart continues to pound in my chest as I get down on the slippery rocks. I sit my ass flat, grateful for the friction of my jeans to keep me from completely slipping down to the ledge below. I know what I'm doing is risky, but I can't leave him down there.

It takes me only a few seconds to slide down, rocks digging into my skin as I do. I send a thank you to the sky when my feet land easily and I manage not to slip to my death. I feel Reed's presence still with me, keeping me calm and collected. I don't know if he's really here, but it feels like it. Like he's guiding my limbs to the right destination.

I take my phone from under my chin and flash it toward Kade. We're level now, which makes it easier for me to see him. It looks like his arm is bent funny, and then there's the blood on his head, but the color of his skin looks okay. He must have fallen only minutes before I arrived.

"Kade!" I holler, but he doesn't move.

I look down at my feet and see the rocky ledge beneath me isn't super wide. If I trip, I might send myself over it. I shiver and try to silence my thoughts, because if I think about tripping, I probably will.

"You can do this, Blake. You can do this," I chant to myself. Bending at my knees, I keep myself low and move.

"*One foot in front of the other*," Reed instructs. "*Take your time, Blakey girl.*"

I breathe steadily, counting some of the smaller rocks in front of me as I move the distance to Kade, using the count to keep my balance. Time suspends as I get closer to him, though I don't look up in case it makes me lose my balance. As I move my hand to wipe rain from my eyes, thunder booms and Willy whinnies. The simultaneous sounds startle me, and I let out a yelp as I fall forward. For a split second I think I've killed myself, but when my body hits the rocks and dirt below, my gaze is level with Kade's jean clad legs.

"Holy shit," I huff. With no time to waste, I scoot myself so I'm near Kade's head. He's incredibly lucky he landed on this wide ledge. Another couple feet to the side or over and I probably wouldn't have even been able to see where he landed. I put my fingers to his neck, and I don't feel a pulse. Fear racks my body.

"No, no, no, no, no!"

I place my hand on Kade's chest and rest my ear near his mouth, I don't feel any breath either. The rain continues to soak both our faces. It takes me only a moment to use my strength to rip his shirt open. I learned CPR a long time ago, but I remember it enough to at least try. I can't let him die. Not like this. Not today. I find the spot between his nipples, right below his sternum. I link my fingers together and press my palm down rapidly.

"Come on, Kade! Come on!"

Nothing happens, which means he needs air. I place myself near his mouth, tilting his airway open before putting my lips to his. I breathe into his mouth twice, then move back to chest compressions.

"Come on, Kade," I plead, my tears mingling with the rain. "Gavin needs you. Your Momma, your Gran. You can't leave them this way."

My compressions go deeper, and I hasten the speed, putting my pleas into my movements. "Come on, Kade!" I cry again. The loudest crack of thunder booms through the sky and I jump. At the same time Kade's eyes open and he sucks in a wheezing breath. I let out a cry of relief, my hands gasping his cheeks as he stares at me wide-eyed and afraid.

"You're okay, Kade. You're okay," I yell over the storm.

"Blake?" he moans in pain.

"Don't move. You fell, and you're injured." The rain batters down around us as he stares into my face. He begins to shiver, his body in shock from whatever the hell happened that caused him to stop breathing.

"It's raining," he says in awe, his body shaking more violently.

I rest my body against his, attempting to give him my warmth while not touching his arm. "It is raining," I say back, unsure of what to do now. I pull my phone and see it's dead, probably waterlogged at this point.

"Gavin," Kade says after a second. "Where's Gavin?"

I open my mouth to answer that he isn't here, but then a bright light shines above me. I squint and let my eyes adjust, relief filling me when I see it's a high-powered flashlight.

"Blake!" Gavin bellows.

I let out a laugh of relief and thank my lucky stars that he's here. I press my forehead to Kade's shoulder, exhaustion settling in my bones. Reed's voice is no longer in my mind, but I know we're safe now.

"Help is coming!" Gavin yells down.

With a shuddering breath, I turn my head skyward and send a silent thank you to my brother for doing more than guiding me here, but for sending Gavin to me. To us.

"Hold on!" Gavin screams, his voice distressed.

"We will," I yell back. We all will.

CHAPTER 36

Gavin

I HATE HOSPITALS. I mean, I'm not sure I've ever met a person who says they love hospitals—that would be a little strange—but I hate them. They're cold, smell like antiseptic, and are full of people who are scared for their loved ones. Just like me.

"Gavin Montgomery?"

I bolt up, the blanket search and rescue gave me falling to the floor in a heap. "How's my brother?"

The petite brown-haired doctor smiles. "I'm Dr. James, and I was in the operating room with Kade. He's in recovery now. Once he's out, you can see him in the ICU."

"How is he?"

"His arm is broken, and he'll have to wear a cast, but he should regain full motion. He has a concussion, no brain bleed. He did go into cardiac arrest and his heart stopped for a few minutes, so he'll have to go through some tests this week, but we believe it was caused due to adrenaline as he doesn't have any blood clots. We'll keep him the next week to monitor everything, but let's just say he's a very lucky man."

I rub my hand over my face and let some of the tension from my shoulders fall. "Is he at risk still, or..." I can't even bring myself to say it.

"We have no reason to believe he won't make it out of this. But he has a lot of healing to do."

"Thank you, Dr. James."

"Of course. Let me know if you have any other questions."

"Can I see Blake Tanner?" I must've sounded eager because there's a small smile that plays on the corner of her lips.

"I'll ask the nurses. We're swamped tonight with the storm."

My heart rate picks up as I think of holding Blake in my arms. "I'd like to see her."

"I'll see what I can do." She nods.

"Thanks again, Dr. James."

"Of course. Your brother's a fighter. You can relax a bit."

Not likely, I think to myself as I shake her hand.

After she walks off, I pace, not knowing what to do with myself while I wait. When I went to bed last night, the last place I expected to end up was here. The image of Blake at Devil's Rock holding my shivering and injured brother will haunt me for the rest of my life. Emotion wells in my throat, but I work it back down.

"Are you Gavin Montgomery?"

I turn at the voice to see an older nurse in floral scrubs smiling at me.

"I am."

"Ms. Tanner has been asking for you. More like demanding." She grins.

I huff out a laugh as she gestures for me to follow her. I fall instep behind her, and we walk down multiple hallways until we reach the last room at the end of one.

She pushes open the curtain. "Ms. Tanner is in here."

Before I can get fully inside, a body hurtles into me, and I almost fall backwards from the force.

"Gavin!" Blake cries.

I wrap my arms around her, walking us back so we're fully inside the room. Her body is warm and pliant against mine, reminding me that she's alive. Tears burn my eyes as I squeeze her tighter.

"I've got you, baby," I whisper against her now dry hair. "I've got you," I repeat. More for myself than her.

"I'm so happy you're here. I've been asking for you for a while but they made me wait."

Her hands fist my shirt around my waist, and she presses her face into the crook of my neck. When her tears pool against my skin, I pull back and hold her face in my hands. I check her over, making sure there's nothing wrong outwardly.

"I'm okay," she assures me. "When they took me in the ambulance, I was in shock and a little cold. I have a few scrapes on my knee and legs too, but that's it."

I brush my thumbs over the apples of her cheeks, recommitting everything about her to memory. It's my futile attempt at trying to erase the image of her being carted into the ambulance with my brother from my mind.

"You're sure?" I press her.

"I'm fine, Gavin. They told me Kade's going to be okay."

I press my forehead to hers. "Thanks to you."

Blake pulls me back and her eyes are full of tears. "Thanks to both of us."

I gently kiss her before leading her to a small, padded bench in the corner of the room. Once seated, she molds herself as close as possible to me, holding my hands.

After a moment she asks, "How did you find us?"

"I woke up and you weren't in the room. I tried to call your phone, but you didn't answer. When I saw your keys and truck still there, I thought maybe you couldn't sleep and went to the barn. That's when I found the missing ATV and saw Willy gone too and the tracks you both left. I don't know how to explain it but, something told me to follow you. So, I grabbed an ATV we had in another barn and went after you. Then it started raining," my voice catches. "I didn't know what I was going to find when I got to you."

Blake places her head on my shoulder and squeezes my hand back. "Maybe it was Reed bringing you to us."

I swallow the lump in my throat. "You think?"

She nods, the story of what happened after I fell asleep spilling from her mouth. How she woke up and followed Kade. How they fought, what he said that made her think he was going to do something bad, and how she risked her life to save him. By the end of the story, I can't stop the tears that fall. This time, I pull her to me and press my face into her shoulder.

"Thank you, Blake. Thank you for saving my brother. Thank you, thank you, thank you."

Blake holds me, rubbing her hand up and down my back as we cry silently together. The events of today, what could've happened if she hadn't followed Kade, comes crashing out of us in waves. I grip her harder, thanking Reed, God, or just sheer luck that both are safe. The question still remains if my brother fell or jumped. It's one that will have to be asked. Though my gut tells me he slipped, maybe due to his heart, because the brother I know wouldn't do that. However, I've been wrong about shit a lot lately, so I don't really know.

I mull in my thoughts and try to focus on Blakes breaths against my skin to stop me from falling apart. A minute later, a knock on the doorframe breaks our little cocoon. Blake's the first to pull back and we wipe our tears. The older nurse is back, and she has a gentle smile on her lips.

"Kade's awake and asking for you both."

I puff out a shaky breath. "Thank you." Making eye contact with Blake, I offer her my hand. "Are you okay walking in that gown?"

She looks down at it like she forgot she was wearing it. "My clothes were soaked, so they made me change. But yeah, I want to see him if you want me to come with you."

I squeeze her hand. "I wouldn't have it any other way."

"Follow me," the nurse says to us.

I continue to hold Blake's hand as we walk to the ICU. During the walk, I stroke my thumb over her knuckles to soothe her. When I feel her tense, I ask, "What is it?"

"Did you call my parents?"

"Yes, they're on their way. They're stopping to pick up Momma and Gran. I didn't want them driving in this weather, so your dad offered to pick them up."

"How did they sound when you called?"

"Shocked, worried, but glad you're safe. I imagine they won't let you out of their sight for a while after this."

"No, I imagine not."

I kiss Blake's knuckles, completely in awe of her. I almost can't believe this is the same woman I found on the side of the road with no shoes, the same one that basically told me to fuck off all those weeks ago. She just went through another traumatic experience on the anniversary of her brother's death—yet here she stands, strong and composed. I have no doubt she'll get through this, even though I know what happened hasn't completely sunk in. It hasn't for me either. We'll all need to do a lot of healing after this—and not only because of tonight, but for all of it.

"This room here," the nurse motions. "Just make sure you stay calm. He's on some good painkillers, so he may be out of it, and we want to make sure he rests."

"Thank you." I remove my hand from Blake's and press it into her lower back, leading her into the stark white room. When my eyes find Kade in a hospital bed, I stop in my tracks. His tan skin is sickly pale, and he wears a bandage on his forehead with his casted arm suspended in air. Blake doesn't seem to notice my immobility though, because she moves right to his bed as I gawk.

She puts her hand over Kade's. "Kade? It's me, Blake."

It takes a second, but Kade's eyes flutter open and he smiles softly at her. The look reminds me of how you would look a sister or an old friend, instead of a woman he hardly knows.

My heart cracks open when Blake cups his face gently and she smiles back. "How are you feeling?"

"Like I died and came back to life," he says groggily, his eyes finding mine.

I remove my hat and hold it against my chest, stepping closer to his bedside. "You'll be okay," I mutter, finally finding my voice. My words are lame, but I don't know what to say. When he left tonight we had so many words left unsaid—now it all feels trivial.

"Thanks to your girl." He tries to wink but it looks ridiculous given his current painkiller filled state. That doesn't stop Blake's skin from turning pink at the attention.

"You're strong, Kade," she says. "You wanted to live."

He shifts at her words and grimaces. His reaction makes me wonder if he did jump. I rest my hand on his leg and give it a light squeeze.

"Take it easy, little brother."

He puffs out air through his teeth and puts his gaze on Blake again. "I asked you to come so I could make sure you were okay, and to say thank you."

She fights tears back. "I'm perfectly fine. I'm just glad you're okay."

"I don't feel okay, but I know I will be."

Blake reaches up and brushes a bit of his long hair behind his ear. "Yes, you will." Her voice combined with her touch is a sweet assurance—to both me and Kade.

"Do you mind if I talk to my brother before I fall asleep?" He flashes her a half-assed Montgomery smile, and I fight a laugh. Even while injured and drugged, he's trying to be a charmer.

"Of course. We'll talk later." Blake stands and kisses my cheek before heading toward the hall.

"Thanks again, Blakey girl," Kade slurs sleepily.

A noise leaves Blake's throat, and she stops walking. She turns on her heel and stares at Kade like he has three heads. For a moment, she's too stunned to speak, then tears fall from her eyes. "No thanks needed," she whispers, then bolts out the door.

I make a mental note to ask about her reaction later, but right now, Kade needs me. I sit where Blake was a second ago and Kade opens his eyes to meet mine. He's struggling to stay awake, but he finally manages to talk.

"I'm sorry," he exhales, sadness in his tone. "I didn't mean for this to happen. It was an accident."

A small bit of relief fills me at his words, and I debate my next question carefully. "Blake told me what you said before you drove off. It made me wonder if this wasn't an accident."

Kade squeezes his eyes shut for a moment. "Maybe there's a part of me that meant what I said to her. I was drunk, upset, and not thinking clearly. But it was an accident, Gavin. I swear to you. When I got to Devil's Rock, I was less angry. I felt bad for how I treated Blake and was going to go back and apologize, but then I slipped, and next thing I know, Blake's next to me and now I'm here."

I study my brother and try to see if he's being untruthful, but by the way he's speaking and how his body is reacting to his story, I believe him. However, I know we'll have to talk about this more when he's better.

I squeeze his hand. "I'm very glad you're here, little brother. Never forget that." Kade's eyes turn glassy, and he gives me a curt nod. "And I'm sorry for not telling you about everything going on with our ranch, and for being a dick."

Kade lets out a painful sounding laugh. "Apology sort of accepted."

I shake my head and grin. "We can talk about it later when you're better."

Kade hums, his eyes closing and his body relaxing. Just as I think he's asleep, he opens his eyes a bit.

"We'll be okay, won't we, Gav?" He asks softly.

I rub my hand over my jaw. "It will take some work," I answer honestly. "But we'll be okay, Kade. I promise. We're Montgomerys after all." That settles him, and he shuts his eyes again.

"Dad would be pissed at me," he murmurs as he starts to fall asleep. "I think he sent the rain to make things difficult."

I let out a huff. "Maybe. Or to help us."

Kade doesn't answer, but his lips are upturned in a smile as he falls into sleep. I sit next to him for a while, taking in my younger brother: His long sandy blond hair, angled features, and the cuts on his cheeks and forehead. He looks a lot like Dad when he was in his twenties. Sometimes I wonder if that's why Momma has always let him get away with shit. I don't know why, but that makes me smile. It also has me thinking of how much work our family has ahead of us—not only emotionally, but regarding our ranch. But for now, I'm content knowing that Kade is safe.

My phone buzzes, and I see it's a text from Momma that they've arrived. When I stand, I'm surprised to see Kade open his eyes.

"Leaving me for Blake already?"

I smirk, placing my hand gently on his shoulder. "I'm going to go get Gran and Momma, they're worried sick. You rest and we'll be back in a bit."

He nods, putting his hand over mine before I can walk away. "Don't ever let that woman of yours go, Gav. She's special."

I take a shaky breath. "I don't plan on it, little brother. Not even slightly."

Epilogue

BLAKE

NINE MONTHS LATER

"That looks great, Kade!" I jump excitedly. "Doesn't it look great, Gav?"

Gavin squeezes me into his side, kissing the top of my head. We gaze at the upgraded golden sign hanging high above the freshly paved road while Kade stands on the ladder, polishing the large letter M of Montgomery.

"It's fancy," Gavin answers.

I roll my eyes and hip check him gently. "You say that about everything new."

"She's right, old man." Kade laughs as he walks down the ladder. "You do say that about everything new."

Gavin just shrugs as Kade joins us in admiring the golden sign. It's a beautiful afternoon with lots of fluffy clouds in the sky. It's been an insane nine months, but we're on track to soft open the Montgomery Family Dude Ranch right on time. Tonight, we're having a barbeque with a band to celebrate, and half the town is planning to come.

Kade pats me on my upper back. "You were right about the gold. It looks better than red."

"Thanks." I grin at the man who's become like a brother to me. Every time I see him, I'm reminded that life works in strange ways. That night at Devil's Rock changed me. It changed all of us. When I was leaving his hospital room and he called me Blakey girl, I knew for sure that Reed led me to this family. I'll do anything to help them, to save their ranch—and not only because I'm completely in love with Gavin and his family, but because I know this place is important. That the land holds memories and maybe even some magic.

"Alright, I got to head out," Kade says, breaking me from my thoughts. "Presley and her band are going to be here any minute. I promised I'd help her set up."

Gavin and I grin stupidly when he says Presley's name.

"Make sure you're on time tonight," Gavin teases, and I see Kade grit his teeth. Everyone knows that when Kade and Presley get together, they often can't be found for hours on end. Where they go, we don't really know. But we can guess what they're doing by how they always come back flushed and smiling, if they bother to return at all.

"Yeah, yeah. We'll be there." He huffs in embarrassment, walking off to his truck.

Before he's even out of sight Gavin turns me in his arms and admires me with a cheeky look on his face. "You're amazing, you know that?"

"You tell me often," I chuckle.

He brushes a piece of hair behind my ear as I look into his evergreen eyes. I've spent many hours these past months getting to know every part of this cowboy's body, heart, and soul. Since he found Kade and me that night, he's practically been glued to me. We've spent hours with his family, my parents included, figuring out how to save their ranch. It hasn't been easy. There have been lots of tears and frustration. It's not a cake walk working with a family that's about to lose everything, and I knew that the situation was delicate from the beginning.

But we've worked it out and continue to. I have every faith that The Montgomery Family Dude Ranch will be a success. And I've told Gavin, I don't care if I don't make my money back—I just want this place to live on for future generations.

Maybe even for our children if we have any, but first, we have so much left to experience together. We even planned a trip to Iceland to work with famous sheepherders, a trip Reed always wanted to experience.

Gavin presses the pad of his thumb into my lower lip. "What are you thinking about, baby?"

I grin at this choice of words. "The future."

He smiles back, his happiness radiating out of him like a drug. He's done a lot of work on his own grief and guilt these last months, and I'm proud of how far he's come. We both decided once we began waking up to mutual nightmares that it was time we got help. Kade inspired us once he started seeing someone in the city that Presley recommended. I think Mom about fell over when I finally asked her to connect me with her psychologist's office.

It was difficult to talk to a stranger at first, but now it feels easy. I think it's even brought Gavin and I closer together. Now when I think of Reed, the pain is easier to handle. It's the same for Gavin and his dad, and for what happened at Devil's Rock.

"How's the future looking?" He pulls me even closer so I can feel the hard planes of his body against my softness. I reach up and kiss him gently on the lips, lingering until I can feel him smile.

"Endless," I whisper against them.

He sucks in a breath, cupping the back of my head to kiss me again. I use my free hand to pull off his cowboy hat like I always do, granting him access to my mouth so we can deepen our kiss. Before I can put my hands on his ass to take things further, he surprises me by spinning me out. I let out a bark of laughter as he pulls me back into his chest. He holds me in his arms and dances us around as he hums the notes to the song "5 Foot 9" by Tyler Hubbard—the tune he says must have been written about me.

I gaze into his eyes after he spins me again. "When are you going to enter another two-step competition?"

He shakes his head with mirth. "When are you going to enter a rodeo?" He's got me there. Ever since I rode Willy that day, I've started riding again—but it's been a process.

"I'm not ready for that yet," I say, even if it's not the truth. I just don't know if my mind is ready for it.

He squeezes me to him and continues to sway. After a moment, he stops us. "I have something for you," he says nervously. For a split second, I wonder if he's going to propose, but there's something in his eye that tells me that's not it, at least not yet.

"What is it?"

"Come with me." He tugs on my hand and leads me to his F150. It takes only a minute before we're settled in and he starts the truck.

I raise an eyebrow at him. "Where are we going?"

"You'll see."

Gavin drives at a cautious speed down the newly paved road to the main house. I smile happily at our progress with their ranch in the last nine months. Most of the work we've completed has been on guest quarters and permits. They already had good bones to work with, so we spent less money on the revamp than we thought. Which is good because the debt we covered was a large one. Kade also had so many great ideas that we were able to cover many of their monthly expenses by leasing out land to schools and other companies—even to cattle ranchers in Mexico. Things were working out better than we ever dreamed.

My curiosity rises as we pull up to one of the large red barns that houses the ranch horses that guests will use, including my now good pal, Willy. Kade lets me ride him whenever I want, which is nice, especially when Gavin rides with me.

"Are we going for a ride?" I ask. "I don't think we have time."

Gavin chuckles. "Patience, baby."

Once he's put the car in park and pockets his keys, he hops out to open my door for me, an action he always insists on doing. Before I can walk ahead, he stops me with his hand and pulls a black scarf out of his pocket, looking nervous as he does.

"Are we going to do that kinky thing you want to try?" I blush nervously. Not that I would mind, but there are a lot of people milling around getting ready for tonight. I'd rather not get caught tied up somewhere.

He clears his throat, his body obviously responding to the image I've conjured up at my question. "No," he says, leaning forward so his lips are at my ear. "But we will soon." Gavin holds the black scarf up to my eyes. "It's for the surprise. Do you trust me?"

"You know I do," I say sincerely.

He kisses my cheek, then moves behind me so he can tie the soft silk around my head. Once it's secure, he makes sure I can't see anything by asking me how many fingers he's holding up. When he's happy with his work, he grabs my hand. We walk for a minute, the sounds of outside changing to the whinnies of horses. The smell of hay alone makes serotonin course through my body. This is where I feel the most at home, especially with Gavin's hand holding mine.

After a short time, he stops us, facing me toward something.

"Are you ready?" he asks in my ear, his hand at the tie of the blindfold.

"I'm ready."

Gavin pulls the knot, and when it falls my heart thumps in my chest at what I see. There, right in front of me, is a horse I never thought I'd see again. When my eyes set on the new golden name plate outside his stall, tears start to flow.

"You didn't," I choke, my voice thick with emotion.

Winchester pops his head over the stall and lets out a small nicker. By the way he responds, I know that he remembers me. I place my hands on either side of his handsome face, stroking the soft midnight hair before I rest my forehead on the white star between his eyes. Tears drop down my cheeks as I feel Gavin's hand on my lower back.

After a time, Gavin leans down and kisses my neck. I turn and face him, one hand still on Win. There are tears in Gavin's eyes too as he watches me with my old horse.

"How did you get him back?" I ask.

"When I called them, the owners said their daughter ended up being more interested in boys than horses, and they were planning to sell him. When I told them a bit about what's been happening with you, with this ranch, they offered him to me for free. I suppose you can say it was meant to be."

The story washes over me, and I can't help but think yet again Reed had a hand in this. It seems too easy, too perfect. But no matter how this came to be, I'm so grateful.

I lean down and kiss Winchester's nose. "Hey, boy. I missed you; did you miss me?" He nudges me again, and I let out a quiet laugh. "He looks the same, just more mature," I tell Gavin.

"They took good care of him. He's got lots of years left in him. Even some racing years."

I step into Gavin's arms and hug him. "I don't know if I'll ever compete again."

"You will, baby." His words are so sure that even I believe them. "Especially with your partner in crime."

I look back at Win, then to the cowboy I've grown to love. I gently press my lips to his before leaning back to gaze into his eyes.

"Thank you for bringing Win home to me. I love you, Gavin Montgomery."

He brushes his finger along my chin, wiping the tears as he goes. "Anything for you, Blake. I love you, too."

"Want to go for a ride?" I grin slyly. "I'll race you."

Gavin's face lights up in surprise, and he gives me his megawatt smile, one he now reserves only for me. "Blake Tanner, I thought you'd never ask."

Also By Kayla Grosse

I LIKE YOU LIKE THAT
a second chance, rock star romance with a plus-size female lead

W.I.S.H. REVELATIONS
a contemporary fantasy romance

FALLING FOR THE MANNY by Kayla Nicole
a sweet and spicy, single-mom and her manny romance

Next Up
REIN ME IN: The Cowboys of Night Hawk
Audiobook produced by Tantor Media

W.I.S.H. BOOK 2

Find Kayla:
Website: www.kaylagrosse.com
Facebook: Kaylaholics Facebook Group
TikTok: @kaylagrossewriter
Twitter: @kaylagrosse
Instagram: @kaylawriteslife

Acknowledgements

It's been a wish of mine for a while now to write a book about a plus-size cowgirl...and I finally did it! Thank you so much for picking up Gavin and Blake's story, and hopefully you loved reading about them as much as I loved writing them.

This book idea started out from a night on the town with my friends in San Diego when we happened upon a bar with a mechanical bull. We didn't go in, but we could watch people ride the bull from outside through the window. The man who was working the bull saw me and kept trying to get me to come in. My friends were all for it, but I was too embarrassed (plus the bar had a ridiculous cover, lol). Did I miss my meet-cute? Maybe. But I made sure Blake did not miss hers with Gavin!

This book also originally did not carry all the themes it does now. I started writing this book after my grandpa unexpectedly passed away and went through the editing process after one of my best friends passed away. I was able to pour my own feelings of grief into this book, and work through a lot of my own process while writing these characters. My hope is that maybe you were able to as well.

Now to the people I could not have written this book without. Nic—my friend, my writing partner, my formatter, the person who gets all my funny memes and TikToks—this book would not be what it is without you. Thank you for always having my back, for helping me write summaries, and giving me opinions on my book cover, and doing a read through before my final read through. I could not do this without you. You inspire me with your strength and courage daily. Never lose your light, your love, your passion. I put a lot of you in Blake, and I hope you know that YOU are one of the strongest people I know.

To Taylor, my beta reader extraordinaire. You put your heart and soul into the comments you give my books. You are always up for the challenge, and when I asked if you could get the beta read done during the holiday season, you stepped up to the challenge. Thank you for caring so deeply about my work.

I also have to shoutout Melissa—you started out as a reader who found me through, I LIKE YOU LIKE THAT, and now we've become great friends. Thank you for becoming one of my beta readers and a most trusted source of insight and input. You are a true champion of indie authors, and I can't thank you and your Crockpot Baddies enough—I love you all!

Then there's Deanie, one of the first champions of my books. You've been with me since 2019 when I published, W.I.S.H. REVELATIONS, and you've continued to help me gain more readers and give me great notes during your beta reads. You also got my book into its first ever library in NEW ZEALAND. I can't thank you enough for all your love and support.

I can't forget about my editor, Swati Hegde! This is the first time I had the privilege of hiring a line editor, and you've taken the cake. Thank you so much for everything you did to help bring this book to life and to make me a better writer.

I'd also like to thank all my readers. You put me on the map by blowing up I LIKE YOU LIKE THAT, the first book I ever wrote about a plus-size woman. You've all shown me how important our stories are. How important it is to see ALL bodies represented in media. You've made my dreams come true, and I seriously can't thank you enough.

Lastly, I'd like to take a minute to talk about my friend Sally. She passed away in January from a long battle with cancer. Sally was my rock, more than a friend, almost like a soul sister. Sally fought cancer multiple times and came out on the other side. She showed me how important it is to always find the joy in living while going through a struggle. She showed me that you can find joy in something as simple as a cup of Earl Grey tea with cream and honey. She called them her "milkshakes." The pain of losing her was unlike anything I've ever experienced—but it also taught me again the importance of doing what makes you happy in life.

So if you're reading this, and you're wondering if you should write a book, take a trip, do something crazy…DO IT. I know that life has its limitations, but if you really desire something, you will find a way. Remember that life is short, and we must grab the bull by the horns! If you were looking for a sign to do that thing you've been wanting to do, this is your sign to do it. DO THE THING!

Until next time…

Xoxo,

Kayla